T
RELU
PASSENGER

For Lars

THE RELUCTANT PASSENGER

A NOVEL

MICHIEL HEYNS

JONATHAN BALL PUBLISHERS
JOHANNESBURG & CAPE TOWN

Originally published in 2003 in trade paperback by
JONATHAN BALL PUBLISHERS (PTY) LTD
P O Box 33977
Jeppestown
2043

This edition published in 2008

ISBN 978 1 86842 300 2

Design and reproduction of text by
Etienne van Duyker, Cape Town
Reduction of text by Maxine Borsato, Cape Town
Cover design by Flame Design, Cape Town
Printed and bound by Paarl Print, Paarl, Cape Town

AUTHOR'S NOTE

Some aspects of the Silvermine laboratory are based on the Roodeplaat Research Laboratories, as reported in the press and as described in *Secrets and Lies: Wouter Basson and South Africa's Chemical and Biological Warfare Programme* by Marléne Burger and Chandré Gould (ZebraPress, 2002), which I can recommend to anybody interested in the gruesome details of this appalling chapter in our history, and in the law's inability or unwillingness to deal with it. The authors are not, however, to be held responsible for the considerable liberties I have taken in adapting their material to my purpose. In particular, my characters are not based upon any of the actual people involved in Roodeplaat and Project Coast. I like to think that my characters are more human.

I am grateful to my friends David Waddilove and Rudi van Rooyen for providing me with environmental and legal advice. Since, here too, I freely adapted the information they so generously supplied, they should not be held accountable for any distortions and inaccuracies in these pages.

... manmade environments are often and increasingly hostile. To be cornered between nature and culture is the human condition. This has not changed: opportunities to find beauty, truth and love abound.

Imre JP Loefler: 'Cornered between Nature and Culture', *Lancet* 1997; 350 (Suppl III): 5

CHAPTER ONE

There is a rumour at work that I tidy my wastepaper basket, but that is an exaggeration – I just make sure, when the basket is more than usually full, that the content is … well, *contained*. Nor do I regard this as grounds for apology or embarrassment: it seems to me that, as sharers of an overcrowded planet, we owe it to one another not to clutter up the place more than is absolutely necessary.

So on Sunday 24 April 1994 I woke up with every intention of mowing my lawn. It had been slightly too short to be mown the week before, and was now slightly longer than the general standard of my neighbourhood, generating unease amongst my neighbours, in whose view any aberration from the general standard impacts negatively, as they like to put it, on the bottom line – the bottom line in this instance being whatever exorbitant sum they've projected as the selling price of the family home when they emigrate to Australia after the Elections. Although not actively planning to emigrate myself, I naturally did not want to be held responsible for the collapse of property values in Pinelands. Nowhere is it truer than in a Garden Suburb that no man is an island.

As it happened, though, Leonora phoned just as I was changing into my mowing clothes and asked me had I read *Middlemarch* yet, which she'd been not quite *insisting* but suggesting fairly pointedly and of late almost irritatedly, insofar as Leonora can ever be even *almost* irritated, that I should read; so, having read only about three of its several thousand chapters, I said no not quite yet, but I had put today aside for just that. About the only thing that works for Tidiness is Guilt, especially the kind induced by Leonora, which works for just about anything. So that took care of Sunday 24 April and of about another three chapters of *Middlemarch*, but it left my lawn exactly where it found it, only a couple of centimetres longer.

I could have mown the lawn on any other day of the week, I suppose, one afternoon after work, for instance, but I find that if I allow chores like that to stray from their appointed slots they sprawl all over the week and start impinging on other duties, and before you know it your schedule has gone to hell and your life's a mess, like my Uncle William who ended his days in a caravan park because he borrowed money against his own annuity. So I kept the lawn for the following Wednesday, which conveniently was a public holiday, proclaimed as that in order to accommodate our country's first democratic election. By this time my two hundred and twenty square metres of lawn was an embarrassment to me and a cause of disquiet to the rest of Pinelands, with adults frowning and children jeering and estate agents taking prospects the long way round to see the house next door and the dog from across the way leaving a huge pile in the middle of the lawn as if to say if you want a jungle I'll give you jungle, all of which indicated that, in suburban terms, we had a State of Emergency. I resolved to deal with my civic as well as my national duty by first mowing the lawn, and then casting my vote.

My mower is the push-pull kind, because the size of my lawn doesn't really warrant the expense of the motorised type. But pushing and pulling can be heavy work in the heat of April, especially given the extra days' growth that I now had to contend with thanks to *Middlemarch*, so I was careful not to over-exert myself, taking frequent breaks for a glass of water and a salt tablet to prevent dehydration and heat exhaustion. At lunch time I was hungry. I thought a beer would probably not be wise, but I discovered some Castle Lights left over from a *braai* I'd gone to the previous month, so I had one of those and a Snackwich, which I made with a mixture of cheese and leftover chicken, not very tasty – dry and sticky at the same time – but good for protein and carbohydrates. I finished the actual mowing at about half past four and spent another hour trimming the edges, after which I switched on the sprinkler so that the grass could recover from the trauma of being cut in the heat of midday.

I was now quite tired. Although I exercise regularly at the Health and Racquet Club, I don't always have very much energy, so I had a shower and sat down in my sitting room, which is the coolest room in the house because of the double curtains my mother gave me from our old home after my father died and she moved into a town house, and I read another chapter of *Middlemarch*, but when I got to the end I discovered the slip of paper I had used the week before as a bookmark – I detest people who mark their idiot's progress through a book by mutilating it with turned-down corners or whole pages folded in – and realised that I'd already read that chapter. This was discouraging – with all those chapters to get through you don't want to read any of them twice. I'm fond of reading, but sometimes find it difficult to concentrate on very long books. My friend Gerhard says my attention span is adjusted to the sonnet rather than to the nineteenth-century novel, but I don't seem to find poetry very interesting either: there's such a lot of unassimilated emotion around for so little reason, as far as I can see. Gerhard says the point of the sonnet is exactly that it tidies up the emotion, but I'm not sure that uncontrollable passion succumbs that easily to a few quatrains and a rhyming couplet. I once saw a man transporting his Rottweiler in a shopping trolley through a No Dogs Allowed area: the beast was clearly well trained, and stayed put, but you could see that all it really wanted to do was chew the wheels off all the trolleys in the universe. That's the sonnet.

By now it was late enough to have a glass of white wine – I never drink wine before six in the evening – so I poured myself a glass of chardonnay from the bottle I had opened on Friday evening, and had the rest of the leftover chicken, this time with mayonnaise, and went to bed. It was very early, but I like going to bed early sometimes. My father used to say that nothing useful had ever been accomplished after eight o'clock in the evening, to justify his going to bed at eight every night of his life (not that he ever achieved anything very useful before eight o'clock either). I wouldn't want to go quite to his lengths, in this respect as in others, but I do try to keep my bedtime hours fairly regular, as part of a general scheme to lead a rational and moderate life.

I woke up at two a.m. and realised that I'd forgotten to vote.

The problem with leading a rational and moderate life is that one is condemned to leading it surrounded by people to whom reason and moderation are strangers at best, impostors at worst. Thus, waking up on Thursday morning after an excellent night's sleep only slightly disrupted by my belated recollection, sparkling with rationality and moderation, my intellect and perceptions nicely spiked with a cup of coffee, my newly-cut lawn sleek and spruce in the morning sun, I had to make my way to central Cape Town where I earn my living.

Cape Town is built on a narrow strip of land between the mountain and the sea, which was more than adequate, in the seventeenth century, to grow fresh vegetables for the scurvy-and rickets-ridden Dutch sailors on their way to the East, but has since proved ill-adapted to the various and often conflicting needs of a large motorcar-owning populace and an even larger minibus-taxi-commuting populace. Between my orderly house in Pinelands and my orderly office in the city, I had to negotiate Settler's Way, a three-lane highway clogged with every neurosis, addiction, psychosis, obsession, phobia, mania and perversion known to science and a few yet to be classified, amongst the latter being a form of demonic possession visited upon minibus taxis, manifesting itself as a compulsion to hop kerbs, push into lanes that are already crowded beyond capacity, reverse into the face of oncoming traffic, make u-turns in the fast lane, and shed wheels and bumpers at random, all the while hooting indignantly at everything obstructing or deemed remotely likely to obstruct their frenzied progress.

More sedately but no more serenely the white middle classes in their one-person alienation bubbles seethed, simmered and slugged along, resenting every other similarly seething, simmering and slugging motorist. Ranging from the relatively quick to the almost dead, they were crammed into equality by the great democracy of the traffic jam: the red-eyed wrecks, who had spent their mid-week holiday in reckless pursuit of pleasure and had now burnt out or decibelled out whatever higher faculties they might have had two days earlier, were stalled together in coerced comradeship with depressed leaders of lives of quiet desperation, who had meekly devoted the day to the multifarious demands of spouses and offspring, apart from queuing in the sun for hours to cast their futile vote, and were now visibly more exhausted and dispirited than on Tuesday afternoon, wondering why this morning was so depressing when the break had been so little fun. Either maniacally aggressive or catatonically passive, hurling obscene signs or fast asleep behind the wheel, applying lipstick or picking their noses, the whole bumping and grinding conglomeration of pleasure-burnout, hangover, mild disappointment, existential anguish, universal ennui, vague despair, terminal depression and natural bad temper gradually congealed into a seething and indistinguishable mass of near-stationary sun-baked tin as we approached the city, and I felt a headache coming on as the caffeine wore off. I try to cut down on coffee, but I find that if I don't have two cups before work, one just after getting up and one just before my first appointment, I get agitated in the traffic and impatient with clients. Mr McKendrick has spoken to me about what he calls my intolerance of irrationality; he says if everybody were rational the world wouldn't need lawyers, so lawyers, even more than psychiatrists, should be patient with irrationality. Lawyers, Mr McKendrick says, are paid to remain rational; and the people who pay them are the ones who don't.

So that's why I have one cup of coffee when I wake up to propel me through the traffic and another when I get to work to sustain me through the morning, stopping by the coffee machine on my way to my office for the latter. The only disadvantage is that the coffee machine is the place where people congregate in the morning to delay going to their offices, especially on mornings after a weekend or a holiday break, and although I like my colleagues, I'm not always interested in their accounts of their new wetsuits or their failed relationships, water sports and sex being what most people in Cape Town devote their free time to. Not having very much to contribute on either subject – I don't even possess a snorkel – I normally just grab a cup and go to my office.

Today, though, the conversation seemed less dispersed and desultory, more as if people were actually discussing something. In fact, they all seemed to be trying to talk at the same

13

time, but for the time being Willy Wilson, who had the loudest voice, had the floor. He was saying, 'I taped the whole thing so one day I can show my grandchildren. I mean, it's history, isn't it?'

'Did you vote in a township?' Sammy Wentzel asked, to the evident dismay of several other people who wanted to chip in but would now have to wait for Willy's answer.

'Hell no,' Willy replied. 'Why drive out all the way to Guguletu to stand in a queue with all sorts of people when you can just walk into the Scout Hall in Monte Vista? It took me only about …' but he had lost his audience. Anybody could vote in a Scout Hall.

'That was clever of you,' declared Kitty Jooste, the chief typist, shamelessly availing herself of the praise-the-previous-speaker gambit, the most effective but most underhand way of getting the floor. 'My boyfriend insisted that we had to drive all the way to Langa, and then when we got there we had to wait for ever because of all the people. God, I tell you, the *people.*' Her gesture was so wide that she spilt half her coffee and had to grind it into the carpet with the point of her shoe. 'You'd think they'd issue tickets or something to keep out the riff-raff. But Geoff was all excited; he kept on saying it was like a rugby match only with everybody on the same side. You'd think he'd never fought in the army against the ANC; he was full of how we must forgive and forget. I told him it's all very well for him to forgive and forget, but how about the other people there, you know who were voting for the first time, and now we say forgive and forget but it's not that easy is it? Geoff said that attitude would get us nowhere in the new South Africa, but then when we got back to the car after hours in that hot sun somebody had stolen his new bee-sting aerial, and he said there you have it they're not even in power yet and already crime is rampant, and where are the bloody police when we need them, probably all swanning up and down in front of the TV cameras, and I said this is a good opportunity to forgive and forget, and he said fuck forgive and forget do you know what a bee-sting aerial costs?'

Nobody else could claim a personal sacrifice of this magnitude, most people having been content to vote in more suburban

14

surroundings. 'Democracy or no democracy,' said Clarence Clarke, the company accountant, 'you don't want to spend your public holiday staring at the back of the neck of a total stranger. I voted first thing in the morning at the Durbanville Town Hall, and spent the rest of the day next to my pool. We checked the telly, of course, every half-hour or so to see how it was going.'

'Yes,' agreed Chris Evans, the Property man, 'They say that in lots of the townships they still haven't voted.'

'I heard that the ballot papers were stolen and had to be replaced at the last minute,' contributed Kitty.

'The story I heard,' said Paul Williams, a rather senior junior partner, 'was that the Far Right bombed some of the voting stations, but that it wasn't being reported otherwise nobody would go and vote.'

'I can't see why you waste your time with these speculations,' growled Cedric Watts, a very senior senior partner. 'Haven't you heard of African time? From now on we're on African time in this country, and you'd better get used to it. What's more, you can forget about your aerials and your swimming pools, once we have the majority government you're all so excited about.' He turned and went into his office, leaving an uncomfortable silence behind. Cedric's views were often embarrassing to the rest of us. We prided ourselves on being the most progressive law firm in Cape Town ('for what *that* is worth,' my friend Gerhard said), and Cedric's opinions had not progressed along with those of the firm as a whole: he still had the ones that had served him well enough in the sixties, the seventies and even the eighties. Cedric was not adapted to the nineties; but since he was in charge of the Commercial section, which brought in most of the money, the firm could not afford to offend him.

'Now what, I wonder,' mused Dikeledi Modise, 'could African time be? Is it something I have that you don't have, Nick? Like natural rhythm?'

'I don't know, Dikeledi,' I said, laughing. 'But then, I'm African too, remember.'

'Gmf,' she snorted, 'you're about as African as those prissy little Ray-Bans you wear.'

Dikeledi was a recently appointed partner, what she herself described as 'a prudent investment in a democratic South Africa', part of McKendrick, Jolly, Wirthenburger, Smith, Watts and Koekemoer's attempt to marry the business of litigation with the pursuit of justice. It was not in all respects an equal match. We did have a whole floor devoted to Public Interest work, and I myself owed my junior partnership to the firm's progressive policies, being in charge of environmental issues – 'Our Green Initiative', as Mr McKendrick liked to refer to my section, partly to justify to Cedric Watts my paltry contribution to the partnership, but also, and this is where the inequality kicked in, partly to justify to me the meagreness of my office and furnishings compared with all the other sections apart from Public Interest: 'Our corporate clients naturally expect an ambience of prosperity and affluence; but our environmental and public interest clients are suspicious of what they regard as wasteful consumerism.' The result was not so much Spartan as shoddy: unsoundproof offices, irredeemably pre-owned furniture, carpets helplessly refraining from looking plush. I didn't really mind the lack of grandeur, but I was worried about the lack of hygiene and privacy.

My friend Gerhard handled Gender Issues, another progressive initiative of Mr McKendrick's devising, very much against Cedric Watts's will ('Gender Issues?' he'd exclaimed, 'the only gender issue I was brought up with was what's sauce for the goose is sauce for the gander, and I can't see that we need a special section to make the sauce.') Gerhard had done his Master's dissertation on gender discrimination in the workplace, and was hoping one day to take a groundbreaking case in this area, but so far all that his portfolio entailed was taking divorce cases on the wife's side. If the client was the husband, he was referred to Casper Jacobs, the Tough Litigation expert. I had once asked Gerhard if it wasn't a gender issue if a woman mistreated her husband, and Gerhard said, 'Is it a case of cruelty to animals if a dog bites its owner?' I suspected there was something wrong with the analogy but couldn't work it out.

'So where did you vote?' asked Angie Philips as we walked to our adjacent offices. Angie was nominally my assistant, though in practice I preferred to do things myself rather than delegate them to her – not because of any deficiency on her part as much as a reluctance on mine to relinquish control of a case for which I had to take responsibility. She was from England, and claimed to detest South African men in general, on the grounds that they could not distinguish between a woman and a surf-board, except insofar as they tended to fall in love with the latter. This did not prevent her from spending all her spare time shuttling amongst a fair cross section of Cape Town's eligible or at any rate relatively unattached young men. Indeed, quite a few of her working hours went into complicated negotiations with one or the other of these undeserving chau-vinists – as I could not but know, given the flimsiness of the partitions between our offices.

'I'll tell you if you promise not to tell anybody,' I replied.

'It's not like you to have lurid secrets,' she said. 'Promise.'

'Well, then,' I said, 'I forgot to vote. I was mowing my lawn.'

She paused outside her office. 'You mean that while history was being made at the polling stations you were pottering in your garden?'

'I don't see why working – not pottering – in the garden is a less appropriate way to prepare for the dawning of democracy than getting drunk next to a swimming pool.'

'Well, you heard Willy Wilson. What are you going to tell your grandchildren?'

'I'm not planning on having any grandchildren.'

'Doesn't that rather depend on your children?'

'Not if I don't have them either,' I said, and went into my office.

Arranging my work on my desk for the new day – not that there was much to arrange: I like to get my office in order for the next day before leaving in the afternoon – I wondered if I could be blamed for forgetting to vote. It wasn't as if I *chose* to forget, after all. My friend Gerhard maintained that forgetting was a deliberate choice – 'You don't catch people forgetting to cash their salary cheques' – but Gerhard himself was extremely selective in what he chose to remember.

There was a light knock at my door. It was Dikeledi. 'What's this I hear?' she asked, but I could tell she was teasing. 'Our first democratic election and you forget to vote? Mowing your lawn?'

'You don't want our young democracy to choke in over-grown lawns, do you? I'm making the world tidy for democracy.'

'Viva Pinelands,' she said, and went back to her office.

At noon my mother phoned.

'Darling, are you all right?'

'Yes, mother. Why shouldn't I be?'

'I'm worried about you down there in the Cape with all that pillaging going on. It doesn't sound safe.'

'Mother, Pinelands wasn't pillaged. It's perfectly safe there.' I was trying to read an office memo while talking to my mother, which I could normally do quite easily, her conversation being as a rule gently unchallenging. Today, though, her questions were if not more searching then more persistent.

'Yes. But where did you vote?'

'I didn't vote, mother. I forgot to vote. I was mowing the lawn.'

'You were mowing the lawn? Everybody goes to vote and you mow the lawn?'

'Mother, I forgot that there was an election on.'

'But it was all over the television – I don't know how you could have forgotten.'

'By not switching on the television, that's how.'

'Yes, I know you say you don't like the television, and I must say there's an awful lot of rubbish on it half the time, but on a day like that one would think you'd take the trouble to watch.'

'I've told you mother, I forgot.'

'That's because you don't watch television. You should be more outgoing.'

'By sitting in my lounge watching telly? I did go out. I went out and mowed my lawn.'

'You know that's not what I mean. Anyway, I'm pleased you're all right, dear. It's a pity, though, that you didn't vote, they say the ANC is going to win by a landslide.' Before I had time to deprecate responsibility for the imminent landslide, her

18

reproach yielded to her maternal solicitude. 'You must be careful, dear. They say that they're planning all sorts of things for after the election.'

'Who are the *they* that are saying this?'

'Oh, they, you know, people.'

'And the *they* who are planning all these things?'

'They … you know, *them*.'

'I see.'

'Yes. And how are you otherwise? How's Theodora?

'Leonora. She's very well, thank you, mother.'

'Yes. Remember, dear, as long as you're happy, we're happy.'

'That's good to know, mother. But who are we?'

'Your sister and I, of course.'

My sister Iris lived in Durban and saw my mother daily, I suspect to discuss me.

'Oh. How is Iris?'

'She's very well, dear. Only a bit depressed about the heat and the children's rashes. I'll tell her you asked after her.'

'Please do.'

'Yes, dear, I will.' There was a brief silence, which I recognised as my mother counting off on her fingers the number of things she had made a mental note to mention to me. Evidently she had run through her list, because she said, 'Yes. Anyway. I mustn't chat. You have work to do, and I must go and do my shopping.'

'Are you going into Durban?'

'Oh, no. I never go into the city any more. Nobody does. They say it isn't safe.'

'Well, you have everything you need in Kloof, don't you?'

'Yes. Still, it was nice in the old days, with the beachfront and the rickshaws. Your father and I used to enjoy the rickshaws, before your father decided they were … Do you think they are still there?'

'I should think so, mother. As long as there are tourists there will be rickshaws.'

'Do you think there *are* still tourists? Nobody seems to want to come here any more. Everybody's leaving.'

'Who's leaving, mother?'

'The Simpsons next door have left. They've gone to stay with their daughter in Perth.'

'You must be pleased. You never got on with them.'

'Yes. Still, they were a goodish sort of people. There are some Afrikaners moved in now next door.' She pronounced it Aff-ricanders.

'That'll be nice for you, mother,' I said, not unmaliciously. 'You can brush up your Afrikaans.' My mother had, as far as I knew, never spoken a word of Afrikaans in her life.

'Yes. Still, for new people they are a wee bit forward, I think.'

'Forward?'

'Yes. They had hardly been here a week when the woman came over to *make acquaintance*, as she put it, as if acquaintance were something one made in ten minutes, like an instant pudding or something. And she brought me some avocados from their tree because she said she'd noticed that I didn't have one.'

'That's very neighbourly, mother. Sounds like an improvement on the Simpsons.'

'Yes. Very kind. Still, one misses the old ways. And if one had wanted avocados one would have planted an avocado tree.'

'I don't know, mother. I like milk but I wouldn't keep a cow.'

'Don't be silly, Nicholas. A cow is not an avocado tree.'

'I didn't say a cow was an avocado tree, mother. But I'm afraid I must go now; I've got a client waiting.'

Turning towards the door of my office as I told my lie, I saw that I had in fact not told a lie: standing in my door with every appearance of waiting, and also some appearance of listening to my conversation, was someone who, however unlikely in appearance, was presumably a client. He was very tall, very young and very dirty, with a mop of wild red hair. He was dressed in a pair of denim shorts, tyre-soled sandals and a t-shirt that bore the faded memory of a subversive slogan; I could make out only the word 'sucks'.

'Of course, dear. Look after yourself, won't you?'

'Of course, mother.'

Myrah Williams, my secretary, appeared behind the young man, her frantic gestures signalling, as far as I could make out, either that I should stop talking or that she was going to cut the throat of the young man. Not thinking it advisable to put the matter to the test, I put down the phone.

20

'I am sorry, Mr Morris,' Myrah began, 'I did explain to this gentleman that you are available only by appointment, but he insisted on walking right in ...'

'I didn't insist, I just walked. You said he had a client in here, and I could see he didn't.'

'It is quite usual for lawyers to consult by telephone, you know,' Myrah pointed out in her most governessy manner.

'Consult?' the young man said. 'You mean he was *consulting* his mother about cows and avo trees?'

I object to being referred to in the third person in my own presence, but did not want to seem in any way eager to secure the attention of this presumptuous young man. So I asked, in a tone that I hoped conveyed civilised tolerance rather than interest, 'Since you have come this far, Mr ...?'

'Oh,' he said, reverting startlingly to the stance and idiom of a polite schoolboy. 'Sorry, Tomlinson, Luc Tomlinson.' He extended his hand. 'Call me Luc. That's Luc as in L-u-c.'

I took his hand reluctantly; this was not what I had envisaged. I had intended to be freezingly polite, not sociable. I certainly had no intention of calling him Luc.

'Nicholas Morris,' I said, as unencouragingly as possible, then winced as he squashed my hand in his. He was obviously much stronger than his slender build suggested, and needed to demonstrate that fact.

'Yes, I know that,' he said. 'Mind if I call you Nick?' As in N-i-c, presumably.

I hate being called Nick, especially by total strangers. 'I prefer Nicholas, actually,' I said. In truth I'd have preferred him to call me Mr Morris, but I thought it would sound starchy if I said so. Myrah nodded fiercely behind the young man's back; I nodded back, as if to say it's okay, I'm in charge, whereas in fact I was feeling decidedly out of charge and didn't want her to witness my impotence. Myrah was sometimes like an overprotective dog that won't stop barking even after it's discovered that there's no reason to bark. Fortunately she accepted my hint and retreated to her office reluctantly, clearly disappointed that I had not asked her to show the intruder the door.

'Well,' I said, relieved not to have an audience to what I

suspected might be an awkward interview, 'what can I do for you, Mr Thompson?'

'Tomlinson,' he said, and stretched himself. His t-shirt and shorts parted to reveal a flat brown stomach sloping down into loins that seemed untrammelled by civilised amenities like underpants. He completed his stretch and sat down without being invited to do so. 'But Luc's what I'm called. Mr Tomlinson is, you know, sort of collar-and-tie-and-boxer-shorts.' These sartorial affectations he clearly held in the deepest contempt.

I had the choice of remaining standing and being interviewed by him as if I were the interloper and he the incumbent, or of sitting down somewhat lamely and conducting the interview that he was clearly intent on having. I sat down somewhat lamely.

The young man put one foot on a grubby knee. His tyre-sole sandals imperfectly concealed the fact that his feet were very dirty. There was about him a strong smell of sweat and something else, partly vegetable, partly animal, something vaguely agricultural but *wilder* somehow than the standard stable-and-barn mix.

He had very blue eyes, disconcertingly clear against the tan and dirt of his skin. His features were regular, except for a nose that dipped up at the end unexpectedly. He gave me a smile that I suspected of regarding itself as disarming: the teeth were whiter than one would have expected from the state of his feet. I couldn't escape the impression that the cavalier disregard of good form was quite conscious, a calculated effect rather than an artless candour. His attempts to affect a slangy proletarian turn of speech did little to conceal the fact that, like me, he had been brought up to speak 'good' English, the rather painful cultivation of which characterises the more affluent suburbs of South Africa.

He seemed in no hurry to get to the point. He looked around the office with a brutal inquisitiveness that had none of the flattery of curiosity about it. Most people, gratifyingly if a trifle predictably, admire my view of the mountain and of Greenmarket Square, but he seemed indifferent to those. He was inspecting my interior, with its neat rows of Law Reports and

22

its framed Daumier prints, as if he was a termite eradicator looking for the centre of infestation. As he turned his head I noticed, half concealed by the profusion of hair, a large gold ring in his right ear.

Through the partition between my office and Angela's she could be heard negotiating one of her complicated relationships. 'Well, it's not as if you gave me much of a choice, is it?' she asked, clearly at the point where defence turns into attack.

'Rubbishy walls, aren't they?' Luc Tomlinson asked. 'You couldn't fart in here without being heard at the other end of the building.'

'That is not something that has ever bothered me.'

He looked at me as if seeing me for the first time. 'Yeah, I shouldn't wonder,' he said after an assessing pause, his tone relegating me to the craven company of unflatulent ninnies. 'Mind you,' he added, looking with undisguised distaste at the flower arrangement on my desk, a tightish composition of vague hybrids in regulation colours, courtesy of Rentaflora, moved down here after a day in Commercial. This being the day after a public holiday, they were even more tired than usual, 'I don't know how you do it.' His tone suggested incredulity rather than admiration.

'How we do what, Mr Tomlinson?'

'Spend your life in a cardboard box, like a laboratory mouse.'

'We are not all of us fortunate enough to earn a ready income in the great outdoors,' I replied, in what I thought was a nicely pointed way. I was willing to bet that the young man had very little of a ready income; I couldn't think of any form of paid employment that he could pursue looking as he did, except possibly rat-catching.

'Well, it's all a matter of choice, really, isn't it?' he said, the question purely rhetorical. 'Plenty of jobs in the great outdoors if you're prepared to do without a secretary and a shiny desk and a pretty-posy-a-day.'

I did not think this called for a reply. Through the wall Angela could be heard saying, 'I didn't say I would, I said I *might*.'

'What is it that you wanted to consult me on?' I asked, since the young man – Luc – showed no sign of coming to the point.

He looked around him again, as if he was not to be rushed. 'You're the environmental chap?' he asked.

'I do environmental work, if that's what you mean.'

'Well, then. I reckon you saw off the bugger who was going to stuff up Sandy Bay, right?'

'Yes,' I replied, and added conscientiously, 'though it's not quite true to say that I won the case. I had the best counsel in Cape Town.' I hoped George Plimsoll would appreciate this wholly insincere compliment. Privately I thought that I had in fact won the case, in spite of some bad blunders on George's part. If I hadn't briefed him so well there would by now have been an upmarket development of desirably exclusive residences on Sandy Bay, the only unspoilt beach on the Atlantic coast.

'Yes, well,' Luc said, his tone implying a total lack of interest in such recondite distinctions. 'Point is, you're a sort of green James Bond, the ghost-buster of the environment, that kind of thing?' He seemed amused at his own metaphors.

'Listen,' I said, 'perhaps you'd better just tell me what it is you want me to do, then I can tell you whether or not I can take it on and on what terms.'

'It's not for me,' he said. 'It's for the chacs.'

'The chacs.'

'Chacmas,' he explained, as if this was a point that should really have been self-evident. As I still stared at him in un-enlightened interrogation, he stooped to the elementary. 'Baboons.'

'Baboons.'

'Yeah. The baboons at Cape Point. I live with them.'

That would explain the smell, then.

'And you want legal advice on the rights and responsibilities of co-habitation with non-human primates?' I asked.

'No, that's no sweat. Baboons can sort out that sort of thing without lawyers. As long as the humans keep away.' He looked at me piercingly, as if I had insisted on moving in with him and his chacmas.

'Like you?'

'No, not like me.' His manner was impervious to irony; he had the kind of earnestness that I had often noticed among the very young, the very religious, and the very environmental. 'The chacs and I have no problem. The humans I mean are the developers.'

The young man started picking absent-mindedly at a scab on his shin. The dark-brown edge of the scab lifted from the golden-brown skin, exposing a sensitive-looking pink area underneath; then, as the finger released the scab, it snapped back into place, only to be lifted again, this time slightly further. I tried to look away, but found it impossible to ignore the gross impropriety of this strangely intimate little procedure. Could I ask a client to stop picking at his scabs in my office? It was not a point of etiquette that I'd had to confront before.

'I mean,' he was saying, 'the chacs were there first.' The scab lifted and took a sliver of skin with it; a drop of blood appeared in the lesion.

'That may be so, but that is not enough to establish property rights. Animals have no rights, at any rate not in the same sense as human rights.' The young man had left the scab for a moment to scratch his right ear and tug at the ring in it; then the prying fingers, strangely slender appendages to such broad arms, but with squarish fingernails, marginally cleaner than his toenails, started pick-picking again at the scab.

'Yes, well. I know that. That's why I'm here.' Pick-pick. 'You must get them rights. Isn't that what lawyers are for?'

It irritated me that the young man's manifest contempt for lawyers did not prevent him from coming to one when he was in need. 'Not really,' I said. 'Lawyers can't create rights where none exist; they can only ensure that people are given their lawful rights.'

'So you're just there to perpetuate the status quo?' The cliché was all wrong on his lips. I wondered whether he was a University of Cape Town dropout. I knew the type, from my own days at UCT: son of rich parents, opting out for a few years of surfing and grass and girlfriends who grew bean sprouts for a living in a commune at Noordhoek or Kommetjie, before returning to the fold and becoming successful in Daddy's business. The young Koekemoer had recently joined the firm after just such a cultural break, and had taken effortlessly to three-piece suits – a lot more comfortable than

a wetsuit, he said when teased about his apostasy from surfing.

'What exactly is it that you expect me to do?'

'Yes, well. Have you been apprised' – his affectation of formal speech was even more offensive than his attempts at prole-
talk – 'of an extremely upmarket hotel and golf course at Cape
Point?'

'Impossible. Cape Point is a proclaimed nature reserve.'

He detached the scab from its last remaining integument of
skin, inspected it briefly, and dropped it on my carpet. I suppressed a shudder. 'Yes, right, I know that,' he said, 'but there's
this one tract of private land inside the reserve, right? Place
called Rocklands?'

I nodded. I had heard that a plot of land had been ceded to
a private person years ago, and that his family had retained the
right to the use of the land in return for the incorporation of the
tract into the reserve.

'And you know that the present owner wants to develop the
property?' To my relief he reverted to standard English.

'No. Should I?'

He shook his head. 'Not really. It hasn't hit the headlines
yet.'

'And you know just because you live out there?'

'Yes.' Then he shook his head gloomily. 'Well, no. I know
because the developer is my father.'

Of course. Brick Tomlinson was one of the more colourful
and successful building contractors in the Peninsula, the
descendant of the original Trick Tomlinson who had been
granted the piece of land by Cecil John Rhodes – according to
unconfirmed rumour because Rhodes had been infatuated
with the young Tomlinson. The Tomlinsons were famous for
their money and their good looks. I was amused to think that
this scruffy dropout was the latest in the line.

'I've heard of your father, yes.'

'Me old famous dad. So you'll know he's a big-time builder
and developer, but big-time as in BIG-time. He's also almost
totally fucking ruthless.'

I'd heard that, too, but I didn't say so, and he continued. 'My
father's scheming to do the actual development and share in

26

the big-lolly profits, but basically he'd be selling the rights to this American conglomerate. Which is worse, because the old man, to give him his due, still feels *something* for the area, but the Americans will fuck it up all the way to Disneyland. To them it's just another theme park with scenery.'

He became quite animated in his anger, and his irritatingly languid manner brisked up. 'I grew up there, you know,' he said, 'that is, apart from school, I spent all my time there. I know all the chacs by name. They were my friends.'

I nodded. 'Of course. And how will your friends be affected by this development?'

'It'll just be the end of them. People don't want baboons around. They steal food and they wank in public and they crap all over the place.'

'I can see how that would make them unpopular.'

'That's nothing to what humans do. But point is, you bring people near baboons, never mind that the baboons were there first, the people start complaining that the chacs are dangerous or unhygienic or immoral and they get shot or sold to Groote Schuur.'

'The zoo?'

'No, the hospital. For medical experimentation. They get put in cages and infected with diseases. Or they have their organs transplanted into one another. You don't want to know what happens to them in those places.'

'Wouldn't that happen to them anyway?'

'We've been able to stop that as long as the chacs were on our ground.'

'Your father shares your concern?'

'Not really – I mean, my father, *concern*. But he did feel, you know, bossy about his baboons when all he was offered for them was about R20 a chac.'

'I gather he's being offered more than that now.'

'He's being offered several million. In hard dollars, at a time when the building industry, that end of the market, at any rate, isn't exactly gearing up for great things now that … you know, things are changing. And the old man doesn't care a shit what happens to the chacs in the process.'

'And what exactly do you want me to do?'

'If I knew that, I wouldn't be here, would I? You're the expert.' He made it sound vaguely disreputable. I swallowed my irritation and took refuge in my professional manner, what my friend Gerhard calls my razor wire mode.

'In order to develop that property your father will have to apply for rezoning of the area. Do you know if he has done that?'

'I'm pretty positive he hasn't. I'd know if he did.'

'Well, then, I suggest you wait until he does apply, and then lodge an objection or get somebody to lodge one. There should be plenty of people who'd oppose development on that coast-line.'

'You suggest I wait ...' he mimicked my manner offensively, '... and then what? So we wait and in the mean time the old man lines up all his contacts and all his pals and by the time we get off our arses the coastline is crawling with golf carts and glitter palaces.'

'You must realise, Mr Tomlinson, that if you want to stay within the law you must follow the correct procedures. I'm here to explain the correct procedures to you, not to tell you how to break the law.'

'Of course, that's why you lawyers never changed anything in this fucking country.'

'I don't think that's relevant.'

'Yes it is. I'm telling you about an injustice and you tell me that as long as it's not against the law you can't do anything about it. So if the law is unjust that's just fine by you as long as it's the law?'

I felt a surge of impatience with this unkempt young person shedding dead blood on my carpet and feeling superior to me because my professional code prevented me from being as rude to him as he was to me. He represented everything most antipathetic to my sense of an ordered existence: rudeness, long hair, body odour, dirty toenails, linguistic incoherence, ear rings. 'If we can return to practicalities, Mr Tomlinson,' I interrupted. 'I'm not quite sure whether you're here to abuse me or to instruct me, but forgive me if I point out that in the normal course of things lawyers' fees are beyond the means of most baboons.'

'I thought you were an environmental lawyer.'

'And you thought environmental lawyers worked for nothing.'

'Of course not. But I didn't think they were so fucking frantic to secure their fee that they didn't wait to listen to what you had to say.'

'Look, Mr Tomlinson …'

'Call me Luc.'

'I don't particularly want to call you Luc. I want to tell you that I have no responsibility to you or to your friends the baboons, and no reason to put up with your rudeness and your bad language and your lack of personal hygiene, just because you think you've cornered the market on the environment.'

'What does my personal hygiene have to do with the merits of the case?'

'I don't have to judge the merits of the case in order to decide whether I want to take it or not.'

'You mean you're judging the merits of the client?'

'In a manner of speaking, yes. I don't want to work with a client who takes no trouble to hide his contempt for me.'

'Relax,' he said in an insultingly patronising tone, as if placating a child throwing a tantrum. 'I didn't reckon lawyers were so sensitive.' He seemed pale under the tan, but there was nothing apologetic in his tone.

'You probably didn't reckon lawyers were human,' I said.

'If I needed a human being I wouldn't come to a lawyer to find one. I scheme that's not what lawyers are paid to be.'

'Then why do you scheme I'll work for nothing?'

'I thought you might be an exception. But I guess I was wrong. I'm sorry.' He didn't look or sound in the least sorry. His eyes strayed to my neck and I wondered if he was going to strangle me.

'That a Milton College tie?' he asked. I nodded. 'It figures,' he said.

'And where were you at school, Mr Tomlinson?'

'Bishops,' he said, and I thought he flushed under his tan. 'But I didn't want to go there. My mother insisted.'

I didn't reply. In my case it had been my father who had insisted: he believed that if one had a good schooling it would

29

never be necessary to work afterwards, a principle he had applied with some success, though at considerable inconvenience to other people.

Luc Tomlinson seemed slightly at a loss, but wasn't going to forgive me the reference to his schooling. 'And then you went on to UCT,' he said, pointing at the framed degree certificate on my wall. 'And ... what's this? The University of London?' He got up and pretended to inspect the certificate.

'I don't suppose you are here to inspect my credentials, Mr Tomlinson,' I said.

'Bloody right I'm not. But I don't think we're getting anywhere. Think about it. I'll phone you if I can't get anyone else to take the case.' He put his hand under his t-shirt and scratched his stomach. 'And no, I don't expect you to do it for nothing.'

As he turned round to leave Gerhard appeared in the door. For Gerhard to appear in a door is to fill it: he is at least as tall and as broad as your average doorway. He paused, raised his eyebrows, and said, 'Oh, I beg your pardon.' He did not, however, move out of the way.

'That's all right,' Luc Tomlinson said, 'I was just leaving anyway,' this last with what I thought was, for him, a nicely understated implication. Gerhard took the implication, but with a slow deliberateness that I'd learned to recognise as signalling at best interest, at worst an intention to close in. To my relief he stopped at interest this time.

Luc Tomlinson paused at the door and looked back at me. 'I reckon the connection between the environment and environmental lawyers is the same as that between whales and whale fishermen.' His eyes flicked in Gerhard's direction for perhaps two seconds and then he turned on his heel and left.

Gerhard turned round and watched him leave. 'Well,' he said, raising his eyebrows in an exaggerated way which I found strangely irritating, 'and what was that?'

'A misguided environmentalist who wants me to work for nothing.'

'And did you decline?'

'Of course I declined.'

'For somebody who looks like that you might have stretched a point.'

'Oh, he's not as poor as he looks.'

'I don't mean he looks poor.' Gerhard grinned in a way I had learned to recognise and fear as the mobilisation of his worst instincts. 'I mean he looks absolutely irresistible.'

'Well, I found him quite resistible, indeed ever so slightly repulsive.'

'He looks like the angel of dawning refulgent with the first light of creation.' Gerhard claims to have a poetic imagination; I tell him it's just pretentiously sublimated lust. 'And he has a most shapely butt, a happy union of strength and grace.'

'Spare me your erotic imagination,' I said, uncomfortably aware of Myrah hovering. Fond as she was of Gerhard, she had problems both with his Afrikaans origins and with his fluent English – 'I think he wants to prove that he can speak English,' was how she reconciled her somewhat contradictory misgivings to herself and to me. Gerhard, having grown up in an entirely Afrikaans environment, but with a preternatural aptitude for languages, had picked up most of his English from literature. Since his favourite authors were Jane Austen and Charles Bukowski – 'exponents, in their different styles, of the pleasures of not working for a living' – his speech was at times a disconcerting hybrid of the erudite, the archaic and the downright filthy.

'And are you not going to take the angel of dawning's case?' he asked.

'Absolutely not.'

'And is his case not perhaps one that could resort under gender law?'

'*No*,' I replied, as firmly as I could. Sometimes Gerhard was extraordinarily sensitive to nuance, but at other times one had to be unambiguously categorical with him. I had more or less learnt to distinguish between the two kinds of occasion.

'Don't distress yourself,' he said. 'There are more ways than one of plucking a turkey.'

He sat down in the chair recently vacated by the Angel of Dawning. 'Where were you yesterday? I phoned at least three times.'

'I was at home, but I was mowing the lawn, so I suppose I didn't hear the phone.'

'You were mowing the lawn? The whole country is exercising its hard-won democratic right and you're mowing the lawn?'

'Listen. Do you realise that at least six people have asked me that identical question today? Why does everybody regard voting as more important than lawn mowing?' Then, as Gerhard raised his eyebrow ironically at my ill-considered question, 'Let's just say I rejoice greatly with my compatriots that we seem to have had free and fair elections, but I can't see that my mowing the lawn interfered with the democratic process. Having been born into the sin of having the vote, and having felt guilty for 25 years for having it, I'm not going to start feeling guilty now because I didn't exercise it.'

'What if everybody had been mowing their lawns?'

I glanced at the front page of the *Cape Times* on my desk. 'There'd have been less chaos at the polling booths.'

'The rest of the world sees the dawning of a new era; what does Nicholas see? – Chaos at the polling booths!'

'I'll believe in the new era when I see it on the front page of the *Cape Times*. In the mean time all I see there is chaos at the polling booths.'

'You must have faith. Faith sees through chaos to the emergent order.' Gerhard's pedantic air, though it pretended to be parodying itself, was only partly jocular. 'But you need not justify your horticultural pursuits to me. Maintaining your lawn in the face of profound social change is an act of faith in something, even if only in the survival of middle-class values. *Il faut cultiver notre pelouse* and all that.'

'Stop trying to cast me as a closet optimist. And what did you do to proclaim your faith in the new social order?'

'I cultivated my garden in my own way.'

'Explain,' I said, and then regretted it, as Gerhard's face assumed the blend of salaciousness and mischief that always signalled his intention of shocking me. Fortunately Myrah came into my office with a document for me to sign, so he contented himself with making big eyes at me and saying, 'Come for lunch and I'll tell you.'

'I can't. I said I'd see Leonora.' Myrah went out, and Gerhard relaxed into what I recognised as his provocative mode.

'Wasn't she mowing the lawn with you yesterday?'

'No, she was in Paarl with her family.'

'Oh? To ensure a block vote for the ANC in the rural areas?'

'You must be joking.'

'I am. So no lunch?' He got up and the room went dark. Gerhard had that effect on all but the largest of rooms.

'Not today. How about after work ?'

'I wanted now. I'm playing squash after work. With, if all goes according to plan, a night of mindless and ceaseless carnal delights to follow.'

I ignored the bait. 'Tomorrow – assuming you survive the night?'

'Tomorrow. I always survive the night; it's the *days* that get me. Which reminds me, I must go and catch up on my sleep.'

He was on the point of leaving, but when he got to the door he turned back to me and said, 'You know, I really don't understand you. You throw the Angel of Dawning out of your office and have lunch with Rageltjie de Beer.'

'And who is Rageltjie de Beer supposed to be?'

He smiled, still in his provocative way. 'Didn't they teach you anything at Milton College?'

'They certainly didn't teach us who Rageltjie de Beer was.'

He turned to face me fully, put his right hand on his heart, and intoned in his most pedantic manner, 'Well, then. Rageltjie de Beer of immortal memory, when caught in a snow storm with her little brother, heroically hollowed out an ant hill, put the little boy inside, took off her own clothes to cover him and then sealed the ant hill with her own naked body. He and his line survived but she quite literally froze her ass off. For this she is venerated as a heroine of the *volk*.'

'She sounds like a truly admirable woman.'

'Excellent company in an ant hill, I daresay, but for lunch, personally, I'd go for the Angel of Dawning any time.'

'You, yes,' I said, 'but you can't expect me to run my life according to your depraved preferences. Can't you accept that there's more to life than sex?'

'Who mentioned sex? I said lunch.'

'Yes, but I know your foul imagination.'

He shook his head. '*I* talk of lunch, *he* thinks of sex and then *he* accuses *me* of having a foul imagination. I'll never understand the Anglican mind.'

He left with an exaggerated shrug of the shoulders, playing down what I sensed was a potential point of conflict between us. Gerhard didn't really like Leonora, and Leonora didn't really like Gerhard, but given their different styles, his dislike was more overt than hers: he called her Little Nell and Joan of Arc and Fanny Price and the Snow Queen and The Iron Lady and Patient Griselda and Helen Burns and now Rageltjie de Beer; she just called him 'your friend Gerhard' with a very slight sigh.

I sometimes wondered whether Gerhard was jealous of my relationship with Leonora. I asked him once and he said, 'I'd as soon be jealous of your relationship with your great-grandmother's crocheted rug.' I had inherited a rug from my great-aunt – not my great-grandmother – that she had crocheted while my great-uncle was in the Great War, and that I had once unwisely confessed to Gerhard I liked to keep on my bed. He referred to it as Great-grandmother Penelope's blanket.

I'd arranged to have lunch with Leonora at the coffee shop we had regarded as 'ours' ever since we met there a year previously. I, trying to juggle my book, my newspaper and my cup of coffee, had spilt the coffee in her lap; she, though clearly suffering extreme discomfort, had been so forgiving that I had decided that she had a beautiful nature. In this I had been proved right by time, if by a beautiful nature is meant extreme self-denial in deference to the wishes, real or supposed, of others. After a year I was starting to wonder whether being forgiven was enough, somehow, as both the main contribution to and the primary benefit of a relationship, especially where the grounds of forgiveness seemed to be my own lack of commitment to a relationship of whose nature and expectations I had only a very hazy notion. So far I had not voiced this misgiving, nor even articulated it to myself. Leonora was a librarian.

The coffee at Michelangelo's was abominable, and the service seemed dedicated to the discouragement of future visits from the unwary wanderer who chanced to stumble into the uninviting interior, but we didn't have the heart to abandon the place for a more congenial rendezvous, as if our relationship depended on our remaining faithful to its origin. It was characteristic of my relationship with Leonora that I lacked the courage to confess to her that the place irritated me beyond measure, whereas she would never presume to express or indeed even feel anything as selfish as an irritation.

'What was your Election Day like?' I asked her, after we had managed to intimidate a waiter into taking our order for two toasted chicken mayonnaise sandwiches and two cappuccinos, which was more or less the limit of the culinary resources of Michelangelo's. The coffee arrived almost immediately, in spite of our request that we be brought our meal first.

'Oh, it was very good. My Uncle Paul and Aunt Betty and their two children came from Malmesbury and we all went to vote together.'

'Wasn't that a bit much?'

She looked puzzled. 'There were only seven of us altogether. And we like to do things with … with people we're close to.'

I sensed or imagined a didactic edge to her voice. I knew that she'd wanted me to accompany her to the occasion, and had been hurt when I'd said that I couldn't imagine casting my vote in an environment where voting was a rearguard action rather than a leap into the future. What I had not told her was that I was also unwilling to go home with her to be subjected to the suspicions of her father, Oom Casper le Roux, a prominent wine farmer who thought I was wooing his daughter because I had designs on his farm, a theory as unflattering to Leonora as to me. Her mother, Tant Cremora le Roux, on the other hand, thought I was 'sweet', which was almost worse than being suspected of farm-grabbing. Since the Le Roux clan, with the exception of Leonora, spoke almost as little English as I spoke Afrikaans, communication was a rather strained affair of taciturn grunts from Oom Casper and inarticulate twitters from Tant Cremora. Still, I felt guilty for turning down Leonora's invitation, and irritated with her for making me feel guilty.

'Were there pancakes?' I asked, as a way of consolidating my irritation with irony. Leonora had told me that her mother had baked pancakes at a pre-election meeting of the National Party.

'No,' she said, 'my mother was scared that all the pancakes

would be eaten by ANC supporters. But my aunt brought a picnic basket, because she'd heard that we'd have to wait all day to vote. But we voted at the Co-op, and there was hardly anybody there, so we took the picnic basket to the Language Monument because my Uncle Paul said we don't know how long it will still stand once the new government is in power.' The Afrikaans Language Monument is a famously and unignorably phallic construction on Paarl Mountain.

'Oh, I should think the Language Monument would survive a little matter like a democratic election,' I said nastily. 'You don't lose an erection like that overnight.'

She frowned slightly, and said 'I beg your pardon?' in that polite way she had been taught at school. Leonora was the only person I knew who could say *I beg your pardon* without sounding sarcastic. Unfortunately I now had to repeat my inane comment. I looked around hoping our sandwiches would arrive, but our waiter was engrossed in the conversation of the only other two customers in the place; a large woman was saying to a depressed-looking man, 'You must learn to honour and obey your natural instincts.'

'I said you don't necessarily lose an erection when you lose an election, but let it pass.'

She blushed scarlet. *Erection* was not a word that I or probably anybody else had ever used in her presence; indeed it was not a word I customarily used in anybody's presence. One of the things that attracted me to Leonora and yet irked me was the fact that she was just as inhibited of expression as I was. In this case, in my suppressed irritation, I pronounced the word much more loudly than I'd intended, and the intense couple and the waiter looked at me as if ... well, as if I'd pronounced the word *Erection* loudly in a confined public space.

'I suppose not,' Leonora said. 'And where did you vote?'

'I did not vote.'

'Oh ... but why not? I thought ...' I had explained to her at some length the week before that it was everybody's democratic duty to vote, however little one felt one could endorse any particular party unconditionally.

'I don't want to talk about it,' I said, resenting my own brutality and Leonora for driving me to it. Leonora didn't answer, just stirred her coffee once more.

'You've stirred your coffee six times,' I pointed out.

'Have I? I'm sorry, I'm … *ingedagte* ?' appealing to me for the English word she probably knew but wanted me to feel I had helped her with. Leonora's English was considerably better than my Afrikaans.

'Preoccupied,' I played along. 'What are you preoccupied with?'

'Oh, nothing in particular.'

'Funny sort of preoccupation,' I said. 'Sounds like a contradiction to me. Like a box full of nothing.'

She smiled wanly, hoping I was teasing her. Teasing was the closest we ever came to expressions of affection. It was also at times dangerously close to an expression of aggression on my part. I put my hand on hers – again one of the few overt gestures of affection I allowed myself, or persuaded myself she would allow me – in appeasement, contriteness, I wasn't quite sure which. To my horror she started crying. Not loudly, indecorously, not even very visibly, but unmistakably and, worse, unignorably.

'Leonora,' I appealed to her in a tone of concern that I hoped hid my exasperation, 'is anything the matter?' and guiltily caught myself hoping that she wouldn't tell me. I really didn't want to know what was the matter.

'Oh, nothing in particular,' she said. But that was not all she said. 'It's just that you're so … so disrespectful sometimes.'

'Disrespectful of what?'

'Of everything. Of values and principles.'

'Whose values and principles?'

'Other people's.'

'You mean yours.' This was an unfair accusation; Leonora would never appropriate even a value or a principle as her own.

'Mine, too, but they're mine because they're other people's as well.'

'And what about mine?'

She looked at me through her tears, and whereas there was something touching about this, I had to admit that it was not in

37

itself an attractive sight. 'That's just the trouble. Your values and principles.'

'What's wrong with them?' I asked, deliberately lightly. 'I think they're very good values and principles.'

'Yes, I know they are,' she said, taking me absolutely seriously. Leonora always took me seriously, which I told myself was a compliment. 'But they're not … not always your own.'

'How can my values and principles not be my own?' I asked, genuinely mystified.

'Well, sometimes I think they're your friend Gerhard's,' she said with a slight sigh, looking down and making patterns in the sugar she'd spilled on the table. For such a tidy person, Leonora was quite clumsy at times.

'And what's wrong with that?' I asked, illogically driven to defend Gerhard.

'It's just that sometimes he's so basic. So superficial.'

'You mean he's interested in sex.'

She blushed again. *Sex* was a word that didn't occur often in our conversations: talking about it might remind us of its absence in our relationship. 'No, it's not just that. It's the way he talks about things and people. You don't understand – but if you're Afrikaans, like me and Gerhard, then you can see the way he talks about things is deliberately … disrespectful.' The waiter deposited our toasted chicken mayonnaise sandwiches on our table as if he wanted to get rid of them surreptitiously and was afraid of being apprehended.

'That's what you said five minutes ago about the way I talk,' I said, biting into a sandwich very carefully; I had once speared the roof of my mouth with a chicken bone at Michelangelo's.

'Yes. That's what I mean.' She prodded delicately at her sandwich with the point of her knife. It exuded tired-looking mayonnaise. 'You get it from him.'

'Can't I even be credited, if that's the term, with my own disrespect? Why must you assume I get it from Gerhard?'

'Because I know you're not really like that,' she asserted with the quiet conviction that I had so much admired in her until I had discovered it was indistinguishable from obstinacy. She spilt a blob of mayonnaise in her lap without noticing. I felt I couldn't relax until she'd cleaned it up.

'Then why don't you just take comfort in what I really am and ignore the bits that come from Gerhard?'

'I can't ignore them. They detract from your true nature.'

In my student days I would at this point have had an animated argument about essence and accident ('What do you mean by *true* nature?'), but on this hot April day in a stuffy coffee bar with a dry chicken mayonnaise sandwich on my plate I felt only exasperation and exhaustion.

'Listen, Leonora,' I said, 'I appreciate the flattering view you have of my true nature, but you must accept that I can't spend the rest of my life living up to some Platonic ideal of myself – by the way, you've spilt some mayonnaise in your lap – and perhaps you'll just have to accept that Gerhard and I are friends for a reason, and that perhaps somewhere under my pinstripes and school tie and nice manner and boxer shorts' – she paled visibly – 'there is a superficial, disrespectful, completely basic person.'

This didn't sound plausible even to me, but Leonora took it seriously enough to start crying in earnest. Our meal ended damply, our sandwiches half-eaten, the inefficient and by now openly eavesdropping waiter over-tipped to buy his forgiveness for our premature departure. Somehow I didn't want him to know how bad his service and sandwiches were. Leonora went back to her library and I went back to my office, both of us feeling, in our different ways, what unsatisfactory things human relationships were.

I went home later than usual, after a session in the Health and Racquet Club, vainly trying to generate enough endorphins to make the day seem worthwhile. Even so, the battle of the road was still at its grimmest, the general aggression only slightly tempered by the disappointments that the first working day after a break is both heir and midwife to, the average speed only marginally faster than the morning crawl. Through some inscrutable stroke of engineering, there is a stretch on the way home where all the vehicles in the right-hand lane have to squeeze into the left-hand lane and vice versa. This causes, on a bad day, near-immobility, and this was a bad day. The traffic was blocked solid.

I don't normally take much notice of other drivers, believing in this relation as in others that before you know it you're involved in something you can't control, and that to show anything, especially goodwill, on the road, is to risk ignominy, insult and possibly injury; but with our enforced immobility I had leisure to survey my neighbours. I checked the range of bumper stickers – five fishes, an average sort of haul; one person who needed the world to know that he or she was losing weight with Weigh-Less; one person who proclaimed that he or perhaps even she bonked like a bastard.

The car to the right of me, an ostentatiously nondescript Far-Eastern corporate issue clone, one of those trying unsuccessfully to look as if it was not trying to look like a Mercedes, harboured, I noted with approval, something other than burnout and impatience. The driver evidently had brought his dog, a woolly white Maltese poodle, along with him, and the animal was exuberantly if rather dangerously hopping up and down in his lap. I'm not a great lover of dogs – their naive emotionality is always a bit painful to contemplate and awkward to negotiate – but the man's evident enjoyment of the animal's antics made a pleasant change from the grim-faced determination of his fellow-commuters; so, as he noticed my attention and caught my eye, I smiled at him and gave him a thumbs-up sign. To my indignation he retaliated with a finger sign that had nothing of the thumbs-up about it, and snarled something which, though I'm no lip-reader, was a fairly unmistakable instruction as to how to dispose of myself. He said something to the poodle and the next moment the dog's face – in fact the lipstick-smeared face of a woman with a very curly dead-white hairdo – appeared at the passenger window next to me, and then she, too, gave me an extremely insulting sign. My car window was open for air – my little CitiGolf does not have air conditioning – but the Clone of course had all its functions hermetically sealed inside its bland shell. So I sat pretending to be so engrossed in the fish symbol on the rear end of the car in front of me that I did not notice the taunts and demonstrations of the couple whose way of battling boredom I had so unfortunately and unwittingly interrupted. Not willing to be ignored, though, the Poodle opened her window, or rather commanded an electric impulse to glide it open smoothly, and yelled at me, in jarring contrast to the elegant control of the window, making me nostalgic for the days when people were better behaved than their motorcars, 'What's the matter, Snootface? Never seen a blowjob before?'

The obvious answer to this was no, not in peak traffic on Settler's Way (the honest answer would have been no, period), but I did not relish the prospect of a public altercation on the incidence of oral sex on motorways. An absurd impulse to exonerate myself made me explain lamely, 'I'm sorry, I thought you were a dog.' This, as I might have foreseen, produced howls of incredulity, mock-indignation and hilarity. Then she yelled at me, so loudly that I was sure all the surrounding cars could hear, 'If you can't tell the difference between a dog and a blowjob I'm going to report you to the SPCA!'

I closed my window with what dignity I could muster, but had to endure the visible ridicule of the Poodle and her companion for another five minutes at least. To my relief they turned off to the left on the Liesbeek Parkway; as they cut in rudely in front of me to turn, the woman mouthed something at me which I interpreted as 'Get a life', though I suppose it could equally have been 'Get a wife', and then she dived in under the dashboard again.

I was heartened by the sight of my lawn, trimly cut and tidy, silent green testimony to order and restraint and man's dominion over the natural universe. Except that the dog from across the road, probably offended at the denuding of his forest area, had deposited a large heap exactly and conspicuously in the centre of the otherwise immaculate surface. The dog was a rather neglected, very young, very bouncy but already calf-sized bull mastiff with correspondingly substantial stools. I sighed and fetched a Woolworths plastic carrier bag and the scoop I had bought especially to deal with Tornado's visits. I hate dog stools. I don't suppose anybody is actually sentimentally attached to them, but mine is a principled aversion: I believe that people who, for reasons of hygiene and emotional reserve, choose not to keep dogs should not have to put up with the effluvia of other people's enthusiasms.

Dogs, however, in their no doubt admirable but to my mind abject consideration of their owners, make a point of leaving their reeking piles everywhere except at home in their owner's back yard where they belong.

As I bent over the offensive heap, I was sent sprawling into it by a violent blow to the lower back. I had forgotten that Tornado's favourite trick was to rush upon unsuspecting strangers, preferably, but it now seemed not exclusively, elderly people weeding their gardens, and bounce off their backs. My next-door neighbour, a widow of gentle gardening habits, had once had her spectacles rammed into a rose bush by one of Tornado's playful rushes. I got to my feet. My hands and the knees of my best suit were soiled with more than the honest soil of my lawn. Tornado grinned at me as if he expected to be praised for his energy and initiative.

'Come here, Tornado,' I said in my best imitation of a dog-lover's infatuated coo. He came up to me, his tail wagging his body in that idiotically indiscriminate palsy of gratitude that makes dogs such undignified creatures, and I wiped my hands on his back and on his head, everywhere where I thought his owners might unwarily pat him when they eventually returned home. 'Tell your mommy and daddy you made them a little present,' I said vindictively, feeling in some measure compensated for a day that had not been in all respects successful. I had alienated a prospective client, almost quarrelled with my best friend, deeply hurt the woman I was supposed to be in love with, and made a fool of myself on the motorway. I reflected also that for millions of people this had been their first day of freedom, and I wondered whether they had discovered yet what an overrated commodity freedom is.

I washed my hands and buried the remaining dog stools neatly under a rose bush.

CHAPTER TWO

My friend Gerhard is a homosexual. I don't *mind* homosexuals, of course. They've never done me any harm, and I can see that they didn't ask to be *made* homosexual any more than – well, than I asked to be made heterosexual, I suppose. I'm pleased for them, naturally, if they're happy to be what they are, and I support our Constitution's entrenchment of the right to the sexual orientation of one's choice or inclination, but it's not as if there's very much in it for me. It's enough of a job coping with my own sexual preference, if anything so involuntary and unavoidable can be called a *preference*. It's not as if people rationally elected their own sexuality, like picking dishes from a menu – 'I'll have the shrimp cocktail, thank you, followed by a well-done T-bone – no, no chips thanks, can I have rice instead?' It – life, sex, *destiny* – is more like those intriguing but invariably unsatisfactory packages distributed to us as children by fake Father Christmases at village Christmas trees in the Natal Midlands, phoney men in cotton-wool beards sweating in the heat of the African December, handing out with unconvincing but even-handed jollity the useless and the hideous, the desirable and the disappointing, it being a rule of these occasions that the disappointing is what you get and the desirable what somebody else gets. I once tried to swap my set of coloured pencils for my friend Walter Feinauer's toy helicopter, but his mother came to complain to mine that I had 'sheeted' him (Mrs Feinauer was German, a fact to which my mother ascribed all her imperfections of temperament and culture and pronunciation), and I had to give back the helicopter, only to discover that Walter had already broken all the points of the pencils. If life hands you a set of pencils with broken points that's what you get, and better forget about preferring the helicopter. Preferences are nowhere.

The issue of sexual preference would probably never have become very real to me if it hadn't been for my friend Gerhard. He is not really an *obvious* homosexual: he looks quite normal, even more normal than most, if by normal you understand a square chin and big muscles and general bulk. In fact, Gerhard is built like a Toyota Land Cruiser. He got to look that way, he says, by carrying bags of mealies on his shoulders on the farm where he grew up, in the Makwassie district of what used to be the Western Transvaal, and then when he went to school he was always in the first rugby team, because his school had a trainer who believed, according to Gerhard, 'Technique is for sissies; in rugby it's size that counts.' Gerhard came from a conservative Afrikaans home – 'My parents were good, simple people,' he used to say, 'the old-fashioned, humble, obedient, God-fearing kind of racist who fucked up the country.' After school he went to the Potchefstroom University for Christian Higher Education, where he discovered the pleasures of litera-ture, but not as yet the nature of his own sexuality, a failure of imagination he ascribed to the fact that, as he said, 'in a good game of rugby you don't notice that you're not actually getting fucked.'

Had Gerhard remained in the Western Transvaal as an attorney in Klerksdorp, which was the limit of his parents' ambitions for him, he might have settled down to what he called 'Life with Sannie', Sannie being the generic Afrikaans wife who, in Gerhard's mythography, is wife to Piet, the generic Afrikaans husband, and mother to Jannie and Annie, the generic Afrikaans offspring. But Gerhard turned out to be a well-above-average student, so much so that he inadvertently won the Toyota Bursary, a substantial scholarship for study in England, sponsored by one Merv Tollmann, a local car dealer who hoped that overseas study could remedy the many short-comings in the Calvinist temperament to which he, as one of the few Jews in the village, was subjected. So Gerhard was sent to London in the interests of the enlightenment of his clan, with results exceeding the wildest imaginings of Merv Tollmann.

It was in London that I met Gerhard. We were both lodged in Baden-Powell House, a residence intended for the youth of the

Commonwealth, of which South Africa was at this stage, in the early nineties, no longer a member, except in the tolerant regard of the Board of Governors of Baden-Powell House, who had fought with South African troops in the Second World War, and who were reluctant to reject the offspring of their former allies. The fact that Gerhard happened to be the offspring of Nazi sympathisers was an anomaly not dreamt of in their philosophy.

I was, to be honest, less than eager to make the acquaintance of the huge South African whose atrocious English made him even more conspicuous than his sheer size alone could do, and who shook hands with everybody in Baden-Powell House: the social style of Kloof, the aloof hilltop retreat outside Durban where I had grown up, is at least a continent removed from the indiscriminate sociability of the depopulated drought-stricken country town where Gerhard had picked up such social skills as he had. Furthermore, in Kloof everybody tried to sound as if they had been born in deepest Surrey, whereas Gerhard sounded as if he had been born in Makwassie, as indeed he had. But Gerhard persevered in the face of my evident reluctance, and gradually I found in his straightforward bluffness a charm unfamiliar to me from my own background of irony, caution, nuance and intrigue. If Gerhard didn't like somebody he avoided that person and left it at that; at Milton College, if you disliked somebody, you organised a surreptitious hate campaign against him, while treating him with the most cordial geniality. By the same token, if you liked somebody, you hid this potentially humiliating fact behind a facade of mutually insulting banter; if Gerhard liked you, he put his arm around you. At first I was uncomfortable with this demonstrativeness, which could dwarf even quite regularly sized people like myself, but as I got used to it, I developed a sense of security in the uninhibited amplitude of his embrace. His English also improved dramatically, the passive vocabulary he had gleaned from all the nineteenth-century novels he read soon emerging actively if at times rather startlingly into his everyday speech, like a dowager putting in an appearance at a dogfight.

Gerhard, left consciously ravenous by the cultural deprivation of Makwassie, wanted to see everything: concerts, opera, art galleries, museums. The height of my cultural aspiration, on the other hand, was attending the Changing of the Guard and seeing the Chelsea Flower Show. But Gerhard's hunger stimulated my appetite, as it were; and I discovered to my dismay that what I had been brought up to regard as the acme of civilisation was severe cultural philistinism. In Kloof, culture was at best a matter of horticulture, at worst a matter of horses. In my family we'd covered the whole gamut, my mother spending her time gardening, my sister spending her time on horseback, my father spending his time and my mother's money at the races. For the rest, Kloof regarded music with distrust as being too German, painting with disapproval as being bohemian, and literature heavier than Barbara Cartland or Jeffrey Archer as 'depressing' (though every house had its obligatory Folio Society collection of Dickens). History ended with the Second World War, Architecture was Tudor Residential, and Current Affairs was the latest issue of *Majesty*. The London revered by Kloof as the centre of all things was as unlike the real thing as the most uninformed imaginings of Makwassie; and Makwassie, having no preconceptions, had the advantage of being more open to whatever the real thing turned out to be.

Gerhard's most momentous discovery was made one night in a pub called The Stud Farm. He had entered this particular pub for no particular reason other than the wish to have a pint, to which he had taken a liking after an initial reaction of disgusted outrage ('English beer must surely be the closest approximation ever contrived to drinking piss'). On this evening Gerhard was wearing the boots and leather jacket that he had used for hunting in the Western Transvaal, an outfit which in the middle of London had quite an exotic effect. It also made him look even bigger than he was. Inside The Stud Farm, though, there were men even more exotically dressed, almost exclusively in leather – 'There must have been a whole herd of dead cattle in there,' Gerhard said – and he was soon approached by a complete stranger, who complimented him on his boots ('Are they King's Road?' – 'No, Makwassie Co-op') and asked him whether he was into bikes. Now Gerhard had always been a motorbike enthusiast, and when his new acquaintance asked him if he wanted a spin on his Harley-Davidson, he said yes, and, by a sequence of events which Gerhard made seem as natural as the blooming of the daffodils in spring, ended up on a sheet of rubber on the man's sitting-room floor in Shepherd's Bush, wearing nothing but a light grade of motor oil, and discovering, as he put it, the latent meaning of contact sports.

All this he told me at 3 a.m. in my room at Baden-Powell House, having knocked at my door smelling strongly of Valvoline and looking very sheepish but also rather pleased with himself. 'Can you talk?' he asked, and sat down on my desk without waiting for an answer.

'Something tells me you're not here to listen to me talk,' I said.

'Well, can you listen then?'

I got back into bed and resigned myself to losing at least an hour of sleep. 'I'll listen till I go to sleep,' I said, 'so try to be interesting.'

'I will try,' he promised. He sat for a moment, not so much scraping up courage as rehearsing, with evident relish, his story. Then he said 'Do you know what a *moffie* is?'

I thought. My Afrikaans had never been very strong.

'Do you mean a homosexual?' I asked rather uncomfortably. I couldn't see why Gerhard would want to wake me up in the middle of the night to discuss sexual perversions.

'If you prefer, yes. Well ...' he said, getting up from the desk, and putting his hands on my shoulders. He put his face near to mine and whispered melodramatically, 'I have discovered that I am, in all probability, a *moffie*.'

I looked at him in dismay. This was not the sort of confession one made at close quarters, I'd have said, unless one wanted it to lead somewhere where I sincerely hoped Gerhard didn't expect it to lead. 'How – how do you know?' was all I could think of saying, wishing he would take his hands off my shoulders.

He grinned evilly. 'I don't *know*,' he said, 'but I think the chances are reasonable. When you do something you have never done before and you wonder why it took you so long to do it, then I would say you have discovered that you are

47

whatever it is that does that thing regularly as an expression of its nature.'

'You've lost me.'

'To put it more plainly, if you enjoy sucking cocks you are a cocksucker. And *vice versa*, *mutatis mutandis*, *ad nauseam*.'

'Honestly, Gerhard,' I objected.

'Yes, honestly, Nicholas,' he mimicked, pursing his lips in what I suppose he imagined to be a reasonable imitation of my manner, which was understandably a trifle constrained. It was quite within Gerhard's range of possibilities to want to share his discovery with me in deeds as well as words. When he discovered Wagner soon after his arrival in London, he dragged me to *Parsifal*, an ordeal next to which being forcibly fellated seemed relatively mild and mercifully short; even so, I was not eager to participate in Gerhard's discovery of his identity, the more so that, as he expanded vigorously on the details of his encounter, it seemed that this particular identity was considerably more complex than he had made it sound, comprising in fact an almost Wagnerian range of perversity.

'Why are you telling me all this?' I asked, after he had given me what I could only hope was a complete account of his evening in Shepherd's Bush.

'Friendship,' he said, 'but now you mention it, perhaps you would care for a demonstration of the Barrow boy? Or the Grand National? Or the Monkey Puzzle?'

'No, thank you very much,' I said. 'I'm still trying to figure out the Missionary Position.'

'Don't bother,' he said. 'Do what comes naturally. And that is not the Missionary Position.'

'What a lot you've learnt in one night.'

'I got one of the talkative ones. He says they're not all like that. In England, he maintains, a fuck is not normally considered grounds for a conversation. So I shall still need you, you see.'

'I'm delighted to hear that,' I said. 'I was afraid I might have been supplanted by the Love that Dare Not Speak Its Name. Now go away so I can sleep.'

Gerhard's Toyota bursary was generous enough to enable him to buy a car, though only enough so for a second-hand Mini, into which his six feet three inches lengthways and not much less sideways fitted only because he was surprisingly agile for his size. In our second summer in England he invited me to drive to Italy with him – on condition, he said, that I would tolerate his intention of exploring the fabled beauty of the Mediterranean male. In return I would be free to explore anything that took my fancy. I opted for the Uffizi and the Pitti, which my *Cultural Guide to Italy* told me were the jewels of Firenze. I also managed to negotiate an agreement that if we were forced for reasons of economy to share hotel rooms he would acquire and wear pyjamas. Being naturally modest myself, I'm uncomfortable in the presence of naked people. A final stipulation was that he was not to bring any of his conquests home to a shared room. Hearing about them was horrendous enough; witnessing them was unthinkable.

Gerhard's clue to the fabled beauty of the Mediterranean male turned out to be the *ManMeet Guide*, a lurid but terse publication listing in graphic shorthand the nature, location and attractions of the apparently innumerable places on earth where men intent on sexual intercourse with other men could meet others similarly inclined. LBAYOR, for instance, stood for Leather and Bondage, At Your Own Risk; BSRS was Beware: Sincere Relationship Seekers, and BB was Bargain Basement. Since most of the *ManMeet* recommendations turned out to be truck stops on the Autostrada (PSBB: 'Probably Straight but Bored'), we initially saw less of the art treasures of Italy and more of its heavy transport than I had contracted for. I found our conspicuous presence in a Mini, surrounded by ten-ton trucks, excruciatingly embarrassing: whereas it did not bring us any of the kind of attention Gerhard was hoping for, it did attract plenty of another kind, expressed with extreme volubility in rapid Italian and accompanied by a larger range of arm, hand and finger gestures than I had thought physically possible even in Italy. Gerhard remained unshaken, ascribing it to what he called the eternal conflict between Machismo and Eros. He had complete faith in his own mastery of Italian, having spent the fortnight before our departure listening to *Teach*

Yourself Italian tapes on his Walkman. He had also brought with him an Italian phrasebook entitled *Italian for Pleasure, Leisure and Business*, supplemented with a multilingual guide to safe sex he had picked up in a London pub, which usefully listed all known sexual practices in most known languages, divided into the safe and the unsafe.

My deliverance came one early evening outside Vicenza, at the Monte Berico truck stop ('good scenery' commented the *ManMeet Guide* helpfully), where Gerhard at last engaged in an exchange of what he thought were erotic negotiations with what he thought was a promising truck driver, a young man in charge of a truckload of live sheep. It turned out, though, that what Gerhard intended as an offer of a quite different kind was interpreted by the young man first as an offer to buy his sheep, and then, after Gerhard's best efforts with the *Multilingual Safe-Sex Guide*, as a bid to engage with one or several of the sheep, as Gerhard explained to me as we drove off in haste, in *sesso orale*.

'What's that?' I asked.

'A blowjob.' Then he started laughing. 'Except what I proposed in my thoughtful and I thought gently reassuring though possibly pedantic fashion, was what my safe sex guide calls *sesso orale senza ejaculare in bocca*.' He pronounced the words with a kind of unctuous gusto, as if he was anointing a Pope or selling dubious pastries on some street corner. 'Sounds like a chorus from Verdi, doesn't it?' he asked, and sang, to the tune of the *Chorus of the Hebrew Slaves* from *Nabucco*, '*Ses*-so or-*ale* senz-a e-jacul*aaaa*-re in *bo- o- o- c*ca', beating time with his huge fists on the Mini's tiny steering wheel. 'That means …' he started to explain.

'I can work out for myself what it means, thank you. He must have thought you were very considerate of his sheep.'

'If he did, it did not placate him. He was furious. And for an Italian he was quite big. So I cleared out.'

'So did he, apparently,' I said, looking behind us. We were being followed by a ten-ton truck filled with bleating sheep.

'You think he has repented of his fury?' asked Gerhard, regaining the evil glint in his eye that I had learnt to dread. 'Shall I pull off at the next stop?'

'Not unless you want to blow the whole of the Common Market,' I said. 'He's got company.'

Behind the sheep truck were what seemed like twenty ten-tonners, all blasting their horns like rogue elephants on the rampage. And they were chasing us.

We escaped only because a Mini can get into places a ten-tonner can't reach.

With one memorable exception, the rest of our Italian trip was relatively uneventful. Firenze did much for our compatibility, in that the Accademia was one of the few places in Italy recommended by both my *Cultural Guide* and Gerhard's *ManMeet Guide* ('Sooner or later every gay man in the world visits the David, so hang around'). Gerhard discovered to his delight, as he put it, that Michelangelo had also had a taste for truck drivers – 'Look at the muscles on the man,' he said, pointing to the David, 'he didn't get those from doing interior decorating.'

I had some bad moments when Gerhard started singing, albeit under his breath, his version of the *Chorus of the Hebrew Slaves* in public places. I was less concerned that the Italians would resent the unasked-for advice on how to conduct their sex lives than that it might incense their notorious sensitivity on the score of their national composer. 'For heaven's sake, Gerhard,' I pleaded. 'Can't you let up? You've managed to become probably the only person in history to be hounded off the autostrada by a convoy of juggernauts for proposing oral sex to a flock of sheep – do you want to get chucked into an Italian jail on charges of public disrespect to Verdi?'

'Do you want to hear the second verse I've composed?' he asked, assuming his evil look.

'*No* thank you very much.'

'Then don't tempt me to perform it.'

Knowing Gerhard, I was careful not to give him grounds for doing what I knew would be at best irresponsible, at worst illegal, and in any case highly embarrassing. I should have known, though, that he would find an excuse anyway, it not being in Gerhard's nature to desist for very long from doing anything he wanted to do. In the event, he contrived a setting of near-operatic splendour.

We were concluding our holiday with a visit to Venice, which, since this was July, was crowded, expensive, mosquito-ridden and noisy, and rank with the smell of diesel fuel, dead rats, unidentifiable general putrescence and the all-too-identifiable effects of clam poisoning on the tourist constitution. The absence of cars, which I had looked forward to as a blessed relief from Italian traffic, turned out to be merely a substitution of pedestrian traffic jams for the vehicular kind, and of the near-tangible aura of garlic and sweat for the fumes of exhausts. Instead of the whine of Vespas and the roar of Fiats to keep us awake, we had, in our very basic *pensione* on a particularly evil-smelling little canal, with all the windows open for air, the groans, gasps, grunts and shrieks of American honeymooners, Swedish backpackers and German lesbians intent upon profiting by or contributing to the fabled erotic ambience of Venice.

The whole place, this over-elaborate and over-priced city where nature had intended only water, seemed to me an arrogant and ultimately futile gesture, a cultural-commercial construct that had passed itself off as a civilisation for longer than its means permitted, and was now gradually and with bad grace decomposing back into the murky waters of the Adriatic that it had done so much to pillage and pollute. Gerhard, though he admitted that it was all 'a bit of a crush and a pong, somewhat redolent of labouring humanity's armpit and groin', seemed actually to enjoy it all. 'It's not Kloof, certainly,' he said – I had made the mistake of expressing nostalgia for the cool green hills of home – 'but then, Kloof was never the centre of an Empire, whatever its inhabitants may have assumed.'

The main advantage of Venice, as far as I was concerned, was that there were no truck drivers. I should have known, though, that Gerhard wasn't going to be deterred by a detail like that. He decided that we couldn't leave Venice without an outing in a gondola: 'The gondola is to Venice as the black taxi is to London or the yellow cab to New York or the donkey to Santorini or the camel to the Sahara or the minibus taxi to Cape Town; it's more than a form of transport, it's a *symbol*, an encapsulation of the spirit of the place. A trip in a gondola is a ritual sacrifice to the ancient Venetian trading spirit. Besides, they say the gondoliers fuck like rattlesnakes.'

'Eels, surely, in Venice?'

'Don't be pedantic.'

'We can't afford a gondola. And you probably can't afford a gondolier.'

'We can find an affordable gondola. You just have to bargain for long enough. And once we've found a gondola the gondolier is thrown in, as it were.'

I suspected that the bargaining was in itself the main attraction for Gerhard; whereas I found the process deeply humiliating, he seemed to enter into the negotiations with an avidity at least matching that of the seller. He had, after his unfortunate encounter with the sheep farmer, improved his bargaining skills and his Italian considerably.

So Gerhard negotiated an 'affordable' trip in a gondola selected on the basis of his assessment of the gondolier's appearance and potential, what Gerhard had taken to calling the eel factor. The cut rate entailed sharing our transport with another group of bargain hunters, George and Martha Plimstick and Martha's sister Emily, all from Yampa, Colorado, as they informed us almost immediately after we'd all shakily settled into the shabby interior of the gondola. The general merriment and excitement was dampened by the discovery that at the reduced fare the gondolier didn't sing: 'You want Pavarotti you pay for Pavarotti,' the darkly handsome but ungracious young man explained sulkily. 'You pay fuck-all you get fuck-all.' Emily blushed deep scarlet and George explained to her that foreigners didn't really *understand* what they were saying. The gondolier looked as if he understood exactly what he was saying, but said no more, and we set off, a rather dour little group in our non-musical gondola. 'It's no better than a goddam row-boat if you don't have singing,' complained George. 'Or a canoe,' added Martha. 'Except that the mosquitoes are bigger than at home.'

This was Gerhard's cue to offer to treat them to an authentic Italian song. He smiled in his most charming manner – Gerhard's most charming manner is to human relations what chemical warfare is to diplomacy – and said: 'Of course, it's not the same thing, but I have made a study of old Venetian troubadour songs. You know of course that Casanova was a Venetian …?'

'Honestly, Gerhard,' I protested, trying to kick him without capsizing the gondola, 'I really don't think that's a good idea.' But Gerhard just smiled demonically, and Emily said, 'Oh yes, please, we've had no singing this trip.'

Gerhard, who actually has quite a good voice, launched into a stirring rendering of *Sesso orale senza ejaculare*. Martha got tears in her eyes and Emily asked Gerhard to start again so that she could get out her video camera to tape the occasion for their Italian grandmother in Wisconsin. After one run through George and Martha took up with sentimental gusto what they took to be the refrain, '*senza ejaculare in boo-o-occa*', with Emily happily recording the performance. I didn't dare look around me, but I did catch the spellbound horror of a group of respectable Venetians waiting at a vaporetto stop. Emily recorded them too.

'Don't you think you've delighted us for long enough, Gerhard?' I asked in my most restrained tones when we came to the last ringing '*in bocca*.'

This was a mistake.

'No, I do not think so,' said Gerhard with a grin like Jack Nicholson's in *The Shining*. 'Should we try a second verse?'

The Plimsticks enthusiastically agreed, and Gerhard launched into a melodic rendering of his second verse, which turned out to be '*Rapporti annali con preservitivo e lubrificante*'. By the time we got back to the landing stage our fellow-passengers were completely enamoured with Gerhard: 'Thank you so much for the most romantic evening of my life,' said Emily, and 'I guess that's what you'd call a real Venetian experience,' said George. Even the gondolier seemed less sulky, especially after he was given a huge tip by the Plimsticks. Gerhard prevailed upon him to tie up his gondola for the evening, and the two of them disappeared down the narrow alleys of Venice. I returned to the *pensione* and tried to go to sleep through the gasps and shrieks of the honeymooners and the backpackers.

I can still not hear the *Chorus of the Hebrew Slaves* without breaking out in a light sweat, which is a pity, because it is a very beautiful chorus.

Given, then, the history of my and Gerhard's friendship, I can hardly be suspected of intolerance on the score of his sexual exploits. But what the expression on his face most reminded me of, as he lubriciously watched Luc Tomlinson's retreating backside, was the Jack Nicholson grin. If I had been religious, Gerhard would have driven me to believe in demonic possession; as it was, my agnostic rationality was at a loss to account for the charge of evil energy that could transfigure Gerhard from a well-behaved and generally ultra-polite Afrikaner boy into a kind of super-intelligent animal, a two-footed beast of prey. I swear that at such times his pupils contracted into slits, and his golden-brown eyes glowed with a yellow beam that transfixed anything it focused on. Gerhard told me that he once delayed the departure of flight SA 243 to Miami by 20 minutes when he caught the eye of the captain in the departure lounge. I believed him, because I have seen for myself an unsuspecting young man on the up escalator in Cavendish Square, fixed by that beam from the down escalator, turn round and run down against the direction of the escalator to where Gerhard was waiting for him below; I have seen an earnest cyclist buckle his front wheel against the kerb, totally disoriented by that magnetic stare; I have seen a sensible-looking bank teller drop a few thousand rand in small notes on meeting that glow through the bullet-proof glass. I have seen a businessman in a three-piece suit park his BMW in a no-stopping zone and get out to take up the golden invitation extended from a pedestrian crossing. But Luc Tomlinson glanced at Gerhard and walked on. So I knew that the grin meant that Gerhard was resolving to return to the chase. And I was irritated by this, though without quite being able to say so to him. Normally I regarded Gerhard's exploits as his own business, even when they to some degree inconvenienced me, as in his pursuit of Italian truck drivers and gondoliers; but in this instance it was literally my business, in that it was open to me to regard Luc Tomlinson as a potential client, even though I had declined to take his case. By this logic, Gerhard was jeopardising the possible development of the case. I knew better than to tell him this, for it would only have intensified his interest in the young man. There was thus very little I could do, except mutely resent Gerhard's unprofessional intervention in my professional affairs. Luc Tomlinson certainly did not need my protection, even had I been tempted to extend it.

CHAPTER THREE

My friend Gerhard professes amazement at my choosing to live in Pinelands, 'proof,' as he puts it, 'of the triumph of domesticity over every other human instinct.' He does not seem to recognise that the admittedly uneventful tenor of life in Pinelands might, to somebody less addicted than he to the unpredictable, the random, to what he calls 'the *randiness* of the city', constitute its attraction. Gerhard, of course, lives in a flat in the City Bowl, which serves him more as a launching pad, really, than as a home.

I bought my house when I was left a small legacy by a maternal uncle in England who felt sorry for my mother but didn't believe in leaving money to women. I decided on Pinelands because I believed or hoped that by leading a quiet existence in a totally unassuming suburb I might be spared the major inconveniences that plague more glamorous areas of the earth. Would muggers stalk the streets of a suburb that has outlawed liquor stores? Would hijackers risk an escape route through a place where every street is a Circle, a Square or a Crescent? The very origin and design of Pinelands, what one might call its conception if that word did not imply so crudely physical an origin for a place that had sprung fully fledged from its creator's brow, constituted a victory of human rationality over contingent and random nature: traced geometrically on the shifting sands of the Cape Flats, settling their uncertain superficiality with pine trees and lawns and white picket or paddock fencing, Pinelands the Garden Suburb arose with twee self-assurance from the ancient ocean bed, each cosy huddle of thatched cottages arranged around a Green or Glen or Close. My own little stake in this paradise of planning blended harmoniously, which is to say inconspicuously, with the general ambience of hobbits, horse brasses and roses: intended for what estate agents call 'beginners', on the assumption that life follows a trajectory of multiplication and accumulation, it had only two bedrooms downstairs, one of which I had converted to a study, and upstairs, under the thatch, an attic with a dormer window, where I accommodated such few visitors as I attracted. For all Gerhard's jesting, it exactly suited my needs and my temperament. It even had just enough garden: large enough to establish a polite distance from my neighbours, small enough to be controllable. The only aspect of the Pinelands ethos that inconvenienced me was its tolerance of free-range dogs, but I could see that as nuisances went in the new South Africa, dog droppings were relatively mild.

It was becoming evident, though, that even the most uneventful existence is shaped by events outside itself, unless you can contrive to live in one of those fortunate countries more boring as a whole than as the sum of the boredoms of its citizens, and known mainly for scenery and dairy produce. And even then, history has it surprises, as witness the experience of a friend of my father's in the nineteen seventies. Intent for reasons of his own on retiring to the spot on earth least likely to be disturbed by event or catastrophe or debt collector, he argued sensibly that it would have to be a remote, under-populated island, preferably under British dominion to guarantee the peace and the plumbing. Acting on this calculation, he arrived on the Falkland Islands just weeks before the Argentinians seized it. He was one of the few civilian casualties, shot by a female British sergeant while in the act of indecently exposing himself. There was an inquiry into the incident, and the sergeant was fully exonerated on the grounds that she thought that he was reaching for a concealed weapon.

This seems to suggest that even the stragglers, the deserters and the flops end up in the passenger compartment of the juggernaut of history – or in our case, perhaps more accurately, the minibus taxi of history: overcrowded, hospitable, unroadworthy, unlicensed and completely unpredictable as to destination. So the year following the Election of 1994 affected me as it affected all South Africans, if not yet materially, then in a gradual and sometimes abrupt change of perspective, a sense of moving very fast in an unspecified direction, with a novice

58

driver not necessarily elected for his driving abilities. The Government of National Unity was a bit like a crowd of passengers trying to agree on a route when they all had different destinations in mind, National Unity being about as precise a designation as Utopia or Shangri-La. At times it seemed as if one half of the country would continue to drive on the left-hand side of the road, and the other half would switch to the right.

My friend Gerhard was euphoric: 'We have outlived the dinosaurs and survived the Ice Age. We are entering a springtime of hope, democracy and blue movies. Not to mention LOTS of foreign ships in the docks.'

Others were less sanguine.

'About all we've got to show for the new South Africa,' pronounced Cedric Watts one morning around the coffee machine, 'are squatter huts and car hijackings.'

'Worried about your new Mercedes, Cedric?' Dikeledi asked.

Cedric was torn between ignoring Dikeledi, whom he disliked, and sharing with the company his latest Gadget. Cedric was famous for his Gadgets, possibly his way of combating the impending chaos that he was perennially predicting. 'No, the Merc is safe,' he chuckled. 'I've seen to that.'

The company subsided into silence, knowing that we were about to have a Cedric Exposition.

'I've had this anti-hijack device fitted,' he said. 'It's quite simple really, but devilishly efficient.' He chuckled again.

'But how does it work?' Kitty Jooste asked. Cedric's Expositions demanded a minimal amount of audience participation, just enough to keep him inflated. Gerhard had once likened him to a blow-up doll with a small puncture.

'Well, they install a cylinder of gas – quite a small one, the size of a shoe box – in your boot, and then connect that to a system of pipes lining the side of your car, just below the driver's door. Now you have a foot pedal inside your car, and when your Gentleman Caller, Mr Would-be Hijacker, knocks at your window for admission, you step on the pedal, the pedal feeds liquid gas to the jets and ignites it, and whoosh! Your hijacker has a ball of fire spewed out at him.'

'But is it safe?' asked Willy Wilson.

'For the hijacker? Of course not, but that's not the idea, is it?'

'No, I mean for you, fooling around with a bottle of gas in your boot.'

'You drive around with a tankful of petrol all the time, don't you? Listen, the system is guaranteed safe; it won't even damage your paintwork – but it will certainly set fire to the chaps with the guns.'

'But is it legal?'

'As legal as any other form of self-defence.'

'Isn't that a bit harsh – I mean, setting someone on fire for trying to hijack your car?'

'Harsh? What do you think they'd do to you once they've jumped into your car? Take you to the Mount Nelson for tea and cakes? No, I'm not taking any chances in this country of ours. If the police can't protect us we have to protect ourselves.'

My mother, too, reported frequent onslaughts upon the hapless and helpless senior citizens of her acquaintance. She phoned me daily with either a new horror story of urban terrorism and depredation visited upon the propertied classes, or a new suggestion as to a 'nice place to move to, now that this country is heading for untold disaster or worse.'

'They say,' she said, 'that it's a deliberate strategy, called the Informal Redistribution of Wealth.'

My mother had already once had her wealth redistributed by my father, but I refrained from pointing that out. Besides, although less apocalyptic than my mother in my vision of my country's future, I was considerably less optimistic than Gerhard. We might have got rid of the dinosaurs, but history has taught us not to expect the bunnies and daisies to inherit the earth.

For the time being, Life in the sense of the things we do each day changed very little. The only development in my relationship with Leonora was that I finished *Middlemarch*, but without this having the transformative effect she'd hoped for. 'It's such a noble novel,' she sighed; I suspect she saw it as a counteragent to Gerhard. 'Yes, I can see that,' I replied, 'but in essence it's about people failing. Just about everybody fails.'

'It's about people accepting their limitations. That's not the same thing as failing.'

This seemed to me an unhopeful basis on which to build one's life, as I suspected Leonora intended for us to do, once we were, in the natural course of things, married. She was accommodating my limitations in advance.

As for Luc Tomlinson, it seemed that I needn't have resented Gerhard's appropriation of him. He disappeared completely from my ken, and even Gerhard reported no sightings, in spite of his cherished belief that nothing indefinitely escapes the observation of the truly alert: 'If you have a strong enough desire to see somebody, you *attract* him by the sheer magnetic force of your lust.' I accepted, with a mixture of relief and something else – something resentful and yet slightly rueful – that Luc Tomlinson had returned to his chacmas, unless indeed, as was more probable, he had returned to the bosom of his family and was helping his father develop a hotel complex at Cape Point, accepting, in the manner of *Middlemarch*, the limits set to his ideals by his environment.

Eventually, however, Gerhard's faith in his own magnetic powers was vindicated. One Monday morning, a good eighteen months after Luc's first and only appearance, Gerhard strolled into my office as he often did on a Monday morning, usually with an account of some disreputable encounter that I listened to only because resistance encouraged him to dwell on the unsavoury details. On this occasion he looked even more arch than usual.

'Do you remember the Angel of Dawning?' he asked, taking his accustomed place on the corner of my desk.

I thought, or pretended to think, for slightly longer than necessary, while pointedly extracting a document from under Gerhard's considerable bulk. I didn't think I wanted to hear his story. 'Yes – that red-haired chap with the baboons. Not so?'

'Quite so, as you know very well. You'll never guess where I ran into him this weekend, though come to think of it, neither of us was running.'

'Angels? The Bronx? Rondebosch station? Sandy Bay? Sea

Point Promenade? Steamers?' I tidied up the document and stapled it neatly.

'Wrong, wrong, wrong, wrong, wrong and wrong,' he said. 'And if I may say so, thoroughly ungenerous of you. Stop fixating on sex, and think nature, think wide open spaces, think healthy outdoor exercise.'

'I think all those things without somehow seeing you in them, if you know what I mean.'

'You suffer from a starved imagination. Well, then – on top of Table Mountain.'

'You climbed Table Mountain?' Gerhard made no secret of his distrust of mountains, having grown up in a landscape where the highest outcrop on the horizon was the neighbour's windmill.

'What's a man to do? Last Wednesday lunch time, minding my own business on my way down Adderley Street –'

'When you were supposed to meet me for lunch, yes.' I'd spent a solitary half-hour over a plate of pasta in Nino's.

'Was I? Oops. Well, anyway, I shall we say *allowed* myself to be followed by this person wearing the most intriguing boots with red socks, so I thought, well that's a new kink, why not?'

'You mean Luc Tomlinson followed you ...?'

'No relax, relax, relax and be informed. My pursuer, it transpired upon closer enquiry, was a *mountaineer*, which explained the red socks ...'

'You mean you hijacked him from a mountain club outing?' Gerhard claimed once to have diverted a scoutmaster from a troop of boy scouts on a route march through Newlands Forest, 'thus providing,' according to him, 'the young scouts with their first invaluable lesson in survival: what to do when your leader gets his ears shagged off behind a tree.'

'No, I tell you this was in Adderley Street; but you know what mountaineers are like, they wear their mountaineering kit or togs or gear or whatever they call it, wherever they go – did I tell you I once met someone in Angels who was wearing crampons? Quite stylish, but hell to dance with –.'

'*Ger*hard.'

'Right, anyway, this person, actually a very sweet chap, had put on his boots and socks, not to mention the most fetching pair of canvas shorts, to come shopping for a kettle at Board-mans, and what with one thing leading to another but him having for some complicated reason to get home with the kettle for lunch – I think he lives in some outdoorsy beansprouty commune and they were having hot water for lunch – and of course, with me being anxious not to keep you waiting –'

'You lie.'

'– we agreed that it might be of mutual pleasure and profit to see each other again, and what he proposed was an early morning climb up Table Mountain on Sunday, and you know me, always accommodating, so I suppressed my bathophobia and put on my hiking boots and followed him up the mountain. Sublime, I must say.'

'The view?'

'That too, what I saw of it. But mainly the red socks. But where was I?'

'The Angel of Dawning, reappearance of.'

'Of course. I knew it was something good. Anyway, as luck and timing would have it, when Clive and ...'

'Clive?'

'Yes, he's called Clive, isn't that sweet? So colonial. He smokes a pipe and his grandfather was a missionary.'

'You were saying?'

'Oh yes, but you keep interrupting. When Clive and I reached the top exactly at sunrise ...'

'You climbed Table Mountain before *sunrise*?'

'I tell you, I'm accommodating. And Clive is quite demanding in his sweet way. Everything is traded off against something else. Any normal person would just say yes, yes, yes please, thank you very much, but not Clive; Clive says Only if you climb a mountain with me to prove you're serious. Isn't it romantic?'

'You're turning my stomach. Let's get back to the Angel of Dawning.'

'You're so *impatient*. I knew you were just pretending ...'

I aimed the telephone book at his head. 'Gerhard, get to the point or leave my office.'

'I am trying, believe me. Well then, there we are on top of the

63

mountain in the first rays of the new day, and I vaguely sense a presence behind me even more blinding in its beauty than the sunrise, and I turn round and see, on a rocky outcrop as if hewn from Table Mountain sandstone, resplendent in the dawn ... you've guessed it ...' he got to his feet, opened his arms as if announcing a star turn, and declaimed, 'Mark POPLINGTON!'

'Luc Tomlinson.'

'I beg his pardon. Luc Tomlinson.'

'It's all right, Myrah,' I reassured my startled secretary, who had put her head round the door. 'Did he recognise you?'

'If he did he didn't let on. He was communing with nature or something.'

'On his own?'

'On his own. Unless there was a troop of baboons behind the rock.'

'And did you speak to him?'

'What do you take me for? Of course I did, to Clive's most gratifyingly obvious chagrin. I said to him Excuse me but I never forget a butt, are you not my friend Nicholas Morris's environmentalist client?'

'You didn't.'

'Not quite in those words, but in essence.'

'And ...?'

'And he's more devastating than ever. You should see him without his shirt.'

'That's not what I mean. What did he *say*?'

'He said Nicholas *Who*? No, only joking. What he in fact said was, and I quote verbatim, "Yes, except he didn't want me as a client."'

'Oh, but that's a *lie*, I ...'

'Don't shout at me, I'm only repeating what he said. And then he said "You can tell your friend Nicholas that the development has been approved and will probably go ahead soon."'

'Gerhard, you're not joking?'

'Would I joke about the environment? Would I joke about the Angel of Dawning? That is exactly what he said, scowling ferociously in that charmingly *farouche* way he has. Do you think he's a bit ... you know ... retarded?'

'You didn't ask him for more details?'

'Nothing would have given me more pleasure, but Clive was getting restive, so I bade the Angel a wistful farewell and Clive and I rushed off the other side of the mountain like a pair of Gadarene swine. After all, a bargain is a bargain and I had kept my side of it ...'

'And you don't know what Tomlinson is doing now?'

'No, I tell you I didn't want to seem too avid in Clive's presence. But he did say ... yes, he said something about staying out at Cape Point while he still had it to himself.'

He got up and stretched himself. 'Let me go and catch up on my sleep. The problem with mountaineers is they always have to get up on top of everything *because it's there.*'

'I hope he took off his red socks.'

'You have no imagination. Without the red socks there would be no point to it.'

I turned to the work Gerhard had interrupted, an application from a Concerned Citizens Group to have the Crossroads squatter camp declared a Protected Wetland. But I found I couldn't concentrate on the intricacies of the argument; for some reason, I was disturbed by Gerhard's 'He didn't want me as a client.' Had I really refused Tomlinson? He had struck me as robust enough to come back if he'd really needed my services – but then belligerence was sometimes a front for diffidence – and then again it was near-impossible to believe in Tomlinson's diffidence, for heaven's sake. And it was absurd to suggest, as he was apparently doing, that my reluctance was to blame for the imminence of the development. I didn't care two lumps of Table Mountain sandstone for Luc Tomlinson, but I hate misunderstandings, and this seemed like a misunderstanding. I had not *not* wanted him as a client; I had just tried to make clear to him what a proper lawyer-client relation demanded.

I hadn't seen anything about the Cape Point development in the press. There would have had to be a call for objections to the rezoning, but it was of the essence of such advertisements to be hidden between the funeral notices and the second-hand laundry mangles, and deadlined for the third blue moon after the previous leap year. Thus it was entirely possible that the call had come and gone without my seeing it. The most natural way of finding out the details would be, of course, to ask Tomlinson; but getting hold of a person who affected to scorn the refinements of civilisation was a complicated business, it being one of the fallacies of natural living that it simplified existence. I might have to drive out to Cape Point – I thought I knew where Rocklands, the Tomlinson property, was: on the coast, well away from the tourist routes conveying visitors to the tip of the Point. I could drive out there on a Sunday: it was unlikely that I would have to see Luc himself. He had the look of someone who doesn't sleep at home very often; indeed he had the look of someone who slept in a cave. I could simply go and inspect the area for signs of imminent development. If I happened to bump into Luc Tomlinson, that would be all to the good, but the chances of doing so were too remote to constitute a reason either to drive out to Cape Point or not to drive there.

On Sundays the route to Cape Point, along a narrow, winding, and therefore officially 'scenic' mountain road, is liable to clogging, especially where your usual morons ignore the No Stopping and Feeding of the Baboons signs, not deterred even by the prospect of having their windscreens urinated on. So to take the road to Cape Point on a Sunday morning was a radical step for me. Indeed, the outing acquired something of a clandestine tinge from the fact that I couldn't tell either Gerhard or Leonora about it: Gerhard because I didn't want his lubricious aspersions on what he would certainly regard as a visit to the Angel of Dawning, Leonora because she would have expected to be taken along, though she wouldn't have presumed to say so. Sunday drives were exactly the kind of thing Leonora wished I'd do more of with her. And somehow Leonora and Luc Tomlinson did not strike me as a happy combination – assuming, that is, that Luc Tomlinson would be at home. Of course, if he weren't, there would be no reason not to take Leonora, but that was not a chance I wanted to take.

Partly to avoid the Sunday crush, then, and partly to escape detection, I set off early on Sunday morning, after a brief hesitation as to the appropriate dress for a visit to Cape Point. If I were to bump into Luc Tomlinson, he would almost certainly be snide about any attempt on my part to dress down to his standard, just as he had been rude about my suit and tie. So I put on my usual weekend clothes, a pair of jeans, comfortable shoes, short-sleeved shirt, half annoyed with myself for considering the matter at all. I couldn't imagine that Luc Tomlinson would waste two seconds of his time planning a wardrobe to see me. I hesitated before taking my Ray-Bans: Luc Tomlinson would certainly have some comment to make about them. But I wasn't going to be intimidated by his cheap scorn; I took the glasses and suspended them from their cord round my neck.

Cape Point, as the name indicates, is a kind of secondary peninsula jutting out of the Cape Peninsula proper, and can thus be reached by either of its two coastlines. Both routes are celebrated in tourist brochures for their beauty, but I opted for the eastern route because that was where the sun would be coming up over False Bay, and, though not deeply versed in the intricacies of scenery watching, I assumed that the sunrise was what one went for when given a choice.

The early start proved to be wise. With only some early-morning runners and cyclists abroad, the world seemed for once able to escape the stranglehold of traffic. The clear, windless light of morning lent an independent existence to the sheer rock faces, the gently swelling ocean, the rounded rocks shiny in the early light, and the abundant greenery of the mountain, making them seem less passively enslaved to the motorcar than usual. It was going to be a hot day, but as yet the air was fresh, with just an intimation of spring. It would be too much to say that the world seemed newly created, but it did look less trampled-on than usual.

The gate at Cape Point had just opened when I arrived.

'First visitor,' said the gatekeeper, as I paid my fee in exchange for a brochure detailing the flora and fauna of the reserve. Fortunately there was a sketch map of the area in the brochure, and I guessed that the Tomlinson leasehold was the part marked Private: No Entrance. I followed a minor road to a gate that said, unambiguously enough: *'Private Property. Turn Round.'* I hesitated. It was unlike me to disregard injunctions of

67

this kind, but then, it was unlike me to drive out to Cape Point on an impulse, and to turn back now was to have wasted a trip.

I got out and opened the gate, drove through, and got out and closed the gate again, reflecting on how elaborate the measures were whereby people tried to preserve a natural way of living, every wilderness surrounded by a fence, every unspoilt territory rigorously policed to keep it unspoilt. I bumped along the road, which by now was little more than a track. It made its unemphatic way towards the sheer eastern face of the Point, then, taking a sharp curve downwards, descended into a cove overlooking the wide expanse of False Bay. Nestling at the base of the cove, set against the slope, was a sizeable stone house, thatched, surrounded by a wide stoep; for all its substantial size, it had clearly been intended to merge with its surroundings. I could see how the place could have awakened every impulse of greed in a property developer's bosom: the setting, against a heather-covered slope, was spectacular, with a sandy beach of its own and a view that seemed to stretch out forever across the hazy breadth of False Bay, to the ring of mountains surrounding it on the far side. As a house, it was sublime; translated into real estate, it spelt dizzy dollars.

I stopped as close to the house as the track allowed me. The sun was just appearing over the Hottentots Holland mountains, the first rays striking the elevated stoep at the top of a flight of stone steps. There was no sign of life, not even a motorcar: young Tomlinson was probably living it up in the city. But as I got out of my car, the front door opened and a figure moved out of the obscurity of the stoep into the new sunlight on the steps. The figure was very tall and lean, its wild mane of coppery-red curls shining in the ruddy glow of dawn: unmistakably the Angel of Dawning, refulgent in the first light of creation, I thought reluctantly, and then realised that Luc Tomlinson was naked.

I paused. Approaching with aplomb a naked person on whose property I was trespassing was a social skill I had not had occasion to master, but nor could I very well turn tail and drive away, the more so that Tomlinson had obviously seen me. He shaded his eyes against the low sun, then waved.

Awkwardly, I waved back, not sure whether he had recognised me; the wave, at any rate, did not seem overtly hostile. I was expecting him to retreat modestly into the house and reappear in a clad state, but he stood there as confidently as if impeccably dressed for a formal reception, in a passable imitation of one of Ayn Rand's more insufferably chiselled heroes. He could not, I suppose, have anticipated the arrival of an audience, but the very act of standing naked on an elevated stoep had something *posed* about it, as if he was trying to impress the rising sun.

I have, of course, in a boarding school and university career seen a fair amount of nakedness, but usually in a context that made it possible to ignore the details: dressing rooms, dormitories, showers, not in full sunshine on a stoep. Walking up, clad in my carefully considered outfit, I felt absurdly as if I was the underdressed person, an effect, probably, of Tomlinson's air of complete possession of his surroundings.

'Well, hello,' he said, registering neither joy nor displeasure. 'Fancy meeting you here.' At least he seemed to recognise me.

'Yes,' I said, and for a wild moment considered pretending that I had got lost on my way somewhere else, but there weren't that many other places to aim for in Cape Point. So I didn't offer an explanation of why I was there, and he didn't ask for one.

'Coffee?' he asked, pointing at the cup in his hand.

'Yes, please,' I replied with a desperate brightness, as if coffee was exactly what I'd driven out to Cape Point for. 'That would be wonderful.'

'Well, then. Come on, then,' and he turned round to lead the way into the house. Despite my relief at this change in our relative positions, I couldn't help reading a sort of arrogance into the ease with which he turned his back on me, secure in the knowledge that there was no aspect of the whole flawless length of his body that could not bear scrutiny. The smooth tan skin was overlaid with a sheen of very fine coppery down, which contributed to the effect of effulgence, giving definition to the delicately sculpted cusps and arches and planes of his body. Gerhard should have been here, I told myself with a twinge of conscience, then in the same breath congratulated

69

myself that I hadn't brought Leonora. I don't think Leonora has ever seen a naked man over the age of six.

To say that the house was untidy is like saying Pompeii suffered from unacceptable levels of atmospheric pollution. Although there were quite enough rooms in the house for a proper division of functions, everything seemed to be something else. Nothing seemed to have an appointed place; even the bed, which was little more than a double mattress with some sheets, was in what by other indications – its size, its position just inside the front door, a sofa, some shabby easy chairs – seemed to be the sitting room. The bathroom, I noticed in passing, had a large bookshelf in it, with books and toiletries – I found time to wonder what toiletries Luc Tomlinson could possibly use – ranged indiscriminately on the heavy wooden shelves. Various pieces of jetsam stood and hung around, chunks of wood shaped by time and the sea into fantastical sculptures; shells, animal skulls. Luc led the way with no attempt to apologise for the state of the house. Only one room, leading out of the long passage between the stoep and the kitchen, seemed at all habitable: it was neatly and quite conventionally furnished as a bedroom, complete with a double bed and a dressing table. There was even a painting on one wall, something that looked like somebody's impression of the house and surroundings. For the rest, there were a few doors that were closed. Incongruously, the windows were fitted with burglar bars; presumably then this idyllic retreat also had its criminal population, though it was hard to imagine who and why. Apart from anything else, I couldn't see anything worth stealing.

The kitchen was clearly also the dining room, if a much-used table and four upright chairs constituted a dining room. A large stable door opened to the north of the house; the top half was open, taking in a sweep of rocky coastline towards Muizenberg. The whole place smelled vaguely familiar; then I recalled the smell of Luc Tomlinson himself in my office: there it had been alien, pungent; here it seemed natural, coming as much from the vegetation outside as from the thatch of the roof, exposed above the timber beams.

'Lovely view,' I said, then realised how conventional it sounded.

'Yes, well,' he grunted. 'Black?' as he poured a mug from a kettle standing on the gas stove.

'Please.'

'Just as well,' he grinned unexpectedly. I'd forgotten how white his teeth were in his tawny face. 'I've run out of milk.' He passed me the mug; we negotiated the handle between us without touching fingers.

'Isn't it inconvenient, living so far out?' I asked.

'No, well,' he shrugged. 'What's convenient? Convenient's what suits your particular way of life. I'd find it more inconvenient having to get dressed' – he gestured at my outfit in a contemptuous way that made me feel again that I was the naked one – 'and drive to work every day.'

'Depends on what you're used to, I suppose,' I replied lamely, irrationally compelled to defend my way of life, even those aspects of it that I hated quite as much as Tomlinson could have wished.

'Does it?' he asked to my surprise; I had not thought him capable of engaging in a rational exchange of opinions. 'It's the other way round, isn't it? What you get used to depends on what you choose to do?'

I was still pondering this proposition when he gestured in the direction of the front door. 'C'mon then,' he said, 'come and check out the early sun.'

Walking the other way, I could make out the thinking behind the strange arrangement of rooms: everything was placed so that it faced a window, and all the windows were positioned so as to capture a different aspect of the view over the bay and coast. The front door itself, where Tomlinson had been standing when I arrived, commanded a 270-degree view over the bay and coastline.

'This is lovely,' I said. The word sounded silly even to me; I was conscious of having used it before. 'Do you still notice it?'

'Yes, well. Why d'you think I live here?' he asked. 'Given the inconvenience?' He put an unnecessary spin on the last word. I decided again that I didn't like Luc Tomlinson. I considered suggesting that he should put on some pants, then decided against it; I could hear him mocking what he would certainly see as my prudery. People who live at all basically always have

71

the moral high ground over the rest of us with our toasters and mowers and garbage removal. My Ray-Bans hung heavily around my neck, civilisation's screens against too much reality.

I didn't reply, and we sipped our coffee in silence, watching the light get stronger over the bay. Abruptly he said, 'I reckon this is just about the most beautiful place on earth.' It wasn't offered as a provocation or even a talking point; it was a simple statement of fact.

'Yes,' I said, 'I can see how it might be.'

'It's all right,' he muttered belligerently, 'I don't expect you to agree.'

'It's not something on which one can agree or disagree. I can see that for you this might be the most beautiful place on earth.'

'Yes, well. Has anyone ever told you to get out of the subjunctive mood?' I stared at him, as much surprised by his command of grammatical niceties as by his evident irritation; but before I could come up with a rejoinder, he continued: 'What's yours?'

'My …?'

'Your place. The one that gets you in the balls, unsubjunctively.' He grabbed his crotch by way of illustration.

I considered. I had grown up in Kloof, suburban Durban, and had had annual trips down the coast to Margate, as the name indicated, a depressing attempt to replicate on the Natal South Coast the tatty attractions of an English seaside town; as boy scout I had obediently taken part in weekend hikes in the Drakensberg, and on my return to school had written generally well-received essays on the experience, extolling the beauties of the Berg and the sublimity of nature. But it did not, in Tomlinson's phrase, get me in the balls. That was not where I normally registered my impressions anyway.

I shook my head. 'No, I don't think I had a place like that.' Anticipating some slight on the subjunctive nature of my testicles, I added, searching my meagre store of superlatives for one worthy of the occasion, 'But this is very very beautiful, yes.'

He nodded, apparently satisfied. Then he said, 'Yes, well. Shall I spoil it for you?'

'Please don't. Why should you want to do that?'

'So you can see what I'm on about.'

I suppressed an impulse to decline the opportunity to find out what he was on about – I suspected Tomlinson of being a bit of a narcissist – and nodded; he said 'Well, then. Wait right here,' and slipped indoors, his bare feet making only a dry brushing sound on the stone stoep.

When he returned he had, to my relief, put on a pair of old football shorts. He was carrying a rolled-up sheet of drawing paper.

'Look,' he said, unrolling the paper, 'Xanafuckingdu.' It was an architect's plan. The legend explained that it was the 'Proposed new Southern Safari Hotel at Cape Point, Cape Town, South Africa. Artist's Impression'. The architects were located on Fifth Avenue, New York, but apparently they had taken the trouble to send out a draughtsman to Cape Point, because the Artist's Impression featured a recognisable though considerably prettied-up version of the landscape in which we were standing. Where the *fynbos* now grew, in all its rather arid variety, the artist had envisaged a lush outcrop of palm trees, swamp cypresses and a bewilderingly cosmopolitan array of flora. In the midst of this misplaced oasis rose a three-storey recreation of the Zimbabwe ruins, only of course in the pink of post-Modernised repair, and porticoed, balconied, canti-levered, arched, pinnacled, turreted, buttressed, pedimented, glazed, spired, domed, all but moated, with the trappings of European domestic, military and ecclesiastical architecture. In front of the glittering complex snaked a river that seemed to originate just behind the present house, to form a lagoon a few hundred metres down next to the sea. On the lagoon were dhows, kayaks, canoes, powerboats towing water-skiers, and even what seemed to be gondolas.

I gazed and gazed, appalled.

'And this house?' I asked.

'Yes, well. It's in there somewhere.'

'You're not serious,' I said.

'I'm *fucking* serious,' he said.

'But …' I gestured helplessly around me, at the immensity of sea and sky and silence. 'Do they really think they'll get away with it? This is a *reserve*.'

He looked at me in a pitying sort of way that, coming from a twenty-plus-year-old dropout, was profoundly irritating. 'Wake up and smell the gravy,' he said. 'They've already got away with it. Permission to Rezone from the Department of Nature Conservation and Development.'

'How do you know?'

'I've checked out the letter. My father has a copy.'

'And he has shown it to you?'

'Don't be fucking crazy. But I've got my methods.' For a moment, in his solemnity, he was, almost endearingly, a boy playing at spies.

'But why ... I mean, weren't there any objections?'

'Well, yes. From something called the Friends of Cape Point, apparently quite influential in their way, but the Committee said ...'

'What committee?'

'This Committee, the one that's supposed to decide these things ...'

'The Land Use Committee of the Department of Nature Conservation and Development?'

'Right, yes. This Committee took a long time to decide, and then to everybody's surprise said yes. I reckon there was something fishy in between to make them change their mind. Plenty of cabinet ministers and other lackeys of the old regime around to sell a favour or two. And my father was very thick with that lot. Vorster and Botha and company used to come here for weekends –' he gestured at the house. That would explain the incongruous size of the place, then.

I grimaced. 'What an atrocity.'

'Yes, I know. But is there anything we can do?' Luc Tomlinson asked in a tone that, for him, was almost humble.

'You mean in law?'

'Yes, right. I don't need you to tell me what I can do outside the law, and I'll do it too, but if you tell me I can make a case or something, I'm prepared to do that.'

I decided it was a bad moment to mention the likely cost of such a course, so I stuck to technicalities. 'You must understand,' I explained, 'that in a case like this, the law, that is the court, has no power to change a decision made by a properly constituted body. All it can do is refer back such a decision for review to the body concerned. Furthermore the court cannot pronounce on the merits of the case, only on the procedure followed in reaching the decision.' I was aware of the incongruity of my technical vocabulary with the setting and with my audience, a half-naked youth with dirty feet.

'So whether they fuck up Cape Point is none of the court's business?'

'Yes, strictly speaking. The court can refer back a decision for review only on the grounds of extreme bad faith –'

'Like bribery and corruption.'

'Yes, like bribery and corruption, which you'd have to prove, of course, or otherwise on the grounds that the professional body had failed to apply their minds, as the terminology has it.'

'That should be a doddle. They're clearly a bunch of morons.'

'It's more difficult than you think. Developers may have very rational arguments, in which case the decision to develop could be exactly the result of their application of their minds. To put it differently, what you're objecting to may well be to a moron a perfectly rational application of his mind, such as it is.'

'And what about the chacs?'

'The …?'

'The chacs. You've forgotten that's why I came to see you?'

'Oh. The baboons.' The fate of a troop of baboons seemed insignificant compared with the projected rape of this piece of earth.

'This is their home.'

'It's your home too.'

'Yes, well. But I can go somewhere else – not that I want to, but I could. The chacs can't.'

'Where exactly do they live?'

'Around. But their headquarters are a little bit higher up from here – there' – a not very clean fingernail pointed to the plan – 'there where they're planning the Source d'Eau. You can imagine what the chacs will make of that.'

'I can't really – I mean not knowing baboons.'

'Well, then. They'll shit in the Source and pollute the Eau.'

'Yuck. But wouldn't that give you pleasure – I mean if the baboons made things difficult for the developers?'

'No. Because when animals make things difficult for humans, the humans get rid of the animals. They'll wipe out the baboons. D'you know that in Scarborough, just down the coast, a householder recently caught a baboon and nailed him to a tree as a warning to others?'

'That's barbaric.'

'No, that's civilised, that's what it means to protect your cherished way of life against threats from other life forms.'

'But why ...?'

'The chacs are marauders. They break into houses and steal food and make a mess. They destroy things. They're dirty. Why else d'you think I have burglar bars out here in the middle of paradise?'

'Then why ...?'

'Why do I want to protect them? Because it's fucking arrogant to think that human convenience and hygiene and ... tidiness and ... and cleanliness and fucking *property* is the measure of all things and the law of all creatures.' I got the unpleasant impression that he was lecturing me, but before I could speak up for my own tidiness and cleanliness as non-prejudicial to the rights of baboons, he carried on: 'Because baboons have social structures of their own that are every bit as ... valid, as *legitimate* as so-called human values. *That*'s why I want to protect them, you get me?' he concluded, glaring at me.

'Okay, okay,' I said, holding up my hands, 'I wasn't proposing exterminating the baboons; I'm just investigating the heads of your argument.'

He still glared at me, but with a slight glimmer of reason behind the fanatical glint. 'Does that mean you're thinking of taking the case?'

'Thinking of it, yes. That's why I'm here.'

'Yes, well, I didn't figure you were here for the pleasure of my company. D'you want to visit them?'

'The baboons?'

'Who else? You'll want to know something about them personally if you're going to fight for them.'

Taken aback at the promptness with which my services were taken for granted, I demurred. 'Of course, I have no idea what such a case would entail and if I could commit the firm ...'

'Of course.' He was unusually rational and accommodating; his vocabulary, too, had shed most of its adolescent affectation of cool. 'But either way you'll want to get to know your prospective clients.'

'Do I really need to?'

'Yes, you do. You'll realise why when you meet them face to face.'

If Luc Tomlinson thought I was going to be charmed by a bunch of baboons he was wrong: what little I had seen of baboons had never struck me as particularly appealing. I knew better than to raise the matter of the fee again, but mentally resolved not to make any concessions.

'Well, then,' I said, 'I'm sure it will be fascinating.'

'Right, let's go, before it gets too hot.'

He stepped out of his shorts and gestured in the direction of my belt. 'Get that lot off.'

'Why?' I asked. 'This is quite comfortable.'

'Well, yes, your comfort's not the point. The chacs don't like Levis and Rockports and Polo shirts. Not to mention Ray-Bans.'

'Are we obliged to take into account the brand name preferences of a troop of baboons?'

'We certainly do, if we want to get anywhere near them. It's the smell as much as anything else that puts them off.' Then, as I hesitated with my hand on the clasp of my belt, 'What's the freeze? There's nobody around here.'

In spite of my early experience of the male fellowship of dormitory and ablution block, I had never developed that cavalier towel-round-the-neck indifference with which most of my fellows comported their own nakedness in places of public undressing. In our house we 'changed', never 'undressed'; indeed, my mother had taught us that the 'nice' way of changing entailed a kind of one-garment-off one-garment-on exchange which left one at any given moment covered in at least half one's clothes, preferably with the addition of a towel around the waist to guard against inadvertent exposures of unmentionables. My mother regarded public nudity, insofar as she deigned to pronounce on it, as a German custom that should have been terminated by the satisfactory conclusion of the Second World War. For me, nakedness, where absolutely unavoidable, remained a transitional state between one set of clothes and another, or at most a way of taking a shower without getting my clothes wet – not an end in itself, and certainly not a state to be found in out of doors in broad daylight in the presence of a similarly unclad person. To strip naked before Luc Tomlinson seemed unthinkable.

'What's the matter?' he repeated. 'Not shy, are you?' I thought for a very brief moment that I detected a glint in his eye that could be amusement.

'I just don't see that it's necessary to go clambering around mountains without any clothes on,' I objected. 'It's not … natural.'

Luc laughed for the first time since I'd met him. If it hadn't been directed at me it might have been a pleasant sound. As it was, it was offensive.

'Yes, well. The chacs have their own notions of natural,' he said. 'And if you want to visit them you'll have to respect that.'

I fumbled with my belt. He stood waiting, not even having the tact to turn his back. As I bent to untie my shoelaces he relented. 'Your feet will hurt. I'll lend you a pair of canvas shoes,' he said, and went indoors, leaving me to undress in such privacy as the elements provided.

I was down to my boxer shorts and dark glasses when he reappeared, carrying a pair of shoes that looked as if they harboured significant colonies of fungi and bacteria.

'Well, then. Off with the Calvin Kleins,' he said, I thought a bit more cheerily than the occasion demanded. But rather than risk another pointless altercation, I slid off my shorts and folded them. He looked me up and down without any concession to modesty or decency.

'Right, then. I don't know what the fuss was about,' he said. 'Nothing wrong with the body that I can see. Everything where it should be.' As long as you couldn't be built like Luc Tomlinson it didn't matter very much if you had three arms and two heads and one leg, was what his tone implied.

78

'I hope your friends will share your approval.' I took off my sunglasses and put them on top of the neat little pile of clothes.

'Yes, well. They're not fussy. Except …' – he moved closer to me and sniffed at my armpit – 'You smell funny. Are you wearing deodorant?'

I nodded, speechless with outrage. Nobody had ever presumed to smell at my armpit before. Certainly nobody who smelt like Luc Tomlinson had ever commented on my body odour.

'They don't like fruity smells,' he said, wrinkling his nose in an unnecessarily exaggerated manner. My deodorant was Jean Patou, the least assertive brand on the market. 'Best wash it off.'

'Do you have a bathroom?' I asked, though I knew well that he had.

'What do you take me for?' he returned, picking up my implication. 'But the sea's simpler. Let's have a swim. That way you can mix business with pleasure.'

And without waiting to hear my thoughts on the matter, he led the way to the little beach below the house. He negotiated the rocky ground with the sure-footed grace of an animal on its home ground, while I limped on behind him.

I don't really enjoy swimming in the sea, especially around the turbulent Cape coast. There's something unpredictable about the waves, and the water tends to have a very high sand content, apart from the dubious creatures that lurk just below the surface of even the most placid-looking seas. And this sea was not placid: it bounced and crashed with all the energy and menace of two major oceans meeting head-on. Jumping into it stark naked seemed reckless to the point of folly.

Luc Tomlinson, of course, was plunging into the tumult with the poise and grace of a young porpoise. While I was still reluctantly getting my ankles wet in the bone-achingly cold water, he was diving into the first wave, a gleaming curve of ostentatious ebullience. He surfaced beyond the wave, glanced back and me and shouted, 'Come on in, then – it's much better in here!'

It certainly could not be much worse; so I held my breath and dived under the next wave to rear up before me. It proved

to be much colder than I had anticipated, and full of mysterious undercurrents and vague presences clutching at my
extremities. It was like a short rinse cycle in a load of very dirty
washing. As I surfaced, another, much bigger, wave immediately behind the first broke on top of me, capsized me, and
churned me around, throwing me head over heels backwards
before depositing me head first on the hard sand, and leaving
me for dead. I got to my feet, shaken and bruised. Out in the
deeps, heroic in the morning light, Luc Tomlinson was swimming out to an immense wave on the point of breaking; at the
last moment, he turned round and with a few powerful strokes
incorporated himself into the momentum of the wave, and was
borne swiftly and triumphantly towards the land, his head and
chest protruding dolphin-like from the foaming crest. The
wave, all passion spent, obligingly deposited him next to me,
where I was hopping on one foot trying to get the water out of
my ear. Luc got to his feet; 'Fantastic, isn't it?' he asked. I've
noticed that there's always something rather smug about
somebody who's just successfully taken a wave, not unlike my
friend Gerhard after his night with the gondolier. 'Wonderful,'
I replied, not very enthusiastically. I felt as if I had sand in my
sinuses. My hair was clinging to my head like a limp dishrag,
and my body was covered in sand. I had an ugly red scrape on
my right thigh. My male member was shrivelled into cowed
retreat.

'Still, let's not wait too long,' Luc said cheerily. 'We can have
another swim later.' His coppery hair had already regained its
spring, and his body was shiny in the sun. As for the rest of
him, he was, if not tumescent, then at least confidently buoy-
ant.

'Great,' I said and followed him out onto the beach.

I looked longingly at my clothes, lying discarded on a rock
near the house. 'They'll be all right there,' Tomlinson said, mis-
interpreting my glance. 'Just get the shoes.'

I put on the grubby canvas shoes. They were too big, of
course, and threatened to trip me up, but the terrain was too
rough for my unshod feet; even my Rockports would not be up
to what promised to be a major scramble – apart from the fact
that one final forlorn inhibition prevented me from putting

Rockports on an otherwise unclad body. I wasn't thinking of their gleaming leather uppers as much as of my own dignity. So I laced the canvas shoes as tightly as possible and flopped on in Tomlinson's wake, as he nimbly hopped from rock to rock. As clumsy and inexpressive as he was in the amenities of social living, so unfettered and light-footed was he out here, in what literally was his element. His feet seemed instinctively to find purchase on the unstable rocks, his body counteracting its own momentum for just long enough to touch down, then releasing its energy in another leap, so seamlessly that he seemed hardly to be checked by gravity or topography. If he had not stopped from time to time for me to catch up, he would have disappeared from sight in the first five minutes.

We arrived, after about twenty minutes of low flying on Tomlinson's part and scrambling on mine, at a shallow plateau, covered in coastal milkwoods and fynbos.

'Careful,' he said, 'the chacs shit all over the place.'

'Charming.'

'They know me,' he said, 'but it's still better to approach quietly. They'll know we're on our way.'

He stooped and led the way into a cavern in the milkwood. As my eyes adjusted to the gloom, I made out, right in front of us, a baboon couple copulating. They looked at us but didn't interrupt their activity.

'That's Elise,' Luc said. 'Fucking with Albert again. She belongs to Petrus, the leader of the troop, but she has it off with other males as well.'

'I thought baboons were monogamous.'

'No more so than humans.'

'Doesn't Petrus mind?'

'Yes, well, he'd mind very much if he knew.'

'And they hide it from him?'

'Sure thing. Baboons aren't keen on sharing their mates. You notice that they're both very quiet –' he paused for me to appreciate this bit of natural lore, while Elise and Albert, unperturbed, went about their business. 'I can tell you,' Tomlinson said to me in a low voice, 'normally you hear a couple of baboons fucking before you see them. But when they're cheating they're very quiet.'

I caught Elise's eye and could have sworn she winked at me.

'Come,' Tomlinson said, 'or they'll expect a reward. They've been spoilt by trippers into thinking they can bonk for bananas.'

He parted a branch and led me into a relatively unwooded area. There were about ten baboons around, looking at us, I thought, assessingly, but without fear. I don't mind animals, of course – who has ever confessed to disliking animals? – but it does strike me as slightly hypocritical to get sentimental about a class of creature that, after all, we have decided it is in order for us to eat. So I've always kept a polite distance from animals, as a less drastic alternative to vegetarianism or cannibalism. Nevertheless, I can recognise that there is in many animals a kind of pathos, an acknowledgement, I suppose, of their subjugation to us, which is flattering to the human ego and hence productive of sentiments of affection and protectiveness. But these baboons had nothing of this humble appeal. They looked at us with unabashed candour, returning our stares quite as if we were the animals and they were the humans. They reminded me of those very badly behaved children encouraged by progressive parents to believe that their infant untutored opinions are as valid as anybody else's: where one expected deference one found only challenge. There was nothing wild in their regard; indeed, their demeanour could only be described as streetwise. I had seen the same expression in the eyes of urchins planning to grab a granny's handbag. The young ones were playing around with each other, some of them teasing the adults, some of them being groomed by their mothers. It looked not unlike a scene on one of the more plebeian beaches on the Natal South Coast, only a bit better-humoured.

On a rock overlooking the area sat a large male baboon. Next to him, jabbering away, was another male.

'That's Petrus,' Luc explained, 'with Chris diverting his attention from the fact that Albert is fucking Elise.'

'Deliberately?'

'Of course. It's quite common for two males to team up to steal another male's woman.'

'But what's in it for Chris?'

'You can look at it in the light of a favour-for-a-pal, or you can see it as next-time-it's-my turn. It's more likely to be the latter. I mean, so Chris doesn't get a chance to put it away this time, but this way at least he has a fifty-fifty chance.'

'Can baboons calculate chances?'

'What is evolution but one immensely complicated calculation?' he asked, surprising me into silence. I would have expected him to believe in some New Age creation myth rather than evolution. Luc parted the branches and led me out onto a relatively unwooded plateau. 'Come and pay your respects to Petrus. His wife may be cheating on him, but he's still the alpha male. Once she stops bothering to hide it from him he'll know he's not alpha male any more.'

We went closer. 'You need to introduce yourself to him,' said Luc. 'You put your right hand under your left armpit and then you let him smell your hand. That's why no deodorant.'

I did as Tomlinson suggested – commanded – and, thanking heaven my mother could not see me now, extended my hand somewhat cautiously to the large baboon. I knew that baboons could bite quite viciously.

Petrus sniffed at my hand with a delicate quivering of his nostrils; then, with insulting insouciance, he scratched his undecorative backside in an exploratory sort of way. The action was startlingly incongruous with the rather delicate grizzle of the baboon's regard, and its expression of melancholy wisdom. Whatever it was he found he put into his mouth, still staring at us. His air of sublime detachment gradually yielded to a rudimentary kind of scientific interest, as it dawned on him that he was being presented with two comparable specimens of the same species – or so I surmised from the clinical minuteness with which he proceeded to compare the details of my physique with those of Luc Tomlinson. The scrutiny was in itself offensive enough, without the indignity of being compared with someone who had of course been endowed by Nature with every advantage at her disposal: as I had by now had every opportunity to notice, Tomlinson was equipped like a young centaur.

'Rude beggar, isn't he?' I commented, when it became impossible to ignore the nature and direction of the baboon's interest.

'Well, no,' said Tomlinson. 'He's just inquisitive. Baboons have much smaller cocks and much less variation in size than humans.'

His blithe reference to variation in size clearly implied that he too had made the comparison Petrus was making. Under the circumstances, I thought it an indelicate reference, but for the time being the only alternative to Luc Tomlinson was Petrus, who was hardly a model of sensitive behaviour either. In fact, Petrus was by now sitting back on his haunches in what was unignorably a state of sexual arousal, a fact that he made no attempt to hide. On the contrary, he seemed intent on drawing my attention to it in a particularly lewd manner.

'Bloody amazing,' said Luc, almost admiringly. 'You must have really potent pheromones.' He added with an unconvincing affectation of concern, 'I'm afraid he wants to fuck you.'

This was going too far. If it was a joke it was in very poor taste on Tomlinson's part; and if it was not, it was certainly highly presumptuous on the baboon's. So I tried to keep my tone light but firm. 'I'm afraid that's not included in the services we offer our clients.'

'Yes, well, he can't know that. After all, you offered him your smell. You don't want to get on the wrong side of him.'

'I don't know what you mean by the wrong side.'

'Let's just say it would be unwise to turn your back on him.'

'So what am I supposed to do?'

'Play it by ear.'

'By *ear*?'

'I mean just hang in there.'

'Well, what do *you* normally do? Do you just ... oblige?'

'No, well, he knows me far too well to find me attractive. But you ... I've never seen him as excited as this. You obviously have something. *Fucking* amazing.'

There was something obscurely insulting about Luc Tomlinson's surprise at my sex appeal. 'We've all got our fans, I suppose,' I muttered.

'Sure, but we don't all drive baboons wild. You should patent yourself for perfume. You can call it Go Ape.'

I'd had enough. 'Listen,' I said, 'I'm quite happy for you to amuse yourself at my expense, but either you want me to take this business seriously, in which case I propose that we go back to the house and discuss it, or you brought me here to make a fool of me, in which case likewise I'm going back now with or without you.'

I turned on my heel with such dignity as I could muster in a pair of heelless canvas shoes several sizes too large for me. But I'd reckoned without Petrus. My outburst visibly excited him, if the curve in his tail was anything to go by, and he jumped off his rock and started circling me in a disconcertingly single-minded fashion. Mindful of Luc's warning, I turned so as to keep facing the creature, but I was on uneven terrain in shoes that were too big for me and he was very much on home terri-tory. Also, I found that turning round made me dizzy, and I had visions of falling to the ground and being ravaged by a sex-crazed baboon, or perhaps even a whole troop of baboons: I was uncomfortably aware of Chris as an interested bystander and potential participant.

'Do something, damn you!' I shouted at Luc Tomlinson. 'He's your pal, isn't he?'

'Sure,' he said, not even trying to hide his amusement, 'but you know that baboons expect their pals to help them get laid. Just try to calm down; I think your anger turns him on.'

I did my best to calm down by counting to ten and trying to keep facing the baboon without turning round. This did not do anything to allay the passion of the baboon, but it did almost twist my head off my body. I'm not sure how the situation would have developed had it not been for the emergence of Albert from the shelter of the milkwoods, trying hard not to seem nonchalant in a post-coital sort of way. In fact, he needn't have bothered, since Petrus's attention was otherwise engaged; but Chris, who was evidently keeping all his options open, leapt off his rock immediately and made for the milkwoods where, presumably, Elise was awaiting him. But Petrus had not become Alpha Male by turning a blind eye indefinitely to the movements of his comrades or colleagues or whatever baboons called their fellow baboons; he paused in his circling of me, looked back towards Chris, who was just disappearing into the bushes, and with an abruptness that I would have been justified in finding insulting had I been at all inclined to take his previous attentions seriously, bounded towards the milk-woods.

'One baboon in the bush is worth two on the rock,' Luc commented.

I was not amused. 'Thanks,' I said bitterly, 'you were a real help.'

He shrugged. 'They wouldn't have done anything to you. Baboons mount other males more to make a point than to have it off. It's a power thing. You just need to relax around baboons.'

'Oh, great,' I fumed. 'Close my eyes and think of Africa. Let's get out of here.'

As we made our way back through the milkwood cavern Petrus was just getting seriously involved with Elise, with Chris standing sheepishly at a distance, if a baboon can be said to look sheepish. Elise looked at us with a what's-a-girl-to-do expression, but Petrus was too much engrossed to spare us a glance.

'Yes, well. Fickle buggers, baboons,' said Luc Tomlinson. 'You mustn't take it personally.'

'That's not funny,' I repeated.

By the time we reached the house, it was blazingly hot. My skin, not used to such exposure, was turning a painful red, overlaid with the deeper red scratches of branches and undergrowth. Luc Tomlinson, of course, looked as unblemished as ever, only slightly burnished by the sun and a light sweat. I was looking forward to the cool touch of my cotton clothes, and the dark coolness of the stone house. Perhaps Tomlinson might even be prevailed upon to produce a cup of tea, though it would probably be some ghastly herbal blend. As we approached the house, I felt vaguely disappointed to see a Land Rover parked behind my little CitiGolf. I had not exactly looked forward to a tête à tête with Tomlinson, but the prospect of other company did not appeal to me either; Tomlinson on his own was bad enough without the kind of friends he was likely to have. My main anxiety, though, was getting to my clothes before I had to face whoever the visitor was; but reaching the spot where I'd left my clothes, I was disconcerted to discover only an empty rock.

'What's the matter?' asked Tomlinson, halfway to the house.

'My clothes,' I said. 'Gone.'

'Not to fret. Mom must have taken them in.'

'Mom?'

'Yes,' and he pointed at the Land Rover, 'my mother often comes out on a Sunday. Come meet her.' He turned round.

'Hey!' I shouted.

He stopped and looked at me enquiringly.

'My clothes,' I explained. 'Get me my clothes. I'm not going to meet your mother like this.'

But the front door had already opened; there was a flutter of light fabric, and a tall, blond-haired woman, recognisably Luc's mother, appeared at the head of the stairs, where her son had made his appearance a couple of hellish hours previously.

'Come in!' she called. 'Your clothes are up here. I thought they might blow into the sea or something.' There wasn't a breath of wind about.

'Come, then,' said Luc. 'And relax – Mom is used to bare bums about the place. Just pretend you're fully dressed.'

In a day of humiliating experiences, this was perhaps the worst, dragging my sore, burnt and scratched body up a flight of stairs, with a strange and clearly amused woman waiting at the top. Pretending for all I was worth that I was fully dressed, I mounted the steps in what I thought was a passable imitation of Luc's nonchalant manner.

'Hello, darling,' Luc's mother said to him, as she kissed him and patted his bottom. 'You're looking gorgeous as always.' She turned to me without hiding the fact that she was inspecting me from head to toe, only marginally more discreetly than Petrus. It was all I could do to refrain from cupping my hands over my genitals. 'And who's your friend, sweetness?'

'This is ...' Tomlinson turned to me and I realised he had forgotten my name.

'Nicholas Morris,' I said, extending my hand. I hoped she would not kiss me, or pat my bottom.

'Hello, Nicholas,' she said in a tone of voice that I'd heard described as *vibrant*, looking deep into my eyes and keeping hold of my hand. 'I'm delighted to meet you. I thought the little car belonged to one of my son's girl friends, but then I found the clothes, so I knew …' she trailed off, leaving us in the dark as to what she knew. 'I'm Joyce Tomlinson,' she concluded, as if that disposed of all questions

'Hello, Mrs Tomlinson.' Joyce Tomlinson was almost as tall as her son, and had a paler version of his colouring, though the eyes were green rather than his brilliant blue, and the skin had been preserved in milky whiteness. She seemed not to be wearing very much under her billowing summer frock. She was very thin.

'Joyce, please, dear. I'm always quite pally with Luc's friends. I spend so much time with young people – the Outreach programme, you know, and the Young Artists Project.'

'Quite,' I said, though I had no idea what she was talking about. 'You say you kindly brought in my clothes …?'

'If you insist,' she said, giving me a last lingering examination. 'I put them in my room – down the passage on the right. Lovely shorts, by the way. I *adore* Calvin Klein.'

Joyce Tomlinson's room was the one that I had noticed earlier as being in a better state of furniture than the others. The painting that I had noted was indeed of the house and surroundings, with, on the stoep, a tiny figure that could have been Luc Tomlinson in his habitual state of undress. On the dressing table was a framed colour photograph of a handsome, rather brutal-looking man, blond and blue-eyed; unlike Luc except for the wide white grin that seemed to take so much for granted while conceding so little. I decided that the Tomlinson family was bad news.

My clothes were neatly folded on Joyce Tomlinson's bed. The Levis were lying tag up, announcing my measurements – Waist 32 Inseam 34 – to anybody interested in the information. I was sure it was not lost on Mrs Tomlinson.

I emerged, reinvested in the security of brand-name identity, to find that Luc and his mother had moved to the kitchen and were making tea. Luc had had the rudimentary decency to put on his football shorts for the occasion.

Mother and son were having a domestic discussion.

'Of course daddy's wrong, my love,' she said, 'but that doesn't mean you can't *talk* to him and discuss your differences.'

'Yes it does,' growled Luc in his ungracious way. 'He doesn't want to discuss our differences, he's just trying to co-opt me.'

'Well, it's natural for him to want his only son in the family business. You know how his own father ...'

She turned to me. 'Excuse us washing the family linen in public like this. Fathers and sons, you know what it's like. I believe you're going to help Luc in his campaign against the bulldozers?'

'Is that what he said?'

'I said you were here to discuss it,' said Luc.

She gave me one of her lingering smiles. 'I'm so pleased for Luc, Nick. Of course, I shouldn't be saying this, it seems so disloyal to one's own husband, but really, I *do* hate it, this eternal money-money-money, don't you?'

'I wouldn't know. I haven't been subjected to it.'

'But you know what I mean, I'm sure. As an environmental lawyer, surely you must feel deeply about nature.'

'I suppose so,' I replied, not very truthfully. I had stumbled into environmental law partly because my supervisor in London had thought that anybody from Africa should be passionate about the environment, not having anything else to be passionate about. My MA thesis had been on the conflict between democratic development and natural conservation. I had argued that conservation was, etymologically as well as in practice, a conservative enterprise whose aims could only to a limited extent, if at all, be reconciled with those of development, but which nevertheless needed to be given priority over short-term development, on the grounds that losing a natural asset for good was a greater evil than postponing the development of non-existing amenities. I was slightly nervous: in the political climate of the eighties this could easily be seen and penalised as a reactionary attitude, but in the event the external examiner – a South African legal scholar – was almost effusive in his or her praise of the thesis.

'Well, then,' she said, as if that settled that. 'I am so pleased that you'll fight for dear old Rocklands.' This last was addressed to her son, with whom she shared a rich-person's oblivion of other people as having plans, preferences, even personalities of their own.

'We have to discuss this first,' he replied – 'I mean me and Nick.'

I looked at him, surprised. This was the first indication he had given that he regarded me as anything other than a hired assistant.

'Then why don't you boys do just that while I get on with a bit of painting?' she asked. 'I won't ask you to pose for me today, honey. I dabble a bit in most of the arts, you'll find,' she explained to me. 'It keeps me sane. It's so important to keep a little space for oneself, don't you find? Space is so *relative*, isn't it? We own five acres of mountainside in Constantia, and would you believe that today of all days my husband invited 45 business associates for a braai next to the pool? And expected me to play hostess to them all? Now that's what I call crowded. Thank heaven for a housekeeper and a cook, is what I say. Who wants to sit and fry next to a pool in Constantia when you can have unspoilt nature?' and she gestured vaguely in the direction of the sea. After my late encounters with unspoilt nature, a pool in Constantia struck me as possessed of definite advantages.

'I was quite sorry for poor Andrew,' Joyce Tomlinson said to her son. 'He arrived just as I was about to set off, and was obviously disappointed, but I wasn't going to stay just to keep him company, and of course he couldn't very well leave immediately after his arrival. So he's stuck with the wheeler-dealers and the influence pedlars. Besides, I didn't think you'd want him to come along. He sends his love, by the way.'

Luc grunted non-committally. I couldn't quite imagine anybody's sending him love, but Joyce was probably exercising maternal licence. The world could not exist if mothers had no illusions about their offspring.

'Oh, darling, I wish you'd be nicer to Andrew. He's so fond of you.' She turned to me. 'An old friend of the family – of mine, really, whom Luc doesn't appreciate as he should. But let me get myself out of your way.' She gathered her artist's paraphernalia, chattering and cajoling all the while. It was clear that she was fond of her son, with a demonstrative fervour that my mother, shying away from overt and indeed covert expressions of affection, would have regarded as all but indecent. He accepted her blandishments with rough good humour, condescending to being adored, guarding his own hostility to his father without entering into a conspiracy against the man.

'I won't be far, if you need me to make tea or coffee or breakfast,' she said, struggling with an easel that Luc made no effort to help her with. 'Oh, thank you,' to me, as I stepped forward, 'just as far as the veranda. I want to get the effect of the light on the waves.'

I saw Joyce Tomlinson settled to her satisfaction in relation to sea, sky and light, and returned to Luc, who was sitting at the kitchen table moodily nursing a mug of coffee.

'So what d'you think?' he asked.

'Of what?' I hoped he didn't want my opinion of his mother.

'Of the case. Of the chacs. Of our chances. Of your involvement.'

I considered. 'Let's take the baboons first. What I don't understand,' I said, 'is why you thought meeting the baboons might persuade me to take their case. They're just about the least loveable group of creatures I've met since my first day in kindergarten.'

'I didn't take you to meet them for you to love them,' he said. 'I took you to them for you to experience them.'

'That I think I did, thank you.'

'And I don't reckon it's necessary for you to like them to take their case.'

'True,' I said. If I had to restrict my clients to people I liked I'd be out of business in a week.

'Yes, well. I reckon it's necessary for you to know just how bloody disagreeable the chacs can make themselves, so you realise you're not fighting for fucking Bambi or Winnie the Pooh here – you're fighting for a bunch of creatures that nobody out there is exactly mad about. The baby seals and the pandas, even the whales and the elephants, they're easy causes because they're so *cute,* but the chacs, they shit and they fuck and they steal and they break things, and because they look so … so *humiliatingly* human, the humans won't have anything to do with them. They're humans without the trimmings.' It was the longest uninterrupted speech I had heard Luc Tomlinson make. Clearly, baboons engaged his primal sympathies. 'What I want to know from you,' he said, his manner still

91

locked into urgency, 'is whether you're willing to take the case.'

'Yes, but willing is one thing – it's a start, but it doesn't get us very far.'

'Well, then, if you're worried about the money, you can relax.'

'That's not my main concern, contrary to your suspicions; but now you mention it, yes, my firm will expect me to bring in some income for my time.'

'Yes, well. I think it's time I explained to you my situation,' he said with a gravity masking, I thought, his slight embarrassment. 'I don't know if you've heard of my grandfather. They called him Trick Tomlinson.'

I nodded. He was part of the mythology of Cape Town.

'Well, then, he loved this place, and often came out here, and I used to come out with him when I was very small. Later in his life my grandfather used to leave my father in charge of the business for long stretches and just come out here with me. This was before I went to school. So we got very close, my grandfather and I.'

This was new light on Trick Tomlinson. Most stories about him suggested that he was barely human.

'And when he died he left me most of his money. In a trust fund, payable when I was 21. And I turned 21 last year, just before I came to see you.'

So Luc Tomlinson was a Trust Fund kid. Things fell into place.

'There's a problem. My grandfather's will is not very clear. He left me the use of the house but said nothing about the land on which it's situated, so that technically belongs to my father. He wants to evict me from the house, but so far it hasn't been necessary for him, and of course he knows I'll fight the eviction. But the point I'm making is that I have more money than I can spend.' He gestured at his football shorts as if to indicate the extent of his material needs.

'When my grandfather died, I came here less often, because my father was not very eager to bring me or even to let me come on my own. But gradually my mother started to bring me here, and for most weekends then it was just the two of us. Except when my father brought his guests.'

'Who were they?'

'Important people. Politicians, businessmen – sanctions busters, arms dealers, you know the type.'

I nodded. I knew the type, the bloated carrion birds of international trade that had been attracted by the stench of the dying regime. 'My father said it was not a company for women and children,' Luc continued. 'From what I saw of it, it was not a company for human beings. But all this has nothing to do with you, I suppose.'

'I don't know. I suspect we'll be hearing more of your father's business associates in this matter.'

'You said money wasn't the main problem. So what *is* the main problem?'

'It's quite a big one. I don't know if we have a case.'

'Isn't that what you're for? To think up a case?'

'I know that in the general perception lawyers manufacture cases out of thin air,' I said, 'but in practice we do need just a smattering of fact and, if at all possible, proof of actual misdemeanour, in order to proceed.'

He laughed again. 'If you're going to sound like that you'll win hands down.'

'Like what?'

'I don't know. About fifty years old and very tight-arsed.'

'Thank you.'

'You needn't be pissed off, I'm saying you sound like a good lawyer.'

'And an insufferable human being.'

'Who wants a human being when he can have a good lawyer?'

He got up and stretched his arms behind his head in a good imitation of lazy unconcern. This had the effect of exposing his whole torso to what I suspected he assumed to be my admiring gaze. I poured myself a mug of coffee as a way of diverting my attention from my own irritation. 'Do you have any idea how far advanced the development is?'

'Yes. Mom says they're about to get in the earthmoving equipment. For which read bulldozers.'

'You've left it very late. Or had you given up?'

'More or less. Or no, I knew I wasn't going to stand for it, but I didn't know what I was going to do about it.'

'You didn't think of going to a lawyer.'

'That's a bit much, coming from you, after the welcome you gave me. But yes, I did go to another firm after I spoke to you. The chap seemed interested, but then when I went back he said sorry, they didn't do environmental work.'

'That seems odd. Why didn't he tell you that in the first place?'

'That's what I figured, but I'm trying not to say anything nasty about lawyers.'

'I didn't say all lawyers were faultless. Which firm was this?'

'Van Niekerk, de Villiers, Segal and Brigstock. Does that mean anything to you?'

'I know about them, of course. Very prominent. Strong connections with the previous government.'

'Like my father.'

'Yes, and like half the corporate world in South Africa. It doesn't necessarily mean anything. Still, we've lost time. I'll have to apply for an interdict.'

'What's that?'

'A court order to stop your father from starting the building and earthworks.'

Joyce Tomlinson wafted into the kitchen. 'It's murderously hot out there,' she said. 'Shall we make brunch? I always bring a couple of groceries,' she continued to me, without waiting for a reply, 'otherwise this great savage eats nothing. I brought a lovely ripe avocado. Luc adores avos.'

'Don't you have a car?' I asked Luc.

'No. I prefer my bicycle.'

'It's a long pedal to Cape Town.'

'I have time.'

Mrs Tomlinson started unpacking groceries – croissants, avocado pear, cheese, butter, orange juice. 'I couldn't help overhearing,' she said. 'You're planning to stop daddy's building.'

'For the time being,' I replied when Luc didn't respond, 'to give us time to prepare a case. But I'll have to have a good reason.'

She laughed, a low vibrato that modulated into a giggle. 'Daddy's going to hate you,' she said to Luc.

He nodded gloomily. 'He hates me anyway.'

94

She took his arm. 'No, he doesn't, you must never think that. But he has put his heart on this project.' She turned to me. 'It's very big.' She giggled again. 'The project, not his heart. His heart is very small. The project is huge.'

I nodded. 'It's a priceless site.' I didn't know how much I could say in front of her. She was clearly on her son's side of the quarrel, but she was after all married to Brick Tomlinson, and with the best of intentions might easily pass on to him the details of whatever strategy we opted to follow – assuming we had a strategy. I felt fairly helpless: if Brick Tomlinson had legitimately been given planning permission, our only hope was to get a review of the decision. It was up to me to find the reason for such a review.

'Grab something to eat,' Luc said, helping himself to a croissant. I poured myself a glass of orange juice. Joyce Tomlinson started buttering a roll.

For a moment there was silence as we busied ourselves with our food; then, apparently out of nowhere, a young woman appeared in the door: very wavy hair and lots of it, the surplus tied in little plaits that stuck out at all angles from her rather large head; gauzy clothes, a generous mouth, very large vacuous eyes. She was festooned in more beads than I had ever seen on one human being: plaited into her hair, wound in strings round her neck, sewn to her garments, draped around her arms, embedded in her nostrils. Instead of shoes she wore a string of beads draped around the ankle and looped around the middle toe of each foot. She smelled of weeds and smoke, and was carrying a piece of pinkish rock.

She looked about her in a dazed fashion, without seeming to register the presence of anybody but Luc; ignoring my presence, she went up to him and kissed him on the left nipple. She was short enough to do so without stooping. 'Strength, energy and power be with you,' she said.

Luc put his left hand on her head – he was holding his croissant in his right hand – and said, 'And with you.'

She kissed him on the right nipple. 'The seven shakras of sympathy and the nine levels of consciousness be with you.' The nipple responded slightly.

'And with you,' Luc repeated, I thought rather awkwardly.

95

'This is Fiona,' he said to nobody in particular. 'Fiona, this is my mother Joyce and this is …' he hesitated, and I deliberately refrained from helping him. If he couldn't remember my name he could squirm for it.

'Oh hi,' said Fiona, not noticing that she had not been told my name, and waving vaguely in front of her as if chasing away flying insects. 'The energy be with you both.'

'And with you,' said Joyce Tomlinson, and for the first time since I had met her I thought I noticed a glimmer of irony in her manner. 'Would you like something to eat … Fiona?'

'No,' said Fiona languidly, 'Food … ' and she dismissed it with an ethereal wafting sort of gesture.

'Well, you'll forgive us if we go ahead anyway.' Joyce deftly halved the avocado on the kitchen table. 'Do help yourself,' she said to me. 'I can't stand avos myself, but I'm told this one is good if you like that sort of thing. Salt and pepper over there. You too, darling.'

I was in fact quite hungry again by now, but as I approached the table, Fiona put out a hand to restrain me and said in a low, dramatic tone, surprisingly intense after her ditzy manner of earlier, 'Don't.'

I froze. 'Don't what?'

'Don't eat that avocado. It has a black aura.'

'I bought it at Woolies,' Joyce Tomlinson declared, as if that settled the matter. The Southern Suburbs believe in Woolworths the way good Catholics believe in the Pope or children believe in Father Christmas.

'It has a black aura!' Fiona hissed again. 'I could sense it the moment you cut it – a vile aura, lethal.'

'Shouldn't the boys eat it then and relieve it of its aura?' Joyce asked. 'It looks delicious to me – I mean for people who can tolerate the stuff.'

'Please don't,' Fiona pleaded with me. 'You will destroy your life chakra.'

'And that is bad?' Joyce asked.

'Fatal.' Fiona had gone even paler than she naturally was, and her eyes were huge with distress.

'Well,' Joyce said to her son, 'it seems you have to choose between your avo and your chacma.'

'*Chakra*, mom,' Luc Tomlinson muttered, looking thoroughly uncomfortable.

'Whatever. Come on, darling, I brought it specially for you – I know how fond you are of avos.'

'Oh, please don't!' Fiona pleaded again, this time with Luc. 'Why don't you just have another croissant?'

Luc, divided between the impassioned pleas of his girlfriend and the quiet insistence of his mother, muttered, 'I guess I'll just have a croissant,' avoiding his mother's eye, or rather her sarcastically lifted eyebrow.

'Nick?' Joyce asked me, her friendliness to me increasing in proportion to her displeasure with her son. 'Are you going to risk your chakra?'

'I'm happy with a croissant,' I lied, far from happy at fore-going a delicious-looking avo, creamy and yellow-green, for the whimsical mumbo-jumbo of a beaded person whose own chakra had probably been over-stimulated by toxic or at any rate illicit substances. And yet, to have accepted the avocado would have been interpreted as siding with Joyce against her son, which I did not want to do either.

'Well, perhaps you can have the avo later when we won't be upsetting anybody.' Joyce made no secret of her displeasure at having her breakfast disrupted. 'I'm going back to my painting.'

'Let's all go outside,' said Luc. 'No point in sitting inside on a day like this.'

We obediently followed. I was the last to leave the kitchen, and as I did so I was startled to see a large grey shape bound over the closed bottom section of the back door. Before I could raise the alarm, the baboon had seized the two halves of the avocado and disappeared through the open door again. That solves that problem, then, I thought.

I did not stay much longer. Joyce seemed to be sulking, and Fiona made little sensible conversation, confining herself to stroking Luc's navel whenever she had an opportunity. Luc was uncomfortable with the conflicting demands on his atten-tion, and though he, to my surprise, urged me to stay, he was probably only too relieved to be rid of one complicating factor in his menage.

97

'I promised you we'd have another swim,' he said.

'That's quite in order,' I replied. 'One swim a day does me just fine.'

He walked me to my car. 'I'll be in touch,' he said. 'About the court order.' I left, not envying Luc his diplomatic task of coordinating the two women. Not that I thought he would bother with diplomacy: he would probably just treat both of them, united in admiration, to the spectacle of his naked assault upon the breakers of the Atlantic.

As my little car struggled up the slope from the house, wheels spinning slightly on the stony surface of the track, I saw a baboon lying next to the road, flat on its stomach, with its head turned sideways. I stopped the car, got out and approached cautiously: there was no telling what subterfuges baboons would get up to. But I needn't have bothered. The baboon was clearly dead, its eyes open, its teeth exposed in a grimace of surprise. Its face was smeared with the green paste of an avocado.

CHAPTER FOUR

It is one of my friend Gerhard's convenient convictions that one is more likely to regret the things one did not do than the things that one did. I have never really given myself an opportunity to test this proposition; indeed I seldom seem to be in a situation where I consciously have to decide between doing or not doing, life generally taking the decisions for me without too much fuss on its part or mine. But for once, waking up on Monday morning, I realised I had *done* something: I had taken the initiative, travelled a considerable distance, braved the hostility of an obnoxious young man, risked being drowned in the ocean, burnt by the sun, raped by a troop of baboons, and poisoned by an avocado, and I had undertaken to save an unspoilt stretch of natural beauty from the predatory greed of unscrupulous developers. It was a profoundly depressing realisation.

I'm not what you would call a troublemaker. I became a lawyer to please my mother. My ambition had been to become an accountant, ever since being introduced at school to double-entry bookkeeping, with its satisfyingly absolute insistence that every credit has a debit somewhere else, the whole intricate system reaching a sort of apotheosis at the end of the financial year in a balance sheet that tolerates no aberrations or vagaries: a vision of order that in its clean abstraction made most of human life seem messy and imprecise by comparison.

My mother, however, demurred. She was a dedicated reader of courtroom dramas, from which she had imbibed the notion of lawyers as steely-eyed but soft-hearted fighters for the underdog, combining morality, law and order, retribution and genteel sexuality in seamless narratives with happy endings. 'Yes, dear,' she said, 'accounting is all very well, and excellent in its own way, I'm sure; I can see that building societies need accountants to make their books balance, but don't you think accounting lacks a – a *heroic* aspect?'

'Heroic aspect be damned,' said my father. 'Heroes are bloody fools, one and all. Stands to reason. You can't be a hero without taking risks, and only bloody fools take risks. Accountants are fine, steady chaps who make a lot of money in their quiet way. So what if people don't write silly novels about them? The boy doesn't want to be a hero – make him an accountant for my money, every time.'

But since it was in fact not his money but my mother's (he'd spent his several times over by this time), my mother prevailed, not so much by convincing me of the heroic aspect of law (on which score I secretly shared my father's sentiments anyway), as by representing to me the power and the prestige that would be mine once I was a judge, which, in her version, it was only a matter of time for me to become. As judge, I saw, I could make the books balance in a more profound way than as an accountant: blind Justice holding aloft her scales presented an awesome emblem of impartiality and order. It helped, also, that I had fairly clear notions of what justice was: something conducted according to well-defined, commonly agreed-upon rules, in a public, well-lit space, in clean and tidy clothing, not unlike a well-run cricket game – as opposed, for instance, to a game of water polo, a sport notorious at my school for the ungentlemanly transgressions committed under water. So though not my profession of first choice, the law promised me a career disinterestedly dedicated to the restoration and maintenance of order.

By the time I became embroiled in Luc Tomlinson's case, I had admittedly had to revise my notions of the law and of lawyers to some extent. However sublime the principles upon which the law rests, it is necessarily practised by lawyers, most of whom stand in relation to Justice as undertakers stand to Life, that is, as a necessary abstraction the regrettable termination of which makes possible their real business. At the commercial end, I found, the Law enables Big Money to chase Big Money while enriching itself out of all proportion to any expenditure of skill and intelligence. At the ceremonial end of the law, the end of trials and judges and juries, the end that had so appealed to my mother, the Majesty of the Law turned out to be an arcane costume drama of obsolete robes and rituals bequeathed by England to her colonies, and jealously guarded by a power elite intent on preserving itself: in practice mainly a covey of touchy old men and ambitious younger men confusing their own vanity with the dignity of the Court. Such good judges as there were, were there in spite of rather than because of a system designed to uphold an order that it could do nothing to change, even had it wanted to do so. Hence – and here Luc Tomlinson had been right – the ease with which the South African legal system, for all its self-vaunted independence, could survive, more or less cynically, by and large amicably, and certainly prosperously, in a political system that was the disgrace of the free world.

Of course, I didn't dare articulate these conclusions of mine to anybody in just these terms, not even to myself; I was still trying to believe in my original ideals. Though, as I've said, environmental law was hardly a vocation with me, nevertheless it seemed a branch of law in which there were fewer opportunists and crooks than elsewhere, mainly because there was so much less money in it. Nevertheless, this belief – hope – was not immune to some misgivings on my part about the chances of a troop of baboons against the combined forces of Brick Tomlinson, his American allies, and whoever it was who had been persuaded to grant development permission in the first place. Justice, though blind, has both her nostrils wide open to the smell of money. What counted in Luc Tomlinson's favour was not the nobility of his cause, but his grandfather's trust fund. And substantial as this no doubt was, it seemed more than likely that the other side had considerably more extensive reserves.

Which is where I came in, explaining that trouble was not really what I had been looking for in my choice of profession, and that Gerhard's dictum, like so much else of Gerhard's philosophy, did not apply to me. What I had done seemed unmitigatedly stupid: why had I gone prying into an affair that would have settled itself quite adequately without my interference, even if at the expense of a few baboons? There was something very disquieting about the sight of a dead baboon, especially so soon after its having consumed food intended for human – *my* – consumption. The sensational interpretation was that the avocado had been poisoned; the dotty theory was that Fiona had been right and that the avocado had been inexplicably, mystically, malign; the theological speculation was that the baboon had been struck down by God for eating stolen fruit. The likely explanation was that the baboon had died of natural causes coincidentally after eating the fruit. The fact remained that I was now embroiled in a case that had produced its first corpse, even if not of the glamorous kind elegantly littering the novels that had in a sense dictated my choice of a legal career.

I had of course driven back to the stone house to report the death to Luc and his womenfolk. Joyce Tomlinson was distraught, it was not quite clear whether at the potential implication that she had tried to poison her own son, or at the shock to her faith in Woolworths; Fiona seemed vapidly pleased that her foreboding had been vindicated; Luc was upset about the death of the baboon, and set about getting the corpse into his mother's Land Rover for an autopsy. He promised to let me know the results as soon as they were available, and I set off home again.

Monday morning, then, dawned with more than its normal balefulness; I had undertaken, with whatever reservations, a case that could only disrupt the even tenor of my professional and even private life. Besides, I had a colourful case of sunburn, extending all over my body except for my feet, and exacerbated by multitudinous scratches and bruises. Driving to work, never exactly a pleasure on a Monday morning, was rendered positively painful by the sunburn on my buttocks and the back of my legs.

I was not inclined to join the usual Monday-morning congregation around the coffee machine, but I needed the coffee. Fortunately my change of colour attracted little notice, or if it did, it was overshadowed by Kitty Jooste's latest episode in the saga of the New South Africa. I was late for the opening, but gathered from the unusually attentive silence that Kitty had her audience enthralled. I joined the outskirts of the circle, next to Dikeledi, who opened her eyes as wide as they would go and put her tongue in her cheek in mock-moronic amazement. Dikeledi had recently, as she said, 'as a precaution against the New South Africa', been made a full partner in the firm.

'… and then my friend's friend noticed that a car was trying to attract her attention,' Kitty was telling her rapt audience, 'but of course at first she took no notice, you know how it is nowadays, but then the car passed her, flashing its lights and pointing at her boot, and the man didn't look like a thug or anything, I mean he was *white* and he was driving a *Merc* and all, so why should he want to steal her Datsun, for heaven's sake? – so when he gestured to her to stop at the next garage, she thought hell, he wouldn't try anything in a crowded place in broad daylight, and she pulled in, and he jumped out and gestured at her to be quiet, and when she got out of the car he explained that while she was putting away her trolley, you know after loading the groceries in her boot, right there outside Pick 'n Pay, I swear to God, a black man had *jumped into her boot and was still in there.*' Kitty paused for effect, but only long enough for the pause not to become an opening. 'Fortunately,' she continued, 'the driver of the Merc had a gun with him, so they opened the boot, and there, on top of her groceries, I promise you, was a black man with a knife *this* long –' she indicated a quite implausible length, eliciting ribald guffaws from Paul Morris and Chris Evans – 'and obviously, you know, waiting for her to stop at her house. You can just *imagine* what would have happened if the man hadn't stopped her …' Kitty shuddered dramatically. 'You'd think Pick 'n Pay would have guards or something to stop people from jumping in on top of your groceries.'

'What happened to the groceries?' Dikeledi asked.

'Well, give us a break, obviously I didn't ask that, but you can just imagine – he probably squashed them all to maggots. Would you want to eat a tomato that someone's been sitting on in the boot of a car?'

'It just goes to show,' Dikeledi said, winking at me, 'a woman can't go anywhere alone any more, not even shopping.'

Kitty didn't seem pleased at Dikeledi's implication that the Crime Wave was not something visited exclusively on whites exclusively by blacks; she just said, 'You can say *that* again,' and gulped down her coffee.

'It is my theory,' said Dikeledi to me, as we walked towards our offices, 'that urban legends proliferate in times of uncertainty. I mean, just how many car hijacking stories have you heard in the last two years?'

'A fair number,' I admitted, 'but isn't that because there are more car hijackings than before?'

'Mm,' said Dikeledi, 'probably. But it's not as if there wasn't any crime before, only people weren't so eager to talk about it. It's as if they need to prove to themselves that the country is going to hell now the blacks have taken over.'

'Speaking of the country going to hell,' I said, as we stopped at the lift, 'can I ask for your help? I need information on a man called Brick Tomlinson.'

She raised her eyebrows. 'He's not exactly an unknown to those of us who read our newspapers and watch our tellies.'

'Yes, even I have heard of him, but I want more information.'

'You want the dirt, you mean.'

'Not necessarily dirt. Just the stuff that doesn't get into the press.'

'And what makes you think I'm the woman to give it to you?'

'I happen to know that you see a lot of a certain journalist on the *Mail & Guardian*.' Dikeledi was seeing one Mhlobo, an 'investigative journalist' of the sharpest kind. He had a nose for corruption and a stomach for exposure that under the previous government had cost him several spells in detention. I told Dikeledi the essentials of the case, that is, the threatened development at Cape Point, without elaborating on the personalities involved. She listened with the slightly quizzical air that she evinced towards most new ideas. Dikeledi had an entirely understandable conviction that the world was trying to take advantage of her.

'Since when am I expected to mix business with pleasure?' she asked.

'Since you became a partner. I'd do the same if I had any pleasure to mix with my business.'

'You did at least get to spend the weekend on the beach, to judge by your tan.'

'You call this a tan? I call it a burn, and I did not acquire it on a beach or in any other vaguely pleasurable way.'

'Then how did you acquire it?'

'I'll tell you when you tell me about Brick Tomlinson.'

'Are the two stories related?'

'Intimately, believe it or not.'

As usual on a Monday morning, Gerhard strolled into my office at about ten o'clock. I was standing at my desk, trying to work in the only relatively painless position I could find. 'Stap my vitals and shiver my timbers,' he exclaimed when he saw me, 'you have been exposing yourself to the sun.'

'And what's so unusual about that? It's what half of Cape Town does every weekend.'

'Yes, but not usually the half with you in it. What's up? Picnic with Leonora next to the Paarl Reservoir?' He hummed the first few bars of Beethoven's Pastorale Symphony.

'That's not funny, Gerhard.'

'Funny is not what I am trying to be, dear Nicholas. Inquisitive, yes; funny, no.'

I sighed, resigned to the inevitable: when Gerhard wanted to know something he was not deterred by delicacy, discretion or decorum. He simply kept on asking. 'If you must know,' I said, 'I drove out to Cape Point yesterday to investigate that environmental case – you know, the business about the threatened development.'

'That environmental case' – he mimicked my speech in his most offensive manner – 'you would not be referring, would you, to the case involving the Angel of Dawning?'

'You could put it like that – you being you *would* put it like that.'

'And you being you, how would you put it?'

'As I said – an environmental case. And the man's name is Luc Tomlinson.'

'Well, then, as lawyer to lawyer and friend to friend, sit down in your chair and tell me all about this case, and of course, Luc Tomlinson's part in it. By the way and between friends, just why are you *standing* at your desk?'

'Honestly, Gerhard, what's it to you whether I do my work standing, sitting or lying down?'

He sat down on my desk. 'Don't stall me, Nicholas. The truth is mighty and shall prevail.'

I sighed again. 'Well, then, what do you want to know?'

'Why you're not sitting down.'

'Because my – legs, the backs of my legs are sunburnt.'

'Do you habitually sit on the backs of your legs?'

'Partly, yes; don't you?'

'No. I sit on my bum.'

'To each his own.'

'Bullshit. Almost the only thing all humans have in common is that they sit on their bums; it's what defines us as human, for God's sake. Now if you don't want me to pat you quite hard on the bum to test my hypothesis, tell me why you're not sitting down.'

'If you must know, my ... sitting area is sunburnt.'

He leapt to his feet. 'I don't *believe* it! Nicholas here, whom I in all our years of intimate acquaintance and regular squash games have never seen without his pants on, goes gallivanting bare-arsed with angelic youths! You call that safeguarding the environment?'

'Please Gerhard. Myrah will hear.'

'And so she should, so that she can know what a hypocrite she's been harbouring to her maiden breast.' He put his hands on my shoulders and looked into my eyes. 'I am shocked, Nicholas, deeply shocked – and profoundly hurt, I might add. I, your closest friend and faithful companion at home and abroad, have never as much as seen your belly-button, and now you bare your all for the first upstart whipper-snapper who wags his butt at you – a very good butt I grant you, but I hadn't suspected you of having preferences in these things. And what does Rageltjie de Beer say?'

'I haven't told Leonora yet, if that's what you mean.'

'Oh-oh. Cheating on the girlfriend already? When did the magic go out of your romance?'

'For God's sake, Gerhard, will you shut up?'

'Only if you tell me the whole story. In *detail*.'

'Well, then. Sit down and shut up and listen.'

To give Gerhard his due, he listened attentively and without too many lewd interjections. When I had finished, he whistled through his teeth.

'You're tangling with trouble. Daddy Tomlinson is a determined sort of animal.'

'Do you know him?'

'I know of him. He wiped out a client of mine who was trying to compete with him for a contract to build a casino in one of the Bophuthatswanas.'

'Wiped out?'

'Well, he ruined him financially. No foul play could be proved, of course, just a matter of a wink and a nod in the right place and a word in the right ear, and my client's contracts and credit dried up overnight. He shot himself.'

'Thanks.'

'Well, I thought you had better realise in advance the calibre of person you're dealing with – an ambitious, determined, influential man – not to put too fine a point on it, an unreconstructed arse-hole.' Gerhard was being unusually serious, making even the obscenity sound momentous. 'But I hope you also know that if you need any help, I'm your man –' then he relapsed into his frivolous mode again '– and not just because of the Angel. I promise you to leave him to you. Clive has very old-fashioned notions. Inconvenient but sweet.'

'Thank you very much, that won't be necessary. I mean about leaving him to me. But your help may well be necessary.'

'Count on me, then.'

One thing about Gerhard, I knew I could.

To my surprise Luc Tomlinson phoned me. I shouldn't have been surprised, I suppose – after all, he'd said he would be in touch – but I didn't think of him as someone who availed himself of the usual technological advances. Even to imagine him at the other end of a telephone was difficult. But whatever his concessions to the rudiments of communication, his style remained his own.

'That chac,' he said, without preamble.

'Yes?'

'Yes, well. It died of natural causes, according to the autopsy.'

'What natural cause?'

'Heart failure.'

'That's like saying it died. Which we know already.'

'Well, yes. But they couldn't find any traces of poison.'

'Who are *they*?'

'Them. Some laboratory at Silvermine – my mother knows one of the high-ups there, so as a favour they dissected, I suppose, the chac.' He sounded upset; I had to remind myself every now and again that Luc Tomlinson had feelings, at any rate as far as baboons were concerned. I couldn't very well point out to him that if there was poison in the avocado, his mother would be a prime suspect, and hardly the person to suggest post mortem procedures for what was conceivably her victim.

There was a brief silence. I wondered if he'd hung up, but in his abrupt way he blurted out, 'Well, then. About the court order.'

'Yes?'

'Will you go ahead with it?'

'If you instruct me to do so, yes.'

'Well, then.'

'Well, then what?'

'Well, then I'm instructing you.'

Normally the concept of *instruction* is a polite fiction between lawyer and client, the flow of coercion being mainly the other way, but Tomlinson lent an unpleasantly literal emphasis to the term. He could have been instructing me, against my express desire, to mow his lawn.

'Certainly,' I said in my briskest and most professional way. 'I'll set the process in motion immediately and keep you informed of progress. Where can I reach you?'

'Yes, well. Don't call me, I'll call you,' he said and hung up. Not for the first time I had an impulse to call Luc Tomlinson a name that I'd never called anyone else before. This time I succumbed.

'You *prick*,' I said into the dead receiver, just as Myrah came into my office.

For somebody who likes his life to be under control at all times, this was not a good start to my week. To add to my obscure sense of being somehow at fault, I was due to lunch with

Leonora, as I usually did when I had not seen her on Sunday. Apart from the sheer discomfort of Michelangelo's hard little chairs on my sunburn, I would have to explain the unusually ruddy glow of the parts of me that were open to observation. Thank heaven, Leonora would never make indelicate inquiries as to the rest of my anatomy; but she was bound to feel hurt at not having been taken along to Cape Point, though of course she would not say so plainly enough to be contradicted or quarrelled with.

There is in Cape Town an odd law of restaurants: a restaurant's chances of survival stand in inverse proportion to the quality of its service and food. So while around it excellent restaurants came and went, Michelangelo's remained, a bastion of what Gerhard called fuck-you cuisine, unchanged as to décor (phoney Italian murals), menu (sandwiches, chicken and steak) and service (a single morose waiter dispensing gloom and food with equal indifference). I kept resolving to propose to Leonora that we change our meeting place, but I didn't quite have the heart to kill the fiction that Michelangelo's was *our* special place. So week after week we braved the soggy chicken mayonnaise sandwiches and thin cappuccino, earning not even the gratification of being recognised by the waiter who had served us for two years, or by the owner who for two years had impassively rung up our weekly contribution to his welfare. They still seemed vaguely puzzled when we arrived, as if they thought we were delivering something, or had come to clear the garbage.

Leonora was waiting for me. I am never late, but Leonora is always early, thus rendering me in effect late. Predictably, she commented immediately on my sunburn. I reminded myself that she couldn't be expected to know that she was only the latest in a whole sequence of people who had made more or less the same comment to me today, and said as neutrally as possible, 'Yes, I had to go out to Cape Point yesterday in connection with a case I'm taking. Some development that needs to be fought.'

To my relief Leonora seemed less interested in my sunburn than in the reason for it. 'Development? At Cape Point? But that's terrible.'

'Yes, it is rather, isn't it? That's why we're resisting it.'

'Oh, I'm so grateful that there are people like you to stop that sort of thing.' Without wanting to, I'd turned myself into the hero of the story, or Leonora had done it for me. I suppose you couldn't blame her for wanting me to be more exciting than I in fact am – but it's not as if I had a deep need to see her as Florence Nightingale or Winnie Mandela or somebody.

'Well, let's hope we can stop it; it's by no means sure that we will be able to. We're up against big money and big influence.'

'Yes, but you have right on your side.'

'That's never been an advantage in a court case.'

'You're so cynical.'

I looked around, trying to catch the eye of the waiter, who was inspecting the nails on his left hand with more interest than he had ever shown in any aspect of his job. 'Then explain to me why the world is full of rich crooks and poor good people.'

'I don't mean that the bad people are always caught and the good people always win, but in the end, on balance, you know, things do get better, and they can only get better if more good people than bad people have their way.'

I didn't think I wanted to get involved in a metaphysical discussion with Leonora. 'Well, then, I hope that whoever decides these things up there won't think that developing Cape Point is in the long-term interests of culture and civilisation.'

'*Nobody* can think that.'

As often in my conversations with Leonora, I was perversely driven to disagree with her, even when she was defending my own point of view. 'Really?' I asked. 'So what do you think of … the Parthenon?' Leonora had been on a librarians' tour of Europe the previous year.

'It's beautiful, of course,' she said, 'but that's …'

'Wait,' I said, warming to my theme, 'and how do you know what the concerned citizens of Athens thought when Pericles built the Parthenon smack on top of the Acropolis – and that to celebrate a military victory? And the Arc de Triomphe – you've seen the films of Hitler's army marching through it to occupy Paris, haven't you?'

'Yes, but what does that have to do with Cape Point?'

'What is has to do with Cape Point is that culture is not a neutral quality, it is decreed by those in power, and what seems like culture to you and to me was in fact an abomination in its time. Think of the pyramids, built by slaves and … and Chartres cathedral built by wretched peasants who thought they were going to go to heaven for it. Who knows, in a thousand years' time this atrocity at Cape Point will be admired as the cultural achievement of a minor African tribe.'

'Are you ready to order now?' the impassive waiter demanded at my elbow, apparently galvanised into service by the unaccustomed opportunity of interrupting what seemed like an animated conversation between Leonora and me.

'No, we're not,' I snapped at him. 'We're still trying to decide between the toasted cheese and tomato sandwich and the chicken mayonnaise sandwich.'

'Call me when you're ready,' he said impassively.

Leonora giggled, which for her was a surprisingly original and emancipated response, suggesting as it did amusement, detachment, even intellectual superiority to my irritation, rather than her usual anxious deference to my moods. Part of me thought this rather presumptuous of Leonora, but part of me welcomed it as a sign of an independent existence. And then it did seem rather funny, and I also laughed, and for once we had a pleasant meal, though the sandwiches were as awful as ever and the waiter was deeply offended because he thought we had laughed at him.

A few days later Dikeledi stopped me in the corridor.

'Mhlobo says to come for a drink tonight.'

'Has he got something for me?'

'The drink is guaranteed. The rest you'll have to take on trust. Come to our place after work.'

Mhlobo and Dikeledi rented a flat in an old but recently revamped block in Vredehoek. 'You know you've arrived when people try to steal your doorknob as an antique,' said Dikeledi as she let me in. 'We found somebody unscrewing it last night. Mhlobo invited him in and asked him why he wanted it and he said that Deco doorknobs are selling on Greenmarket Square for a hundred rand each.'

111

'Did you hand him over to the police?'

'No. Mhlobo let him go on condition that he could publish an edited version of their conversation. He says it's good for people to read about blacks being burgled by whites, what he calls a salutary exercise in reverse stereotyping.'

I smiled. I'd read Mhlobo's columns in the *Mail & Guardian*: he tended to the polysyllabic.

We went into the sitting room, a large underfurnished room overlooking the city. Mhlobo was watching television; he was sinewy, very dark-skinned; with an unnerving stare and a disarming smile.

'Hey, man,' he said, zapping the television set into silence and darkness, 'nothing there but dark foreboding and gloomy prog-nos-ti-ca-tion.' He punctuated each syllable with a twirl of a long index finger. 'Grab a seat. I'll get you a beer. Dikeledi?'

'Nothing at the moment, thanks.' She sat down next to me on the sofa. Mhlobo handed me my beer, sat down and came straight to the point. 'Dikeledi tells me you have a professional interest in Brick Tomlinson.'

'That's right – really just background to a case.'

'Bullshit. Tomlinson's not background. You don't venture into a bull-ring with an interest in the bull *as background*.'

'Well, yes, I see the point of your analogy, but the thing is, this case … it's not about personalities, it's about principles.'

'Bullshit,' he said again, slapping the palm of his left hand with his right. 'When you've worked for a newspaper as long as I have you know every principle in-var-i-ab-ly has a personality attached. Mind you, not all personalities have principles attached, but that is, as they say, another story.'

'Fair enough,' I said, 'as long as you remember I'm not writing a story, I'm preparing a case.'

'If you insist,' he shrugged. 'For my part, everything is a story. But you're welcome to what I possess, and Dikeledi can fill in on anything I leave out. Where should I begin?' He looked down at a little notebook on the coffee table in front of him. 'The official version or the unofficial?'

'Both; starting with the official.'

'Right, of-fi-ci-a-lly, then, Mr Bernard Richard Tomlinson, more commonly known as Brick Tomlinson, is, as you are no doubt aware, CEO of Tomlinson and Tomlinson, the largest construction company in the country. He is the only grandson of the founder, Rock Tomlinson, who was a personal favourite, for reasons much spec-u-lated about, of Cecil John Rhodes, and who built most of the mansions in Bishop's Court and Constantia, at any rate those not built by Herbert Baker. He is also the only son of Trick Tomlinson, who first squandered most of the family fortune in the forties, after he took over control, if that is the term I'm looking for, of the firm after his father's death – Rock Tomlinson died in 1940 – and then remade it several times over by winning or wangling government contracts in the nineteen fifties and sixties to build low-grade township housing. This, you will remember, at a time when new townships were arising outside our major cities only slightly less quickly than blacks could be kicked out of those cities in terms of the miraculous and wondrous Group Areas Act, passed, if memory serves me, in 1950.'

'If you ever lived in one of those townships,' Dikeledi cut in, 'you will know that Trick Tomlinson sacrificed quality to expedience, or possibly profit – '

'Or both,' Mhlobo said. 'Either way, Trick's houses were a far cry from daddy's solid stone edifices, though his bank balance was soon very solid indeed, enabling him to move back into one of said edifices in Constantia, where young Richard was born and bred and in the fullness of time, to be precise' – he glanced at his notebook – 'in 1965, joined the firm. This is where Tomlinsons's Construction became Tomlinson and Tomlinson and moved firmly up-market, though without abandoning the lucrative lower end of the market. You get the picture, marble for show and ticky-tack for quick profits, during the building boom fuelled by the almost total silencing of black resistance in the sixties, after Sharpeville and such. And then Brick's rise to power was consolidated by the construction of grandiose administrative blocks and dream-palace casinos and luxury hotels in the Bantustans that were popping up all over our country in the seventies as Homelands to black people who had the temerity to be born in white South Africa.'

'You might say,' commented Dikeledi, 'that the Tomlinsons

built South Africa as we know it – the plush white suburbs, the little-box townships and the unreal homelands.'

'Yeah, right,' said Mhlobo, 'and Brick's contribution was duly recognised by a grateful nation.' He glanced at his notes again. 'He was given a President's Award for services to the country in 1985, and an honorary doctorate by the University of Cape Town in 1987, just after donating a new Building Sciences block. He has built almost every single public building put up in the last ten years in Cape Town. In short, for an English-speaking person he has done uncommonly well under a regime notorious for reserving its big projects for its Afrikaner Broederbond allies, and he looks set to do very nicely thank you out of the construction of hotels made necessary by the fact that people are coming to visit our country in such gratifying numbers just at present. Which is, I believe from Dikeledi, where you come into the story.'

I nodded. 'Where do you get all this information?'

'Oh, it's quite easily available, with someone as well known as that, Who's Who in Construction, that kind of thing. The rest we have on file at the office. Miraculous thing is that a history that may strike you and me as one dismal account of collaboration with an evil regime is, of course, from another angle, simply the cur-ric-ulum vi-tae of a highly successful person and useful member of the community. And Brick runs a tight ship, with lots of grassroot support from his workers, at any rate those who think the fact that he kicks a ball around with them means that he regards them as equals, without asking him whether they can join in his games of golf.'

He glanced down at his slip of paper again. 'Do you know about the casino bid?'

'No,' I said, 'no, that wasn't mentioned.'

'Well, then, hear this. You will remember, of course, that the shall we say outgoing government professed ab-hor-rence of evils like gambling and pornography, thereby reassuring their followers that this was an im-pec-cably Christian country, and at the same time guaranteeing their puppet rulers of the homelands a tidy income from the gambling and prostitution dens to which the said Christian supporters flocked in their thousands every weekend – in hotels, of course, constructed by Brick Tomlinson and his ilk.'

I nodded. One of my father's last indiscretions had been to blow what remained of his money in one of the homelands casinos, which enabled my mother to blame his downfall on the Nationalists, conveniently forgetting that the rest of his – and her – money had been squandered on the Sport of Kings.

'Well, then,' said Mhlobo again, 'hear this too. The new government is planning to grant casino licences to selected individuals –'

'The right to gamble being one of the inalienable human rights we struggled for,' interjected Dikeledi.

'Right. And licences will be granted on a strictly limited basis, a casino licence being as they say a licence to print money. The only snag is in order to be granted the licence you have to submit a proposal which will convince the powers that be that you will be contributing to the welfare of the region, that is creating jobs, improving the environment; you can't just convert your back room in Pinelands or your flat in Vredehoek. And Brick is gearing up to apply for a casino licence. The long and short of it, Nic-ho-las, is that your man Tomlinson has plenty to gain by developing his property at Cape Point, and plenty to lose by being prevented. He'll already have sunk a couple of million into design, planning, surveys, applications, that kind of thing – and those are just the legitimate expenditures. Add to that the bribes that he will have paid to any number of people just to be in the running, and you have a sizeable investment, promising some very determined opposition. Prepare yourself for a good fight.'

'That I'm doing,' I said, rather dejectedly. The more I heard about Brick Tomlinson the less I really wanted to be involved in this case. A good fight has never been one of my priorities.

'Any assistance I can give you, let me know. To be honest, I'm not a green, because too much of what claims to be conservation tends to be whites hanging onto the wide open spaces for themselves. But I'd gladly help you in any way I can to stop this man Tomlinson – I reckon I owe him something for the shitty little house in Guguletu that he built for us.'

'Thanks for that. I hope in any case that Dikeledi will work on the case with me, so you're bound to hear about it one way or another.'

'Bound to,' said Dikeledi. 'In this house we bring our work home and share it out.'

Dikeledi and Mhlobo saw me to the door. As Mhlobo turned the knob, it came off in his hand. The outside knob had been stolen again.

CHAPTER FIVE

It is one of the misfortunes of being a lawyer that one spends so much of one's time trying to get information out of people who distrust lawyers. Furthermore, anybody in possession of any information whatsoever immediately assumes that a lawyer's interest means that it is worth money. When I lamented this fact to Mr McKendrick, he said: 'That is true. However, there is comfort to be derived from the fact that we usually sell the information for considerably more than we pay for it.' My friend Gerhard, on the other hand, maintains that we have human nature on our side, in that the kind of person we are interested in is usually disliked by somebody else. 'The trick,' he says, 'is to find that person and get him, or more frequently her, talking.'

The Rocklands affair promised to be, as we say, information-hungry. It was clear that if we had any case at all we'd have to dig for it: on the face of it, Brick Tomlinson had followed the correct procedures in getting his land rezoned for development, however outrageous the result might seem to a naive environmentalist. The most fruitful line of inquiry might be to find out how such a result had come about, so obviously in conflict with professed environmental policy. Mhlobo had hinted that any number of people would have had to be bribed, but that was just a general speculation, however plausible.

'What I want to know,' I said to Dikeledi, 'is who *exactly* would have had to be bribed for Tomlinson to have been given planning permission?'

'Easy,' said Gerhard, who had dropped in for one of his visits. 'Find the person who had the authority to give permission for the planning to go ahead. That is the person who was bribed. Stands to reason.'

117

'Not necessarily,' said Dikeledi. 'Somebody higher up may have been bribed to put pressure on a subordinate to grant the permission.'

'Yes, Clever-Clogs, but it is to be presumed that said subordinate will have been aware of pressure being put upon him. I say go for the person who signed the document. *Cherchez l'homme*, is my motto.'

'Yes, dear, we know,' said Dikeledi. 'We've seen some of your finds.'

'Well, the Minister of Nature Conservation and Development was and for the time being still is Sam Stanford, of course,' I said, 'who sold out to the Nationalists when the going wasn't so good for the Progressives. He's capable of anything to save his own skin. But I don't know whether he actually signed the document.'

'You haven't even seen a copy of the planning permission?'

'No,' I said. 'I don't imagine that Brick Tomlinson will pop one in the post for me.'

'But how about the Angel?' asked Gerhard. 'He must have seen a copy.'

'I don't ... or yes, I do. He did say that he'd seen a copy.'

'Well then, Bob's your uncle. Ask him.'

'Mmm. Problem is, I don't know how to get hold of him.'

'Oh, for heaven's sake, Nick,' said Dikeledi. 'How do you propose to run a case when you don't have a single document, and don't know how to get hold of your client? It's all very well having an angel for a client, but the court's going to need good old-fashioned un-ethereal documentation.'

'Don't you start on the angel bit,' I said morosely. 'The man is called Luc Tomlinson and he is not an angel.'

My phone rang.

'I'm sorry to interrupt you, Mr Morris,' said Myrah, 'but it's that young man. He says he's phoning from a public telephone on Simon's Town station and he has only 40 cents.'

'Right, Myrah, put him through – or why don't you ask his number and phone him back?'

'If you say so, Mr Morris.' It clearly did not accord with Myrah's idea of professional decorum to phone a client at a public telephone.

'That, as it happens, is Luc Tomlinson,' I announced. 'Phoning from a public telephone.'

'See?' said Gerhard. 'Angelic apprehension of your need.'

'Angelic apprehension is all very well,' said Dikeledi, 'but a cell phone might be more reliable.'

'He probably thinks they fry your brains,' I replied as my phone rang.

'Hello, yes, Mr Tomlinson,' I said.

'Hello, yes, Mr Morrison.'

'Morris,' I corrected before I could stop myself. Gerhard made a pursed-lip face at Dikeledi, the one he makes to mock what he calls my Little-Miss-Priss manner.

'Yes. *Morris*. I said I would phone.'

'Yes, last week.'

'Yes, well. How's the case going?'

'Awaiting your input.'

'Right, then. What do you want from me?'

'A copy of the document granting your father permission to develop Rocklands.'

'Well, yes. I had it somewhere.' There was an unhelpful pause.

'I suggest you find it and get it to me very quickly, by carrier pigeon if necessary.' Dikeledi made a chopping motion with her right hand in her left, which did little to alleviate the irritation I felt with Luc Tomlinson for having made me seem so remarkably ineffectual.

'Yes, well. I'll have to think.'

'You have 20 seconds.' Gerhard made two rapid chopping motions with his right hand.

'Hey, what's made you so ratty?'

'I am not being *ratty*, Mr Tomlinson, but this case has been badly, perhaps even irretrievably delayed by your non-communication. I take it you are serious about pursuing it?' Gerhard and Dikeledi nodded solemnly at each other, as if to say Now he's telling him.

'Of course I'm fucking serious.'

'Then when can you let me have the document?'

'I'll have to think … okay, okay, don't blow, you'll have it today. Tell you what, my mother has a copy, I'll ask her to bring it in, how's that?'

'That seems admirable. And please, in future, either give me a contact number or be in touch once a day. I cannot proceed with this case by telepathy, finely attuned as our sympathies are.' Gerhard and Dikeledi gave each other a high-five.

'You *are* being ratty, aren't you?'

'No, I am not.'

'Yes, you are. You're as ratty as a bad drain. Right, then. I'll phone you every day about this time.'

'Do that. Goodbye, Mr Tomlinson.'

'Cheers, Nick.' Then, as I was about to put down the receiver: 'Hey, Nick!'

'Yes?'

'Were you ever called Nick the Prick at school?'

'Only by my friends,' I said, put down the receiver, and chased Gerhard and Dikeledi out of my office. At times their high spirits were indistinguishable from childishness.

I did not relish the prospect of a visit from Joyce Tomlinson. I remembered her as taking rather a lot for granted. I have always preferred to have some control over the level of sociability governing any particular relation; Joyce Tomlinson, however, did not seem to recognise the other person's – my – right to consultation. Having been brought up to treat older women with deference and respect, I found it difficult to deal with one who seemed intent upon flirting with me – insofar as I could judge of these things, never having been much given to flirtation myself.

In a remarkably short time Joyce Tomlinson appeared in my office – instructed, no doubt, by her much-indulged son. I wondered where he had found another 40 cents – probably begged it from a gullible pensioner. Joyce was dressed, as before, in a dress that suggested, without quite revealing, an absence of what my mother used to call foundation garments.

'Well, hello, Nick. We meet again.' Her manner was, to my relief, slightly less charged with meaning than before. She was indeed a bit perfunctorily flirtatious, as if she felt it was expected of her but wasn't really in the mood for it.

I decided my professional manner would be the most congenial for both of us. 'I appreciate your visit, Mrs Tomlinson, at such short notice.'

She sat down at my desk, put down her handbag, and picked a petal off one of the Rentaflower specimens on my desk. 'These flowers are very tired.'

'Yes. I get them second-hand.' I didn't want to look at the flower because I thought she might think I was trying to peer down her dress.

But she wasn't listening. She picked up her handbag again, took out a letter, and placed it on my desk. 'I've brought you this letter. I could …'

'Ah, thank you, that is …' I began, but she held up her hand.

'Please. I was going to say I could have faxed it to you quite easily, but I wanted to bring it personally.' Her manner veered alarmingly towards the intimate; she seemed to have quite a narrow register of response.

'I appreciate that,' I said, as politely impersonal as possible.

But she wasn't listening. 'Look, Nick,' she said, her deep voice dropping several octaves, and her manner becoming startlingly grave. 'To be honest with you, I'm wondering why I'm here. Except that I had a sense that it was important to talk to you.'

'And you kindly brought that document.'

'Oh yes, that, of course. But I would have had to come to see you anyway.'

'Of course, as your son's lawyer …'

'No, not as my son's lawyer, or rather as that, yes, but as more than that.' She leant forward and looked deep into my eyes. I had to return her gaze or stare down her dress. 'You see, I have this sense that you are about to become quite deeply involved with our family.'

This was a sense I had also had, to my considerable discomfiture.

'And I think,' she continued, 'that you should understand the family before you proceed any further.' It occurred to me that I would have been spared this sort of thing if I had opted for accountancy. Balance sheets did not have family complications.

'Of course,' I ventured lamely, 'legal principles take no cognisance of personal elements …'

'Then legal principles leave much to be desired,' she

121

returned, quite sharply for somebody who in general so favoured smooth surfaces and rounded edges. 'The law is about people, isn't it?'

'Certain branches of it, yes, the law of persons, say, as opposed to the law of property …'

'Please,' she held up her hand, 'don't try to confuse me with jargon. You know what I mean. Without people there would be no law, would there?'

This was unexceptionable enough, except that the same proposition applied to garbage removal and astrophysics. 'True,' I ventured, 'but I thought this case was about baboons …'

'Oh, Luc's baboons!' she shrugged. 'That's his thing. But there's much more at stake here than a few baboons.' She selected another flower and started demolishing it. 'I suppose you could say that I'm here to *equip* you for the case.' She gave me another melting-green gaze from over the ravished flower.

'That is very kind of you.'

'Oh, *kindness*,' she shrugged again. 'If you were to ask me why I should want to provide you with this information, I could say to you it's because you're a charming young man with a fetching line in underwear, but that wouldn't be the whole truth.' She threw away the husk of the flower. 'Nick,' she said abruptly, 'have you ever been in love?'

I was taken aback. 'I … I have a girlfriend,' I said.

She smiled, and for a moment her manner recaptured something of its disquieting challenge. 'That's nice, darling, but not necessarily the same thing. *Girlfriends* are what boys have. *In love* is what adults are.' Her voice deepened again. 'I mean have you been in love so that you measure time by when last you saw the person you love, so that a sunrise has only happened if you've shared it with that person, and the night is meaningless without him? I mean have you been in love so that nothing else and nobody else on earth mattered to you?'

'No,' I said. 'Definitely not.' It was difficult to forget that I had stood naked in front of this woman, and there was something in her manner that suggested that she hadn't forgotten it either.

She smiled again. 'You needn't look so alarmed. I'm not here to confess a guilty passion. I want you to understand that the

122

only person I have ever loved or ever will love is Brick Tomlinson.'

I was relieved at this unexceptionable confession, though puzzled that anyone should declare her love for her husband so much as a matter of wonder and surprise. 'It's fortunate, then, that you're married to him.'

'So I would have thought … oh, more than twenty years ago, before I married him. When I look at Luc I see the young Brick, beautiful, talented, loving, joyful, passionate.'

This seemed to me a somewhat idealised description of Luc Tomlinson, but I was willing to make concessions for the perceptions of a mother. She sighed and shook her hair away from her face. 'But, to abbreviate a very long and not very sensational tale, my husband fell out of love with me. Not an unusual development, you will say; but my husband did not fall in love with another woman: he fell in love with success, with achievement, with acceptance, approval, praise – praise from inferior people, whom he respected because they had positions of power and authority. At heart, you see, my husband is still a boy trying to please his father.'

'But I thought …'

'Yes, yes, of course, he's been dead for years, but Brick can no more shake off his dread of his father's disapproval and his desire for his praise than if the old man was still head of the firm and head of the house. All his life he laboured to please his father, but the harder he worked and the more successful he was, the more his father resented him – because he couldn't stand the idea of being superseded, as his father had been by him. So that the more Brick achieved, the more his father hated him. And Brick never knew why. It took a woman – me – to understand them, because Brick married me to impress his father – I was a woman who impressed men in those days –' she gave me a quick smile, but not so as to invite the obvious demurral – 'and the old man hated him for that, too, being married himself to a narrow, cold drudge of a wife.' She stopped for a moment and sighed lightly again. 'And he hated me for marrying his son. Which is why he lavished all his affection – for he was not naturally a cold man – on our son, who thus became the unconscious instrument of his grandfather's hatred, and in due course the conscious object of his father's jealousy.'

'And the object of his mother's worship.'

'Worship?' she repeated pensively, as if considering it. 'That may be too strong, but it's true that Luc has become for me the consolation for a life misspent. But I am almost scared to love him, when I consider what love has done in our family, for what is the whole mess but love gone wrong?'

She smoothed her dress with her long, strong fingers. 'There. Now you have the Tomlinson family from an outsider's point of view. For I was always an outsider: it's a male dynasty, with no room for women outside the nursery and kitchen. There's no room for culture, either; it's all a matter of making money. I honestly believe my husband has not read a book since he left school, and I don't think he's ever listened to a symphony or a concerto or a sonata from beginning to end. Imagine, then, how I must love him, to tolerate his complete lack of the qualities I look for in human beings.' She paused again, as if to give me time to make the effort of imagination to which she had enjoined me. 'So I want you to know that in helping you and Luc with this case I am violating my feelings for my husband, except if you can say that I'm punishing him for not loving me. And I want you to know that you are taking on more than a dispute about some land: you are taking on the ancient house of Tomlinson – well, relatively ancient, as these things go in this country – and the implacable resentment of Brick Tomlinson.'

'Thanks,' I said. 'You're not the first person who's told me that.'

'Well, yes. Brick's resentment is famous. He has ways of making himself very unpleasant. Think of him as a little boy with power.'

I nodded bleakly.

'Which is why I'm willing to help you.' She pushed the letter towards me. 'I hope this will be of use to you.'

She got to her feet. There was now nothing flirtatious about her manner. 'Brick is going on one of his business trips this weekend to one of the former homelands. I'd like you to come to lunch on Sunday.'

'I ... I ...' My default response to most invitations is to try to think of an excuse not to accept; but this invitation paralysed even my normally inventive avoidance mechanism, and I just gaped stupidly.

'Bring your *girlfriend*, of course,' she said with a slightly satirical edge to her voice, evidently guessing that I had been alarmed at the prospect of a lunch tête-à-tête with her. 'And I want you to meet an old friend. The most civilised man I know, not excepting yourself. I have told him about you, and he is anxious to meet you.'

I wondered what exactly she had told her friend. 'Oh, well, then ...'

'You can come?'

I belatedly remembered my manners. 'Yes, certainly, thank you very much.'

'Wonderful. Luc will be there too, I hope.'

She might have told me that before I accepted, I thought, but smiled bravely.

'Come at about noon. Very informal. Bring your bathing costume if you insist on wearing one.'

'Thank you. I will.'

'There's my card.' She slipped a vaguely scented card onto my desk. 'Bye now,' and with a last glance of green she selected the least faded flower from my depleted arrangement and drifted out of the room.

It is not in my nature to distrust women. Something in my upbringing, possibly my mother's precept, more probably my father's example, imbued me with the irrational conviction that whereas men cheat and lie all the time, women never do. It may even have been this conviction – illusion – that attracted me to Leonora in the first place, an instinctive recognition that she would leave my faith in women intact – as indeed she had done, albeit at a certain price in mystery and excitement. Thus it was not easy for me to imagine that Joyce Tomlinson might have had undeclared motives in telling me her family history; might even have given me a partial or distorted version of that history. Her self-consciously tragic air, though hardly spontaneous, was not necessarily insincere; indeed, self-pity is one of the most genuine of emotions. And yet it was also difficult to believe that a woman who loved her husband as much as she said she did would choose to side with his enemies against him, or at any rate with his son, which in the Tomlinson book seemed tantamount to the enemy. In short, either Joyce Tomlinson was lying to me or she was betraying her husband.

The letter she had brought me was from the Western Cape office of the Department of Nature Conservation and Development, and had pleasure in informing Mr Richard Tomlinson that at its meeting of 1 September 1995 the Land Use Committee had, acting on the recommendation contained in the attached report of its Chief Conservation Officer, decided to approve his application for the rezoning of the land known as Rocklands, etc., etc., and, subject to certain height restrictions and the provision of amenities as set out in a separate annexure, also the development of the leisure facility as applied for by him in his capacity as Chief Executive Officer of Tomlinson and Tomlinson and special adviser to Safari Investments. The letter was signed, with the kind of flourish that I had been taught was vulgar, by the Chief Conservation Officer himself, Dr HC Visser. There was no trace of the report mentioned.

The only useful aspect of the letter was Visser's name, which was unfamiliar to me; my previous dealings with the Department of Nature Conservation and Development had gone through a man called Hartshorn – a man whom I had never met, but whose occasional letters had been helpful enough in a vague, bureaucratic kind of way. I wondered what had happened to him. I decided to consult Cedric Watts – not because he knew anything about Nature Conservation, but because he had an almost uncanny knowledge of movements in official circles.

His secretary answered the phone. 'I'm sorry, Mr Morris, Mr Watts is unavailable.'

'Any idea when he will be in?'

'I'm afraid not.' Then she giggled. 'I'm afraid he's in prison.'

'Cedric Watts in prison! Whatever for?'

'I couldn't tell you, Mr Morris. He didn't turn up this morning and when I phoned his home I got Mrs Watts, who was hysterical and couldn't tell me anything. Mr McKendrick is down at the police station now to sort it out.'

I consulted my friend Gerhard.

'Easiest way of finding out anything,' he said, 'is to ask.'

'Yes, but ask whom?'

'This man Visser. Make an appointment to see him, and ask him what's happened to the other chappie, and ask him at the same time to give you a copy of his report.'

'You don't seriously think he's just going to say sure help yourself to all the information you need?'

'Perhaps not just at first, but this is where the new dispensation, of which you are so sceptical, kicks in. Haven't you read your Interim Constitution?'

'No. Should I?'

'Yes, most definitely. Both as New South African and as lawyer. In particular you should inform yourself of Section 23. It's expressly designed with a view to squeezing the balls of the likes of your Dr Visser till they squeal.'

I did as Gerhard had suggested, and, fortified with the authority of the Interim Constitution, felt emboldened to phone the office of the Department. A brisk female voice answered: 'Nature Conservation and Development.'

'Good morning. I am Nicholas Morris of McKendrick, Jolly, Wirthenburger, Smith, Watts and Koekemoer. I should like to make an appointment to see Dr Visser.'

'What is the nature of your business?'

'It's about a proposed development that he – his department approved. Out at Cape Point.'

'The Rocklands development, yes. I can make an appointment for you to see Dr Visser at 10 a.m. tomorrow morning, but Dr Visser prefers members of the public to submit a short memorandum a few hours in advance, stating the nature of their business. Dr Visser finds that saves time.'

'Of course. Will this afternoon do?'

'What time this afternoon?'

'Three o'clock?'

'Three o'clock will be acceptable. You can fax your document to this number.' She measured out a number in two-digit bytes.

127

The offices of the Department of Nature Conservation and Development were in downtown Cape Town, on the 12th floor of a nineteen sixties block, above a multi-storeyed car park. The lift smelled of urine and sweet sherry, and it took a very long time to reach the 12th floor. When at last it did so, the door sighed open to reveal a featureless and windowless vestibule, with a swing-door at the far end. Opening this, I found myself in yet another featureless and windowless vestibule, this one, though, furnished with a desk, behind which sat a stern-looking middle-aged woman, peering attentively if somewhat disapprovingly at a computer screen. She did not look up as I entered, although the door must have signalled my arrival quite audibly.

'Good morning,' I said.

The secretary looked up enquiringly, but did not reply to my greeting.

'I'm Nicholas Morris,' I explained. 'I have an appointment to see Dr Visser.' I pointed at the door at the far end of the vestibule, which had a large brass plaque on it saying *Dr HC Visser, Chief Conservation Officer*.

'Yes,' she said neutrally, 'at ten o'clock.'

I glanced at my watch. It was three minutes to ten. Clearly, in her book it was as reprehensible to be early for an appointment as to be late.

'Please wait here for your appointment with Dr Visser,' she said, and prepared to resume her typing. At the last moment she relented and reluctantly asked me, 'Would you like a seat?' as if offering me something of great value that she couldn't really spare.

'Yes, thank you, if you don't mind,' I risked, taking a seat.

She shrugged. 'No, I don't mind,' she said, in a tone implying that even if she had minded nobody would have taken any notice, and went on with her typing. I took up an old copy of *Veld and Flora* – it was either that or *The Civil Servant* – and examined her over my magazine. She sat up very straight, and stared at her screen and keyboard sternly, as if she suspected them of potential misbehaviour. She was about fifty-five, and had the regimented, dedicated tidiness that in women of her age often takes over from mere vanity. Her hair had obviously been 'done' that morning, in a style which would have been frivolous had it not been glued so rigidly into place. The same tension between the decorative and the functional was maintained in the unexpectedly ornate gold chain dangling from her primly pointed glasses. The total effect was one of stern silliness, as on those unfortunate photographs of Mrs Thatcher steering some cowering male around a dance floor. I guessed that she had been a fixture in the department for much longer than anybody else, and that she disapproved of the whole new dispensation, though compelled by her sense of duty to be loyal to her superiors in the face of intruders like me.

At ten o'clock exactly she got up, walked purposefully to Visser's door, and said, 'You may go through now to Dr Visser.' I tore myself away from an account of the growth habit of *Sparaxis grandiflora* and followed her. Without knocking, she opened the door and announced, 'Mr Morris.'

I smiled at her in passing and murmured 'Thank you,' but she stared straight ahead like a Horse Guard determined not to be importuned by a tourist. I went into the immoderately large office, and the door closed behind me with the understated firmness that marked all the actions of this paragon of secretaries. As far as I could see, Visser was not doing anything that would have prevented his seeing me when I arrived; he was in fact sitting at an absolutely empty desk, with his hands folded in front of him on the solid surface. His hands were small and plump, and the surface was very shiny. Behind him a large window afforded a splendid view of Table Mountain, its brilliance in the morning light slightly dimmed by the state of the window, which was such as to make one want to reach for a bucket and a squeegee.

Visser did not get up, but with one fat little hand gestured at the chair in front of his desk.

'Good morning, Mr Morris,' he said, and smiled. He exuded a kind of affability that I had come across in cardio-thoracic surgeons and samoosa vendors, a blend of professional civility and private contempt, based on a consciousness of being one up in any game. He had a strong, slow Afrikaans accent, which he used to good effect to give a certain ponderous emphasis to his words. My name, in particular, lent itself to strong guttural stress.

129

'You must rrrealise, Mr Morr-rris,' he explained, after I had reminded him of my business, 'that the decision was taken by a committee. I am not the committee.'

'But it was your report that persuaded the committee to approve the rezoning and development.'

'I am a public servant, Mr Morr-rris, and in the spirit of public service I prepared a report to guide the committee. I was of course happy that they accepted my recommendation, but if they had not accepted it, I would not have been aggrrrieved.' He nodded in a pleased sort of way, as if that concluded the matter.

I decided to take a different tack. 'How well do you know Mr Brick Tomlinson?'

He looked down at his hands, as if fascinated by their pale plumpness; he twirled his thumbs as if experimenting with a new gadget; then he looked up at me and said, 'Mr Morr-rris, I can answer that only if you will tell me why you are asking it.'

'I'm asking the question because it may be necessary in court to establish the likelihood of his having tried to influence the decision in some way.' I was taking a chance here: I knew from experience that the mention of legal action either intimidated people or rendered them sullenly uncooperative. Visser, though, retained his air of suave accommodation.

'I know him just well enough, Mr Morris, to know to keep my distance. I know Mr Tomlinson, of course, as a leading builder, and I respect him for what he has achieved and for what he has contributed to the South Efrrrrican economy. But I have heard rumours, which I must strrress are merely rrrumours, that he is unscrrrupulous in his methods, and for that reason I take care not to compromise myself. I am speaking, of course, in the strrrrictest confidence. You will appreciate that as a public servant I must at all times avoid the taint of scandal.'

'Of course,' I said, smiling brightly. 'It's just that we have to cover all angles.'

'Of courrrse,' he concurred, also smiling, his eyes as cordial as pebbles. 'But I think you will find, Mr Morris, that there has been nothing whatsoever irr-rregular in the handling of this application.' Visser leant back in his swivel chair, displaying to unpleasant effect his considerable paunch. 'You see, Mr Morr-rris, we believe in this department that honesty is the best policy. You will hear people say that in the New South Efrrrica democracy is being bought at the expense of justice, and without prronouncing on that one way or the other, I want to assure you that in this department we are keeping up the old standards.'

'The old standards?' I asked sceptically. In my experience the old standards had left much to be desired.

'Yes, Mr Morris, the old standards,' he said gravely. 'Justice, fairness, accountability, transparrrrency.'

'Then I take it you will have no objection to letting me have a copy of your report to the committee.'

He chuckled plumply and wagged a short index finger at me skittishly. 'Ah, no, no, Mr Morris, we must distinguish between transparrrency and irrrresponsibility. That report is confidential.'

'I think you will find, Dr Visser,' I said, grateful that my friend Gerhard wasn't there to comment on my manner, 'that in terms of Section 23 of the Constitution of the Republic of South Africa Act, no 200 of 1993, and I quote, "Every person shall have the right of access to information held by the state or any of its organs at any level of government in so far as such information is required for the exercise or protection of any of his or her rights." I think you will agree that this seems to mean that a government department such as yours no longer has the right to confidentiality in cases such as that of my client, whose right of residence is self-evidently affected by the development approved by the committee as a direct consequence of your report. If you need some time or help to familiarise yourself with the content you may want to study the relevant section at your leisure or have it perused by your own lawyers …?'

As I had hoped, he shied away from this suggestion. In fact, he probably knew Section 23 of the Interim Constitution better than I did: it had so obviously been drafted to counter the best efforts of such as himself to hoard and control information, a much-protected commodity under the previous government. 'That won't be necessary, Mr Morris,' he said, with admirable restraint. 'I can still make up my own mind about such things in my own office.'

131

'Of course,' I said. 'May I ask you, then, and this is really why I came, for a copy of your report to the committee?'

'Of courrrse, of courrrrse,' he said. He leaned forward and pressed an intercom button on his desk.

'Brrrenda,' he said into the intercom, 'please make a copy of my report on the Cape Point development and bring it through.' The intercom light flashed acknowledgement, as taciturn and inscrutable as Brenda herself.

In a much shorter time than could have been expected, the door opened noiselessly and the secretary slipped a document onto his desk. Visser nodded curtly, took the document and passed it to me. 'There you are, Mr Morris. Transparrrency, accountability: my report as tabled to and approved by the Land Use Committee of the Department of Nature Conservation and Development.' I had to admire the aplomb with which he managed to present his surrender of the document as a personal achievement.

'Thank you very much, Dr Visser,' I said, 'and thank you for your time. I take it if I have any questions about this document …?'

'Any time, any time,' he said, getting to his feet and rocking slightly as his paunch redistributed his centre of gravity. He extended a small moist hand. I shook it, trying to touch as little of it as possible. 'Have a good day, Mr Morrrrris.'

As I left Visser's office, I paused in the anteroom to put the document into my briefcase. His secretary got up and pointedly closed the door that I had left open. I smiled at her and said, 'Sorry.' There was not a flicker of acknowledgement; but quite impassively and in a very low voice, she said, 'My name is Brenda Booysens. You will hear from me.'

I froze, taken totally unawares by this dramatic overture. It was as if a painting in a museum had winked at me, or an animal in a zoo had spoken to me. I'm afraid I simply gaped at her gormlessly, incapable of any rational response; but Brenda, retaining her air of unimpeachable probity, pointed her nose at the intercom and mouthed the words 'Brick Tomlinson'. I nodded, relieved: it seemed that I had met the Deep Throat of the Department of Nature Conservation and Development. Also pointing my nose at the intercom, I whispered 'When?'

She put a finger to her lips and whispered: 'When the time is right.' Then she returned to her typing and I ceased to exist for her.

Getting back to my office, I took the Visser report from its brown envelope and skim-read it. It was headed 'Department of Nature Conservation and Development: Land Use Committee: Application for the Amendment of Conditions of Rezoning to Permit the Development of a Hotel Complex: Cape Point (Rocklands).' It was a lengthy document, sketching the history of the land, and outlining the proposed development, together with a small copy of the plan Luc Tomlinson had shown me. The main import of the document was contained in the section headed 'Desirability'. Much is made of the natural beauty of the area: 'To have an area of such outstanding natural beauty in such close proximity to Metropolitan Cape Town is such a unique situation that development of any nature must be undertaken with the utmost care and sensitivity to ensure its sustainable amenity value. In terms of the Coastal structure plan, this area is identified as an area warranting full conservation measures.' Slightly inconsequentially, the report then continues: 'It is accepted that the most appropriate use of the existing structure and property be permitted and in this respect a form of holiday accommodation is considered appropriate. A low-density high-quality development in which the existing dwelling is incorporated would be preferable to large-scale commercial exploitation.' It then transpires that the proposed development is exactly the kind of low-density high-quality development that would be appropriate and acceptable: 'The impact on the coastal environment will be kept to a minimum and repaired as soon as possible.' The report concludes with a recommendation that, subject to certain conditions mainly pertaining to sewage, the proposal be approved. The signature beneath was the by now familiar swirl of the Chief Conservation Officer, Dr HC Visser.

The report was as poorly argued as it was formulated, in that all it managed to say was that in view of the sensitivity of the area, the proposed development would be less hideous than some other things that could be envisaged there. One of my first lessons as environmental lawyer had been that committees often seem to find the threat of a larger development sufficient reason to approve the one actually contemplated – the 'At least it's not Disneyland' justification, as a disillusioned older lawyer had explained it to me. But Visser's adoption of this argument might imply nothing more sinister than committee thinking: the fact that he was stupid and could not write a decent sentence did not mean that he had not applied his mind or had acted in bad faith.

My phone rang.

'It's that boy again,' said Myrah. 'He's calling from the curio shop at Cape Point. Shall I put him through?'

'Yes please, Myrah.' Myrah never ceased hoping that one day I would instruct her to tell Luc Tomlinson to *stop bothering us*, as she put it ('I wish the Government would *stop bothering us*' being one of her more implausible hankerings).

'Hello, Nicholas Morris speaking.'

'Hello, yes. Nick. This is Luc Tomlinson!'

'Yes, I know. And you needn't shout, I can hear you quite well.'

'Sorry, there's such a racket here, people buying post cards and crap – yes, all right ma'am, I'm sorry, I know they're high-quality souvenirs – anyway, there's a lot of noise here.'

'Just speak in a normal tone of voice and you should be perfectly audible.'

'Well, then. Crisis. The bulldozers are coming.'

'How do you know that?'

'Well, I can fucking *see* them, can't I? – sorry ma'am – coming down the road to Rocklands like a bloody invading army.'

'Oh-oh, that's bad.'

'Well, yes, I f – know *that*. I want to know what we're going to do.'

'I'll have to apply for an urgent court order.'

'Well, then, get your arse into gear, otherwise there's not going to be much point to it.'

There were excited voices in the background. Tomlinson seemed to be having an argument with several people at the same time, some of them apparently speaking Japanese.

'You seem to imply that the present crisis is somehow attributable to undue delay on my part.'

'I'm not implying any fucking thing, I … yes, yes, all right, ma'am – listen, Nick, they're trying to take the telephone away from me – yes, ma'am, I'll stop now – I'll phone you again …' The call was abruptly terminated.

My first step was to institute proceedings to apply for an urgent temporary court order prohibiting Brick Tomlinson from proceeding with any earthworks or any other building activity at Rocklands. I cited the legitimate interests of my client, Mr Luc Tomlinson, who had been bequeathed life use of the residence on said property, which would be rendered uninhabitable by the building activities. It struck me that this kind of thing was what I had an assistant for, and managed to disengage a surprised Angie from a heated telephone disagreement, apparently on the relative aphrodisiac qualities of oysters and abalone, and entrusted the application to her.

'About time you did something for the environment other than plunder it for seafood salad,' I said, and she made a face at me.

A fulminating Cedric Watts told us the story of his arrest the following morning around the coffee machine.

'Talk about inefficiency! Sheer bloody moronic incompetence!'

'Whose?' asked Kitty Jooste.

'Everybody's! It's a conspiracy of ineptitude. In the first place the bloody firm who fitted the device – Flamesafe indeed – I mean I ask you, imagine linking a bloody bottle of liquid gas to a pedal as sensitive as a bloody …' – he ransacked his stock of metaphor for an image of sensitivity – '… as a bloody nun's conscience, and then the bloody traffic cop, stopping me for jumping a yellow light – I mean I ask you, maniacs are killing women and children all over the Cape Peninsula and I get stopped for jumping a yellow light in a residential area.'

'Yes, Cedric,' Sammy Wentzel said, 'we know; but carry on with the story.'

'And then the bugger starts getting stroppy when I point this out to him, and he says would you mind showing me your licence please sir, knowing bloody well I won't have it on me, I mean I ask you who drives with his licence on him, it's just

135

one more thing to get stolen when you get hijacked, but I thought I'd go through the motions of looking in my cubby-hole, and of course, as I lean over I step on the bloody Flamesafe pedal and the next moment there's this … this …'

'WHOOSH?' asked Dikeledi, with slightly more energy than the occasion demanded.

'Yes, exactly, this WHOOSH, and the traffic cop is on fire with his little book and all.'

'Jee-sus, Cedric!' Kitty Jooste exclaimed. 'What did you do?'

'I ask you, what could I do? I couldn't very well jump out, I mean my car was still shooting out flames like a bloody Primus stove, the damnfool Flamesafe system turns out not to have an off button, well it has a shut-off valve but the stupid thing is in the boot I ask you, and there wasn't much point in setting myself on fire as well was there, so I just had to watch the cop roll around on the sidewalk like a dog with fleas except he was such a big bugger it was more like a bear. And he's burning seriously, otherwise it would have been quite funny, but of course it wasn't,' he added sternly, looking at those members of his audience who were grinning or sniggering. 'Fortunately somebody drove by who had a fire extinguisher in his car, a black chappie but very decent I must say, and he stopped and sprayed it all over the cop, but by this time he didn't have much of his uniform left and not much in the line of eyebrows or moustache – you know how traffic cops wear these big moustaches to intimidate you – and of course bugger-all of his temper, not that he ever had much control over that.'

'So he wasn't too badly injured?' asked Melissa Strydom, a gentle woman who was inclined to assess situations in terms of their human consequences – an eccentricity which had prevented her from making much of an impression in the legal profession.

'Well, he was making a hell of a fuss, you can imagine, and insisted on being taken to hospital, and now he claims of course that he's suffered all sorts of burns in unmentionable but expensive places, and I'm being charged with assault and grievous bodily harm, and he had the cheek to tell me I was lucky he wasn't going for attempted murder, but he backed down pretty quickly when he discovered I was a lawyer, I can tell you. And then, you won't believe it ...' he glared at his audience as if daring them to believe it. 'On top of it the damn fool leaves his motorbike behind when he's taken to hospital and somebody drives off with it and gets slammed at one of those pubs on the Waterfront and drives it off the Victoria bloody pier and now they want to hold me responsible for that, can you believe it? And I don't even want to tell you how I was treated at the police station, you'd swear I was a criminal or something, absolutely blow-all respect for my position or my ... my ...'

'Race?' asked Dikeledi.

'Age?' Gerhard suggested.

'My *standing* in the community. There was a policeman there who couldn't even spell my name, he wrote it *W-h-a-t-s*, I ask you. And you know what the worst of it is?' he paused for dramatic effect and encouraging noises. 'The paintwork on my brand-new Merc is totally buggered up. I'm going to have the whole of the side panel resprayed, and the bloody *pointless* insurance company won't pay because they say I *voluntarily caused the conflagration*, and the Flamesafe company says they don't guarantee that it won't damage paintwork, it just says *with normal use* it won't damage paintwork, and I ask them what the flipping hell is *normal use* for a bloody flamethrowing machine? You know what the problem with this bloody country is?' he demanded from us.

'Vehicle anxiety?' Dikeledi suggested, but Cedric ignored her.

'I'll tell you what the problem with this bloody country is: ten percent of the people are doing the work while the other 90 percent are dividing up the country for themselves.'

'It makes for a change,' said Dikeledi. 'Time was when 90 percent of the people were doing the work and the other ten percent were dividing up the country for themselves.'

Cedric glared at her. 'And a damn sight better it worked, too.'

'The *real* trouble with this country,' said Dikeledi, as we walked back to our offices, 'is that everybody's in favour of transition, but nobody wants change.'

CHAPTER SIX

The Law in its infinite cynicism has made it possible for almost anyone willing to pay large sums of money to be a serious nuisance to society. Obstructing the ends of justice is the legitimate and highly paid occupation of the majority of lawyers. It is only fair, then, that this capacity of the law should now and then extend itself to a cause truly worthy of its protection. To my relief, the application for an interim court order was granted, and Luc Tomlinson phoned – from a cell phone charmed out of a Finnish visitor to Cape Point – the news that the bulldozers had halted their advance upon Rocklands, although, ominously, they had not retreated, but were merely stalled there, creating a nuisance to traffic.

'The bulldozers – should I put sugar in the petrol tanks?' he asked.

'Not unless you want three bulldozers cluttering up Cape Point into all eternity,' I said. 'Besides, you're supposed to be the injured party appealing to the protection of the law.'

'Yes, well. I wish I had more faith in the protection of the law.'

'Thank you. You can of course resort to your own terrorist tactics if you feel you can dispense with regular procedures.'

'Don't be so touchy, will you? Can't a man say what he thinks?'

'That depends on whether a man thinks before he says it.'

To my surprise there was a laugh at the other end of the line. 'I find it sort of reassuring that I've got the snootiest lawyer in Cape Town. They can outsmart us and outwit us but fucked if they can outsnob us.' The phone went dead, whether because of one of the vagaries that cell phones are heir to or, more likely, because Luc Tomlinson regarded telephone etiquette as one of the many dispensable niceties of civilisation.

Dikeledi was in my office discussing the success of the application for a court order – 'Probably an administrative error,' she said – when Myrah put her head round the door. 'I'm sorry to interrupt, Mr Morris,' she said, 'but there's a gentleman who insists that he must see you immediately.' She lowered her voice. 'He's not very polite.'

'Can he be a gentleman, then?' asked Dikeledi, but her humour was lost on the distraught Myrah.

'May I show him in? He's really most insistent, really almost … abusive. He just *stormed* into my office …'

Dikeledi shrugged and got up. 'Deal with the gentleman first, Nick. Ladies can wait.'

'Thanks, Dikeledi,' I said. 'Right, Myrah, who is this … gentleman?'

'He won't tell me; he says that his business is highly confidential, and even when I told him that all our business is highly confidential and that that is why we appoint only people who are worthy of the confidence that is placed in them …'

'Of course, Myrah,' I said. 'But you can't expect …' I didn't quite know what it was that Myrah couldn't expect, so I said safely enough, 'the man in the street to appreciate these things. Why don't you just show him in?'

'Of course,' she said, hardly mollified. 'But I hope he doesn't get violent.'

The man who entered was not, on superficial evidence, a gentleman. He was dressed carelessly, though his clothes were of good quality: a windbreaker, a pair of khaki shorts, long socks, stout boots, none of it exactly dirty, but none of it very fresh either. His manner was too distracted to be rude: you felt that he wasn't aware enough of you to intend any slight, and yet of course that oblivion was in itself a reflection on your importance in his world.

He extended his hand almost as an afterthought.

'Afternoon,' he said. 'I'm Brick Tomlinson.'

Of course. The photograph in Joyce Tomlinson's room – though the real thing was rather more rugged than the smoothed-out studio version. When he did look at me, the bright blue of the eyes marked him immediately as Luc's father, though the physique was much more chunky. He had coarse blond hair touched almost imperceptibly with grey, and a chin so square I wondered whether that was where he had got his nickname from. He looked in his forties, which, allowing for the Tomlinsons' trick of looking younger than their age, probably put him in his early fifties. He would be violently attractive to a certain kind of woman, the kind who wasn't looking for understanding and support as much as for uncomplicated forcefulness. His handshake was like a declaration of war. He sat down and pulled up his socks.

'You'll know why I'm here,' he said.

'I can guess, but I don't want to jump to conclusions,' I replied. 'Perhaps you can …'

'If you've got time to waste, I haven't,' he said. 'It's about this damnfool nonsense of Luc's.' He chucked a piece of paper on the desk in front of me. I recognised it as a court order.

I nodded. 'The interdict.'

'I'm not going to put up with it,' he continued.

I nodded again.

He raged on. 'He had the flaming gall to tell me when I went to talk to him, father to son, when I had the *bloody decency* to drive out to that stinking house of his that used not to stink when decent people were living in it, to drive out and sit down and talk to him like my father never would have talked to me … you know what he had the balls to say to me?'

'I have no idea,' I replied, though I did in fact have a fairly good idea.

'He told me that he could only communicate – co*mmuni*cate, I ask you, when his own bloody father was sitting opposite him like I'm sitting here with you – *communicate* with me through his bleeding fucking *lawyer.*'

I nodded again, intent on charting my course through the vagaries of Brick Tomlinson's syntax.

'Why don't you say anything, damn you, and stop nodding like one of those moron dogs in the back windows of cars?'

'I'm listening, Mr Tomlinson. I'm the bleeding fucking lawyer.'

'Well, listen carefully then, damn you. I'm not going to be stopped, not even by interdict, by my whippersnapper of a son and a crowd of monkey-hugging environmentalists and a

140

poncy lawyer all the way from Milton bloody College.' One strong finger pointed accusingly at my throat, as if my tie were an incriminating piece of evidence I had tried to hide.

I smiled, amused that even in his rage he had noticed the tie. 'Your son also objected to my schooling. I take it you, too, went to Bishops.'

'That's absolutely none of your bleeding business.' For some reason my reference to his schooling outraged him even more.

'Perhaps if you explained your business to me I could concentrate on mine.'

'Oh, very smart, very smart. But if you must know, my business is to build; if only smarty-pants lawyers with nothing to do but sit on their arses in little glass boxes and issue interdicts would let me be and get on with it. I'm a *builder* and I've been *building* ever since I left school, and, if you must know, it wasn't bloody Bishops either and I left it when I was sixteen and I've *built* up with my own hands the largest construction company in South bloody Africa, what's left of it.' He held out his hands as if in evidence: they were large and strong and hard and certainly looked as if they'd done some building in their day.

'I thought Tomlinson and Tomlinson was an old family firm.'

'Old family firm be blasted, of course it's an old family firm, but my father blast his memory transferred every asset worth a monkey's fart to a so-called bloody trust fund for my worthless bare-arsed beanpole layabout of a son and left me to build it up all over again. He *bequeathed* me' – he made a large gesture with his huge hands – 'the name of the firm and the lease on the premises and the bulldozers and cement mixers and 60 boys to pay and not a cent to do it with. D'you realise that the day after he died I didn't have money for a packet of fags? That every bleeding cent of ready money was immediately frozen rock-solid in a trust fund for a spoilt ten-year-old who I in my stupidity gave the best education money could buy so he could in due bloody course become the spoilt 21-year-old who wiped his arse on the firm and who's been squandering the trust fund on lawyer's fees?'

His questions were so clearly rhetorical that I didn't dare reply, but he thundered at me, 'I asked you a question! Do you realise that?'

'Your question has several heads, which, if I understand them correctly, cohere around the matter of your financial situation, which naturally I have no insight into.'

Brick Tomlinson turned red, of a shade that suggested an alternative source for his nickname. 'What in God's name has happened to a good honest yes or no? Bugger and blast your little games, Mr Milton Several Heads! – what I'm telling you is that you're getting blood money, blood sweat and tears money. When I went to work for my father he made me carry bricks for the first six months so that I could get a *feel* for the job, and to this day I'm called Brick – not that I mind, I'm proud of it.'

He held out his hands again. 'I'm a hands-on builder, and to this day, when the boys are too slow with the concrete I get in there and start mixing, Mr Whatever-your-name-is, and I have no time for fancy tricks.'

'I still don't see how this affects me, Mr Tomlinson. And my name is Morris, Nicholas Morris.'

'Well, Mr Nicholas Morris, how this affects you is that you can tell that monkey-fucker of a son of mine that I won't leave him a stone to wipe his arse with, and furthermore you can take note that I'll make sure that you and your firm don't get another job from any self-respecting business in Cape Town.'

'Thank you for the warning, Mr Tomlinson, but I think you'll find that the legal fraternity is not entirely dependent on the building industry for its clientele.'

'And did I say it was, Mr Smart-arse legal fraternity? I think you'll find, Mr Morris Nicholson, that Brick Tomlinson is bigger than the building industry, and that he's got a clientele that will make yours look like extremely low-grade chicken shit.'

'So if I understand you correctly, Mr Tomlinson, you're threatening me that if we proceed with the case you'll exercise undue influence on unnamed influential people to discriminate against this firm?'

'You make of it what you like, Mr Influence Influential. I can tell you one thing more, and that is that you don't have a turkey's hope at Christmas of succeeding with your so-called case. You can take that from me as my free contribution to your education.'

'Then why should you try to intimidate me, if all you need do is sit back and watch us lose the case?'

'Because the money you'll squander on the case is my money, for all that that son of mine carries on as if it belonged to him. I don't want to see him pay out millions to a lot of lawyers to write letters to my lawyers which I then have to pay them to *peruse* and answer. And if you charge me for this visit I'll refuse to pay.'

'That's all right, Mr Tomlinson, we don't charge for a first consultation.'

Brick Tomlinson went his eponymous shade of red again. 'This is not a fucking consultation. I am giving *you* ...' he jabbed a square finger at me as he spoke, 'free gratis and for nothing my very good advice, which is to keep your long nose out of my business or to keep your arse very well covered, because as God is my witness we'll have your balls for ornaments in the resident's lounge of the hotel which I swear to you we'll build at Cape Point in spite of anything you can do, you and that red-haired throwback dropout *pansy* of a son of mine.' He got to his feet, wiping the foam off his mouth, and left. At the door he paused and said, 'So think about it very carefully.'

'What was that all about?' Myrah asked, appearing at my door.

'An avalanche of mixed metaphors,' I said. Oddly, the formidable Brick Tomlinson had come across as more of a blustering bully than a real threat. Though no doubt he could make himself unpleasant enough, he had seemed out of his depth: his language had the kind of schoolboyish profanity that hides lack of true confidence. And yet, of course, a schoolboy with power was a powerful schoolboy.

I phoned Joyce Tomlinson to confirm the lunch invitation, and incidentally to make sure that Brick Tomlinson would be out of town.

'Why yes, of course I meant it, Nick,' she said. 'I'm counting on you to be present. I've told Luc and he's *thrilled*.'

'I'm sure.'

Her guttural laugh was more sincere than her compliment.

'Okay, I concede, that's not really my son's mode. But he did say "Yeh, fine" when I told him.'

'That does sound more like him.'

'And your girlfriend? Have you asked her?'

'Yes, I have. She'll be delighted to come.' In fact, Leonora had said, 'Yes, if you think I should go.'

'Oh, I'm so pleased. What is her name, by the way?'

'Leonora. Leonora du Toit. She's Afrikaans.'

She laughed again. 'You say that as if it required special preparations. It's all right, I speak perfect Afrikaans.'

'Oh, she speaks perfect English. I just meant … I meant …' but since I did not in fact know what I had meant, I left it at that.

'And Andrew is looking forward to meeting you too.'

'Andrew?'

'Andrew Conroy. I told you I had a friend who wanted to meet you.'

I guessed that this was another amiable exaggeration. Presumably her friend had also said 'Yeh, fine' when informed that he would be meeting a totally unknown and undistinguished lawyer for lunch.

The Tomlinson mansion was, as I had expected, impressive. It was one of the homes that Rock Tomlinson had built at the beginning of the century in Constantia, in the colonial style of Herbert Baker: British assurance incorporating some Cape Dutch elements, lots of stonework and woodwork, a discreet statement of solidity and prosperity marginally redeemed from pomposity by a grace of style, a respect for materials, an attention to detail that modern building methods and budgets could no longer afford.

'Mrs Tomlinson is in the morning room,' we were told by the woman who opened the heavy teak front door for us. As she led us through a stone-paved entrance hall with a massive wooden staircase ascending from it, Leonora whispered to me, 'Am I dressed smart enough?'

'You look lovely,' I said, which was true enough – her dark hair and eyes looked their best in the simple white dress she had put on – but did not address her question, of which indeed

144

I took the point as I saw the scale and opulence of the house. We were taken to a large, light room at the back of the house, understated as only very self-explanatory rooms can afford to be. Its large spaces implied discretion, comfort, ease, wealth, not so much emphasised as left to the imagination by the simple furniture, coir matting, a single painting on the white wall. The furniture was arranged so as to look out, through open French windows, upon a large swimming pool with a diving board at one end; beyond that, the garden disappeared into the distance, apparently merging with the natural vegetation of the mountainside. The whole effect was of a landscape framed by the window, luminous with the new light of spring, the unnaturally vivid green of the lawn in the foreground setting off the duller shades of the indigenous growth.

Joyce was sitting on a low sofa covered in straw-coloured linen. Her light cotton dress was, I was relieved to note, even less formal than Leonora's. On a matching easy chair sat a middle-aged man who got to his feet as we entered. He was dressed, like me, in slacks and a short-sleeved shirt.

'Ah, Nicholas,' Joyce said from behind her drink, a tall affair with a sprig of greenery. 'And … Leonora? This is my old friend Andrew Conroy.'

Conroy extended a hand to me and then to Leonora. He was tall and slim, his dark hair streaked with grey. Matinee idol, I thought, except that the smile was more diffident, the dark eyes warmer, the wrinkles around the eyes more good-humoured than the type allowed for. He seemed familiar; and as he shook Leonora's hand I got the profile: the aquiline nose, the strong ironic mouth, familiar from photographs in the *Mail & Guardian* – Judge Andrew Conroy of the Cape Supreme Court, the man whom some credited with single-handedly saving the reputation of the South African judiciary during the years of the Emergency, by fearlessly ruling against the State on many a sensitive point; favoured to chair the Truth and Reconciliation Commission or at least to become the Chief Justice in the new dispensation, the man whom universities were rushing to give honorary doctorates to, now that there was no danger attached to the tribute. I should have recognised the name earlier, but had not connected Joyce Tomlinson with this kind of eminence.

'I know Judge Conroy, of course,' I said, 'as a public figure ...'

'Andrew, please.' His request was unperemptory; he made it sound like a favour he was asking. 'I believe you are also a member of the profession.'

I nodded dumbly.

'Andrew is an old friend,' Joyce explained. 'He is Luc's godfather, in fact.'

There was not much I could make of this information, except silently condole with Conroy, and the conversation splintered into offers of drinks and seats, and other civilised noises of various kinds, as we settled into a loose circle around a large low wooden coffee table. Leonora and I sat down on another sofa facing the windows and pool, with Andrew to the left of us and Joyce to the right. There was the sound of activity from the pool – splashing, a woman's scream ending in a gulp, a man's laughter.

'The young people will join us presently,' Joyce said, animatedly, as if announcing a delightful prospect. 'They've only just got up, and wanted a little splash before lunch.' After this she said relatively little, leaving it to Andrew Conroy to keep the conversation going, which he did with practised ease, involving both me and Leonora in topics that were universally accessible without seeming trite, even engaging enough to seem to constitute a discussion. He recommended the wine – a Thelema Sauvignon Blanc – as if he was seeking our opinion on it. Leonora, having grown up on a wine farm, could venture a judgement, whereas I, brought up to regard the relative merits of Lion Lager and Castle Lager as exhausting the possibilities of disagreement on alcoholic refreshment, could only nod in what I hoped was a knowing manner. Leonora also recognised the picture on the wall as a David Hockney, prompting Conroy to ask in good-humoured provocation: 'Isn't there something abject in a working-class English lad's idealisation of Californian values as the ultimate good? Is the swimming pool the apex of civilisation? As subject, how deep is the swimming pool?'

From this, conversation moved to physical exercise, keeping fit and gymnasiums, which it turned out we all belonged to.

'What a sad reflection on our society,' said Conroy, 'that we should pay sizeable sums for the privilege of performing physical labours that our ancestors would have been only too happy to escape. What do you do at the Health and Racquet Club?' he asked me.

'I play squash after work, and for the rest I mess around on the equipment. I don't really ...' I trailed off, aware of the fact that Leonora's attention had shifted from me to the scene outside. I followed her gaze and saw Luc Tomlinson emerging from the pool into full sight, pursued by a laughingly vengeful Fiona. She was dressed in a bikini, a somewhat frivolous costume, I thought, compared with the earnest dowdiness of her previous apparition. She also turned out to be not at all as shapeless as her New Age raiment pretended. Luc, consistently enough, was dressed in nothing at all. I tried to concentrate on the conversation, but was disconcerted by the unprecedented situation of sharing with Leonora a view of a naked man chasing a scantily clad woman into a shrubbery, as Luc was now doing, having turned flight into pursuit. My main concern was that he would catch her, with results I dreaded to contemplate. Fortunately Fiona chose to turn back to the pool and jump in, shrieking joyfully; Luc, to make absolutely certain that his every angle had been exposed to our inspection, did a long slow backward somersault off the diving board. They both mercifully disappeared from view, though the shouts and shrieks were now unignorable.

'It's time those two got dressed for lunch,' Joyce said. 'Andrew, won't you chivvy them along?'

Conroy went out and said something to the two in the pool, then returned to the company. After a pause just long enough not to seem abjectly compliant, Luc reappeared from the pool, helping Fiona out. They stood in the bright sun, he hopping on one foot to clear the water out of his ear. Fiona picked a branch from a bay tree, evidently intent on wreathing his brows with it. As she approached him, he ducked and made a grab at the wreath; she pulled it away and tried again to crown him with it. The four of us sat in silence, like an audience at a play gazing at a brilliantly lit tableau, the two people outside intensely visible and yet remote in their self-absorption. Joyce

147

seemed impervious to the rompings of her son, which I thought inconsiderate: Leonora, after all, had not come prepared to have her lunch spiced up by a full display of the physique of the son of her hostess. She came from a family in which the children were not allowed to appear at table with bare feet, and the father always wore a suit on Sundays. I did not dare look at her, but I was sure that she must be blushing vividly.

'Luc regards clothes as a bourgeois affectation,' Andrew Conroy said in the relaxed tone that made it impossible to gauge the ironic content of his statements. I was grateful to him for finding a way of acknowledging the unignorable and mentioning the unmentionable.

Joyce laughed. 'I've stopped noticing,' she said. He's never worn clothes when he could help it. For some reason it infuriates my husband.'

This was the first point of correspondence I'd found between myself and Brick Tomlinson, but I contented myself with saying, 'I'm pleased that we seem not to be underdressed for the occasion.'

'You're dressed beautifully,' Joyce said, recovering something of the velvety tone that had so disconcerted me at Rocklands. Outside, Luc had submitted to being crowned, and the two young people, laughing, disappeared into a side entrance, his hand on her head.

I could feel Leonora relax back into the sofa as they disappeared; she had probably been holding her breath for the duration of Luc and Fiona's performance.

'They should be along any minute now,' said Conroy. 'I told them they were delaying lunch.'

The young couple duly appeared, joined at the hip. They were both somewhat cursorily dressed, he in cut-off denim shorts and a pink singlet, she in a loose cotton shift and little else, as far as I could make out. Both were barefoot, and she was carrying the pink stone that she had had with her at Rocklands. She had divested herself of some of her beads, and the hair was now frizzed out into a carefully contrived chaos. Joyce introduced Leonora to Luc and Fiona. 'Hello, Nick, hello Leonora,' Luc said, favouring her with a blinding smile. Fiona said, 'Oh hi,' at the company at large, and remained attached to Luc.

'I suppose you two young people are starving,' Joyce Tomlinson said brightly.

'Not at all, really,' Luc replied ungraciously. 'We had a late breakfast.'

'I know your breakfasts,' Joyce laughed, a little forced. 'Not exactly substantial. Lunch will be ready in a sec. Have a seat and a drink in the mean time.'

The couple collapsed leggily into a two-seater sofa. Fiona giggled and whispered something to Luc; he got up languidly and returned with two glasses of water.

There was a silence. Luc put his hand on Fiona's knee and she put her hand on top of his, not so much restraining as teasing it. I tried not to watch. I had been taught that Public Displays of Affection were vulgar; indeed, I think my mother regarded even Private Displays of Affection as not quite the done thing. Whereas in many respects I have emancipated myself from my mother's perhaps over-strenuous standards, I find that I do still as if instinctively avert my gaze from the spectacle of a couple uninhibitedly kissing or embracing or even holding hands in a way too much lingering on possible developments. There is something demeaning in being trapped in the company of two people who would obviously rather be somewhere else having sexual intercourse. The company sat in silence once again, perhaps wondering, as I was, whether they weren't going to do it anyway.

Luc himself unexpectedly broke the silence. 'You Nick's girlfriend, then?' he asked Leonora. Given that Leonora and I had never discussed the status of our relationship, this was an impertinent question. I wondered if I should intervene to spare Leonora the harassment, but she smiled pleasantly and said, 'I'm a friend, but I wouldn't call myself a girl.'

Andrew Conroy gave her a supportive smile. I turned to Fiona and asked, 'And are you Luc's girlfriend?'

She focused on me with an effort of will, then giggled and said to Luc, 'Well, Ell, answer the man, *am* I your girlfriend?'

'If you're not, you've been taking some *huge* liberties of late,' he said, and they subsided into gales of laughter that effectively excluded the rest of the company.

Andrew Conroy got to his feet. 'What do you say, Joyce, that we take our seats for lunch? I'm ravenous, even if the young people aren't.'

'We've only just sat down,' objected Luc puppyishly, and I was gratified to note Conroy quelling him with a glance, which Luc clearly resented, though he had the grace to blush. Joyce led the way into another airy room overlooking the garden, where a meal had been set out as if by an invisible company of fairies.

Meals have the advantage over other social occasions in serving up, as it were, ready-made topics of conversation. The company, with the exception of Luc and Fiona, energetically availed itself of the opportunity, though here too I was at a disadvantage. My mother's culinary ambitions had stretched, on very special occasions, to Coronation Chicken (which my father scornfully rejected as 'outlandish'); for the rest, it was Bangers and Mash, Bubble and Squeak, or more frequently, meat and two veg. The dish which appeared on Joyce Tomlinson's table I could have identified only as curried chicken; but Andrew Conroy said, 'Ah, your famous *Hare masale wali murghi*,' in what sounded to me like a perfect Indian accent, and proceeded to explain the ingredients to Leonora, who had done a course in Indian cookery at some stage. Leonora had done a course in almost everything at some stage.

Conroy would in fact have been insufferable had his universal informedness seemed to be posited on our universal ignorance, but his statements were presented as ideas for discussion, intended to elicit the opinions of his interlocutors, rather than as pronouncements – 'Don't you think the fresh coriander is what prevents it from being just another curry?' he asked me, who would have been hard pressed to tell fresh coriander from fresh lucern. The effect of his manner – style, technique? – on Leonora was extraordinary: her normal slightly exasperating diffidence and deference yielded to a readiness, tentative but articulate, to defend her own position: Conroy indeed seemed to make her aware of the fact that she *had* a position, whereas with me all her energies were

150

intent on discovering my position so that she could adopt it as her own.

Luc and Fiona drank only water and ate only rice and vegetables and spoke mainly to each other. I wondered, given their limited consumption and their even more limited contribution to the occasion, why Joyce had thought it worth her while including them at all. Luc did, surprisingly, seem less indifferent to Leonora than to the rest of the company, and once even filled her glass, managing, in stretching across, to display to advantage all the muscles in his right arm, from his index finger to his armpit. Sitting to the right of him, I also got a whiff of the body odour that even a swim in chlorinated water could apparently not dispel. Leonora thanked him with her shy smile and he rewarded her with a close-up of his spectacular teeth.

I saw Conroy looking at Fiona, and I wondered whether even his social skills would be up to the task of drawing her into the company.

'Is that a rose quartz?' he asked her, when we had finished eating.

She looked up at him, taking a second or two to transfer her attention from Luc's forehead to Andrew's politely interrogative regard. Then she nodded briefly. 'Mm.'

'What is its significance?'

'Its significance?' she repeated. I wondered whether she was drugged or just naturally slow.

'What makes it special?'

She shrugged. 'It's a foundation stone, sort of.'

'Foundation stone?'

'Mm. That means it contains the full spectrum of colour.'

'And does it have any special powers?'

'Oh yes, that's the point. It helps you to love yourself, and to accept all you are, and to release your psychic energies so that … so that …' While she was talking, her gaze on him became more and more fixed, and her speech became more sporadic.

'… so that … so that …' She stopped altogether. Then, muttering something inaudible to Luc, she jumped up from the table and disappeared into the house.

'Excuse me,' Luc said, with uncharacteristic politeness,

'she's upset,' and followed her out of the room, his lazy saunter suggesting that he did not regard Fiona's terror as life-threatening.

'Upset seems mild,' said Joyce. 'What could have got into her?'

Luc and Fiona remained absent, and the company relaxed into a discussion of the garden, Leonora wanting to know whether it contained many indigenous trees. Leonora was too polite to say so, but she regarded exotic trees as a form of dis-loyalty to local flora. She had done a course on the indigenous trees of the Cape.

'Don't you find it a bit tedious that most of our indigenous trees are evergreen?' Conroy asked her.

Leonora laughed, and I noticed, almost with surprise, how attractive she was when she was not frowning anxiously. 'No, why should it be? Evergreen means forever young, immortal – that's what we all want to be.'

'*Do* you?' he asked, and I was surprised to see how serious he was. 'Do you really want to be forever young, immortal?'

'I accept my own mortality, of course …'

'It seems to me you don't have a choice, dear,' said Joyce, perhaps a bit fretfully.

'Well, yes,' Leonora persisted, 'but there is something – I don't know – *symbolic* about evergreens.' I groaned inwardly. Leonora was not at her happiest when she ventured into the symbolic. From symbolism to religion was a disastrously short step for her. But Conroy took even this unoriginal proposition seriously.

'Don't you think that a tree, like a human life, needs a sense of transience, of its own death-directedness? Don't you think there's something *shallow* about a tree or a human being that seems immune to time?'

'I've never thought of it like that,' said Leonora, slightly alarmed at the thought of approving of shallowness, even in plants. 'I suppose I'm too young to have thought about such things.'

'Come,' said Conroy, 'if the others will excuse us, I'll show you the most beautiful tree in the garden. It's an oak and it's at least two hundred years old, and what makes it beautiful is not that it looks young, but that it seems to welcome its own death, to be slowly withdrawing into the darkness at its own core. Do you mind, Joyce, if I steal your guest?'

'By all means, go ahead,' said Joyce, 'as long as I can keep Nick. We'll have coffee when you get back.'

Conroy got to his feet. Leonora looked at me as if for permission. I smiled encouragingly and she got up too, and the two disappeared into the garden. I felt the company was the poorer for Conroy's departure, and I was slightly apprehensive that Joyce might have engineered the situation for purposes of her own.

She refilled my glass and her own and said, 'Perhaps it's no bad thing for the two of us to have a real chat.'

'Yes,' I ventured, somewhat inadequately.

'I'm pleased you've met Andrew,' she said.

'So am I,' I said, and realised that in fact I was.

'My oldest friend,' she continued. She clearly wanted to tell me about Conroy, though I wasn't quite sure what bearing her friendship with him could have on the case. Although I was interested in hearing more about Conroy, I hoped Joyce Tomlinson would not pay me the compliment of her full confidence. I have the unfortunate propensity to give people the quite mistaken impression that I am a sympathetic recipient of their most intimate revelations. I have even on occasion been thanked for my *empathy*.

'I've known him since my first year at university. I was a Fine Arts student, he was a Law student. We were both from dirt-poor families, studying on bursaries that we had to supplement with part-time jobs, but what little time we had left over from that we spent together. We believed that we had to learn something new every day.'

She paused while the discreet serving woman removed the lunch dishes. 'It was,' she continued at length, 'in some ways the happiest time of my life: free of the constrictions of a poverty-stricken, crabbed existence at home, daily conversations with an intelligent, beautiful man, the widening world of drama and music and art and literature. Andrew read everything, saw everything he could afford, and shared it all with me.'

153

'Then why …?' I stopped myself.

'Then why did I marry Brick? Because, as I've said to you before, I fell in love with him. My friendship with Andrew had everything I could want except passion; my relationship with Brick had nothing I wanted except passion. I met him one weekend when a group of us were invited to the house at Cape Point, which at that stage still belonged to Brick's father. And Brick in those days …' She shook her head. 'Poor Andrew, who was part of the company for the weekend, had to watch as I fell in love with somebody who was in almost all respects his opposite: uncultured, rough, rich, a man of action – well, you've met Brick.'

'I have.' This was the first indication she had given that she knew of Brick's visit to me. I wondered if this was a slip on her part, inadvertently admitting that she was in her husband's confidence.

'And you have met Andrew. You may think that I was a great fool. Sometimes I think I was a great fool. But I was very much in love, and I can honestly say I've never regretted my choice.'

'But then,' I asked, 'did Andrew want to marry you?'

'Oh yes, very much. We were always talking about *one day* when we would be married. But it was to be later, after he had gone overseas, after we had both made our careers – we were both absolutely determined not to be poor like our parents. You may say that that was part of Brick's appeal, that he was the heir to a fortune, to …' she gestured vaguely around her, 'all this. It's what everybody else said; everybody except Andrew: ooh, she's marrying for money, they said. And perhaps I was, perhaps his money was part of the intoxicating mix that Brick represented. I had by now – I was in my fourth year at university – seen enough of art and culture and everything I valued to realise that they flourished best in the medium of money, that one couldn't spend the rest of one's life queuing in the rain and standing in the back row on student concessions. But mainly I was just in love with Brick Tomlinson in a way that I was not with Andrew Conroy.'

She took a sip of wine. Sensing a presence in the doorway, I looked up to see Luc Tomlinson standing there. She followed my gaze.

'Oh hello, darling, you always move so quietly. Have you been there long?'

'No.' He came slightly closer. 'I'm taking Fiona home. She's feeling too grotty to drive.'

'Yes, we noticed that she was not feeling well. Do you want to borrow my car?'

'No,' he said, 'I'll use hers. I'll stay at her place, then she can take me back to Rocklands when she's feeling better.'

'As you wish, darling. But aren't you going to say goodbye to the guests?'

He favoured me with his attention. Unexpectedly, he smiled. 'Goodbye, guest,' he said.

'I meant Andrew and Leonora too. They're in the garden.'

'Tell your girlfriend goodbye for me,' he instructed me. 'Fiona is sort of nervous on her own.'

'Say goodbye to her for us,' Joyce said. 'Is there anything …?'

He shook his head. 'No. She gets upset like this sometimes. It has to do with auras. It passes. Bye, mom.'

Joyce watched him leave with a smile half fond, half rueful. 'I wonder if he's in love with that strange girl,' she said. 'I hope he doesn't get carried away with all her gobbledygook. He's not normally so solicitous.'

This I could believe; in fact, even his alleged solicitude struck me as hardly overwhelming. I had no desire, though, to discuss Luc Tomlinson's heartless treatment of his sexual partners. Unexpectedly, I found I was interested in Joyce Tomlinson's recollections, though still without any inkling as to their relevance to the Rocklands case.

'And Andrew? How did he …?'

'How did he take his disappointment? Badly, at first; accused me of selling out to the forces of Mammon, pleaded with me, predicted disaster, tried to persuade me that Brick was a barbarian and a Philistine – which, of course, he was and is. But then Andrew won a Rhodes scholarship to Oxford, and when he came back after three years he seemed to be over his disappointment, and he became a family friend.'

'Of your husband too?'

'Yes, amazingly. Of course, Andrew and I have things in common that he doesn't have in common with Brick, but that's just as well. It makes for variety in the friendship and the marriage. When I asked Andrew to be Luc's godfather, Brick, as you can imagine, was not exactly what you might call effusive in his support, but now they're ... well, if not the best of friends, then still surprisingly close, in a man-to-man sort of way. Andrew and Brick have even been involved in a couple of business ventures together. I don't really know the details, but Andrew seems to have put away a good deal of money over the years.'

'He never married?'

'No, somehow not.' She tried in vain to hide her pleasure at the failure of her old lover to find a substitute for herself. 'The only rift in the lute is that Luc does not like Andrew.'

That did not surprise me. Andrew Conroy was too civilised for the likes of Luc Tomlinson. 'Oh, why not?' I nevertheless asked.

She shrugged. 'You know Luc, he doesn't explain, not to me at any rate. Perhaps he will to you. He seems to like you.'

'He seems to me to despise me.'

'That's because he doesn't want to let on that he likes you. He's rather shy of affection. He used to be very fond of his father, you know, and then when Brick rejected him ...'

'Why was that?'

'Mainly because the old man, Brick's father, took to Luc – and then, as you know, left him the use of Rocklands along with most of his fortune.'

'And your husband held this against his son?'

'Yes ... well, you've met Brick, you know what an impulsive sort of person he is. And his father was no longer available to be hated. So Rocklands has really become a site of conflict for them; it represents more than a plot of land, it's a battleground. In developing Rocklands Brick would be avenging himself on his father and on his son at the same time, and destroying what they had in common.'

'And Andrew – has he taken sides?'

'No – of course, he has spoken to me about it, but he is far too tactful to take sides in a quarrel as divisive as this one.'

She got to her feet. 'But Andrew and Leonora will be back soon. I have something to give you that may be of help to you in the case. Come to my study.'

I followed her through the house that now, in the Sunday afternoon heat and stillness, seemed deserted. As we walked, I asked her, 'What would you gain if your husband lost the case?'

'I wouldn't gain anything, but I would get to keep everything that means anything to me now. Going out there to paint. Being with Luc. And as I've said, I'd have my revenge.'

'On your husband?'

'Only incidentally. Mainly on Tomlinson and Tomlinson, the firm, the father-and-son obsession that has stolen my husband from me, the firm with all its shady associates and shabby deals. I tell you, Nick, I don't really share my son's feelings for the baboons, let's face it they're an ungrateful and ungracious and undecorative bunch, but they're models of civilised behaviour compared with the lot who used to go there for weekends until … well, until Luc inherited the place.'

We had reached her study, a smallish, cosy room also overlooking the garden. There was a painting on the wall, evidently one of Joyce's own, showing the beach at Rocklands at dawn, with a figure emerging from the waves, silhouetted and haloed by the rays of the sun behind him. 'You remember,' Joyce continued, 'the Sunday when I met you, I said my husband was entertaining a crowd of business associates?'

I nodded. She sat down behind her desk and gestured at the chair opposite her. I sat down, feeling as if I was being interviewed for a job.

'The guest list would make interesting reading. Almost anybody who is anybody in government, in planning, in property. But always there and always fawned upon, the two grand panjandrums.'

'De Klerk and Mandela?'

She laughed. 'No, they have bigger business at the moment. But below them are the fat and overfed who are facing a spell in the wilderness, the sharks and vultures and hyenas who kept the last lot going and were handsomely paid for it, still making it for the time being in the Government of National Unity, but unsure how long it will last. And from Brick's point of view, the two big ones are Nature Conservation and Defence.'

'I can see Nature Conservation, but Defence …'

'As environmentalist you will have noticed that all the missile testing ranges are in National Parks.'

'Yes, I have.' There had been periodic protest in the press against the devastation of large tracts of indigenous vegetation, but the South African government had learnt that the best way to deal with protest was to ignore it until it went away.

'So we need a good relationship between Conservation and Defence – which means, in this instance, the ministers supposed to be representing the interests of those portfolios.'

'Yes.'

'Which means Sam Stanford in Conservation and Walter Kotze in Defence. Good friends to each other and to Brick, who gets lots of Defence contracts, and the planning permission to go with it. To give him his due, Brick does not share in their tastes; he just exploits them.'

'You're being very cryptic now.'

'Yes, let me be clear.' She opened a drawer in her desk and took out a small parcel, really no more than a fat envelope. 'Rocklands has quite a history. In Brick's father's time, it was used as a retreat for the big men of the time – Verwoerd, Vorster, ostensibly for the men of destiny to escape the cares of office for a weekend, in reality for Trick, Brick's father, to curry favour and make deals. I don't know if you know that Trick for a while had a near-monopoly on constructing low-cost housing in the townships spawned by the Group Areas Act – I mean, even Verwoerd and Vorster realised that you had to move people *somewhere* if you kicked them out of the white cities.'

'Yes, I did know that – I mean about Mr Tomlinson Senior's involvement in low-cost housing.'

'Right. Well, after Trick's time, and after Vorster's fall from favour, the place reverted for a while to a rather run-down beach cottage, until Brick started building up his contacts in business and industry. And more and more this became the military-industrial complex, and eventually a rather exclusive little group around Kotze and Stanford, a club consisting, as in all truly corrupt regimes through the ages, of the absolutely powerful and the absolutely powerless.' She nodded at the package in her hands; I tried to interrupt, but she held up one hand.

'Let me explain. As Minister of Defence, Kotze had at his disposal any number of young officers, recruits, a whole generation of young men with very little say in their own destiny. And who in many cases were probably only too pleased to get out of camp to a place where there were no rules, and lots of food and liquor.'

'I'm not sure that I understand you ...'

'You do make one spell it out, don't you? Well, then, what I'm saying is that one of the things Kotze and Stanford shared was a taste for young men, and that Kotze provided the young men, and what Brick provided them with was a discreet retreat where they could indulge their tastes.'

I looked at her incredulously.

'But ... how could they possibly get away with ... I mean, what you're saying is that two ministers in the government openly indulged in homosexual activities.'

'Not openly, no. Rocklands was very remote, very private.'

'The young men ...'

'Were subject to military discipline. And were implicated by their own participation. And if those deterrents didn't work there were others.'

'Others?'

'Young men on active duty have been known to disappear without a trace – or to get shot by accident by one of their mates.'

'But how can you possibly know this?'

'Part of it is speculation, but based on scraps of conversations I've overheard. And once a young man phoned here; he'd found Brick's business card at Rocklands, and he had to speak to someone, and the fact that Brick hadn't taken an active part in the proceedings ... you know, made him think that perhaps he could talk to him. At least, that is what I gathered from his disconnected talk; he kept on saying he didn't want to disappear like the others. I told him he could talk to me, but he seemed reluctant, said he couldn't talk to a woman about it. I gave him Brick's business number.'

'And what happened to him?'

'I have no idea. I asked Brick whether he'd had a call from the young man, but he simply said no and that was that.'

'But your husband …'

'Yes, the whole thing was hardly his cup of tea, I'd have thought, but at a certain point of his career he became … how shall I say? – very ambitious. Power-hungry. And he could see that the way to have power was through the weaknesses of the powerful.'

'Did he tell you this?'

'Of course not. But I know my husband, and I made my guesses. These …' and she tapped the envelope on the desk, 'are photographs taken by somebody who wanted a record of the proceedings for purposes of his own. My guess is that they were taken by Brick.'

'What are they?'

'Records of the proceedings. You can look at them in your own time. I found them stuck behind a drawer in a desk of my bedroom at Rocklands. I've not been able to bring myself to examine them in detail, as you'll appreciate when you look at them, but the nature of the proceedings and the identity of the main participants are unmistakable.'

'And may I ask why you're telling me this?'

'Of course. I'm telling you because I know that if you're going to tangle with Brick you're going to need all the ammunition you can lay your hands on. I don't pretend to know exactly how you would use this, but on the assumption that knowledge is power … there you are.' She tossed the envelope onto the desk in front of me. 'Look after them well, and give them back to me if you don't use them. But come, Andrew and Leonora will be waiting for us.'

But when we arrived in the lunch room, it was to find it still deserted. Coffee had been set out on the table, but was as yet untouched. Andrew and Leonora had clearly found much to discuss in the garden. As Joyce and I sat down to our coffee, they appeared from the garden, talking and laughing, unaware of us in our glass box. In the afternoon sun, laughing up at Conroy, her unwonted animation set off against his grave, ironic charm, Leonora looked again inordinately attractive, and I wondered what it was in this man's attention that so enlivened the timid Leonora.

'Pretty girl,' said Joyce, reading part of my thoughts.

'Yes,' I replied, feeling somehow disloyal to Leonora in concurring in a judgement that, coming from Joyce Tomlinson, could not but be a mite condescending. Joyce Tomlinson was a beautiful woman, and must have known it; must have known, too, that a *pretty girl* is another order of creature altogether. Was she jealous of Leonora's youth and freshness? Of the attention Andrew Conroy was giving her with such evident pleasure? As for myself, I felt what in all my association with Leonora I had never felt, a stab of jealousy.

As we drove home, I asked Leonora: 'Did you like Andrew Conroy?'

'Oh, very much,' she replied, for once not waiting to find out what I thought before venturing an opinion. I found this both refreshing and irritating.

'You don't think he has too many opinions?'

'I don't know. They seem to be quite good opinions.'

'Do you mean you agree with them all?'

'No,' she said, 'but they are opinions you can disagree with without feeling stupid.'

I consciously refrained from finding here an invidious comparison with my own opinions, and contented myself with saying, 'He seemed to like you too.'

'I think so,' she said with something of her old diffidence. 'But he liked you a lot. He said so.'

'He said he liked me?'

'Well, he said he wanted to see more of both of us. He said he'd invite us to his house.'

'He couldn't very well invite you on your own, since he met you as my companion.'

'No, but I'm sure he wants you too. He said so.'

'Thanks,' I said, not quite sure whether I wanted Leonora to reassure me of Conroy's regard for me.

'He's quite well known, isn't he?' she asked after a while.

'Oh, yes. Became prominent in the eighties as one of the few judges who were prepared to pronounce openly against the security legislation, and in his judgements to overturn convictions based on the legislation. He acquitted any number of people charged with crimes against the state – the previous state, of course.' I wondered how Leonora would take this. Though not exactly a Nationalist, her upbringing had given her a horror of anything radical, seditious, *disobedient*.

'He must be a very brave man, then,' was all she said.

'Yes, I imagine he is. He's likely to have a seat on the Truth Commission.'

'Oh,' she said. The Truth and Reconciliation Commission was regarded with some mistrust by many white South Africans, who thought that the Truth might be such as to make Reconciliation unlikely.

We drove in silence, each of us involved in our own thoughts.

'Do you like Luc Tomlinson?' she asked after a silence of some minutes.

'No,' I said. 'Not at all. Or rather, at times he seems to have a … a kind of crude sincerity which is quite appealing; but it can be quite offensive too. What did you think of him?'

'He's … very attractive,' Leonora said, and blushed.

'I should not have thought he was your type,' I said, probably a bit stiffly. I did not think it was proper for Leonora to express such open appreciation of the physical appearance of other men, especially given that in this instance she could be taken to be pronouncing on attributes that I would not have thought her to have an opinion on. On the whole, Leonora had enjoyed the afternoon rather more than was quite appropriate for somebody invited only as my companion.

'No, of course not, he's not my *type*,' she protested. 'But objectively, just as … well, as a physical object,' she added circularly. 'He looks a bit like Brad Pitt.'

'No doubt,' I said. 'I wouldn't know. I don't judge people by their degrees of approximation to movie stars.' I dropped Leonora at the flat she shared with two fellow-librarians, and declined her invitation to coffee. Apart from not wanting to be subjected to the politeness of her flatmates, one of whom clearly wanted me to marry Leonora, and the other of whom as clearly hated my guts, I was curious to see what Joyce had given me, and impatient to be alone with my own impressions of the afternoon.

The photographs were indeed of a compromising kind, so much so that, unversed as I am in the more ambitious forms of sexual expression, I found them at first near-incomprehensible: it seemed so implausible that people would willingly subject themselves to such situations. Of course, some of them might not have been willing: I remembered what Joyce Tomlinson had said about the powerful and the powerless. The situations in the photographs were in fact vivid parodies of power relations: in each shot somebody was being subjected to the domination of somebody else, with some fertility of imagination in ringing the changes on this basic theme. And as Joyce Tomlinson had said, very much in evidence were the faces of Minister Kotze and Minister Stanford, familiar from newspaper photographs, though here in decidedly unfamiliar poses. There were military uniforms enough, but in highly unconventional deployment. The most bizarre photos, though, featured uniforms of another kind: waistcoats of black leather, loin cloths, chains, whips and masks. There were shots of naked young men suspended by chains from staples in the wall and ceiling; of another stretched out in a kind of hammock strung from the walls, with masked figures vying with each other to attend to him in various ways. It was like a vision from Hieronymus Bosch, but rendered particularly horrific by the mundane medium of faded Polaroid.

I was content with a general impression of the activities; it was hardly necessary to scrutinise the detail. In theory, the processes of justice should not be promoted, expedited, facilitated or implemented by means in themselves illicit, immoral or improper; in practice, law thrives on just such means. But I couldn't really see how these photographs could help us in a case involving two parties who had nothing, or very little, to do with the activities recorded in them. By one of the unwritten principles of litigation, whatever is embarrassing to your opponent is helpful to your case, and there was no doubt that these photographs could be highly embarrassing to some people; but whether their embarrassment could in fact advance our case was dubious. I decided to consult Gerhard; he would in any case be able to tell me if there was any aspect of the photographs that in my ignorance I had neglected to notice.

The following day being Monday, Gerhard paid his accustomed mid-morning call. Since he had been seeing Clive, his weekends had, to my relief, been yielding less varied and colourful narratives; but Gerhard, who could make a story out of darning a sock with a blunt needle, found plenty to recount in even the comparatively tame pursuits he shared with Clive, his involvement with whom was lasting longer than any previous relationship. He claimed that this was because it was based on the principle of deferred satisfaction – 'We have to climb a mountain every time before we can fuck. I've lost about ten kilograms since I met him.'

'Perhaps the two of you should buy a house in Pinelands,' I suggested. 'Stuart and Sharon across the way are trying to sell.'

'The dishy-but-dim young daddy with the designer wife? Where are they going?'

'Australia. They're just waiting for their papers.'

'Whatever for?' Gerhard demanded, almost fiercely. I regretted too late my mention of my neighbours' plans: emigration was one of Gerhard's Topics.

'For little Samantha's sake, as they put it.' Samantha was their one-year-old daughter. 'Samantha needs a safe environment to grow up in.'

'A safe environment be stuffed. Did you see that item in the paper the other day about the primary school in Australia somewhere? Apparently they removed the urinals from the boys' bathrooms on the grounds that their presence discriminated against the little girls who had not been issued with the equipment to negotiate urinals. So little Samantha, bless her little heart, condemned by nature and by plumbing to squat forever, will have the safety and security of knowing that some little boy isn't unfairly pissing in an upright position? Is that what Stuart and Sharon want for little Samantha?'

'I hardly think that's why they're going to Australia,' I said, but Gerhard was now in full spate. 'Nick, can you *believe* these people? They stuck out the horrors in this country in the eighties, of State of Emergency after State of Emergency, of people murdered in the name of State Security and Civil Co-operation – and now just when we seem about to live in a respectable country they hive off to a *safe environment* in the Country of Gender-Sensitive Pissing. Can you *believe* it?'

'I can believe that people might want to get away from the insecurity and the crime and the poverty here, yes.'

Gerhard leapt up from his perch on my desk and started declaiming at me and at Table Mountain in turn. 'What makes them think they have the *right* to escape from the ills of a soci-ety they've helped to create and will now do fuck-all to rebuild? And where, pray tell me, will they go to get away from disease and death? From fallen arches and hanging tits and haemorrhoids? From bankruptcy and radiation and glob-al warming? From depression and despair and unhappy mar-riages? From stupidity and greed and religious fundamental-ism? What makes people feel entitled to immunity from the ills of their fallen natures?'

I got up and closed the door. At times Gerhard reverted alarmingly to his Calvinist origins. 'Forget I mentioned it. Does this mean you and Clive don't want to move to Pinelands?'

'Pinelands, the Australia of the Cape Flats? No thanks, I'll take my chances in the City Bowl.' To my relief he seemed for the time being to have exhausted his moral fervour.

'Well, then, sit down again, calm down, and take a look at these illustrations of life in our newly respectable country.' I tossed the envelope onto the desk. He opened it and glanced at the first shot.

'What have we here? Dirty *peec*-tures? Why are you showing me these? Are you trying to corrupt me?'

'Look more closely and you'll see.'

'Bloody sure I'll look more closely … Jeez, what a monster this one has on him, looks like a mongoose sitting up to beg … Hey, wait a minute, who are these mature gentlemen putting it away with the boys? Do I recognise an honourable member of our esteemed Cabinet?'

'You should recognise two members, or at any rate the faces attached to them. Look carefully – at the faces this time.'

'Of course, of course, Walter Kotze … and that's Sam

Stanford, geez, who could have thought the old man to have such a dick on him?'

I explained to him the history of the photos while he flipped through them, commenting in varying degrees of ribaldry on the participants and the situations.

'*Semper paratus* indeed. And this is what they got up to when they were supposed to be safeguarding the country against the forces of darkness?'

'Apparently so. As guests of Brick Tomlinson, who incidentally, according to Joyce, took the photos.'

'No, he did not. Not all of them, anyway.'

'How do you know?'

'Because that's him over there, isn't it? One of the spectators in this extremely busy shot?'

'Let me see. Yes, that's Brick. How do you know him?'

'My dear Nicholas, if you could bring yourself to watch television like well-informed people everywhere, you'd know that Brick Tomlinson is a public figure of some standing. He's forever being asked for his views on the housing problem that it seems he's going to solve single-handedly. He's very photogenic.'

'But ...'

'But what?'

'If Brick didn't take the photographs ... ?'

'Then ...?'

'Then who did?'

'Anybody, surely. What puzzles me more is how Joyce Tomlinson did not recognise her own husband in that photo.'

'She says she didn't examine them closely, which you'll agree is sort of understandable.'

'Sort of.'

'But I'm still not happy that just anybody could have taken the photos. Have you noticed that they're all angled so as to feature Kotze and Stanford?'

'Isn't that because they were at the centre of things?'

'There were clearly any number of other things going on. They're at the centre merely because the camera put them there. And as you'll be better able to appreciate than I, they weren't put there because they were the most beautiful objects around.'

166

'I'm surprised and slightly shocked at your acuity and penetration, Nicholas. But what, then, Holmes, do you deduce from your own observation?'

'That somebody intended to blackmail the ministers and then lost the photos.'

'And the somebody?'

'I have no idea. But it means that there's somebody else than Brick Tomlinson to reckon with.'

Gerhard laughed and rumpled my hair. 'I love you when you're in your Hardy Boy mood.'

'Don't pretend you read the Hardy Boys in Makwassie. And please refrain from disarranging my hair. And tell me what I'm supposed to do with these photos.'

'Nothing at this stage. But hang on to them and wait.'

'You don't think there's something ... well, indecent about wanting to make use of this kind of material?'

'Depends on the use you make. If you intend to make money out of it, yes, it's blackmail pure and simple. But if it's a matter of exposing a couple of low-down high-ups who abused their position to roger young men who had no choice in the matter, then it's a matter of justice.'

'And if it's a matter of revenge? On the part of the person who gave me the photographs?'

'My dear Nicholas, which of us would presume to draw the line between justice and revenge with precision and confidence?' On this lofty declaration Gerhard got to his feet to return to his office, but I stopped him.

'Any idea of a counsel I can use for this case?'

He thought for a moment. 'Yes, I think so. I have just the man for you – John Scheepers.'

'What makes him the right man?' I asked cautiously. Gerhard had been known to base his recommendations on the size of their pectorals, or worse.

'Relax, not because of any allegiance as far as I know to the Persuasion. He is, amongst other virtues, ecologically-minded. He's a member of the Mountain Club, which is where I met him.'

'I keep forgetting that you have become a mountaineer.'

'I'm a mountaineer only as Leander was a swimmer; I do it for love.'

'I seem to remember that Leander got drowned for his pains. What's this John like as advocate?'

'Lively, aggressive, sharp.'

'You make him sound like a ferret.'

'Good description, if you can imagine a ferret with a sense of humour. But tell me more about your lunch party. Was the Angel of Dawning there?'

'You could say he dropped in briefly. With Fiona.'

'Oh, the New Age prophetess. Did she denounce the man-goes again?'

'Avocados. No, but she did abandon us halfway through the meal while she was talking to Andrew Conroy.'

'Andrew Conroy was there? Isn't he rather more politically impeccable than the Tomlinsons?'

'Perhaps so, but turns out used to be in love with Joyce Tomlinson and has remained a family friend.'

'You must hope Brick Tomlinson hasn't lined him up on his side. He's very big.'

'He's also Luc Tomlinson's godfather, though apparently relations are a bit strained.'

'Better unstrain them. He's a powerful man in the present climate of transition. Whites with good left-wing credentials are hard to find.'

'I suspect he's pretty much his own man.'

'What does that mean, *he's his own man*? As far as I can make out, all it means is that one is not influenced by people one does not want to be influenced by. That still leaves the field wide open for all the people that one does want to be influenced by.'

'I can't imagine that Andrew Conroy would want to be influenced by me, especially in a case involving his own entirely obnoxious godson.'

'Ah, would that I had my burning youth!' Gerhard exclaimed in mock despair.

'Would you have influenced Andrew Conroy?'

'No, I would have de-obnoxified Luc Tomlinson. Chop-chop, as we say in Makwassie.'

CHAPTER SEVEN

I am that rarest of creatures, the Average Man. I know, because I have checked my attributes against any number of statistical tables in the magazines in my dentist's waiting room (I have a twice-yearly check-up, and, being more punctual than my dentist, have ample time to catch up on the latest figures). I am exactly five feet and ten inches tall and I weigh ten stone (I still think of myself in the imperial system because my mother refused to adapt to the metric system when it came to South Africa). My waist measurement is 32 and my inseam is 34. Like, apparently, 98% of all men, I dress on the left, as tailors used to say in my father's day. (My father's sole ground of distinction was that he dressed on the right.) As for other measurements, I regard it as indelicate to take a tape measure to myself as if I were an item of haberdashery, but from my limited opportunities of comparison I would guess that here, too, I am entirely average, unlikely, were I ever to enter into an intimate relation, either to disappoint or to intimidate. In appearance I am undistinguished either by great beauty or by startling deviations from the norm: I don't turn heads but I don't frighten horses either. My hair, which I wear a medium length, is between blond and brown, and my eyes are between blue and grey. My features are what is known as regular, my teeth are good without being dazzling, and on my passport, where it says 'Distinguishing marks', is the bald entry: *None*. Were I to get married (and being average, I have an 84% chance of doing so), I would no doubt have 1.2 children and have sexual intercourse 1.4 times per week. As it is, and this is another statistic I supply in the modern spirit of frankness about things which we have no business to be frank about, I masturbate on average 3.1 times per week, not counting holidays, which I am informed is almost exactly right for unmarried men of my age.

All this rather depressingly but also reassuringly suggests that my life conforms to a norm, a kind of Platonic ideal of ordinariness, and that I am unlikely to be taken by surprise by violent aberrations such as have been known to drive perfectly sane men to their destruction. I am aware, of course, of the supposed strength of the sexual instinct, and cannot deny its occasional manifestation in even my life – in unfamiliar dreams, or in sudden and inexplicable arousals which would seem to be sexual in nature, given the nature and location of their incarnation; but the much-vaunted all-consuming nature of love is surely a kind of conspiracy of literature, art and music, vulgarised in our time by the popular media: people have come to expect to be ravished by emotion, and thus induce it in themselves at the slightest opportunity. How else explain the implausible romances and the impossible marriages chronicled by literature and the law courts alike? My friend Gerhard says that writing a love sonnet is the most constructive but least interesting way of getting an erection to subside, which, if it were true, would be one of the more useful functions of art. But since the demise of the love sonnet, art has served mainly to persuade people of their right to a simultaneous orgasm. Thus the very magazines that provide me with the statistics of my own normality paradoxically suggest, if only by implication, that I am a freak celibate in a world insatiably intent upon sexual gratification.

Gerhard, who has few inhibitions on topics that to other people are matters of privacy and discretion, asked me once, 'So I know you don't have sex, but what turns you on?'

'What do you mean turns me on?' I asked, pained by the invasiveness of his question.

'Well, what do you think about when you wank?'

I have learnt that when Gerhard is in this particular mode, the only way to avoid ever-more-outrageous enquiries is to deal with all questions as if they were perfectly neutral requests for information. 'I don't know,' I said, after pretending to consider the matter, 'I'm not sure I think about anything.'

'Think about it: what do you see when you close your eyes?'

'I don't close my eyes. If you must know, I don't want to, you know, soil the linen.' I had painful recollections of my mother brandishing stained sheets at me accusingly.

'Do me a favour, will you?' he said. 'Next time you wank, close your eyes and tell me what you see. Regard it as your contribution to the sum of human knowledge.'

I had no intention of heeding this impertinent request, but found that once the idea had been lodged in my head it remained there, with the predictable result that I did follow Gerhard's instructions, after taking precautions to protect the bedding.

Never one to forget an embarrassing point, he asked me not long afterwards, while we were having drinks after work, 'Well, did you try it?'

'Try what?' I asked, though I knew perfectly well what was coming.

'Wanking with your eyes shut.'

'I can't see that it's any of your business.' I looked around us. We were in the Wig and Pen, a pretentious pub frequented largely by lawyers and journalists, a place where private conversations were easily and frequently picked up for transmission. I lowered my voice. 'But yes, I did.'

'Ah hah. And what did you see?' he asked with unbecoming avidity.

'Well,' I said, 'a … a sort of landscape.'

He snorted. 'You mean to tell me you wank with *scenery*? What sort of landscape?'

'For God's sake, Gerhard, it's not as if I made notes or took photographs. And please keep your voice down, this is hardly something I want to share with every articled clerk in Cape Town. But yes, a landscape … with trees.'

'What kind of trees?' His voice became positively lubricious. 'Long thrusting stems of palm surging out of the desert plain, or low voluptuous tropical growth luxuriating in moist crevices?'

'Oh, ordinary trees – you know, oaks and beeches, that kind of thing.'

'You mean ordinary English trees, yes. And what else?'

'Large bodies of water – lakes, I suppose you could call them.'

'No crashing oceans then, or plummeting waterfalls. Placid. That figures. And what else? Human beings?'

'No.'

'Satyrs or nymphs?'

'No.'

'Shepherds or shepherdesses in smocks, perhaps?'

'No.'

'Not even a lonely-looking sheep bleating appealingly at you?'

'*No.* But if you must know there were flowers.'

'Ah hah. And what kind of flowers?'

'Daffodils.'

'*Daffodils*?' he exclaimed, so loudly that the whole of the Wig and Pen looked up. 'You absolute *pervert.* My god, here you are in the middle of Africa and you wank up the Lake District!' He looked at me incredulously. Then he widened his eyes, put his index finger on my chest and said, 'But wait a minute … you have inadvertently made an important discovery. Listen.' He assumed what I'd learnt to dread as his poetry quoting stance, and intoned: '*But oft when on my couch I lie, in vacant or in pensive mood, they flash upon that inward eye which is the bliss of solitude.* Does that mean anything to you?'

'Of course, it's that poem we did at school – *Upon Westminster Bridge* or *The Daffodils* or something.'

'What a magnificent thing is education. *The Daffodils* it is. And what you and your subconscious have discovered is the masturbatory subtext to the poem– *that inward eye which is the bliss of solitude.* You know they call wanking the thinking man's colour television? Well, that's exactly what Wordsworth anticipated. Fantasising about daffodils flashing him! Tossing their heads in sprightly dance indeed!'

'This really is quite obscene,' I objected. 'Not to mention far-fetched and highly embarrassing.' I looked around us. Fortunately our neighbours had lost interest when Gerhard mentioned Wordsworth. 'But what if it was true? Why would it be such a discovery?'

'Can't you see?' He seized me by the shoulders so vigorously that for one terrible moment I thought he was going to kiss me. 'You've uncovered the sexual base of Romanticism! It stands to reason that all that heavy breathing over nature must have been more than mystic communion – in fact, as your own

172

over-heated but sadly repressed imagination has intuited, it was literally a wank. That means that nature poetry is not so much a sublimation of sexuality as a coded expression of it. I can't wait to get back to *The Prelude*.'

'*You* should talk about over-heated imagination,' I objected. 'You could discover coded expressions of sexuality in the telephone book.'

'But of course: there's nothing more erotic than a telephone book – all those mysterious numbers, each one with a name and address attached, each one harbouring a potential encounter right there, a phone call away, as they say.'

'I am worried about you, Gerhard. You'll be arrested for making dirty phone calls next.'

'And I am worried about you, Nicholas. You'll be arrested for molesting the daffodils in the park next. But seriously, I *am* worried about you. I don't think you need Wordsworth. Try *The Tiger* next time.' He bared his teeth and recited in a ferocious growl, very fascinating to the Wig and Pen, which now redirected its communal attention to us, '*Tiger, tiger, burning bright, in the forests of the night* – now isn't that more exciting than fluttering and dancing in the breeze? *In what distant deeps or skies burnt the fire of thine eyes?*'

'That's William Blake,' I said, for want of anything else to say.

'Very good, Nicholas, very good, if a trifle reductive. But you see, nothing wrong with the inward eye, as long as you can make it a fiery eye. Nothing wrong with nature either, but there's more to it than lakes and daffodils. Go for a romp in the forests of the night next time.'

But as I was saying, I am not a Tiger type of person, and such fantasies as I have tend towards the tame. For this reason my involvement in the ever-deepening intrigue surrounding Luc Tomlinson's baboons was as unusual as it was unwelcome. As far as I am concerned, the Environment should behave itself if it wants us to look after its interests. As a matter of fact, the Lake District is just about my notion of an ideal environment: well-mannered, contained, placidly packaged, officially protected and signposted, with postcards available from licensed dealers.

And now Luc's case was making the concept of Environment expand beyond my most lurid dreams or vivid fears. If not quite the Forests of the Night, Rocklands seemed to have harboured some very exotic creatures. The photographs which Joyce Tomlinson had entrusted to my care and discretion made this point with some force: if not exactly of direct environmental concern, the shenanigans of the two cabinet ministers formed part of a complex of motives surrounding the development of Rocklands that still eluded me. Joyce Tomlinson's part remained puzzling: why should she provide me with incriminating evidence against two of her husband's accomplices? And who had taken the photographs?

Not long after my visit to Joyce Tomlinson, I had a strange phone call. 'Mr Morris,' Myrah announced in the put-out tone which meant that she'd been bested by a caller, 'I have a lady on the line who refuses to give her name.' Refusing to Give One's Name was the First Deadly Sin in Myrah's book. 'She's phoning from a tickey-box.' Phoning from a Tickey-Box was the Second Deadly Sin. Decent people did not phone from public phone boxes.

'Thanks, Myrah, put her through … Nicholas Morris speaking.'

A dramatically lowered voice, husky with intrigue, said: 'This is Brenda Booysens. I think the time is right.'

I searched my memory.

'For what?' I asked apprehensively.

'I told you you would hear from me when the time was right. For my revelation.'

'Yes indeed. Well, that's excellent, would you like to make a statement, perhaps? Can I come to see you?'

'Over my dead body. *Literally*. No, I must not be known to see you.'

'Then would you like to come to my office?'

'I might as well publish my visit to you in the *Cape Times*,' she growled. 'No, Mr Morris, I know what I'm about. Meet me at five minutes past one today in the restaurant of the National Gallery. I take it you know where that is?'

'Yes … yes, of course.'

'Good. Not many people do. Five past one. I shall be sitting with my back to the door.'

I had not given much thought to Brenda Booysens's promise, the day in Visser's office, to get in touch 'when the time was right', because she had not struck me as the repository of important secrets, rather as someone who fancied herself the main figure in a drama in which in fact she was a minor player, even a stage hand. It was more than likely that the information she was now prepared to give me would be some minor detail that we already knew. But in my new role as sleuth I was prepared to follow up any lead.

'Where are you having lunch?' asked Angie, as we got into the lift.

'The National Gallery.'

'Lord, does Cape Town *have* one?'

'Yes, as you'd know if you stopped surfing and started absorbing some local culture.'

'What do you mean? Surfing *is* the local culture.'

I laughed, relieved at not being interrogated about my admittedly unusual lunch venue. The National Gallery, a venerable structure beautifully situated in the Gardens, had its points, but lunch, as far as I knew, was not one of them. In spite of my jibe at Angie, I hardly made a habit of visiting the National Gallery. My friend Gerhard is a regular visitor, but his motives for visiting anything are seldom unmixed.

The National Gallery restaurant was almost empty. Brenda was sitting in the far corner of the room at a table for two, with her back to the door, as promised. As I pulled out a chair, she looked up, startled – her glasses were dangling from the gold chain – then relaxed and said: 'You came.' I did not deny this, and she continued: 'I chose this place because it's the last place on earth Chris Visser would visit.'

She pointed her glasses at the chair opposite hers in a manner more peremptory than inviting, and I sat down, not sure what was to follow. To cover the slight awkwardness I looked around for service, but the single waitress was taking the order of the only other customers in the place. Brenda displayed no interest in the ordering of food. 'You must wonder, Mr Morris,' she said, 'why I should be acting in this unprofessional way.'

I tried to make some feeble demurral, but she held up her hand and said, 'Please don't interrupt. I can't stay for long. If I'm seen I shall also be removed.'

'Removed?'

'Yes, like poor Felix.'

'Felix?'

She nodded portentously. 'Felix Hartshorn.'

'The previous ...?'

She nodded. 'Yes. A fine man, only a bit weak-kneed.' She reminded me again of Margaret Thatcher as she crisply pronounced her verdict on her previous boss.

She continued. 'You are contemplating appealing against the decision to allow development at Rocklands?'

'Yes. More precisely, we want ...'

'Let's not waste time with legal technicalities, Mr Morris. You were looking, weren't you, for the environmental impact report on the Cape Point development?'

I nodded. 'Yes,' I said, 'and Dr Visser kindly ...'

'Dr Visser kindly nothing,' she cut me short. Then she hissed: 'The man's an arsehole.'

I looked at her, too shocked to speak. She seemed, though, to expect some response, so I repeated reluctantly, this not being part of my usual vocabulary, 'An arsehole?'

She nodded curtly. 'An arsehole and a motherfucker,' she pronounced factually, as if identifying two distinct species of dog. 'One day, when he calls me Brrrrenda again in that voice of his like a bad case of diarrhoea, I'll stab him in the neck with my paper knife and staple his tiny prick to his fat belly.'

I glanced around us, hoping that our dialogue was not being overheard. Fortunately the other occupied table was at the far end, around a local artist holding forth on the state of 'Cul-ture' in Cape Town. I risked another intervention: 'You feel that Mr Hartshorn was not treated fairly.'

'He was treated like shit,' she said.

'By Dr Visser?'

She nodded. 'May Chris Visser burn in hell with all his ancestors, and may his seed shrivel in his balls and his prick rot on its stalk.' I was still unpacking this metaphor, which seemed to be drawn from legumes, when she held up her hand and

176

said in a conspiratorial tone: 'But wait.' She rummaged in her bag and produced a brown envelope. 'Don't open that here,' she cautioned. 'But you'll find that it's what you're looking for.'

'But why …?' I said.

She held up her hand. 'I can't explain. Visser is small fry. He thinks he's the dog's dong, but in fact he's being used by people who will get rid of him like the shit-rag he is when it suits them to do so. And please don't ask me any more questions. As it is, I've jeopardised my position and …' she leaned over and whispered dramatically, *'perhaps even my life!'*

'I'm extremely grateful to you, of course.'

She returned to her impassive mode. 'You needn't be. It's not for you that I'm doing it. You seem a nice enough young man, but I am motivated almost completely by a desire for revenge.'

I nodded, fearing another outbreak of vituperation, but she just pursed her lips and said: 'Vengeance is mine saith the Lord, but in my experience He dawdles unconscionably about it.'

She got to her feet, replaced her glasses, and looked again the soul of respectable spinsterhood. 'Goodbye, Mr Morris,' she said. 'May you prevail.'

I leapt to my feet, but she put me down with an imperious hand. 'Stay,' she commanded, for all the world like Barbara Woodhouse, and left. I stayed for what I judged was the regulation period in obedience class, and then followed, to the indignation of the waitress, who had just been preparing to take our orders.

I went back to my office and opened the envelope Brenda had given me. Inside was a report, at first sight identical to the one Visser had surrendered to me. I turned to the last page; there, under 'Chief Conservation Officer', instead of the ostentatious swirl of Visser's signature, was a neat, cramped, legible signature: *FC Hartshorn*. The date was about two months earlier than the Visser report. I paged through the document, then started comparing it more carefully with Visser's version. My task was made considerably easier by the fact that somebody – presumably the helpful Brenda – had marked certain sections in blue pencil. Thus where the Visser version read '… development of any nature must be undertaken with the utmost care and sensitivity to ensure its sustainable amenity value', the Hartshorn version had continued: 'To this end it would be preferable to have no development at all.' After the reference to 'full conservation measures' Hartshorn had added: 'The proposed development does not take cognisance of this requirement,' and had then gone on to list 'the four essential qualities of natural beauty' as 'the landscape character, the scenic beauty, the flora and fauna as well as the peacefulness,' concluding that 'natural beauty, therefore, comprises those qualities which are valued by the nation either for their own sake or for the enjoyment they give.' Hartshorn ends this section with the confident if unsyntactical declaration that 'As an area of outstanding natural beauty, it is encumbent upon public authorities to protect such qualities. A development such as proposed in the application under consideration would impair the condition of the area as well as detract from its appearance. As such it would impact in a negative manner.' The conclusion of the document is that 'The proposal is environmentally undesirable and should not be supported. The scale of the development is excessive and inappropriate to its context.' The recommendation is that the application be rejected.

The whole document was an awkward and yet touching mixture of genuine concern and pompous bureaucratic jargon: it spoke of earnest endeavour, a conscientious functionary self-consciously doing his appointed task to the best of his abilities, a prosaic soul moved to its own kind of pedantic poetry, an orderly person trying to systematise natural beauty. All of this Visser, in his revised version, had dealt with simply by omission – hence the effect of inconsequentiality. His document, in fact, was not a revision as much as a scissors-and-paste job, in which anything unfavourable to the development had been snipped out. It was as insensitive as the vandalising of an exhibition of child art.

I got hold of Mhlobo and asked him to check for any shady or sticky details on the previous Chief Conservation Officer in the Department of Nature Conservation and Development.

In a very short time he phoned back.

'Yeah, I thought the name rang a bell. We ran a minor item on him about two months ago.'

'Oh – what happened to him?'

'Abso-lootly nothing happened to him. On the contrary, our interest was aroused by the fact that he was granted early retirement and a package of several million rands, which, we suggested, was excessive for even as meritorious an employee as the Minister claimed Mr Hartshorn had been.'

'And what happened?'

'Nothing, as usual. These assholes have had fifty years in power in which to get used to being unpopular. We publish these stories telling ourselves we'll at least make the buggers squirm for a while, but let's face it, most of them must be gua-ran-teed squirm-resistant by now.'

'So you don't see Hartshorn as a victim of unfair discrimination, that kind of thing.'

'If he is, all I pray for in life is a spot of unfair discrimination. Listen, I can see how he might have been bought, you know, that they didn't want him to spoil somebody's game; fact remains he took the money and ran.'

'Any idea where I can get hold of this Hartshorn?'

'Yes, as it ev-entu-ates. Our report mentions that he bought himself a mansion on Millionaire's Mile in Hermanus. There's even a photograph captioned *The House that Nature Conservation Built*. Odd thing about small guys when they get corrupted, first thing they do is buy themselves a monstrous mansion. What's with houses?'

'I don't know; I suppose it's like a little bird building a big nest to impress the female or fool the predators.'

'Sounds like a variant of the small-dick syndrome to me. You got what you want on Mr Hartshorn now?'

'Yes, thank you very much. Let me know if I can do something for you.'

'Never give a journalist a break. See you.'

I was grateful to Mhlobo, but also a bit disappointed. Brenda had implied that Hartshorn had been a victim, whereas it now seemed that he had benefited quite handsomely from whatever injustice he had suffered. And, of course, if he had been

179

illegitimately enriched, as seemed almost certainly the case, he was not going to want to tell me the story. Still, there was only one way of finding out.

Directory enquiries was very obliging, once I had succeeded in persuading them that the name Hartshorn did actually exist and was spelt thus and not Hardhorn, Heartshorn or Harthorn. Without quite knowing what I would say, I dialled the number.

'Hello?' a woman's voice answered, a depressed-sounding voice, speaking of a lifetime of receiving unsatisfactory phone calls and of not expecting this one to be an exception.

'Good afternoon. I'm Nicholas Morris from McKendrick, Jolly, Wirthenburger, Smith, Watts and Koekemoer in Cape Town. Could I speak to Mr Hartshorn, please?'

There was a short silence. 'I'll see,' she said and disappeared into the distant hum of a vacuum cleaner. After a considerable time, during which I could follow the progress of the vacuum cleaner through several of the rooms of the Hartshorn mansion, she returned.

'From where?' she asked.

'From … from Cape Town.'

'No – the other bit.'

'Oh. McKendrick, Jolly, Wirthenburger, Smith, Watts and Koekemoer. It's a lawyer's firm.'

'Oh. I'll see,' she said again, and left me to the vacuum cleaner for another few minutes. The telephone was picked up, and after a longish pause a voice, hardly more sanguine than the first, said 'Yes?'

'Mr Hartshorn?'

'Yes.'

'Mr Hartshorn, I am Nicholas Morris of …'

'I know. My wife told me.'

'Oh, good. Well, Mr Hartshorn, I'm phoning to ask if it would be convenient for you if I came to see you at your home.'

'No.'

'I beg your pardon?'

'I said no. It would not be convenient.'

'I see. I wonder if I could explain to you what I want to speak to you about?'

'No.'

'Oh.' I had not counted on such a total lack of curiosity on this man's part. Usually, I have found, people cherish, however irrationally, the fiction-fed hope that a lawyer will have 'something to their advantage' to disclose, preferably the death of a distant, fabulously rich relative. But Mr Hartshorn was made of sterner stuff, or otherwise his windfall had made him indifferent to the uncertain favour of distant relatives. This was not the beaten, rejected man Brenda had given me reason to expect.

'Brenda suggested,' I began, conscious of stretching the truth here, 'that I should speak to you.'

There was a tense silence at the other end. I could hear him breathing. Then he said, 'Brenda?' in a completely different tone of voice, more like that of the man I had envisaged on the strength of Brenda's comments. Apparently her Barbara Woodhouse manner retained its power to quell even over time and space. Slightly disingenuously, I continued in as airy a manner as I could summon up: 'Yes, she seemed to think you might want to help us in a matter of mutual concern.'

'How ... how is Brenda?' he asked, to my considerable surprise. I would not have imagined that Brenda's welfare was a matter ever at issue or of interest: she seemed so immune to mere time and mortality. I decided to push this unexpected advantage.

'Well, that's partly why I wanted to see you,' I prevaricated. 'She seemed ... agitated.'

'Yes,' he said, 'she has always been a sensitive woman.' For a sensitive woman Brenda had a robust turn of phrase, I thought, but judged it diplomatic to indulge this novel perspective. 'Yes, yes, she seemed very ... upset on your behalf,' I replied, truthfully enough.

'Well, then, Mr Morris, if Brenda wants me to see you, I'll see you.' His tone was brave, like a man resolving to go to the scaffold for his beliefs. I marvelled again at the power of this woman; but then, had I not myself obeyed her summons to an assignation in the National Gallery? I sensed that it would be unwise to profess too much gratitude: the man had no desire to do me a favour, he was driven entirely by his awe of Brenda. No wonder she had called him weak-kneed. 'In that case, if you name a time, I'd be happy to drive out to Hermanus.'

'Time is no longer an issue with me. One day is very much like another.' Betrayed into intimacy by his self-pity, he seemed to warm to me. 'But why don't you come to lunch on Saturday, and bring your wife?'

'Thank you very much for that, Mr Hartshorn, but I'm not married ... yet.'

'Well then, bring whoever it is that you're not married to ... yet.' He almost allowed himself a chuckle. 'Then you and I can talk while the ladies chat.'

Leonora was happy to accompany me to Hermanus, even when I explained to her that it would involve visiting an unspecified number of people of indeterminate age and uncertain temperament. I refrained from mentioning that her function would be to *chat* with the ladies while the men *talked*. 'Visiting strangers is something I grew up with,' she said. 'Every Sunday my parents went visiting, and we all had to go along. Daddy believed that families should always do things together.' However little I sympathised with this view of family togetherness – the principle, if applied to my own family, would have produced some truly terrifying situations – I was grateful for Leonora's presence in what I sensed would be more her home territory than mine. The trip to Hermanus, besides, was officially designated as Scenic, indeed even, if one took the coastal route, Highly Scenic, and thus presented itself to my perennially guilty conscience as reparation for my reluctance to take Leonora for weekend outings like normal motorised couples who cement their relationships by sharing Scenery.

The Hartshorn home was not difficult to find. It was, as the *Mail & Guardian* had noted, immodestly large – what is known as a statement, although it was difficult to figure out what it was trying to say. Hermanus is known for the fact that nature rather overdoes things there: the mountains gloat darkly over the town as if contemplating something unpleasant; the waves bang and smash against the rocks like a bad-tempered baby trying to get out of its playpen; the beaches stretch on for ever in sandy vacancy. Faced with this kind of excess, the architect of House Hartshorn had unwisely decided to compete with nature. Where a more sensible architect would have gone for a slightly cowed Blending In, this one had gone for Assertion of the Human Spirit. Unignorably situated above the looming cliffs and crashing waves of the Hermanus coast, the house recklessly piled arches and pediments on top of buttresses and columns and aluminium sliding doors, a Hollywood hybrid of temple, cathedral and squash court, the whole thing wrapped up in a grotesque filigree of razor-wire security fencing.

'It's very post-modern, isn't it?' Leonora commented, as I parked my little Golf in the paved area outside the security gate at the back of the structure. She had done a course in architectural styles at a Summer School.

'It's post-something certainly: it seems to be built entirely of leftovers from other eras.'

'Except for the security fencing.'

'Well, that's post-Apartheid.'

To gain access, we had to shout our names into an uninviting little box next to what looked like a portcullis but proved to be a sliding gate, opening ponderously to admit us. As we reached the front door, it clicked open to reveal Mr and Mrs Hartshorn, an unsmiling couple, who, however, greeted us civilly and professed pleasure at meeting us. I would have judged them to be in their early fifties, both rather spare of outline and upright of bearing, as if life was something to be tolerated with dignity. They were colourlessly dressed, producing a general effect of beige and grey without insisting on it.

They conducted us through a large entrance hall to the sitting room. I was not unprepared, either by my sense of the Hartshorn style or by the rigours of my own upbringing, for a certain amount of formality. My mother, perennially warding off the ruin that my father's habits seemed destined to bring upon us all, had cultivated very high standards of respectability. Thus I am no stranger to the starched tablecloth, the discreet doily, the polite butter knife, the anxious coasters, the cautious antimacassars, the considerate little coffee tables, all the neurotic amenities and treasured relics of gentility maintaining itself against the odds and against the evidence. To be honest, I find these things curiously congenial, as testifying to the determination to Cope, to go down with the band playing *Nearer My God to Thee*, or at least with Vera Lynn singing *The White Cliffs of Dover*, which I had once heard my mother refer to as a hymn. As far as I am concerned, Western civilisation owes its survival to the feather duster and the broom.

But the Hartshorn home and table set entirely new standards of upright discomfort and rebarbative formality. The tidiness I could respond to, the order of the place I could negotiate and accommodate; but the total effect was constricting even to me. My mother's taste running more to Sanderson and Wiltshire, our house had had softer surfaces, slightly more give, more absorption of light and sound, less reflection and resonance, fewer sharp corners and empty surfaces. The interior of the Hartshorn house was less multicultural post-modern, more single-mindedly Pompous Indigenous than its exterior might have led one to expect. The furniture was austerely upmarket Great Trek, massive imbuia chairs and sofas, a shiny modern copy of a yellowwood-and-stinkwood armoire, ball-and-claw feet everywhere straddling gleaming stretches of lacquered parquet flooring, not so much livened up as booby-trapped with little Van Dyck Persian rugs. A petrified arrangement of giant proteas in a copper jug filled the empty hearth, in a fire-place of polished slasto, and watercolours of indigenous flowers adorned the walls. Nature was truly conserved here, in the sense that fruit is conserved in bottles and cans. The Hartshorn house – one would have hesitated to call it a home – was intended to embody and proclaim solvency, probity and Culture.

The whole was if not redeemed then at least upstaged by a large picture window overlooking a particularly bumptious stretch of coastline, which did more for the house than the house did for it.

'What a beautiful view,' Leonora volunteered.

'Yes,' Mrs Hartshorn sighed deprecatingly. 'But it's such a job keeping the windows clean, with the spray from the sea. And we don't have servants over a weekend.' She stared at the magnificent bay morosely. 'Whales come here to calve in spring time,' she said, in the depressed tones in which my mother tended to pronounce on the fecundity of the natives.

184

The subject of whales kept us going though the dry sherry and into lunch, which was, in spite of the dearth of domestic help, an only slightly scaled-down version of the kind of meat-and-starch orgy that I had experienced at Leonora's mother's table. It was accompanied by a KWV wine much sought after not so much for its innate qualities as because it was available only to wine farmers and those favoured by the political-agricultural establishment. Leonora, of course, could identify its provenance and make the noises appropriate to its aspirations.

The Hartshorns spoke English to me, Afrikaans to Leonora, English to each other when I was deemed to be in some sense implicated in their conversation, Afrikaans at other times. This gave a stilted formality to the occasion, an air of ritual polite-ness that made conversation difficult. Fortunately Hartshorn proved to have what my friend Gerhard calls the endemic Afrikaans obsession with family, and whereas my own sur-name meant nothing to him, Leonora's sent him off tracking a tangled web of connections and collaterals, succeeding in proving to his satisfaction that Mrs Hartshorn and Leonora were in fact related on their mothers' side. Leonora's family being one of the largest in South Africa, the process saw us through the meat and vegetables and the sticky pudding and the heavily percolated coffee.

After lunch I felt capable only of falling asleep on one of the uncomfortable sofas, but Hartshorn proved to be more tena-cious than I in keeping to the purpose of my visit.

'Laetitia,' he said.

'Yes, Felix.'

'Mr Morris is interested in the indigenous flora of this area. I think we'll take a walk along the cliff path. Perhaps you and Miss le Roux …?'

'We'll go for our own little stroll and chat, thank you, Felix.'

Felix Hartshorn led me to a garden gate that issued, through a locked gate in the razor-wire fence, onto the cliff path, a cele-brated walk winding through coastal shrub and across rocks, past small beaches and coves, skirting the wide curve of the bay. The constant crashing of the waves on the rocks produced, as Laetitia Hartshorn had complained, a fine spray, smelling of ozone, overlaid with the darker tones of kelp.

'Are you in fact interested in indigenous plants, Mr Morris?' Hartshorn asked, pointing at the expanse of vegetation in front of us, which consisted mainly of to me somewhat amorphous-looking low shrubs.

'I'm afraid I know little about them.'

This was an understatement. I knew absolutely nothing about indigenous plants: my mother's garden had bloomed, not with the rank profusion of Africa, but with the prim decorum of the English garden, the hollyhocks and herbaceous borders, the flowering annuals and hardy perennials, primroses and primulas, conscientiously copied from the English edition of *House and Garden*. It was one of her constant grievances that her bird table, constructed according to dimensions adapted to the size and behaviour of polite British birds, had collapsed under the weight and antics of the voracious, ungainly, noisy hadedas which had gobbled up her titbits and then defecated all over the table.

'The Western Cape floral kingdom is the richest in the world,' Hartshorn informed me severely, as if reproaching me for neglecting such riches.

'I have heard that said, yes,' I replied, not entirely untruthfully; I dimly remembered Gerhard enthusing about the variety of plants in the region.

'But I take it that that is not what you have come to discuss with me,' he said, not without a certain dry humour. 'You must excuse me; nature is my passion.'

I smiled. There was something very unpassionate about the declaration, and yet this was recognisably the blend of pedantry and ... yes, passion, that had animated the recommendation to the Land Use Committee. 'That was clear from your report to the Land Use Committee,' I said.

'Ah, you have seen it, then,' he said. 'May I ask how you gained access to it?'

I decided that honesty would best serve my purpose. 'From Brenda. She made a point of giving it to me.'

'Ah, yes,' he said, and stopped, staring pensively at a pretty but not very spectacular little pink-and-red flower. Then he turned back to me. 'How is Brenda?' he asked, as he had done on the telephone.

'She seems well – healthy and all that – but I suspect that she doesn't like her new boss.' This was putting it mildly indeed.

He nodded. 'She never much liked Chris Visser. His manner is a bit peremptory, perhaps, for a sensitive person like Brenda.'

'She certainly seemed to take exception to his manner.' I wondered how to steer the conversation back to the report, but Hartshorn anticipated me.

'You want to know about my report to the Committee.'

'Yes.'

'You have also seen the report that was finally accepted?'

I nodded. 'That is why ...'

'Of course.' He turned to me, as if to ask me to help him solve a riddle. 'Why should two almost identical reports issue in two diametrically opposed recommendations?'

'That's what I was hoping you could tell me.'

'You haven't told me why I should do so.'

'Yes, of course. I'm representing Mr Luc Tomlinson, the son of the owner of Rocklands, who ...'

He held up a hand. 'Yes, I know, the boy with the baboons. I saw him when I went there to make my report. Unconventional but fundamentally sound.'

'He cares deeply about the area.'

'Naturally. It's a beautiful spot.'

'And about his baboons.'

He sighed. 'Yes, the poor creatures. Intelligent enough to make a nuisance of themselves, but not intelligent enough to realise that man in his arrogance does not tolerate nuisances. I sometimes wonder when we will make so much of a nuisance of ourselves to God that he'll decide to wipe us out. His mistake last time was in saving Noah and his family along with the animals.' He was staring at a long-beaked bird with a brilliant green throat, sipping nectar from a flower.

'The malachite sunbird. It drinks from the aloe but knows not to destroy it. It's infinitely more stupid than the baboon and the human being, and infinitely more intelligent, if we define intelligence as the ability to survive in a given environment.'

Again I wondered how I was going to get him back to the report, but again he anticipated me. 'And the young

Tomlinson,' he said in the same lugubrious tone, 'is intelligent enough to resist his father, but not intelligent enough to take on the whole ...' – he shrugged helplessly – 'the whole crowd, clique, *gang*, call it what you will.'

'Do you mean the Department of Nature Conservation and Development?'

'No, Mr Morris, I don't, although that is the part of it that I had to deal with. But it's much bigger than that.'

'So Dr Visser ...'

'Christo Visser is a small man who was useful and was rewarded. I was a small man who was in the way and I was punished.'

'Punished?' I asked, gesturing ironically in the direction of his clifftop mansion.

'Yes, I know,' he said. 'It must seem as if I'm not doing badly. And I'm not. The point is that I had no choice.'

'But what exactly happened?'

He thought for a while, crushing a leaf that he'd picked from a shrub, and smelling it. 'Nothing that hasn't happened often before and won't happen again. I had to write a report in the course of my duties. I did it to the best of my abilities – you have read it, you say –'

'Yes, indeed, and I thought it was a very thorough and ... thoughtful report.'

'Thank you. I was on the point of submitting it to the committee when my immediate subordinate, Chris Visser, read it and informed ... somebody.'

'Brick Tomlinson?'

'No, but somebody who was acting for Tomlinson. Sam Stanford.'

'The Minister?'

'Yes.'

'But what is in it for the Minister?'

'Brick Tomlinson's gratitude, perhaps. But the Minister also has people to please.'

'Such as?'

He shrugged. 'People. His friends and colleagues. And somebody – a Person, somebody who has taken a personal interest in this case.'

'Do you know who this person is?'

He shook his head. 'No. I couldn't even swear to his existence. But several times while my ... my retirement was negotiated, I sensed that there was somebody beyond the Minister who had to be consulted. It was someone who was either well disposed towards me or wanted to make sure of me. The bribe came from there.'

'So you were bribed?'

'Partly bribed, partly blackmailed.'

'So you did have a choice?'

For the first time, surprisingly, he seemed to resist my probing. 'Mr Morris,' he said, 'I hope that you will never have to make a choice of that kind, between what you believe to be morally right and what you know to be your sole means of support and survival. You understand: I wasn't bribed to resign. I was told that I had to go, but offered an extremely large severance package. I could have left with a clean conscience and without the severance package. And in case you were wondering why a man who professes, as I do, love for nature in all its simplicity should have found it necessary to build such a large house – well, shall we say I thought I owed it to Laetitia. She has not had many pleasures as the wife of a middle-ranking civil servant. I wanted somehow to make it up to her.'

I wondered if I could risk pushing further. Although touchy, Hartshorn was clearly finding some relief in telling somebody his squalid little tale. 'You mentioned blackmail ...?' I suggested as gently as it is possible to mention blackmail.

'You ask a lot, Mr Morris, but if I can have your word for it that I won't be called as a witness in this case ...'

I considered. 'It's not really a matter of calling witnesses. In a case like this, it's likely to remain a question of an exchange of affidavits in court; the judge will refer the matter to oral evidence only in cases of substantial dispute of facts. What you are asking is that we exclude your testimony from our affidavit, which is of course an important omission, what one might call a diminution of the whole truth.'

Hartshorn, clearly at heart a law-abiding civil servant, seemed properly impressed with the gravity of this impediment to the ends of justice, and for a moment I thought he would capitulate; but like most law-abiding civil servants he also had a strong sense of his own advantage. This was, after all, the man who had been victimised to the tune of several million rand. 'I realise that, of course,' he said, 'and I appreciate your situation. But then, if I don't give you the information, you can't use it anyway.'

'Fair enough,' I said. 'I won't use the information without your express permission.'

'In that case ...' He hesitated, clearly embarrassed at what he had to say; then, bracing his narrow shoulders, he continued. 'You see, the temptation of the severance pay – I'm not saying I could definitely have resisted it, but it might have been easier if it had not also meant ... not to be too roundabout with you, Mr Morris ... you have met my previous secretary, Brenda.'

'Why yes, as I said ...'

'Yes. And you will agree that she is an uncommonly fine woman.'

'Certainly. Very ... strong.'

'Exactly. It was her strength that attracted me to her in the first place; but it was her gentleness that kept me captivated.'

I blinked. 'You mean you and Brenda ...?'

'Yes, Mr Morris, we had a relationship for more than five years. I know it was wrong to Laetitia, and I won't try to justify it to you. The point is that Visser found out about it, and informed his superiors. So that the ... suggestion that I should take early retirement included a promise that nothing would be said about my involvement with Brenda – which was, of course, tantamount to a threat that something would be said if I didn't play along.'

'Said? But to whom?' I couldn't imagine that the petty infidelity of a civil servant with his secretary would be information worth anybody's concern.

'To Laetitia, of course. And that would have destroyed her. Laetitia has not had a happy life, Mr Morris. I was very much preoccupied with my work, and we never had children. So I couldn't do it to her – I mean, lose my job and have her told that for five years I had been unfaithful to her. It would have destroyed her,' he repeated. 'So I destroyed Rocklands instead.'

'Let's hope not. If we succeed ...'

We'd reached a point where we would have to turn inland to continue our walk.

'Shall we turn back?' he asked.

I nodded. 'Thank you for taking me into your confidence.'

'It's the least I can do. If you do succeed and Rocklands can be saved, I won't have done quite as much harm.'

He paused for a moment and pointed at a showy pink flower, emerging out of the soil on a single straight stem. '*Amaryllis belladonna,*' he said, 'somewhat more prosaically in the vernacular, the *misrybol.*'

I looked at him in mystification. 'My Afrikaans ...' I said apologetically.

'It means the bulb of the manure-carting time,' he explained. 'You see, in the old days, March and April were the months when the wine farmers carted manure to fertilise the vines. The labourers associated the appearance of the Amaryllis with that time of year. It speaks of a time when human concerns were measured by the rhythms of nature. Nowadays the farmers use chemical fertilisers that kill the Amaryllis. But I'm told our wines have improved immensely.'

'Did you have a useful conversation?' Leonora asked me in the car. I had told her the bare outlines of the case.

'Yes,' I said, still mulling over what Hartshorn had told me. 'Yes, thank you. And how was your chat with Laetitia? I felt a bit guilty about sticking you with her, but ...'

'You needn't feel guilty. We had a very interesting talk.'

'Really?' I asked, still a bit absent-mindedly. 'To be honest, she didn't strike me as very cheerful company.'

'No, she's not very cheerful. But she's a brave woman.'

'Brave? You mean to live in that fortress all alone?'

'Well, yes, all alone with a husband who ... doesn't love her.'

'Did she say that?'

'Yes. Well, she said her husband ... you know ... had a relationship with his secretary for more than five years and never told her about it.'

'And she knew about it all the time?'

'Yes, she says she found out almost immediately when it

191

started, but she didn't want to make a scene, because it might have been bad for his work. She says it would have destroyed him if he had to give up the woman. She found a letter he had written to her, and she says it was clear that he was more in love with the other woman than he ever would be with her.'

I considered this. Felix Hartshorn had not struck me as rampantly virile or even as a man of average sensuality, and yet apparently he had had a torrid and potentially devastating relationship with a woman who had struck me as combining the least accommodating qualities of Margaret Thatcher and Barbara Woodhouse.

Good Lord, what did they *do*? Were Leonora and I the only sane, celibate people in a world single-mindedly intent on sexual intercourse? I put my hand on hers, where it lay primly folded in her lap, and said, 'Aren't you pleased we're spared all that?'

She considered. 'Yes,' she said, but quite wistfully, as if she wasn't sure. It was true what my friend Gerhard said: women didn't know what they wanted.

CHAPTER EIGHT

It is a little-known fact that the collapse of the Government of National Unity in May 1996 affected also the existence of a troop of baboons at Cape Point. Since the respondent in our matter was technically the Minister of Nature Conservation and Development, who had been serving on the Cabinet as a National Party member, the departure of the National Party from the GNU left us without an identifiable respondent. Of course, the Minister as abstraction, that is as legal entity, continued to exist, but the withdrawal of Sam Stanford into the generous retirement benefits which, for the senior functionaries of the previous regime, constituted the wages of sin, caused considerable delay in the serving of papers and other processes which require the presence of a human agent.

'It's in your interests, really,' said Dikeledi. 'While the new Minister is faffing around trying to find out what he's supposed to do, Brick Tomlinson is prevented by the court order from carrying on with his development, which must cost him a hefty sum in interest on his investment.'

'You mean we're bleeding him dry?'

'That's an unpleasant way of putting it, but yes, that's about the size of it. You know the first principle in law is Time is Money and our Taxi Meter is Running.'

'You almost make me feel sorry for the man.'

'Don't think of it as a man being ruined. Think of it as impersonal economic forces driving out the weak and unfit.'

'For a Marxist you've become very hardnosed very quickly.'

'It's the Culture of Entitlement meeting Corporate Culture.'

I took up Gerhard's suggestion and contacted John Scheepers: would he be interested in taking the case?

A cheerfully resigned voice said: 'In these days I don't insist on being interested in the cases I take, but it helps.'

'Then when would be a good time for me to come and see you?'

'Now is always an excellent time, I find.'

John Scheepers was small and wiry, with very bright eyes and spiky hair and a wide, expressive mouth that seemed amused at most things. I told him the broad outlines of the matter.

'Oh lord, the Broeders are still at it, aren't they?' he said.

'I'm not sure that it's a Broederbond deal. After all, Brick Tomlinson, as an Englishman, wouldn't be a member.'

'No, but you can bet your shirt on it that the Broeders have been using him. They're not averse to a bit of hanky-panky with the erstwhile enemy, now that they have to go to bed with whoever will go to bed with them.'

I explained the situation to him in more detail. He nodded. 'Yes – typical Broeder moves; one front man and a whole cabal behind the scenes. Your man Visser – is he overweight, smug, balding and wears shit-coloured Grasshoppers?'

'Yes, do you know him?'

'I don't know him, but I know the species – the classic Broeder. The Grasshopper model is Civil Service; behind, or rather *above*, every successful Grasshopper model is a black toecap and little homburg hat man, usually a cabinet minister.'

'That would be Sam Stanford.'

'Mm. Another Englishman, you see, granted honorary Afri-kaner status as a reward for crossing the floor.'

'How do you come to know the species so well?'

'I was born into the small-town variety of it. My father was a member of the Bredasdorp chapter – he was the headmaster of the high school. The ambitions were smaller but the costumes were the same. They're on their way out now, which is why they're feathering their own nests even more energetically than usual. Not dead yet, though, not by any means. But there's no helping that, we're going to have to proceed as if our case was going to be judged on its merits.'

'As I see it,' I said, 'what we have to do is put in an applica-tion for a review on the grounds that the Land Use Committee

194

either did not exercise its mind or was improperly influenced. Of course we know that at least one of these conditions did obtain, but our job – your job – is to prove that in court.'

'I imagine the matter will be settled by affidavits, except if the judge decides he wants to refer the matter to oral evidence. So we'll submit affidavits based on the discrepancy between the two reports, which is fishy enough in all conscience to make a cat sit up, even without Hartshorn's evidence. But are you positive that we won't get an affidavit out of him or his Mata Hari?'

'Brenda Booysens? No, she's convinced that she's risking her life every time she speaks to me. And Hartshorn has his marriage to think of.'

'He should have thought of his marriage while he was poking Brenda.'

The majesty of the law was duly invoked, and a court date applied for, in the matter between Tomlinson and the Minister of Nature Conservation and Development, with Safari Investments as second respondent, but with the delays attendant upon the change of government, the matter only came to court in early summer of that year. John Scheepers was cautiously optimistic.

'We have a good case, but never underestimate the Broeders,' he said. 'Sam Stanford may be out of office, but his influence persists – and, of course, your man Chris Visser is still exactly where he was. We'll have to go for him, but keep Sam Stanford in reserve. The new minister will oppose our application as a matter of course, but the affidavit will have been prepared by the old guard, meaning Visser.'

'Incidentally, speaking of Sam Stanford, are you planning to use those photographs?'

I had shown John the photographs Joyce Tomlinson had given me, and he had kept them, as he said, on the principle that it's always a matter of national concern when politicians don't keep their pricks in their pants.

'I don't know. It's obviously not the most ethical of means, but the pictures do establish the existence of a relationship of some intimacy between Brick Tomlinson and the minister. Let's wait and see.'

On our arrival in court I was not surprised to see, in the public gallery, Joyce Tomlinson, looking cool and pale; also, next to her, Brick Tomlinson, looking ruddy and hot. A few benches behind them sat Luc Tomlinson with his sunburst of red hair, unusually respectable in an open shirt – and next to him, formally and colourlessly dressed, Felix and Laetitia Hartshorn. I was pleased to see a few court reporters; if we were going to be washing dirty linen, it would be good to have it as public as possible.

We had drawn, for our case, Justice Koos Pieterse – 'Old style, but not Broederbond,' said John. 'A bit conservative, a bit self-important, but sincerely believes he's serving the cause of justice.' The counsel for the respondent was another relic of the old regime, Jurgen van Zyl, affable, easy-going, totally dishonest, according to John: 'I was in kindergarten with him: he used to buy up our sandwiches in first break and sell them back to us at a profit in second break. With the peanut butter scraped off.'

Judge Pieterse preserved a studied neutrality in appearance and manner, which he no doubt thought of as embodying the impartiality of the law. This could be a good sign: in my experience of judges, the more flamboyant they were, the more prone they were to fits of whimsy or prejudice or playing to the gallery. On the other hand, a totally colourless personality was often a manifestation of conservatism, which in an instance such as this would side instinctively with Authority.

John, as counsel for the applicant, Luc Tomlinson, addressed the court at some length on the significance of the discrepancy between the two reports. He was eloquent without being smarmy, pointing out that the only changes in the second document pertained to the actual recommendation to allow the development, in other words, that no new considerations had arisen which could have led the compiler of the report to reverse his predecessor's recommendation.

'I submit, M'lord,' John said, 'that in the absence of any evidence whatsoever as to the reasons for such a radical change in the tenor of a document, the only plausible explanation is that the compiler of the second report, Dr Chris Visser, was motivated not by the merits of the case but by matters extraneous to the case itself. I submit further, M'lord, that the only possible such extraneous matter was the intervention of an interested party, conceivably the second respondent or somebody acting on his behalf, and that this constitutes extreme bad faith on the part of the authority granting the permission.'

'Objection, M'lord!' Van Zyl said. 'Counsel for the applicant is presenting sheer speculation as evidence.'

'Objection sustained. Mr Scheepers, please confine yourself to the facts of the matter.'

'Yes, M'lord. I crave the court's indulgence, then, in re-emphasising the *fact* that the second report offers no reason whatsoever for recommending a course of action diametrically opposed to that based on the same report two months earlier. In not taking this fact into account the committee was self-evidently either not applying its mind, or was being misled by somebody acting in bad faith. Thank you, M'lord.'

He sat down before Van Zyl could object. Koos Pieterse said, 'Mr Scheepers, a self-evident speculation does not constitute a fact. Mr van Zyl, do you wish to address the court?'

Van Zyl, in his address, could not very well deny the discrepancy between the two documents, but he argued, with the impassioned fervour of a deeply insincere person seeking to cloak his lack of conviction, for the sacred right of individual judgement, and for the impossibility, in environmental affairs, of reaching objective conclusions: 'Whatever we may think of Dr Visser's interpretation of his predecessor's report, we must accept that it was an interpretation made in good faith on the basis of the available facts. Even if we ourselves were to disagree passionately with the recommendation, that would not establish bad faith on the part of the authority who made the recommendation.'

Pieterse restricted his own interventions to the occasional question or interjection. When Van Zyl sat down, having effectively kicked dust all over the issue, the judge sat still for a few minutes, ruminating, with that imperviousness to the impatience of others that characterises all civil servants, from the humblest clerk to the Chief Justice. Brick Tomlinson whispered something to Joyce, obviously irritated with the delay. At length Pieterse said 'The matter before the court is clear enough. It is common cause that the second report differs from its predecessor only, but crucially, in its conclusion. This is surprising, but does not, as Mr Scheepers argued, in itself constitute evidence of bad faith. Nor, though, is it as entirely uncontroversial a circumstance as Mr van Zyl suggested. In fact, neither counsel has succeeded in establishing the motive of Dr Visser in overturning the recommendation of his predecessor. Under the circumstances, I deem it proper to refer the matter to oral evidence, in order to hear the evidence of Dr Visser and of Mr Sam Stanford.'

There was a subdued buzz, promptly quashed by the usher who, in the absence of witnesses to call, had not had much of an innings so far; the buzz subsided, and Pieterse instructed the registrar to issue subpoenas to Visser and Stanford, and to allocate an early date for the hearing.

'So what is that supposed to mean?' Luc demanded from John and me, as the court adjourned.

'Just what the man said,' I replied, '– that he hadn't been convinced either way.'

'But isn't it obvious what happened?'

'Not to him. Or it may be obvious to him as an ordinary human being, but not as a representative of justice.'

Luc flung up his hands in exaggerated despair. 'My fuck, so what does that tell us about justice?'

John chipped in. 'Well, it tells us that justice is not an ordinary human being. Which, I agree, has its disadvantages and its absurdities, but may also have its advantages.'

'Like what?' Luc demanded.

'Think of most of the ordinary human beings you know,' John said. 'Would you go to them if you wanted justice?'

'Fuck, no.'

'Well, then.'

Not long before the trial, set for an early date, according to Pieterse's instructions, I was phoned by Felix Hartshorn.

'Mr Morris,' he said, 'I have come to a decision.'

'Yes?' I said as neutrally as possible. I guessed that Hartshorn would not want to feel that he had acted under compulsion from any agent other than his conscience, having once disregarded that faculty so flagrantly.

'My wife Laetitia has … informed me that she has for a long time been aware of my … romantic attachment to Brenda.'

'Really?' I asked, not knowing quite how to react to a piece of information that came as so much less of a surprise than its conveyer imagined. 'How extraordinary.'

'Yes. Needless to say, I was considerably taken aback.'

'Of course.'

'But Laetitia bears me no grudge. She told me, she says, only because she feels uncomfortable about living with something that I don't know – I mean with knowing something that I think she doesn't know.'

'That is very scrupulous of her.'

'Laetitia is the most scrupulous person I know, Mr Morris, with the possible exception of Brenda. But the point is that now that I no longer have to protect Laetitia from the truth, I am in a position to testify in the trial. Do you think that there would be any point in that?'

'Yes, indeed, very much so. It could materially affect the outcome of the case.' In my experience, people who made confessions needed to know that the confession made a difference to people other than themselves.

'That is reassuring to know. And how do I go about … testifying?'

'We'll apply on your behalf to intervene in the case. It's quite common for people who feel they have something to contribute to come forward.'

'I would be very grateful. You can imagine what a relief it is for me to free myself of the burden of deception after five years.'

'Indeed I can.' I thought it would be uncharitable to point out that the liberation had hardly been of his own volition.

John and I were relieved to find, on the day of the hearing, that Judge Pieterse would once again be presiding. He might be over-cautious, but insofar as justice was what we wanted, we were pleased for it to be taken seriously. 'I have certainly taken some cases,' said John, 'that I would have been ashamed to

199

bring before Pieterse. But for once I'm on the side of the angels.'

Visser was the first witness to be called. He looked uncomfortable, sweating slightly even in the air-conditioned court room. John wasted no time in getting to the point, after Visser had been sworn in.

'Dr Visser, can you tell the court why your predecessor's report, which is in almost all respects except its conclusion identical to your own, was replaced by your own?'

'It was found unsatisfactory.'

'By whom?'

'By myself.'

'Thank you. Dr Visser, when did you take over as Chief Conservation Officer?'

'On the first of September 1995. Acting Conservation Officer.'

'And you have since been appointed as Chief Conservation Officer.'

'I have.'

'And before that you were …?'

'The Deputy Conservation Officer.'

'As Deputy Conservation officer, would you have had access to reports produced by the Chief Conservation Officer?'

'Not always.'

'But it would have been possible for you to gain access to such documents?'

'Yes.'

'So you were aware of Mr Hartshorn's report to the Land Use Committee?'

Visser paused, obviously trying to figure out if he was being led into a trap. Then he said, 'No, I don't think I saw that report.'

'You don't *think* so?'

'No.'

'Would you not have been sure?'

'The office deals with many reports. I can't remember every detail about every one.'

'But you took office on the first of September, and submitted a revised version of Mr Hartshorn's report on the 15th, that is only a fortnight later. That would not have given you much time to acquaint yourself with previously unfamiliar documents.'

Visser was pulling at his own tie as if tolling a large and heavy bell.

'I came across it in preparing documents for the meeting of the Land Use Committee.'

'And undertook to revise its recommendation on your own authority?'

'I consulted with the minister.'

'When exactly?'

'I can't remember.'

'Can you remember whether it was before or after Mr Hartshorn's resignation?'

'After, of course. Before his resignation I would not have had access to the document.'

'Except in the course of your ordinary duties, as you have indicated.'

'I suppose so.'

'And you still maintain that you passed the report on to the minister only after taking office.'

'Yes.'

'Thank you, Dr Visser.' John paused briefly. 'Dr Visser, why did Mr Hartshorn retire?'

Van Zyl leapt to his feet. 'Objection, M'lord! This line of questioning has no bearing on the procedures followed by the Land Use Committee in reaching its decision.'

'With respect, M'lord, I'm trying to establish that Mr Hartshorn's resignation was part of those procedures.'

'Objection overruled. Continue, Mr Scheepers.'

'Thank you, M'lord. Dr Visser, can you tell the court why Mr Hartshorn retired?'

'I believe it was for personal reasons.'

'And these personal reasons made themselves evident how long after his writing of his report?'

'About a month, I suppose.'

'And as a result of Mr Hartshorn's resignation you were made Director of Nature Conservation and Development?'

Van Zyl was on his feet again. 'Objection, M'lord. Counsel is implying a connection between two unrelated events.'

'Objection sustained. Mr Scheepers, you may have heard of the *post hoc ergo propter hoc* fallacy.'

'I have, M'lord.'

'Then pray avoid it in your argumentation.'

'I shall, M'lord. Dr Visser, can you tell the court on what grounds you disagreed so radically from Mr Hartshorn's recommendation that you entered a recommendation diametrically opposed to his without altering the substance of his report?'

'Yes. Mr Hartshorn's recommendation was short-sighted.'

'Short-sighted? In what way exactly?'

'In placing what it sees as the ecological interest of the area over the long-term benefits of controlled development.'

'What are the long-term benefits of controlled development?'

Visser was well-briefed in the rationalisations of development. 'Job creation. Sustainable conservation. Benefit to the community as a whole. Income-generation which can be ploughed back into conservation.'

'Why does your report not mention any of these factors?'

'I assumed they were self-evident.'

'And did you discuss the matter with the minister?'

'I did.'

'And these were also his reasons for advising a reversal of Mr Hartshorn's recommendation?'

'They were.'

'And you repeat under oath that the minister did not see Mr Hartshorn's report before Mr Hartshorn's resignation?'

'I do.'

'Thank you, Dr Visser. I have done, M'lord.'

'Mr van Zyl?'

'Thank you, M'lord. Dr Visser, how long have you been in the Department of Nature Conservation and Development?'

'Twenty years.'

'And in that time, have you had reason to disagree with decisions made by your superiors?'

'Inevitably.'

'And what has been your way of dealing with such disagreements?'

'If they were minor, I ignored them; if I felt they were important, I discussed them with my superior.'

'And you have never gone over the head of your superior to, for instance, the minister?'

Visser looked righteously indignant. 'Never. I would regard that as disloyal.'

'So in this instance you went to the minister only because Mr Hartshorn was in fact no longer available for consultation?'

'That is right.'

'Thank you, Dr Visser. Thank you, M'lord.' Visser left the stand, his shiny brow furrowed, clearly not knowing whether he had lied himself into or out of trouble.

Felix Hartshorn took the stand, still pale, but calm and resolute. John went straight to the central question.

'Mr Hartshorn, would you tell the court why you resigned?'

'Yes. I had pressure put upon me.'

'What kind of pressure?'

'I was offered a large sum of money if I would take early retirement.'

There was a commotion in court. Brick Tomlinson could be heard to say, 'What *crap* is this?'

'So you were in effect bribed?'

'I would say so.'

'Objection, M'lord!' Van Zyl shouted.

'Objection sustained. Mr Scheepers, you should know a leading question by now.'

'Yes, M'lord.'

'Continue, Mr Scheepers.'

'As it pleases the court. Mr Hartshorn, by whom were you offered this sum of money?'

'By Mr Sam Stanford, the previous minister in my department.'

'Did you have any idea why Mr Stanford wanted you to retire?'

'Yes, because of my report on the Rocklands development.'

'Did he tell you why he disagreed with your recommendation?'

'No, he just said it was short-sighted.'

'And this was obviously before your resignation?'

'Obviously.'

'Thank you, Mr Hartshorn. Thank you, M'lord.'

'Mr van Zyl?'

'Thank you M'lord. Mr Hartshorn, on oath, would you say that the reason you have just given us for your resignation was the only one?'

'No. No, I would not.'

'And yet you implied that it was.'

'No, I did not.'

'Well, whether you did or not, would you give the court the full details of your resignation?'

Hartshorn looked at Laetitia and smiled his pale smile. 'Yes. I was blackmailed.'

'Mr Hartshorn, that is a serious charge. Are you sure you can substantiate it?'

'Your honour, I leave it to the court to find a name for the pressure exerted upon me. The minister told me that it was known to him that I was involved in an illicit relationship with my secretary, and should I refuse the offer of a retirement package, he would feel it incumbent upon him to discourage open immorality in his department; in short, he would have to tell my wife.'

'Mr Hartshorn, you are a mature man. Are you suggesting that such a threat would be enough to make you give up your job?'

'Yes, it was. My marriage was important to me.'

'Not important enough, it would seem.'

John was on his feet. 'Objection, M'lord. Mr Hartshorn's views on his own marriage are not relevant to his testimony.'

'Objection sustained. Mr van Zyl, please confine yourself to matters affecting Mr Hartshorn's reasons for resignation.'

'Yes, M'lord. Mr Hartshorn, isn't it odd that the minister should go to the considerable trouble and expense of getting you to resign, when he could so much more easily have persuaded you to change your recommendation?'

'No, it is not odd. In the first place, I would rather resign than make a recommendation that I do not believe in; but in the second place, I had to resign so that Dr Visser could be rewarded for alerting the minister to my report.'

'Do you have any evidence for this extremely serious charge?'

'No, I do not. I was answering your question. Not laying a charge.'

'Mr Hartshorn, may I put it to you that having left the department in disgrace, you are avenging yourself on your previous superiors and your successor?'

Felix Hartshorn turned to the judge as if Van Zyl was not standing right in front of him. 'M'lord,' he said, 'my disgrace I have borne as my just deserts. But this accusation is beneath all contempt, and I cannot reply to it.'

'You need not reply, Mr Hartshorn,' Pieterse said. 'The counsel for the respondents is availing himself of his rhetorical privilege. Pray proceed, Mr van Zyl, restricting yourself as far as possible to actual questions.'

'Thank you, M'lord. Mr Hartshorn, do you have any proof that the minister saw your report before your resignation?'

'Yes, he said so to me himself.'

'Yes, but with respect, Mr Hartshorn, that is your word against the minister's. Do you have any documentary proof, such as a letter of acknowledgement of receipt?'

'No, I did not send the report to him. Dr Visser showed it to him.'

'Dr Visser says he showed it to the minister only after your resignation.'

'I cannot answer for what Dr Visser says. I keep to my statement.'

'So that there is in fact no documentary proof or corroborative evidence for any of your allegations. Thank you, Mr Hartshorn. Thank you, M'lord.'

As Hartshorn left the witness box, pale but righteous, I whispered to John: 'That should sew it up, surely?'

'Not for a conservative judge like Pieterse. It's Hartshorn's word against Visser's.'

'What are you going to do?'

'Nail Stanford.'

Sam Stanford was familiar from photographs in the press, where his flamboyant appearance assured him frequent appearances. In the flesh he was a mite more fleshy, a shade more florid, a degree more coarse, but essentially the same dapper, dandified gentleman of the old school as appeared, glass in hand, at politically unfastidious occasions. He had been a pilot in the Second World War, and had kept his clipped moustache, his rakish fringe, his bonhomie and his aviator glasses. If the court was looking for bad faith, he was its embodiment: it wafted from his every pore, with every whiff of his aftershave; it glinted from every perfect tooth, it reflected from the sheen of his perfectly cut hair. He used to be known as the only gentleman in the National Party.

'Mr Stanford,' said John, 'this court has been given two versions of the same event today. You recall, no doubt, the resignation of Mr Felix Hartshorn.'

'Yes, indeed, a regrettable loss of a most able man.'

'And you recall, no doubt, a report that Mr Hartshorn drew up on a proposed development at Cape Point.'

'Oh, perfectly, perfectly. An able piece of work, only a bit idealistic, perhaps.'

'What the court would like to know, Mr Stanford, is whether you were shown the report before or after Mr Hartshorn's resignation.'

Stanford hesitated for a very brief second and his eyes flicked in the direction of Brick Tomlinson. For a moment he looked so shifty that he reminded me of my father. Then he said, 'Oh, before, of course, definitely.'

'Objection, M'lord,' Van Zyl interjected. 'The witness is being led into incriminating himself.'

Koos Pieterse raised a colourless eyebrow. 'Are you objecting, Mr van Zyl, to the witness being given an opportunity to tell the truth?'

'No, M'lord, but the witness does not realise the implications of what he is saying.'

'And is it your contention that if he were aware, he might perjure himself in order to avoid such an implication?'

'No, M'lord.'

'Then it is very difficult to see what exactly your contention *is*, Mr van Zyl. Mr Scheepers?

'I have done, M'lord. I needed to establish that Mr Hartshorn was forced to resign after the contents of his report were made known, and I have done so.'

'Mr van Zyl?'

'No questions, M'lord.'

Stanford left the witness box with the aggrieved air of a man who had dressed up for a party only to find that it had been cancelled.

After this it was purely a matter of wrapping up the bits: with Stanford supporting Hartshorn's contention, he was by implication also admitting to his own part in bribing and blackmailing Hartshorn; John's cleverness lay in not putting him into a spot where he actually had to admit to this.

Judge Pieterse did not take very long to deliver judgement. 'It is clear to me that the applicants have succeeded in establishing extreme bad faith on the part of high-ranking officials in the Department of Nature Conservation and Development. It is not within the province of this court to pronounce on the transparent corruption within the Department, nor on the conduct of the Honourable Minister, except insofar as it affected the decision under consideration. Under that head, it must be said that the conduct of the Honourable Minister was such as to cast doubt on the integrity of the whole process. In this he would seem to have been most ably, not to say eagerly, assisted by Dr Visser, who did not impress me as a witness. I would be failing in my duty to the community if I did not remark that in my view Dr Visser is not fit to hold the high rank entrusted to him. I find in favour of the applicants with costs, and refer back the report of the Land Use Committee for reconsideration.'

'So how did you swing that?' I asked John, as the courtroom emptied. 'How come the minister was so obliging?'

'I happened to bump into the minister in the Wig and Pen not so long ago. Naturally I mentioned the hearing in passing, and commented, in a light-hearted fashion, that for once it would be in his interest to speak the truth.'

'With no mention of certain photographs?'

He shrugged and smiled his expansive smile. 'The merest hint.'

'That does not make it any less reprehensible.'

'Reprehensible? To urge somebody to speak the truth?'

'You're not going to say that the end justifies the means.'

He laughed. 'Not if you don't want me to. But think about it.'

Outside the court Luc Tomlinson came up to me.

'Does that mean we're okay?' he asked.

'For the time being, certainly, and probably in the long run. It would be a very brave committee who persisted in their recommendation after that judgement.'

'I guess I must thank you, then.'

'Don't force yourself.'

He grinned. 'I don't have to force myself. I'm going to enjoy this.' In full view of the street and the courts he put his arms around me and kissed me on the forehead.

Felix and Laetitia Hartshorn were standing on the sidewalk, hand in hand, looking strangely forlorn. I went up to them.

'Can I offer you a lift?'

'No, thank you,' Felix said, 'we're staying in the Town House, just five minutes from here.'

'May I thank you for so bravely offering to testify?'

He shrugged and smiled his pale smile.

'It had nothing to do with bravery. More a need to bring these things into the open. A kind of Truth and Reconciliation,' he said, smiling at Laetitia.

Two days later Brick Tomlinson came to my office. He was very much quieter than the previous time.

'I thought I'd come to tell you personally what you've done,' he said.

'I appreciate that,' I said nervously.

'You needn't. I'm not doing it for your pleasure, although it may well give you pleasure. What you've done is to land me with a debt of several million rand and interest payments which in themselves are more than I can possibly pay.'

'I am sorry, of course, that this should have cost you so much. It was a quite unintentional consequence of my client's attempt to retain his home.'

'Oh bull shite!' he exclaimed with something of his old vigour. 'Do you think I don't know that this is exactly what that son of mine wanted? To ruin me?'

'It was my impression that his main concern was the survival of the baboons at Rocklands.'

'Oh, bugger your impressions,' he said, but without much passion. 'My son wanted to ruin me, and he's succeeded. You can tell him, because I'm not going to speak to him again, you can tell him that he carries his father's curse with him. It's a bitter thing to spawn the cause of your own undoing.' At the door he turned round. 'But I'll get even with you and that baboon freak of a son of mine.'

He left, and I reflected that that might be the last I had seen of the Tomlinson clan. I sincerely hoped so.

I told Leonora the main features of the case, to liven up our toasted chicken mayonnaise sandwiches. 'You'll be interested to hear that our friend Felix Hartshorn was the surprise witness. It seems Laetitia told him that she had known all along about, you know, what she told you about, and that made him feel he could tell his tale in open court.'

Leonora put down her fork, finished chewing, and wiped her mouth. She had been taught never to talk with food in her mouth, which made our lunches seem longer than they were. 'Oh, I'm pleased. We talked about it that day at Hermanus, Mrs Hartshorn and I, and I said to her that I thought it wasn't, you know, fair to know a thing like that and not tell your husband about it.'

I looked at her incredulously. 'So in a sense you were responsible for Felix Hartshorn's testimony.'

She blushed. 'Only very indirectly.'

'I don't know about that. Without you she wouldn't have told him and he wouldn't have … in fact without you, we couldn't have won the case.'

'It's not me. It's just that the Hartshorns both decided to tell the truth. Isn't justice, you know, just a matter of everybody telling the truth?'

'No. That would be too simple and too cheap.'

Under a new minister, the Department was only too ready to reverse its predecessors' decision, and the proposed development at Rocklands was decisively turned down; the new minister, too, prompted thereto by a concerted press campaign, lost little time in implementing Judge Pieterse's recommendation regarding Chris Visser, who accordingly disappeared into the golden sunset of early retirement. He was succeeded, perhaps a bit bizarrely, by his own predecessor, Felix Hartshorn, who sold his house in Hermanus to return to his old position. It was not known whether he repaid the retirement package he had received so recently.

Not long after the trial, ex-Minister Sam Stanford was assassinated by person or persons unknown.

CHAPTER NINE

I'm the most punctual person I know. One of the perennial mysteries of the human condition, as far as I'm concerned, is that people will lament the fugacity of time, the brevity of life, the fewness of opportunities, and then squander time, life and opportunity by *being late*. If we are truly powerless against time's winged chariot, then punctuality at least restores to us a measure of control over our own contingency. Though we cannot make our sun stand still, at least we can draw up a timetable.

One Monday morning soon after the successful conclusion of what Mhlobo reported in the *Mail & Guardian* as the Baboon Rights Trial, I set off from my home in good time, allowing my usual adequate margin to ensure that I would get to the office on time, slightly augmented to allow for the fact that it was Monday, and that the spirit of approaching Christmas was abroad like a large, stupid child on roller skates. I was barely on the freeway, however, when I realised that I had committed myself to a near-stationary block – it would have been inaccurate to call it a stream – of traffic. Indeed, I had hardly driven a hundred metres when the flow of traffic, such as it was, stopped entirely. People were getting out of their cars and peering down the central verge, and even climbing onto the roofs of their cars to see what was happening. The less rational members of the motoring public, which is to say most of them, were sounding their horns mindlessly. A man walking back to his car said to anybody who cared to listen, 'The country's finally broken down.' A woman in the car next to me shouted at him, 'What's happening?' and he said morosely, 'Nothing. They just pulled out all the plugs at the same time.'

'They can't just leave us here!' she exclaimed indignantly. He shrugged and said, 'Welcome to the new South Africa.'

After a few minutes the traffic started moving again, but very very slowly. The 15-minute drive to Groote Schuur Hospital took 40 minutes. As we crawled up Hospital Bend we came upon the cause of the delay: an aged tourist bus, probably brought back from the jaws of the wrecker to cope with the unprecedented loads of tourists now that South Africa was a respectable destination, had caught fire while labouring up Hospital Bend. The bus was beyond saving, little of its body remaining apart from a buckled flank announcing 'Rainbow Tours Get You There', but two fire engines were enthusiastically dousing it with water, creating dense clouds of smoke and foul-smelling streams of water and melted tar. Two ambulances were parked next to the road, though there was no evidence of any injured people. This, together with the stationary cars of the usual crowd of rubbernecks, further clogged the road, not to mention the tourists, who were wandering around taking photographs of their luggage piled on the grass verge, and of one another posing against a backdrop of the burning bus or of Table Mountain. A young couple in baseball caps and dark glasses were perched on the back of a fire engine, to the evident irritation of the firemen. Next to the stack of luggage a scuffle broke out: uttering polyglot cries of outrage the tourists descended on a young man, evidently one of the rubbernecks, who had seized the opportunity to help himself to an expensive-looking suitcase, which was now being reclaimed by its indignant owner. Two men, both wearing t-shirts saying 'I ❤ the Rainbow Nation', were holding the would-be thief, and their fellow tourists were hitting him with cameras, binoculars and, in one case, a crutch. The tour guide, a diminutive blond woman armed, presumably for visibility, with an open sunshade topped with a rainbow-striped pennant, was trying to herd the tourists together in a relatively safe spot off the road, but they were not taking any notice of her. She took a whistle out of her handbag and blew on it: it sounded more plaintive than authoritative, and she was once again ignored: I think I was the only person who noticed her agitation. As I drove past her she put out her thumb in a forlorn hitchhiking gesture, her handbag dangling from her wrist like a dead chicken. She seemed hysterical. I stopped and gestured to her to get in. I

212

don't normally pick up hitchhikers – hitchhikers in my experience invariably have unbearably strong body odour – but the woman was clearly in a terrible state. She opened the door and got in as far as the open sunshade permitted. She paused for a moment, then muttered 'Bugger it' and let go of the sunshade. In the rear-view mirror I could see it bouncing and tumbling in the morning breeze, the pennant gaily streaming behind. The tourists were pointing at it in evident alarm and speculation.

The tour guide sat in catatonic silence. She looked like a very small Barbie doll having a nervous breakdown. She wore a large lapel button, also rainbow-striped, which said, 'I'm Becky and I Want to Help You.'

'Can I take you anywhere?' I asked.

'Yes,' she said, 'anywhere.' She started shivering and muttering to herself. It sounded as if she was saying, 'Anywhere's a very good place, except nowhere's better.' This seemed like an unhopeful view for a professional tour guide to hold, but she was evidently not in a state to have this pointed out to her. She varied this with, 'Nowhere's a good place to be if somewhere's anywhere,' and 'Somewhere's an excellent place to be if everywhere is nowhere.' I couldn't think of anything to say in reply, but she didn't seem to intend her cryptic statements as conversational gambits.

After a few minutes of these incantations she said quite lucidly, 'That was my first job.'

'All jobs have their rough days,' I said insincerely; I couldn't help thinking that she hadn't altogether risen to the challenges of this particular one. 'It's just bad luck to have it on your first day.'

'Yes,' she said 'but to lose a bus full of tourists on your first day is more than bad luck.'

'I suppose so,' I said, my tact yielding to my honesty in the face of this entirely incontrovertible statement.

'Do you think they'll fire me?' she asked, with touching faith in my judgement, considering that I was a complete stranger.

It seemed more than likely that Rainbow Tours would not be anxious to retain the services of a tour guide who had left her charges behind on a highway with a burnt-out bus, but I said, recovering something of my tact, 'I'm sure your employers will understand.'

'Will they?' she asked, her reliance on my words now assuming alarming proportions. I had become a kind of oracle to her. 'Are you sure?'

'It seems very likely,' I said more cautiously, 'especially if you go back to the bus and try to calm the passengers.'

'You must be right,' she said. 'Imagine what it will look like on my report – abandoned group of tourists on Settler's Way.' She started shivering again. 'But they were horrible. They wouldn't stop asking me questions I couldn't answer – I mean, how am I supposed to know the names of all the ships in the harbour, or how far Cape Town is from Fort Worth? I don't even know where bloody Fort Worth is.'

'It's in Texas, I think,' I said helpfully.

'Of course it's in fucking Texas,' she snapped with a disconcerting mood swing to sheer malevolence. 'Do you think I don't know that? But where exactly in Texas?'

'I wouldn't worry about that,' I said. 'I'm sure you did your best.'

'I burn out the bus and you say I did my best,' she said accusingly. 'What do you think of me? You don't understand: that was my first job.' She frowned at me. She was quite young, probably in her early twenties, but her truculent air made her seem ageless, like a tiny Valkyrie. Whatever her lapel button said, helpfulness was not her distinguishing trait.

'But you're quite right,' she continued. 'I'll have to get back to them.'

'Good idea,' I said cheerily, 'I'll drop you in town and you can make your way back to the bus from there.'

'No,' she said, 'you take me back.' There was nothing pleading or even polite in her tone.

'I'd love to,' I said, 'but unfortunately I'm already very late for work.'

'You took me away from my bus,' she said accusingly. 'You take me back.'

'Look,' I said, 'I was trying to do you a favour …'

'Then finish the favour,' she snapped, now quite openly disagreeable about it, 'and take me back to where you found me.'

She paused for a moment, and then added, with startling venom, 'Otherwise I'll tell people you abducted me.'

'Oh, nonsense,' I said, attempting a scornful laugh. 'Nobody will believe you.'

'I don't have time to argue with you. I have to get back to my tour group before they do something silly.' She took out her whistle, opened the window, stuck out her head and blew: at close quarters its sound was much more impressive than it had been in the open. The traffic, however, took no notice: imperturbable in their tin bubbles the workers of Cape Town proceeded workward.

'*Look* at them,' Barbie-Becky spat with infinite contempt, 'I could get raped and murdered and chopped into bits like that poor girl in Salt River for all they cared. It's a good thing I can look after myself.' She rummaged in her handbag and produced a small but efficient-looking pistol, which she pointed at my lap in a businesslike way. 'Turn round,' she commanded, 'or I'll blow your balls off.'

I doubted whether she'd actually execute her threat, but she was not exactly a picture of cool rationality as she sat there aiming at my groin. It occurred to me to reply, 'Blow away sister, I won't miss them,' but in the first place this wasn't entirely true, and in the second it seemed unlikely that in her present mood she'd settle for my testicles: what she wanted was to be taken back to her bus or what remained of it – at, it seemed, any price. And there was, after all, a limit to the price I was prepared to pay for punctuality.

'All right, all right,' I said. 'But do you mind if I find a turn-off first? I mean you don't want me to do a U-turn here?' The traffic had eased up considerably since we left the burning bus behind, and the three lanes of traffic were moving briskly towards the city.

'Don't be a smart-arse,' she snarled – and a snarling Barbie doll is a disconcerting sight, like a rabid Lassie or a rutting Bambi, 'turn when you can.' I marvelled at the resentment she had generated against me for no reason that I could see other than that she was abusing my charity.

We were approaching Cape Town – the office block in which I worked was glinting in the sun, alluring as a fairy castle in its glazed self-sufficiency, its promise of quiet corridors and private offices – and I could turn off to the left into the mountain suburbs, to make my way round tortuously to the outbound route and back again into the incoming lane, which is quite a complicated matter on that stretch of Settler's Way. It requires a cool head, and is not helped along by distractions like a pistol pointed at your groin and a malevolent blond dwarf kvetching at every turn.

Still, eventually we laboured up to what remained of Rainbow Tours: a charred wreck, a pile of luggage, and a group of belligerent tourists. They didn't seem pleased to see Becky, but as she didn't bother to hide her gun as she got out, indeed brandished it at them in a manner one wouldn't have wanted to risk not taking seriously, they mustered smartly enough. Needless to say, Becky did not thank me for my efforts on her behalf: as she got out she muttered, 'What a dildo!' an insult so gratuitous that I was nearly moved to object; but, not wanting to be around when Becky discovered that there wasn't very much she could do with 50 irate tourists without a bus, I drove off, half fearing a bullet through my rear window. In my rearview mirror I saw Becky waving her pistol at her charges, apparently ordering them to pick up their cases and start walking.

I was now seriously late for work. It was past ten o'clock when I walked into my office, badly in need of a cup of coffee. 'Mr McKendrick wants to see you,' Myrah announced as I arrived. She believed it was unprofessional for secretaries to notice in any way the doings of the lawyers, and on this occasion, in all consistency, she refrained from commenting on my unprecedented lateness. I could have told her I'd been hijacked by a Barbie doll, but now that it was over, it lacked any kind of reality that I could have conveyed in the retelling.

So I just said, 'Oh dear. It would happen on the one day I'm late.'

'Well, Nicholas,' Mr McKendrick said, and paused. He was a man of few words, but the long pauses between them made up the time.

'Yes, Mr McKendrick,' I said, as brightly as possible. I had

216

never got over my schoolboy sense that being 'called in' meant at best a dressing-down, at worst a hiding, which was odd, given that I had been a model schoolboy and had never, as far as I can remember, been called in for punishment. Still, there was the perpetual possibility of error if not of misdemeanour, of displeasure if not of chastisement.

'Well, Nicholas,' Mr McKendrick said again. 'If I'm not mistaken you've been with us for close on five years, not so?' His tone did not allow for the possibility of his being mistaken, reinforced as it was by a glance at the information in front of him on his desk pad.

'That's right, sir. Five years in January. Started in 1992.'

'Yes,' he said, 'yes, I know,' and paused again. I wondered if it was incumbent upon me to express my appreciation or gratitude or whatever one expresses on the fifth anniversary of one's appointment, but decided to leave it to him.

'The long and the short of it,' he said eventually, 'is that the senior partners discussed your progress, and we all – or almost all,' – he did not dwell on the conscientious qualification, which I assumed to be Cedric Watts – 'agreed, more specifically in the light of your handling of the Rocklands case, you were the kind of person we would like to encourage to stay with us.'

I wondered what the difference was between *the kind of person* and *a person*, but all I said was, 'I'm very pleased about that, Mr McKendrick.'

'Yes,' he replied, pensively, 'yes, I hope you are. But to get to the point' – he looked at me as if I had been deliberately delaying the process of getting to the point – 'to get to the point, we thought it was time you were given a company car.'

He flushed gently as if he'd announced that the Millennium was about to break on us, but didn't want to take too much personal credit for it. I tried to look impressed, overwhelmed and grateful at the same time. Whereas I was in fact pleased at what was clearly intended as a vote of confidence, the idea of a company car wasn't quite as potent as Mr McKendrick evidently expected it to be. My little CitiGolf had its shortcomings, but I had looked after it well and I was comfortable enough in it: the trouble with driving wasn't my motorcar, it was other drivers.

'Well, that's … that's very gratifying, sir,' I said after a decent pause, into which he could read all the appropriate emotions, 'I hope I shall prove worthy of it.' This sounded phoney even to myself – how does one prove worthy of a company car? By not scratching the paintwork on the first day? By polishing the hubcaps? – but it seemed to satisfy Mr McKendrick.

'I'm sure you will,' he said gravely. 'You can collect the car this afternoon from Foreshore Motors.'

'You mean it's been bought?' I asked. I had imagined that I would be told to go and select a car, within a certain price range of course.

'Yes,' he said. 'We like to keep a certain consistency of profile in our vehicles. We've ordered you a BMW 316.'

'That's very handsome, sir,' I said. 'It's a much more … elegant car than I'd have selected for myself.'

I'd always had a suspicion that BMW drivers were people with image problems – they wanted a recognisable luxury car but they wanted to seem modest about it – and I couldn't quite imagine myself behind the wheel of a 316, but I could see that refusing, indeed anything short of radiant gratitude, would be taken as a slight, so I did my best to radiate gratitude as I listened to the details as to how and where I was to collect the car.

As I was leaving, Mr McKendrick stopped me, saying, 'Oh, Nicholas.' Silence.

'Yes, Mr McKendrick?'

'One more matter, in some senses perhaps in contradiction to what I've told you.'

So I was going to be reprimanded after all. He gestured at the chair that I had just vacated and I sat down again, doing what Gerhard calls my 'all ears and sincerity bit'.

'I should perhaps not be mentioning this to you so prematurely,' Mr McKendrick continued, having given me ten seconds to settle in my chair, 'and I rely on your discretion to keep it to yourself.' Another pause, about five seconds this time. 'The senior partners have for some time been considering opening a London office, to deal at first hand with the increasing volume of foreign business now that we, by which I mean our country, are once again an international presence.'

'Of course, Mr McKendrick,' I nodded, though I had no idea what I was agreeing with.

'And we were thinking – just thinking, mind you – that with your London training and your youth you might be just the person to open, as it were, the office for us.' He looked at me with the same kind of modest deprecation with which he had announced the bestowal of my car.

'That is very complimentary indeed, Mr McKendrick. Of course, it would be a wonderful opportunity ...'

He held up his hand as if to prevent the outpouring of indiscretions. 'No need to say anything at all now, Nicholas. Nothing may come of it after all, and even if it does, it will take some time. But I'm telling you so that *if* the scheme should come to fruition, *if* mind, you will not be mentally and spiritually unprepared. It would of course constitute a considerable promotion; but in return we should expect a corresponding commitment of some time, say at least five years.' He held up his hand again. 'No need to say anything at all now. Just bear it in mind as a possibility. Thank you, Nicholas. You may go.'

I phoned Gerhard to postpone an appointment I'd made with him for a drink after work. I told him about the car, though not about the London prospect, and we agreed on a celebratory supper in Observatory.

'Seven at the Obz Café?' he said.

'Seven at the Obz Café. Don't be late.'

'I'm never late – just delayed on occasion. Enjoy the new car.'

Buying a car proved to be easier than buying a hamburger: there were so many people making money out of the deal that my way was smoothed from start to finish. What about my own car? 'No problem, sir, we'll sell it for you; in fact, if you like we can treat it as a trade-in on this car and give you a cash cheque for the book value? That's probably simplest, then you can just leave the car here? Yes? In that case, just leave the keys with us – is that your front-door key, sir? Wouldn't do to leave that on the bunch, would it? Anything else you want to take out of the old jalopy? It's going to be quite a change for you, isn't it, from the little Golf to the Beem? Your car will be brought round to the forecourt momentarily, we've just been checking the last few details – wheels, engine, that sort of thing, ha ha. Cynthia will bring you a cup of coffee while you wait … Cynthia? Why don't you have a seat so long, sir, it won't be long.'

I took the proffered seat, an angularly shiny contraption of chrome and imitation leather, and helped myself to a booklet from a perspex container labelled 'Please Take One – The Life You Save May Be Your Own' – not so much because I thought I would be called upon to save my own life as because the only other reading matter was a free publication put out by the Auto Retailers for Christ ('Trade in Your Old Model for a Shiny New One – At Half the Price'). My life-saving booklet was entitled *Look Lively and Stay Alive: What You Must Know about Unauthorised Vehicle Appropriation (Car Hijacking)*. By the time I'd paged through it I was tempted to return my new high-risk ('appropriation-prone') BMW with its 'desirability quotient' of eight out of ten, and take back my appropriation-resistant CitiGolf which scored a humbling but reassuring two out of ten, according to a handy reference table in the back of the book ('Your Risk at a Glance'). I was also warned that 'violent appropriation of one's vehicle negatively colours the victim's disposition and attitude towards the State and other individuals, as well as impacting on the individual's productivity.' Clearly more was at stake here than a mere car.

In the event my Beem took rather more time to appear in the forecourt than originally predicted, and I was at leisure to make a thorough study of the dangers I was incurring, as well as the forlorn-sounding defences against loss of life and car (*Put your hand on the hooter and switch on your hazard warning lights.*) What the booklet made alarmingly clear was that there were any number of people out there, categorisable in terms of motive, method and degree of lethality, ready to nab my car, with me inside as an expendable accessory: the 'desperado', the contract hijacker, the shopper, the show-off … all they had in common was that they wanted my car and that they didn't much care what happened to me in the process. It seemed also that they were a touchy bunch, and should not be annoyed or inconvenienced at any cost (*Speaking too fast or swearing could be seen as an attempt to undermine your captor's position.*)

At last the Beem squelched into the forecourt, smelling powerfully of leather and rubber, a bit like my friend Gerhard after a successful night out. Getting into the ergonomically designed, all-leather driver's seat, I noticed that the mechanic had left a greasy handprint on the bonnet. In this time of slipping standards it was probably my duty to insist on the removal of the stain, but I didn't really have the stomach for another wait (I'd read the *Look Lively* booklet in detail by now); I knew I'd want to wash the car when I got home anyway.

On the way home I experimented with the unfamiliar range of controls: the air conditioning, the radio, the electrically controlled side mirrors, the adjustable seats. For once the slow crush on Settler's Way was quite bearable, even pleasant. My delight in the new car was spoiled slightly by the discovery that the same greasy-fingered mechanic had been fiddling with my radio (it had one of those fronts that one is supposed to remove to discourage people from stealing the radio), and left smudges all over the controls. But with the window closed and the air conditioning on and the radio playing (I used my handkerchief to push the buttons), the interior of the car created its own little environment, shut off from the fumes and fury of the road. I'd often wondered what it was that was excluded by 'exclusive' products: in this instance it was obviously the rest of sweating humanity. I twiddled the electrically controlled side-view mirrors; the battered Toyota behind me was too close to me, and I stepped on the brakes lightly to warn him to keep his distance. No fun in being tail-ended by an inferior brand on my first day out in the Beem.

In this car I could learn to love driving; for the first time in a very long while I noticed that the view from De Waal Drive, across the city and harbour, was very beautiful in the late summer afternoon. Mr McKendrick's other offer came back to me. He had called it 'premature', but I knew his caution well enough: he would not have mentioned it if it wasn't pretty much a certainty. I looked at the looming mountain and the peaceful sea: would I be prepared to leave this for London?

Arriving home, I drove onto the lawn next to the house, where I always washed my car, so as not to waste the water. I tried to look nonchalant, in case my neighbours were watching, but I needn't have bothered: there was nobody in sight. Only Tornado came bounding over from his little patch of grass outside his garden gate, ready for aggression or conciliation, it was never quite clear which.

I don't really mind dogs: I can see that people who need to be constantly reassured of their own indispensability and lovability can get this more easily and unconditionally from dogs than from other human beings. I suppose it's even possible to train dogs not to salivate all over one's best three-piece suit. But I don't want to spend much time in the company of a creature that is so naively convinced, in spite of so much evidence to the contrary, that the world is going to treat it well, that its next bone is just around the corner, and that its owner will return in the next five minutes to take it for a walk. Tornado's owners, a bright young couple called Stuart and Sharon, were in fact a pair of inveterate socialites who were hardly ever at home; their tired-looking baby, Samantha, the one for whose safety and security's sake they were planning to emigrate to Australia, went everywhere with them. On the rare occasions that they did come home, Tornado went into a frenzy of joy, a demonstration of blind affection profoundly depressing to more rational creatures who like to believe that affection should be expended roughly in proportion to deserts. If the meek really did inherit the earth, it would be a dog's world.

So, though I couldn't really begrudge Tornado the illusion that he was protecting his territory by bounding up to me every time I parked, or even his conviction that he had to extend his boundaries by marking my lawn with his leavings, I was careful not to encourage him to include me in his area of concern and protection. I didn't think I could meet the emotional expectations of a dog. I patted him in a deliberately perfunctory sort of way and said, 'It's all right, Tornado. I live here. And so does this car from now on.' He gave me a grudging prod with his nose, urinated on one of my gleaming alloy wheels, and went back to his spot on the sidewalk to await the always-imminent arrival of his owners.

222

I had time to clean the car thoroughly before going out to meet Gerhard; he wouldn't notice that it was clean, but he would certainly comment if it was dirty. I removed the face of the radio; I could clean it in my kitchen with ethyl alcohol. Rather self-consciously, though I still had no audience other than Tornado, I pressed the little button on the immobiliser, and marvelled at the prompt obedience with which the car uttered a little squeal of acknowledgement, flashed its lights and absorbed its door levers to make itself inaccessible to all but its legitimate owner. It seemed to establish a private under-standing between us, a relationship I never thought I would have with a vehicle. I pressed the button again, just to savour the promptness of the car's response, the brisk popping of its levers in alert anticipation of its owner's hand. I shut it down again, feeling slightly guilty at disappointing its manifest expectations, and went inside.

I changed into shorts and t-shirt, and found my car-washing equipment: the cloths, the sponges, the chamois and the sham-poo, everything that I had used (I thought with a twinge of conscience) to keep my little CitiGolf, now relegated to a used-car lot somewhere, looking its best. Arriving outside, I was struggling to connect the car-washing nozzle to the garden hose – one of those sticky Gardena fittings – when I felt some-thing jab me in the back. It was quite a hard jab, so my first response was annoyance rather than shock or surprise, but when I looked round, shock and surprise had it all their own way. The jab had come from an unpleasant-looking pistol in the hand of a young black man. I couldn't see much of his face, since he was wearing a baseball cap and a very large pair of sunglasses curving round his face like a windscreen, but what there was of it seemed to match the pistol in unpleasantness. A hijacker: obviously the desirability quotient of the Beem had conjured him up out of even the appropriation-resistant air of Pinelands.

'Right, man,' he said.

'Right?' I echoed. It sounded moronic even to myself.

'Right. Don't move.'

'If you say so,' I said, hoping this would not count as the backchat one was not supposed to give hijackers in case it annoyed them. (The booklet's advice came back to me with strange clarity: *Never talk back at your apprehenders; they're not in the game for the conversation.*) I wondered, though, what good I'd be doing him by remaining where I was. Still, he had the gun.

'Right,' he said, 'let's move.'

'Right,' I said, 'where to?' (*Always obey to the letter any command, after making sure that you've understood it.*)

'Don't be clever. Get into the car. Otherwise I shoot you.' I felt a jab in my back. I now had the choice between disobeying a command or talking back, since I still had the garden hose in my hand; nor could I simply put it down (*Refrain from making any unexpected movement that might be misinterpreted by your apprehender and cause him to panic.*) I opted for the potentially least lethal of the violations of hijacking etiquette, and asked, as unchallengingly as possible, 'Can I put down the hose pipe?'

'Yes,' he replied, and, clearly feeling that any concession might be considered weakness, stipulated, 'slowly.'

I slow-motioned the pipe into place, though it was tempting just to drop everything and run. I felt very vulnerable as I came to my full length again. Another jab in the back.

'Quick,' he said, 'get in the car.'

I obediently but very slowly walked across to the passenger door. There was a battered Toyota parked against the kerb, with someone in the driver's seat (*Be aware that hijackers almost never operate alone*). So they'd followed me from the highway while I was fiddling with all my new gadgets. (*Don't allow anything to distract your attention from your driving and your environment.*)

'Other door,' he commanded. 'You drive.' He followed me as I went round to the driver's door. I pulled at the handle, but it yielded flaccidly, with no interest in engaging the catch: I'd locked the door when I went into the house.

'It's locked,' I said lamely.

'So unlock it,' he said.

'The key's in the house,' I replied.

'Fuck,' he said.

'I'm sorry.' (*NEVER lose your temper.*)

224

There was moment of irresolution while he wondered whether to shoot me.

'Get it,' he said.

'Get the key?' I asked.

'What else?' he asked. 'Move.'

I moved, but very slowly. Walking away from a loaded pistol takes almost as much courage as walking towards it. (*Never give the impression that you're running away.*) I made my wary way towards the side door to my house and was almost there when he said sharply: 'Hey! Stop!'

I stopped dead. (*Obey all commands promptly; don't try to play the hero, you may not live to collect the reward.*)

'I'm not stupid,' he said. 'You think you can get away like that?'

I'd not even thought that far; in fact, I would probably have collected the keys and brought them out without considering my opportunities. I was every hijacker's dream victim.

'Wait,' he said, 'I'll go with you.' I stood still until I felt the by now familiar, almost reassuring, nudge in the small of my back, and led the way into my own house.

'Where's the key?' he demanded. 'Get the key.'

Normally my car keys, like everything else in my home, have their place – in their case, inside the drawer of the hall-stand.

'It's in there.' I pointed in slow motion at the hallstand. 'In the drawer.' (*Never make any unexpected movement that could be interpreted as reaching for a weapon.*)

'Open it,' he said. Nudge.

I opened the drawer. There was the extra front door key, my gardening gloves, the face of the radio, and my loose change for parking meters and beggars; but no key.

'It's not there,' I said, more flustered by this than by anything else that had happened to me so far. My car keys were always in that drawer.

'Find them. Quick.' Prod. 'Otherwise I shoot you.' (*Above all, don't panic.*)

I had heard of people losing keys, and could never understand how they came to do so: after all, if you put your keys in a sensible place, they are invariably there when you need them.

I was now at a disadvantage, having no experience of looking for keys or anything else for that matter. In my experience, things were where I'd put them. How does one start looking for something that could theoretically be anywhere, given that they weren't where they were supposed to be?

'I don't know where they are,' I confessed, helplessly. The change in routine, the excitement of the new car, must have made me lose track of my movements; or otherwise my automatic routine-sequence-checker had registered the face of the radio as the keys.

'Find them,' he said. 'Look for them.' Nudge.

I made my way back to the kitchen, where I'd collected the cloths and sponges. The clean, open surfaces had nothing to hide or declare; there was not a foreign object in sight. My own tidiness had never seemed so barren to me.

'Not here,' I said, redundantly.

'Don't play the fool. Find the keys.'

'Right,' I said brightly, trying to remember where else I'd been. Had I gone to the loo? Yes, I had.

'Right,' I repeated, 'follow me.' As if he wouldn't.

I led the way to the toilet next to the entrance hall.

'They may be in here,' I said, not very hopefully.

Nudge. 'Look.'

I went in, closely followed by the gun in my back. Nothing; the hand towel was slightly crumpled from my drying my hands on it; otherwise no sign of my brief visit.

Nudge. 'Don't play the fool. Otherwise I shoot you. You must find the key.' Prod. There was a desperate edge to his voice; obviously he had almost as much invested as I in my finding the key. Almost.

'Listen,' I tried to explain, 'I'm sorry. I just don't know where I put the keys. I just came home and got undressed …' I stopped. 'Follow me,' I said again, and led the way to my bedroom. It occurred to me that this was the first time I'd ever led anyone to my bedroom. It was also likely to be the last.

My bedroom was as tidy as it always was, with nothing on any surface that could hide a key. My shirt and socks were in the laundry basket; my office suit was in the wardrobe where I always hung it when I took it off … Ah.

226

'I think the key is in my jacket pocket,' I said. 'Inside the cupboard.'

'Open it. But no funny business. Otherwise I shoot you.' Nudge.

There was a loud tweet and *Nkosi Sikelel' iAfrika* erupted jauntily somewhere next to my left kidney. I refrained for all I was worth from making a sudden movement.

'Wait,' he commanded. He rummaged in his jacket pocket (*Hijackers often wear bulky jackets in which they hide a weapon*); there was a fumble and click (*Never look round at your apprehender; he will think you are memorising his appearance*) and he started talking in rapid Xhosa into a cell phone. (*Pay close attention to all conversations between apprehenders, without being obtrusive.*) My close attention was rendered less useful by the fact that I can't understand a word of Xhosa, but my apprehender's tone sounded deferential, anxious, explanatory, even ingratiating. (*Hijackers often work for superior operators.*)

He switched off the phone. 'Hurry. Find the key or I shoot you.' I opened the cupboard and felt in the inner pocket of my jacket. I caught myself praying, against all my rational impulses, that the keys would be there; to my immense relief I heard the compact little jingle of the set of car keys and felt the bulge of the immobiliser.

'Here it is,' I announced, producing the keys and holding them out in my open palm. (*Never take any initiative. It may be interpreted as aggression.*) He took them with his left hand. 'Quick,' he commanded, 'my friends are in a hurry.'

We made our combined way to the car; at the front door I paused, wondering whether to lock it, then reflected that if I ever did come back to my house I wouldn't have my front door keys with me, since they were now on the same bunch as the car keys. So I just closed the door behind me and walked to the car. He zapped the central locking system and the door levers obediently popped open, exactly as they had done for me. So much for the beautiful relationship. I reflected bitterly that the one thing the car couldn't do was tell when it was being hijacked.

'Get in and drive to Khayelitsha,' he instructed, and gave me the keys. 'And no funny business. Otherwise I shoot. And my friend will follow us.'

He glanced at the battered Toyota, which was revving its engine ominously. For the first time since I'd lived there I cursed the determined non-interference of Pinelands with its neighbours; nobody seemed to notice that there was a hijacking going on in broad daylight. Even Tornado was lying in his customary spot, quite impervious to this threat to his neighbourhood. I called down an earthquake upon their suburban complacency.

'Quick,' my hijacker said again. He was sweating profusely, more than the heat of the day merited: he was nervous; more nervous probably than I. (Of course: *Remember that your apprehender is probably more nervous than you are.*) After all, I had no responsibility for the events; I was there simply to do as I was told. I noticed that his shoelace was undone, but that he couldn't risk bending to tie it. There was a kind of security in this, oddly compatible with a general conviction that I was probably going to end the day being shot and thrown into a ditch (*Last year there were 8 740 hijackings in South Africa, of which only 1% ended in a fatal shooting* – which still meant 87.4 dead people).

I reversed into the street and pulled off. The battered Toyota followed. In the rear-view mirror I could see another baseball cap and dark glasses. I drove out on Forest Drive towards the motorway, and took the N2 to Guguletu, a passenger in my own car, if by passenger is meant an occupant not in control of the destination. Yes, Mr McKendrick, thank you very much, Mr McKendrick, London would be wonderful, Mr McKendrick.

I noticed the hijacker had taken a slip of paper from his pocket and was consulting it.

'This is a BMW 316, right?' he asked.

'Right,' I replied.

'Latest model?'

'Very latest. Bought today,' I added bitterly.

'With aircon?'

'Check,' I said sardonically.

'Check?'

'I mean yes.'

He checked his list.

'Radio-tape deck?'

'Yes,' I said, pointing to the empty face of the radio cavity. 'But the control panel is not there.'

'Not there?' he asked, 'Where is it?'

'At home,' I replied. 'I took it out so it shouldn't get stolen. Funny when you think about it.'

But he was not amused. (*Don't attempt to joke with your apprehenders.*) 'Stop,' he snapped at me.

The traffic had subsided from its peak-hour frenzy, and we were driving at a fairly comfortable 60 kilometres per hour.

'Stop?' I repeated. 'You mean here in the middle of the road?' I was in the middle lane. (This was a violation of the rule not to talk back – but surely there was a limit to the deference due to a hijacker's sensibilities?)

'No,' he said. 'Don't be stupid. Turn round.'

'Turn ROUND?' I exclaimed, throwing caution and etiquette to the winds. 'You mean make a U-turn in the middle of a three-lane highway?'

'I said don't be stupid,' he repeated. 'Go back home. I must have the radio.'

'If you say so,' I said.

'I don't say so,' he said, 'this paper says so.'

'A Christmas shopping list?'

'Yes. Instructions.' He made it sound almost grand. (*Many hijackers work to fill export orders for specific makes and models.*)

'By whom?' I asked, genuinely curious.

'The boss,' he said.

'You don't work for yourself?'

'Not yet. I learn first. This is my first job. If I do it wrong –' he left the statement in the air, but drew his finger across his throat in eloquent demonstration. Twice in one day I had been threatened with death by novices anxious about losing their jobs. The work ethic was clearly not as dead as pessimists feared. It was a pity, though, that I seemed destined not to survive along with the work ethic. I had never been a wildly popular person, but nor had I ever, as far as I knew, inspired the kind of unprovoked hatred both my hijackers had seemed to feel for me. (The booklet had the answer even to this: *Remember that your apprehender will have psyched himself up into extreme antipathy against you.*)

229

'An apprenticeship?' I asked, in an attempt to lighten the atmosphere; I do believe I wanted him to *like* me. (*Attempt to initiate dialogue in a calm and rational manner. This may have a calming effect on a tense apprehender.*) But he only frowned and said, 'Don't ask so many fucking questions.' (Quite right: *Don't ask questions.*)

'Go home,' he said. 'I must have the radio. What must I tell the boss?'

'I don't know,' I said. 'I'm just the driver.' It seemed a bit much that I was being expected to advise my hijacker on how to hijack me.

'Shut up!' he snarled. (*Do not make any comment that could be interpreted as a comment on the hijacker's performance. You don't want to push him to demonstrate his cool.*) He took out his cell phone and dialled – punched – a number. In my rear-view mirror I could see the driver of the Toyota put his cell phone to his ear. There was a rapid conversation; my hijacker, as I was starting to think of him, seemed nervous and defensive; I could see the other man gesticulating angrily, and the conversation came to what was clearly an unsatisfactory close. But my hijacker just said, 'Back to Pinelands,' and watched bleakly as I took the Goodwood East turn-off and the Toyota rattled past us. He licked his lips nervously and said, pointlessly, 'Quick.' I reflected that I was going to be very late for my supper with Gerhard, and then it occurred to me that being dead meant not turning up for supper, unless you were Banquo or the Commendatore. Perhaps this was what Gerhard meant by *getting a life*.

Pinelands was as we had left it. Even Tornado was still lying in the same spot. He put up his ears and frowned at us as we drove past, not recognising the new car, then relapsed into patient expectation. I drew up outside the house.

'Drive in,' he said.

I obeyed, and parked next to the car-washing equipment that I now seemed destined never to use.

'Go and fetch the radio.'

I reached towards the door lever; only to be stopped by a prod in my ribs.

'You think I'm stupid. I'm coming with you.'

He got out and slammed the door, pointing the pistol at me in what I thought was a dangerously casual manner. He was starting to relax rather too much into his own possession of a dangerous weapon. He stumbled slightly; he must have tripped over his shoelace. 'No funny business,' he warned, as he bent to tie his shoelace.

There was a blur of movement and he disappeared from sight as if he had been knocked flat by a passing helicopter.

I jumped out of the car, mainly to get its bulk between myself and his no doubt irritated trigger finger. If the booklet was to be trusted, this was the kind of thing that really upset hijackers. Peering over the car I saw Tornado planted squarely on the hijacker's back breathing threats into his ear and drooling down his neck, having performed what must have been one of his more spectacular flying tackles. The young man was lying very still, his baseball cap a few metres away, his dark glasses knocked askew on his nose, and, I was relieved to note, his pistol lying out of reach on the lawn.

I had no idea how long Tornado could be relied upon to keep his man pinned down, so, though I was extremely reluctant to do so (*NEVER handle a gun if you don't know how to use it*), I did what innumerable films had taught me to be the done thing under the circumstances: I picked up the pistol and pointed it at the hijacker.

'Get up,' I ordered, hoping my voice sounded more in command of the situation than I felt.

'I can't,' he replied. 'The dog is standing on me.'

'Okay, Tornado,' I said, trying to sound as if I was used to ordering calf-sized bull mastiffs around. 'That's a good dog. You can down now.'

To my extreme surprise Tornado meekly obeyed, though he hung around in a reassuringly belligerent way. I mentally nominated him for one of those awards one occasionally sees dogs and cats getting for feats of bravery and intelligence, and waved the pistol at my hijacker in what I hoped was a convincing way.

Without his cap and glasses, and at the other end of a gun barrel, he looked shockingly young, little more than a child. (*Hijackers are often very young; this is their entry into a life of crime.*) I thought of my friend Gerhard's saying, 'If there's anything I'm scared of, it's a child with power,' which, coming from Gerhard who seemed afraid of nothing, carried some weight; and I hardened my heart against a fleeting impulse of pity for this boy who had just messed up his first job.

'Get up,' I commanded, 'and no funny business. Otherwise I shoot you.' I was perturbed to discover that I felt quite capable of executing this threat, once I had uttered it. I knew, with an icy kind of clarity, that I could easily, even happily, kill this boy and regard it as a good day's work; and it would not be an act of cold justice, either, but the execution of an irrational, murderous, near-sexual urge. I hated him for what he had done and had intended to do to me, and probably would still do in the life he had chosen for himself. I wanted him dead, and I had the means to kill him with impunity. What was to prevent me? As the boy came to his feet he put up his hands; they were trembling. I felt a stirring in my groin as my finger touched the trigger.

Tornado was watching me with a puzzled frown. What, I found time to wonder, had prevented *him* from tearing the boy to pieces? And at what point of our evolution into the supreme species had humans lost that inhibition? And, absurdly, I realised that I couldn't kill this boy in front of Tornado: it would be like committing a murder in front of a child.

So I said, 'Come with me and don't do anything I don't tell you to do. I can't answer for my actions.' I don't think he understood what I meant, but it was necessary for me to say it out loud, and fortunately for both of us he obeyed me to the letter. I marched him inside and phoned the police. (*Dial 10111 immediately.*) They arrived very promptly and removed him efficiently, not to say brutally (*The South African Police Services are determined to wipe out this cold-blooded onslaught on our lives and property*), having secured without very much trouble the identities and location of his collaborators.

They drove off, forgetting to collect the gun I had put down once the boy was securely handcuffed. I'd have to go and hand it in – just holding it had taught me that people didn't carry guns because they wanted to kill: they wanted to kill because they carried guns. But that could wait: I was going to be very late for my dinner appointment with Gerhard. I locked the gun in my wall safe, which contained nothing else except my passport. Passport and pistol – the New South African's survival kit. Then I showered and changed and once again got into the Hijacker's Delight. It felt as if I had been driving it all my life. On the seat, forlorn, was the hijacker's cell phone. I'd get Gerhard to show me how to activate it; after all, I was entitled to some compensation for my discomfort.

As I drove out, Tornado's owners arrived home. Stuart and Sharon waved at me unexuberantly, making insincere big eyes at the new car. Tornado went into a supercharged version of his glad-you're-back routine, trying to tell them that he'd pinned down a hijacker today. 'No, Tornado,' said Stuart, as he closed the gate. 'Don't jump up.' Sharon patted the dog perfunctorily. Samantha baby looked at me wanly, with black rings of exhaustion under her eyes: social life was getting her down. Things were back to normal.

I drove to Observatory slowly. I was three-quarters of an hour late, but that now seemed completely unimportant. I felt as if the world owed me a vote of thanks for just being *alive*. Then I almost drove into a lamppost as *Nkosi Sikelel' iAfrika* struck up peremptorily at my side. I picked up the cell phone, and pressed the little green telephone. An angry burst of Xhosa greeted me.

'Sorry, wrong number,' I said and switched off the phone.

In the Obz Café Gerhard was sitting alone at a table, looking slightly the worse for the bottle of wine he'd nearly finished. 'So what the fuck detained you?' he demanded. He was thoroughly irritated, I was gratified to note. 'Aren't you supposed to be obsessively punctual?'

I smiled. 'I got held up,' I said.

CHAPTER TEN

I have a temperamental aversion to gossip. Valuing my own privacy as I do, I shrink from invading the privacy of others with impertinent speculations, irrelevant information and salacious confidences. My friend Gerhard, on the other hand, maintains that gossip is all that modern society has retained of the old sense of community. 'Your squeamishness about gossip is not half as high-minded as you think: it's half based on your *pudeur* about your own affairs and half on your callous indifference to the affairs of others.'

But whether for high-minded superiority to petty gossip or for a prudish sense of privacy, I had no desire for the story of my hijacking to become a talking point around the coffee machine at McKendrick, Jolly, Wirthenburger, Smith, Watts and Koekemoer. Apart from anything else, it was bound to give rise to a certain degree of *Schadenfreude* amongst those of my colleagues who had not been given a company car: for some reason connected with people's desire to think themselves invulnerable, they tend to regard victims of hijackings as in some way *deserving* the experience, *asking for it* by driving around in ostentatious cars beyond their means. I know, because that is what I thought before it happened to me.

'I don't want to be the subject of one of Kitty Jooste's dramatic narratives,' I said to Gerhard, 'so please keep the story to yourself.'

'I still think you're depriving the community of their legitimate spoils, but if you really don't want me to, I won't say a word.'

'I really don't want you to.'

And that should have been the end of that, except that the police found they had neglected to take a full statement from me, and turned up in full force at my office – that is, two of them turned up, and while one was taking my statement, the other told Myrah the whole story, or as much of it as he knew, supplemented by what he wanted to believe. By the time the police left, half of McKendrick, Jolly, Wirthenburger, Smith, Watts and Koekemoer was telling the other half how I had single-handedly, with the help of my trained dog, apprehended four hijackers. This might have been gratifying to my vanity if the story had not inspired such evident incredulity: 'Nick *Morris!*' I heard one of my colleagues exclaim. 'I didn't think he could *fart* at a hijacker, never mind apprehend four of them.'

This generally unflattering astonishment continued unabated for a day or so, and then settled into a comfortable communal conviction that the hijackers had been inordinately stupid. 'You won't believe how stupid some of them are,' Kitty Jooste assured her morning audience at the coffee machine. 'I swear, they're just so *thick*, you won't believe it.'

'How do you know, Kitty?' Dikeledi asked in her most sweetly interested manner. 'How many hijackers have you had dealings with?'

'Oh, none myself, thank God, but there's this woman, she's a good friend of a friend of mine, and she had this experience you won't *believe*. She was driving along minding her own business, and then she stopped at a robot, you know the one there by Ottery, to buy a newspaper, and she'd hardly opened her window when this … well, this *man* stuck a gun into the car and told her to get out and hand over the keys. Now you can imagine what kind of a state she was in, so when she tries to undo her safety belt she presses the button by accident, the one that closes the window, I should have mentioned before she had electric windows, and the next minute the bugger is screaming bloody murder and his hand is stuck in the window like a mouse in a trap and he drops the gun into her lap.' Kitty looked at her rapt audience over her coffee cup, secure in the knowledge that she could pause for effect without being upstaged. 'Right in her lap, I swear to God, like a hot potato.'

'I hope she shot the bastard,' Cedric Watts said.

'No she did not, she was too stunned, I can tell you. But what happened next you won't believe. Four black men get out of a car parked behind her, and they take hold of the hijacker and signal to her to let him go, and you can imagine she's now nipping wholesale, but she reckons she's got flip-all choice, and she presses the button again and these four men take hold of the bugger who's now screaming more than ever, and without so much as a by your leave they shoot him right there, dead as a doornail, and leave him on the pavement and get back into their car and drive off. And she's got a pistol on her lap, so when the police rock up eventually they think she did it and she's held for questioning but fortunately the gun hadn't been used recently so they believed her and released her. But it just goes to show,' she said, recalling the point of her story, 'how bloody stupid these hijackers are.'

As I walked away from the coffee machine, I was mulling on a rather different moral – how permeated our lives had become with violence, when every urban legend featured some gruesome encounter with potential death. 'Whatever happened to the urban legends about couples getting trapped behind the steering wheel while having sex?' I demanded from Gerhard. 'Nowadays somebody would hijack the car from under them. However far-fetched some of these stories are, they reflect the state of mind of the country.'

'What country? What mind? They reflect the state of funk of a few whites, that's all.'

'And as one of those few whites, aren't you in a state of funk?'

'No, absolutely not. Of course there are dangers, there are dangers anywhere ...'

'Not to the same extent as here.'

'Perhaps so, but if you're going to go through life scared, you can be scared in ... in London of dying in a fire in a tube station or in Sydney of ... dying of Aids ...'

'Except you're much more likely to die in a fire or of Aids right here than in London or Sydney.' We were in my office now, and I lowered my voice so as not to be overheard by Myrah: discreet as she was, she seldom missed a morsel of information. 'And I must tell you, after my little brush with the new highwaymen, I'm very tempted by McKendrick's offer of opening the new office in London.'

He sat down on my desk. 'You're not serious.'

'I am, Gerhard. Why should I stay here and feel insecure for the rest of my days, and on top of that feel guilty about feeling insecure?'

'Because you stayed here in spite of feeling guilty when the whites were in charge and murdering people to safeguard your traditional way of life.'

'So because I didn't emigrate at the age of 20, I'm totally committed to staying in this country whatever happens to it?'

'Perhaps not whatever happens. But at this stage, yes.'

'What's the point? What's the point of working hard and being given a company car in recognition and having it stolen the same day?'

'You don't work hard to be given a company car.'

'Well it's a … a symbol of everything you work for that can be taken away from you by anybody with a gun. Listen. I don't think I'm ever going to convince you. But I'm telling you as a friend that I'm considering Mr McKendrick's offer – not that it's really an offer as yet anyway – and even if you don't agree with what I'm doing, I'd be grateful if you didn't mention it to anybody else.'

He got up. 'Of course I won't mention it. It's not as if the story gives me any pleasure.'

I tried to concentrate on my work. I wasn't happy with Gerhard's refusal to see my point of view, but I was perhaps even less happy with my own doubts about my intentions. In any case, I kept telling myself, probably nothing would come of the idea of a London office; I was agonising over a decision I'd never be called upon to make.

It occurred to me that I hadn't told Leonora about my little adventure. Not that I was eager to do so – she would find in it confirmation of every pathetic hope she'd ever cherished that I'd turn out to be a hero after all, instead of the nerd she secretly suspected me of being. I never knew whether I was most irritated by the heroic hopes or the nerdic suspicions. I reached for the telephone, steeling myself for another lunch at Michelangelo's; but before I could pick it up, it rang. It was Leonora.

'What a coincidence,' I said, realising that it sounded a bit

237

feeble, even though for once it was true, 'I was just going to phone you.' She very rarely phoned me at work.

'Were you? That's nice.' Leonora sounded genuinely pleased. It was one of the temptations of a relationship with her, that she absolutely believed everything I said. It almost seemed like a waste, that I didn't have anything to hide from her, except possibly my doubts about our relationship.

'Yes. I thought we might have lunch.'

'That would be nice.' Again she sounded as if she actually meant it. 'But I was phoning you about an invitation – from Andrew Conroy.'

'Oh?' I was torn between pleasure at the invitation and resentment at its coming through Leonora. 'To what?'

'To his house. For lunch. Next Sunday.'

'Sounds good. What did you say?'

'I said I'd ask you.'

'But what do you think, then? Shall we go?'

'Oh yes, if … if you think we should.'

'I don't think we *should*, but I think it might be enjoyable.' There was, of course, the fact that I had won a court case against his friend and business associate; but I couldn't see that it need bother me if it didn't bother him. Indeed, the invitation was probably intended to signal Conroy's intention not to take sides in the dispute.

'Then I'll phone him back. He said I should.'

Andrew Conroy lived in Kalk Bay, a pleasantly old-fashioned relic of an English presence at the Cape: modest but substantial stone houses dug in against the slope of the mountain, looking down on the little harbour and the railway line. The place had been spared the characterless ranch-style epidemic of the sixties by the fact that the steep slope wouldn't accommodate its wasteful sprawl, and it had escaped the ravages of the high-rise blocks by never being fashionable enough to tempt developers: situated on the eastern slope of the peninsula, it lost the sun too early in the afternoon to appeal to the kind of people who bought flats in high-rise blocks next to the sea. The people who lived here did not cultivate suntans or have square sun-shades in front of their houses; they did not own four-wheel-drive vehicles or satellite dishes. The general effect was one of unostentatious but reassuring solidity.

We arrived in a light drizzle, more a kind of luminous mist than real rain, which contributed to the un-African gentleness of the surroundings. Conroy's house was next to the fishing harbour, one of the few houses directly on the sea. Like many in the area, it was a very simple stone house, and had been built before the vogue for large windows, although a veranda running round the house provided all the opportunity one needed to enjoy the panorama of mountain and sea. It was a house that could enjoy its environment without trying to dominate it. Conroy was in his garden when we arrived, an understated growth of indigenous grasses and shrubs. He was looking more relaxed, less dressed than when we'd seen him at lunch, though he was as meticulously neat as always, even in the light waterproof jacket and jeans he was wearing. He shook my hand rather formally, and put his arm briefly around Leonora's shoulder, giving her a light hug.

'Come in,' he said, and led the way into what was clearly the main room, a large, informal space stretching from the back of the house to the front. Through the relatively small apertures in the thick walls one had framed views of the harbour, the coastline, the rocks, faraway Cape Hangklip. The furniture was old but comfortable: club easy chairs, a large floppy sofa in front of a fireplace. A music stand perched in one corner, a cello case leaning against the wall next to it. On one wall was an oil painting that I guessed to be by Joyce Tomlinson: again the beach at Rocklands, but this time at sunset, and without any human figures.

The lunch was as relaxed and yet choice as everything else in the house, much of it cooked by Conroy while we sat around in the large kitchen adjoining the main room: a risotto made with dried porcini he had picked in winter in a spot known only to himself but which he promised he'd bequeath to us in his will, a chicken dish that Leonora recognised, from her course in Italian cooking, as a *pollo in potacchio*, for dessert a *zabaglione*.

'Do you always cook Italian?' I asked him.

'No, by no means. Only when I'm cooking for friends.'

'You don't cook for enemies, surely?'

Instead of laughing at my pleasantry, he looked serious. 'I can't always choose my guests. So yes, I may have fed an enemy or two in my day.' He consciously lightened his tone. 'For my enemies, I cook British.'

I had wondered slightly apprehensively whether an extended conversation with Andrew Conroy might not turn into a series of short or even long lectures on his pet topics; he had struck me as prone to elaborate theories which required expounding on his part and intelligent attention on the part of his auditors. But, although it remained true that there were few phenomena, from the behaviour of dogs in the rain to the incidence of the word *ardent* in George Eliot, which he did not enquire into with a possibly excessive minuteness, he was also too good a host or too tactful a human being to impose his theories on a passive or mute audience. He invited, encouraged, *demanded* participation. The surprising thing about his conversation was not only, as I had noted before, that he elicited more opinions from Leonora that I had known her to possess, but that he placed her and me in a totally new relation, one in which we exchanged views like equals, indeed one in which she was in most respects the better informed. This was not an entirely flattering new light for me to be bathed in, but it certainly enhanced Leonora's appeal.

Conversation ranged in a desultory fashion from literature (he shared Leonora's enthusiasm for *Middlemarch* but disliked the Romantic poets), through the new government (he was more optimistic than either Leonora or I about the country's prospects under the ANC), wine (he and Leonora differed on the relative merits of Chardonnay and Sauvignon Blanc), dogs (I told them about Tornado, and Conroy said that he found dogs too abject to serve as companions), and films (we disagreed at length on *Forrest Gump*, *The Remains of the Day*, and *Pulp Fiction*, the favourites respectively of Leonora, myself and Conroy), to crime (he thought that crime had not increased as violently as sensational reporting was making it seem).

My friend Gerhard has a theory that any conversation conducted in a room with a child in it will sooner or later turn to children. By the same rule, a conversation conducted in a room with a cello in it is bound to turn to music. It is not a topic to which I am averse, any more than Gerhard is to the topic of children, but since I am – to pursue the analogy – about as unlikely ever to make music myself as Gerhard is to beget children, my interest is that of a benign outsider rather than a practising or prospective participant. Leonora, who had 'done music' at school, asked Conroy about the cello.

'Yes,' he said, 'it was always one of my life's ambitions to play the cello – it's to me the most beautiful of the instruments. So I took it up about ten years ago.'

'Do you play on your own or as part of a group?'

'Oh, on my own. I was part of a string quartet at one stage, but I found I got impatient; it's bad enough coping with your own mistakes without having to put up with those of others. I don't think I'm a quartet person.'

'Is there enough music for solo cello to keep you going?' I asked, though I would rather have asked him about his impatience with quartets. He had not struck me as an impatient person.

'Oh, yes. Apart from anything else, there are the Bach suites, which are enough to keep me going for the rest of my life.' He became more animated, less ironic as he entered into the topic. 'They are the most complete and inexhaustible expression I know of the principle of controlled passion – you know, the equilibrium between feeling and restraint.' He hesitated and said, to me rather than to Leonora, 'But these are words, words, words. One day you must come round and I shall play you the Suite No 5.'

'I'd love that,' I said, gratified at this unexpected intimacy.

'I find, don't you,' Conroy said to Leonora, 'the cello has the warmth and life of the human voice, but abstracted beyond words and beyond personal feeling? Don't you find that most adult voices are impure?'

Leonora blushed lightly, as even the mention of impurity made her do. 'Are you thinking of opera?' she asked. Leonora was very fond of opera.

'Mainly opera, yes. Not all opera, of course, but yes, I think the large, overblown Austrian-Italian operas *are* impure. I don't mean they're indecent, though it's surprising how much

241

adultery manages to get committed in opera; I mean they're at odds with themselves, torn.'

'But torn between what and what?' Leonora asked.

'Between, let us say, anorexia and bulimia, the impulse to denial and the impulse to excess. All those consumptive heroines, all those massive tenors, whinging and bingeing on their contradictory impulses – *o passione, o passione,* warble the hollow-eyed sopranos, *o pasta, o pasticcino* roar the fat-bellied tenors ...' Conroy was slipping into the mode that I had learnt to recognise, a state of mind in which he generated ideas as much to explore what he was thinking as to generate discussion. 'It's a form of decadence, I think. All decadent music is torn between two extremes, a kind of spiritual gluttony and a kind of death wish, Mario Lanza dying of an overdose of pasta, Dame Nellie Melba lubricating her throat before a performance with the semen of 16-year-old boys.'

Leonora looked faintly ill – we were eating *zabaglione* at this stage – and even I was at a loss for words.

'Or so the legend runs,' Conroy continued. 'It doesn't matter whether it's true or not, it illustrates the extravagance, the *spending* on which opera feeds.'

'But isn't all music torn between extremes?' Leonora asked. 'The beauty of music is that it is ... transient, that we experience it and then it is gone.'

'True; but that is more of a creative tension than a contradiction. In its simplest form I'm talking about the banality of the plots undermining the aspirations to sublimity of the music. The orchestra soars, the soprano takes off, and all she can come up with is that one fine day that fat dummy of a Pinkerton will return to her, because that's what the plot and the words and the physical appearance of most tenors condemn her to. To be truly pure, music should have no words, or at most the stripped-down formulae of religious ritual.'

He went to a cupboard in the corner and opened it. Inside was a sound system and several shelves of records and CDs. He selected a disc and put it on the player.

'Listen,' he said. 'Music that is not torn.'

After a few minutes he said, 'Do you know it?'

I shook my head, well out of my depth. Having grown up

with *The White Cliffs of Dover* and *We'll gather lilacs in the spring*, I knew only as much about music as Gerhard had taught me. Leonora said 'Is it Fauré's Requiem?'

'It is indeed. The Lullaby of Death.'

'But there are words, too, in that' – Leonora pointed to the loudspeaker as if it were the music – 'only they're always the same.'

'Exactly; the music expresses a universal truth, not an individual yearning. There are no stars, no prima donnas, no million-dollar fees for appearances on soccer fields. There is only the pure musical line and the ritual formula.' He hummed with the music: *'Requiem aeternam dona eis domine, Et lux perpetua luceat eis.'*

'Are you religious?' I asked.

'Absolutely not. Christianity has become a form of popular entertainment run by bad actors. But the old formulae do express an impersonal truth, an *acceptance*, you see, of death not as some kind of lurid mistake of one's love life. Fauré said he saw death as *une aspiration au bonheur dans l'au-delà*, an aspiration towards happiness in the beyond.'

'I like Schubert lieder,' said Leonora, I thought somewhat inconsequentially, 'they're not overblown.' For myself, I thought we had pretty much covered the musical field; but Conroy followed up the unexpected tangent of the Schubert lieder with the alacrity, I realised, of somebody starved for argument.

'I grant you that,' said Conroy, leaning forward to Leonora, 'but then, isn't there something neurotic in the eternal, obsessive *sehnsucht* of the German lieder? All that yearning? Less self-absorbed, I grant you, than the plangent *tristesse, toujours tristesse* of the French chanson, but ultimately still an elevation of the emotions as the measure of all things.' He paused, thinking about what he had just said, then continued, 'That is; if you're talking of the Schubert of the *Winterreise* or the *Schöne Müllerin*, with their absurd exaggeration of love-sickness into tragedy, sublime music wasted on trivial emotion. Dying of love – it's at best an absurd idea, at worst pathetic.'

He sounded almost angry; but then, as neither Leonora nor I leapt to the defence of dying of love, he relaxed and his face assumed its more normal expression of animated engagement. 'Ah, but if you're talking about the Schubert of *Der Tod und das Mädchen* ... that's another thing altogether.' He turned to Leonora and intoned in a dark monotone: '*Bin Freund, und komme nich zu strafen. Sei gutes Muts! Ich bin nicht wild, Sollst sanft in meinen Armen schlafen!*'

Leonora shivered. She knew German from school and university. As for me, I didn't understand a word. 'That's dreadful,' she said. 'Very beautiful, but dreadful.'

'No,' Andrew corrected her, 'not dreadful – awful, that is, inspiring awe.'

'What does it mean?' I asked Leonora.

'It means,' she answered hesitantly, looking at Andrew, 'I come as a friend, not to punish – Be of – *gutes Muts* – good courage, I'm not ... not wild, not cruel, you will sleep softly in mine arms.'

'Excellent!' said Andrew. 'Now *that* – that is the proper way of seeing death – not as some messy accident of one's personal emotional life, woe is me, I'm going to die because the miller's daughter has dropped me – but as a great strategist, a stern friend, even a demanding lover, as *inevitable*.'

He turned to me. 'In *Erlkönig* ... do you know *Erlkönig*?'

'No,' I said. 'My ignorance of music is considerable.'

'You will learn,' he said. 'In any case, in *Erlkönig*, you see, the father is riding home one stormy night with his son in his lap, and the terrified boy hears the Erlking talking to him, singing to him, pleading with him, enticing him – *Du liebes Kind, komm, geh mit mir!* he says to the terrified boy, *Gar schöne Spiele spiel' ich mit dir* ... – You lovely child, come, go with me, and I'll play wondrous games with you' – Conroy, directing the German at Leonora and the translation at me almost intimately, entered eerily into the persona of an insinuating tempter. 'And then yet later, *Ich liebe dich, mich reizt deine schöne Gestalt* – I love you, your beautiful form entices me ... *Und bist du nicht willig, so brauch' ich Gewalt* – and if you're not willing, I'll take you by force.' For a brief moment, as he pronounced the last phrase, his gaze locked in mine.

'But that's ... that's rape,' said Leonora, and blushed.

Conroy relaxed the intensity of his impersonation into his

more academic, almost pedantic manner. 'Strictly speaking, yes, but you must remember that the boy alone can see the Erlking, in a sense *wills* the Erlking into existence, and refuses the reassurances of the father – the very terror of the child attracts the Erlking, and the Erlking claims that he is provoked by the child's beauty.'

'You mean that the child *wants* to be taken?' I asked,

'Not consciously, of course, but yes, somewhere in him there is something that calls to the Erlking and answers to him, even while he's calling to his father *Mein Vater, Mein Vater*, Father my father, can't you hear the Erlking's promises?'

Leonora got up from the table – we had finished our meal and were having coffee – and went to stand by the window. She shivered. 'I still think it's horrible.'

'You can find a different version, if you like, a much more *joyful* version of the same theme in *Ganymed*, as it happens also one of Schubert's setting of Goethe – you know it?'

'Yes, I think so,' said Leonora, tentative again, 'but I didn't think of it as about death – isn't it about closeness to nature?'

'So Goethe pretends, but the title tells another tale, literally, tells us that it's about Ganymede's abduction by Zeus, to become cup-bearer to the gods –'

'But that's not death,' I objected.

'Depends on how you see it. From a purely temporal point of view, Ganymede dies – his mother, for instance, on being told that he had been snatched up by an eagle, would have been unlikely to be pleased at her son's being called to higher duties. If you think about it, Ganymede's apotheosis is not too different from the *schöne Spiele* the Erlking promises the young boy. But the point is that in the *Ganymed* Schubert sets to music the young man's total acquiescence in his own abduction – *Umfangend umfangen* he describes himself as he is taken, *embracing while embraced – Aufwärts an deinen Busen, Aliebender Vater*, Upwards to your breast, All-loving father – so it becomes the ecstatic union with a higher being –'

'Fauré's aspiration towards happiness in the beyond,' I suggested, relieved to have something to contribute.

'Exactly,' he replied, pleased. 'And once you accept that acceptance of death, you find even in the Maid's resistance to death, even in the father's despairing denial, an implicit tribute to the power of death. And however much the Maiden doesn't want to die, however desperate the father is to save his son, the music, the music has no doubt, the music is on the side of Death all along.' He paused for effect, then sang '*Ich liebe dich, mich reizt deine schone Gestalt*' in a light, almost mocking tone.

'You sing beautifully,' said Leonora.

'Thank you. I sang in the college choir at Oxford.'

'So the boy dies?' I asked.

Both of them laughed. 'Of course,' said Conroy. 'The boy always dies.' He thought for a moment, plotting another connection. 'In fact,' he said, looking at Leonora almost mischievously, 'consider the parallels with the Christian myth. How well do you know your Bible?' he asked us both.

The day was becoming a quiz show in which I was the dud contestant, the one who goes home with a packet of Surf. 'Not at all,' I said. My mother had sent me to Sunday school because the neighbours' children went, and beyond that she believed that respectable people should be married and buried by the church, but she could not have produced any other article of faith upon pain of everlasting damnation. At school there had been chapel, of course, but it would not have occurred to us to see it as a religious occasion distinct from Assembly and Sports Day.

'I know it quite well,' Leonora said. 'I had to spend half-an-hour every morning and evening reading my Bible.' She smiled shyly. 'I used to win all the prizes for Bible knowledge in Sunday school.'

'Then you'll know that the Gospels have different versions of Christ's last words on the cross.'

'Yes,' said Leonora. 'Matthew has – is it Matthew? – *Eli, Eli lama sabach'thani?* My Lord, my Lord, why hast thou forsaken me?'

'Right,' said Conroy, excitedly, 'and Mark has the same – but of course the Lord that has forsaken Christ is in fact his own father – so my Lord, my Lord is in fact My father, My father, *Mein Vater, mein Vater*. And then when we get to Luke ...'

'I know it in Afrikaans,' said Leonora, 'Father ... into your hands I give my spirit.'

'There you are,' exclaimed Conroy, 'so in this version the son

246

does not feel alienated from the Father, indeed, sees his death as bringing him closer to the Father – into your hands – Ganymede's *Aufwärts an deinen Busen, Aliebender Vater!*'

Leonora looked rather shocked: she was not accustomed to discussing Christianity as one of a set of variations on myths of erotic abduction. 'And in John,' she said, 'Christ just says "It is finished."''

'Yes, *knowing that all things were now accomplished*, says John – so Christ's death is here the fulfilment of the prophecy, a kind of divine success.'

'But talking about contradictions,' I said, 'what do you make of such contradictory accounts of the same event?'

'They're only contradictions if you try to read them as a rendering of a literal truth. But if you see them as interpretations of the myth of the crucifixion, they are all equally valid, in dramatising different aspects of the death – just as Schubert sets different poems dramatising different attitudes to death. But my point is that in all of them death necessarily triumphs – *and there is nothing tragic about it.*'

He got up from his chair and looked out of the window. 'It seems to have cleared,' he said. 'Shall we stroll down to the harbour? I'll show you my boat.'

'A fishing boat?' asked Leonora.

'I suppose you could fish from it, but it's really only a rowing boat, with an outboard motor for emergencies or failure of muscle power. I use it more as a form of exercise than anything else. Do you row?' he asked me.

'Yes,' I said, relieved at being able to claim expertise at something. 'That is, I used to row at school.'

'You must come on a fine day and we can row round to Cape Point.'

'That sounds wonderful,' I said, though in fact it sounded terrifying.

On our way home, I said to Leonora, 'I didn't know you knew so much about music.' I was slightly resentful, in fact, that she should always make herself so small in my company, as if she couldn't afford to show how much she knew in case I felt inferior or something.

'Oh,' she said, almost apologetically, 'it's just that … it's not something we talk about, usually. I did music at school, you know.'

'Yes, I know, but I did Latin at school and I couldn't tell you the … the difference between the first and the second declension.'

'Yes, but music is not like Latin, I still go to concerts, and now, in the library, I listen to all their compact discs.'

'Those Schubert songs – do you have recordings of them?'

'Yes – would you like copies?'

'Yes, I would. I'd like to hear them, of course, after your discussion of them this afternoon.'

'I'll give you copies of the words, too, so you can follow them.'

'With translations, I hope.'

'Of course,' she said, without irony.

The next morning I used Gerhard's Monday morning visit to tell him about our visit to Andrew Conroy. He listened attentively – Gerhard, unlike most good storytellers, was also a good listener – and then said, 'So this man Andrew Conroy – do you think he lusts after you?'

'Oh, for heaven's sake, Gerhard, don't judge everybody by yourself.' My impatience was coloured by my own speculations in the same direction.

'Well, perhaps I am deeply corrupt, but if an unmarried man of fifty-plus starts asking me to lunch I do tend to wonder if it's just the pleasure of my company that he's after.'

'In the first place he asked Leonora as well, and in the second place the reason that he is unmarried is that he cherishes an unrequited but otherwise entirely normal passion for Joyce Tomlinson.'

'In the first place he could have asked Leonora as part of what I call good public relations, which I've often practised myself, also known as the charm-the-girl-and-fuck-the-boy gambit, and in the second place an unrequited *normal* passion is a very convenient alibi for an unmarried man. I myself have consoled any number of *normal* men left inconsolable by the loss of some woman.'

'You're barking up the wrong tree. If anything, Andrew Conroy is more interested in Leonora than in me. He spoke to her almost exclusively yesterday.'

'Are you jealous?'

'No, why should I be? I have no claims on him.'

'I was thinking of your claims on Leonora, but I find your mistake interesting. You're not perhaps cherishing a passion for Andrew Conroy yourself?'

'Honestly, Gerhard – apart from anything else, the man could have been my father.'

'Now *there's* a turn-on. Don't tell me you've never wanted to fuck your father.'

'The idea of a sexual relation with my father is monstrous. To be honest, the idea of any relation with my father is monstrous.'

'The monstrous is very often a source of great fascination, as mythology attests. The gods were forever appearing to human beings in enticing or at any rate irresistible animal shapes.'

'If my father had appeared in animal shape to anybody it would have been as a very old and smelly camel.'

CHAPTER ELEVEN

I don't think I'm a cold person; it's just that expressions of affection make demands on me that I can't meet. With Gerhard this is not a problem: it is a given between us that the only demand he is ever likely to make on another person is out of the question with me. His rough hugs are no threat, no prelude to anything, expressive only of the slightly perplexing fondness he feels for me and which I reciprocate in my more reserved way, just as I return the robust pressure of his embrace with a self-conscious little slap on his broad back. But with someone like Luc Tomlinson, affection is impossible, because there is no such prefabricated compartment in which to accommodate it; it threatens to claim its own space, intrude upon the secure chambers of my emotional retreat. Reticence and reserve have come to seem to me a kind of decency and consideration, leaving other people the freedom I want for myself.

This being the case, I was perhaps unduly disconcerted by Luc Tomlinson's exuberant demonstration outside the courthouse. Our relationship had been posited on the barely-concealed assumption that we found each other only just tolerable; even allowing for the high spirits of victory, his behaviour had been a transgression of our working relationship. Still, I was unlikely to have very much to do with him in future; certainly he would not importune me again with uninvited embraces.

I did see him again briefly one day when he came in to pay some outstanding charges on his account. He presented a cheque drawn on the leading Broederbond bank, no doubt the bank administering the trust fund left him by his grandfather. He seemed for some reason to want to linger, though he did not volunteer a topic of conversation, so I assumed the burden of discourse.

'You're spending your time at Rocklands now?'

'Yes, well. Pretty much.'

I decided to ask him something that had puzzled me for a while: 'Tell me, what exactly do you *do* all day?'

He looked at me with his slow insolence. 'I stay busy.'

'But doing what?' I persisted, conscious of irritating him.

'Do I ask you what you do all day?' he asked, but quite mildly, as if it really was a question he was curious about.

'No, but I think it's fairly obvious what I do.'

'It's obvious that you sit behind your desk all day. That's not necessarily the same as doing something.' I found it strangely unsettling to have my daily activity questioned, as if it was not self-evidently useful and productive. But just as I decided to relinquish the question, he said, 'I work.' With a touch of self-consciousness, he added, 'I'm involved in an alien-vegetation clearing project.' Then he smiled his brilliant smile, and said, 'That means I chop out hakea and Port Jackson. But I do it systematically. I work with Nature Conservation and Development now. I get on well with your friend Felix.'

'Felix Hartshorn?'

'You can't know more than one Felix in Nature Conservation.'

'Yes, it's just that ... well, that I'm so surprised.'

'Because I actually work or because I get on well with Felix?'

'Both, I suppose.'

'You've always thought of me as a useless little rich boy, haven't you?'

I was going to deny it, and then realised that his question wasn't a petulant complaint or a request for a denial; he was actually discussing something – himself – with me. So I said, 'Well, I don't know about *useless*: that would imply a lack of a potential that I wouldn't have denied you; but idle, yes, uncommitted.'

'You'd have taken me seriously if I'd worn a khaki uniform with green Nature Conservation epaulettes. But just because I don't like clothes doesn't mean I don't like work. I said to you the first day I met you that I couldn't work in an office, and I still can't. But you should see me chop out hakea. I'm a demon.' He said this as a simple fact, as if demon was some

251

category of labourer; Demon, First Class, I thought, and smiled.

'Why are you laughing?' he asked, on the defensive again.

'I'm smiling because I'm glad that there are demons on the mountain eradicating alien vegetation.'

'You'd better be glad. Hakea is a bugger. And if you think that's too negative, I've started an indigenous plants nursery at Rocklands.'

'I'm sorry if I doubted your ... your usefulness.'

He got up. 'That's all right,' he said 'I used to doubt your usefulness too.'

The rest of the summer went by uneventfully, unless one were to regard the passing of summer in itself as an event worth recording. I am not a summer person. The heat and drought of the endless Cape summer, the relentless light of its long days, are conducive only to sloth and beach-going; I have heard it said that whereas other cities have culture, Cape Town has shellfish.

Thus the fabled Cape summer in itself was hardly an inducement for me not to take up Mr McKendrick's tentative offer of a transfer to London: however bleak and dark the English February, it must be preferable to the fury and scorch of late summer in Cape Town. Besides, there seemed not to be any very cogent reason for me to stay in Cape Town: my relationship with Leonora was not going anywhere, and if it did unexpectedly and implausibly take off, there was no reason why she could not accompany me to London. Gerhard was probably the most constant presence in my life, and even he had, since the advent of Clive, other priorities to consider and other claims on his time. As for Andrew Conroy, it seemed presumptuous even to regard him as a considerable feature on my horizon; and yet, he seemed to want to involve me in a friendship premised upon an intimacy the exact nature of which I could not categorise. It was not as simple as a sexual advance: inexperienced as I was in this department, I think I would have recognised a predominantly sexual motive for what it was. Conroy's interest was at the same time more subtle and more intense; indeed, at times I wasn't even sure that it was there, as

252

when he engrossed himself in conversation with Leonora on topics I knew nothing about. But if it was perplexing not to know what he felt, it was even more disconcerting not to know what I felt. I dealt with my own perplexity by deciding that I was over-interpreting the natural enough interest of an essentially lonely man in somebody who seemed to offer uncomplicated companionship.

As the long dry summer yielded at last with bad grace to the showers of autumn, the Cape regained something of its freshness and vigour, the sky sparkling again in the clear windfree days, the soil coaxed by the rain into releasing the rich smell of decay and fertility, the days waning gracefully into early darkness. Autumn deepened into winter. Leonora sent me a tape of Schubert songs, the words meticulously transcribed in both German and English.

I phoned to thank her.

'I hope you'll enjoy them,' she said. 'They're the ones Andrew Conroy mentioned, and some others on the same theme.'

'What theme?'

'You know. Death.'

I spent some of the long winter evenings listening to the Schubert, intrigued as much by what Conroy had found in them as by the songs themselves, haunting as these were. In particular, I returned repeatedly to the tense, feverish drama of *Erlkönig*, trying to decide whether the song was most eloquent about the tragedy of the boy's death or about the triumph of the Erlking; in either reading, the ineffectually reassuring father is a near-irrelevant rationalist good intention. But however one interpreted the song, it was clear Conroy's tastes were what my mother would have called *morbid*. A familiarity with death was not what my religious training had inculcated in me, our religious observances having been so much a matter of polite apology and unassertive entreaty to a God who was deemed to disapprove of extremes of emotion. At home, too, death as a topic was delicately avoided, though as actual phenomenon it proved of course less ignorable. In this it resembled sex, which also existed in our home only insofar as my sister and I must have been presumed to have been conceived non-vegetatively, a fact which I think to this day faintly embarrasses my mother. I once heard her refer to adoption as 'so *clean*'.

My father, inconvenient in this as in all other respects, quite literally brought home the reality of death to us by dying one evening on the living room sofa, while I was home for the university vacations. Had he but extinguished himself in that succinct style for which sofa deaths are known, he would not unduly have shaken our family's equable if distant relationship with death: it would at most have entailed a phone call to the undertakers who, after all, are there exactly for the purpose of rendering death no more of a disturbance than installing a telephone or removing some unusually bulky garden refuse.

But my father was visited, on his death-sofa, by all the terrors he had sidestepped so adroitly in life: to judge by his terrified babblings, his last moments were illumined by a positively mediaeval vision of the gates of Hell opening to the gleeful gibbering of a thousand devils, armed, apparently, with paper knives and staplers, possibly in recollection of his extremely brief period of gainful employment in a bank. He died with a mighty roar not unlike that of Don Giovanni under vaguely similar circumstances. A life of petty deceptions and shabby deals, of shuffling evasions and feeble pretences, achieved one moment of honesty and even grandeur in its momentous confrontation with a reality larger than its quotidian exigencies. My mother, to give her her due, kept her presence of mind and forbade my sister and me to call the neighbours until my father had achieved the ultimate discretion of death. After that, decorum reasserted itself, with my father entrusted to the polite and tolerant blandishments of the Anglican Church. At the funeral, the presiding clergyman managed to mention neither God, nor death, nor my father by name, much to the relief of my mother, who thanked the priest for what she called an uncontroversial funeral. But I had glimpsed chaos and abyss, and resolved henceforth to lead an orderly life yielding, ultimately, to a dignified death.

Leonora had supplemented Conroy's examples with other songs on the same themes, and the cumulative effect was not reassuring. The shocking nonchalance of Death's ravishing reassurance to the Maiden, the suave sophistication of the Erlking's blithe promises to the boy, the personification of death as an independent agent, adversary, even ally or lover, embodied an imaginative world infinitely less rational and predictable than the Pinelands assumption of death as a consequence of human mishap, guarded against by life insurance, regulated by actuarial probability. And yet these songs gave expression to something hidden somewhere behind the small anxieties and minor victories of employment, the mundane drudgery of groceries and traffic, something at the back of the rain against the windows of my thatched cottage, something speaking through the wind in the trees.

I listened to the songs frequently, without discovering exactly what that *something* was; I even tried to explain it to Gerhard, in the hope that in articulating my apprehension I would clarify it to myself. But I came no closer to an understanding, except insofar as Gerhard's response could have been said to clarify. He listened carefully, and then said, 'It sounds as if you're suffering from either sexual deprivation or a death wish, probably both.'

'I know that to you anybody who is not in a state of permanent satiety is suffering from sexual deprivation, but I can't see what that has to do with a death wish.'

Gerhard thought for a moment, then said in the lightly bantering tone he adopted to camouflage his more portentous pronouncements: 'The songs express simultaneously the dread of and the desire for the consummation of death, an erotic ambivalence which it is not difficult to relate to the vacillations of repression in the face of the challenge and risk of sexual experience.'

I considered this. 'For a basically crude person you can be very abstruse sometimes.'

'If you really want it in words of four letters, I could say, as each fuck is a little death, so death is the ultimate fuck.'

'Isn't that a very *male* view? I mean, you're equating sexual expiration with death because of ... you know ...'

'You mean because men shoot their wad when they come?'

'Yes, although I was trying to find a more elegant way of

255

putting it. But my point is that for women sex may be linked with procreation, life, birth.'

'Possibly. I can't pronounce on that. I'm anatomising your case as a male.'

We were having this conversation in my office one morning in early July. Myrah appeared at the door, apologetic and yet vaguely remonstrative as always when interrupting one of my conversations with Gerhard. 'I'm sorry, Mr Morris, but Mr Tomlinson is here.'

I groaned. 'I don't think I want to be shouted at this morning.'

'No, not that Mr Tomlinson. The young one. He seems very upset.' She sounded almost well disposed towards Luc Tomlinson.

I glanced at Gerhard. He had assumed his avid expression, or the expression had taken possession of him, the one that I had hoped had disappeared with Clive's accession. I said to Myrah, 'Thanks, Myrah, you can show him in, Mr Naudé was just leaving.'

'No, I was not,' Gerhard whispered as Myrah left.

'At least get up off my desk then.' I did not think this was the time for Gerhard to prove Difficult, but the last thing I wanted was for Luc Tomlinson to walk in on an altercation between Gerhard and me.

Luc did indeed seem upset, though it was difficult to relate the impression to a single symptom; he was upset as an unhappy animal is unhappy, a matter of slack bearing and loss of muscle tone, of dullness in the normally lustrous eye. Even his hair seemed limp. He hardly noticed, to my secret satisfaction, when I went through the motions of 'You have met …?' He merely nodded absently in the direction of Gerhard, who was now pretending to admire the view from my window, and collapsed into the chair opposite mine.

'You must help me.'

I took out my pen and moved my pad closer. 'Perhaps,' I said to Gerhard, 'you wouldn't mind if Mr Tomlinson and I …'

Gerhard had the grace to pretend to prepare to leave. But Luc said, 'It doesn't matter. I need all the help I can get.' His normally challenging blue eyes seemed almost beseeching.

256

Gerhard, giving me his 'So there' look, now took up a position where he could stare unabashedly at Luc.

'What is it that I can help you with?' I asked, trying to give some semblance of professional decorum to the proceedings.

'The chacs,' he said. 'They've gone.'

I sat back. 'Your baboons have gone.'

He nodded. 'That's what I said.'

'And you've come to me as a lawyer to help you find them.'

'You don't understand,' he said. 'They were stolen.'

'Somebody stole your baboons.'

He nodded mutely, lost in his misery. He was tugging pointlessly at a loose thread on the leg of his jeans.

'Have you notified the police?' I asked, impatient with my own rote responses.

He nodded again. 'They say it's none of their business. Baboons can't be stolen. They're not private property. And they can't be kidnapped, because they're not human beings.'

'What do you expect … want me to help you with, then?'

'Get a court order or something against the buggers who took them.'

'And do you know who these … people are?'

To my surprise, he nodded. 'Yes. Fiona saw them.'

'Fiona … ?'

'Yes, you know her. The one …'

'Yes, I know her. Listen, why don't you just tell me what you know and we'll take it from there?'

'That's what I'm trying to do, isn't it?' For a moment his truculence flared up again.

'Don't let us prevent you, then.'

'Well, then. There's not much to tell, really. After the court case things were fine, except of course that my father called me names every time he saw me, which wasn't often if I could help it, and he forbade my mother to talk to me, and I was just starting to think he'd given up his scheme when … well, this morning very early Fiona went wandering around, you know she says there's a very powerful chakra right there where the chacs are, and she saw this van from the laboratory and these men …'

'Which laboratory?'

'Oh. Yes. The Silvermine laboratory. It's been in the news.'

'For what?'

Gerhard cleared his throat. 'If I may interrupt,' he said, 'I happen to know about the Silvermine laboratory. It used to be the State Facility for Strategic Research. Recently privatised under pressure from the government.'

'That's right,' Luc nodded. 'That was where they tested that dead chac – you remember – the one that died the day you were there.'

'You said at the time that your mother knew somebody there ...?'

'Yes, the director or whatever is one of my father's friends.'

'Is he still the director?'

'She. It's a woman doctor, Johanna van der Merwe.'

Gerhard whistled through his teeth, a short sharp sound I'd leant to recognise as his tribute to a crisis. 'The Black Widow,' he said. I ignored him, knowing that I would in due course be informed.

'And what would the Silvermine laboratory want with your baboons?'

'Well, they do all kinds of research, and they use baboons. But that's not really why.'

'What's not really why?'

'That's not why they've taken the baboons, for research. It's my father. He did it to get at me.'

I thought of Brick Tomlinson saying, 'I'll get even with you and that baboon freak of a son of mine,' and had to admit that it was not unlikely. It was the kind of childishness he would be capable of.

'Do you know that for a fact?'

'Yes. I'm convinced of it, I tell you.'

'Being convinced does not in itself constitute a fact. On what do you base your conviction?'

'Well, if you want to be technical about it, I don't *know* it. But I'm fucking sure of it.'

'Have you spoken to your mother?'

'Yes.' He paused. 'No.'

'Yes or no?'

'I spoke to her, but she doesn't want to speak to me. I told you my father has forbidden her to speak to me.'

'Do you think she will speak to me?'

'No. Or she may. She's not angry with me, she's just obeying my father's orders. And perhaps he didn't tell her not to speak to you. But what's the point?'

'It would be useful to know whether this … abduction was in fact initiated by your father, before we decide what to do.'

'I tell you it was. But go ahead, phone her.'

'I'll do that. But perhaps we'd better think up a plan of action, look into the legal aspects …'

'Yes, well I want you to get a court order.'

I smiled at this touching faith in court orders. 'I'll try, but it takes more than a sense of personal injury to obtain a court order. Before I can get a court order I need to establish that somebody's rights are being infringed.'

'The chacs' rights are being infringed, aren't they? You take them away from their natural habitat and you put them in cages and you start transplanting them and amputating them, and you say you have to prove their fucking rights are being infringed?'

'The rights of animals are a much debated area in law …'

'I'm not interested in any fucking debate. Anybody who isn't unbelievably stupid or dishonest *knows* what we're doing to the animals, I mean when an animal hurts another animal it doesn't know it's doing it, but when we do it we know exactly what we're doing, it just suits us to come up with *debates*. The law is …' He looked around my office and seemed to be scrutinising the Daumier prints for a suitable epithet.

'An ass?' I suggested.

He looked doubtful, suspecting irony but not detecting it. 'If you say so. I was thinking of something more useless, like a … a eunuch,' he concluded.

'Eunuchs have their uses. They guard the Sultan's harem.'

'Yeah. Great if you're the Sultan, not so great if you're not.'

'Well,' I said, a bit exasperatedly, 'for better or for worse, the law, for all its shortcomings, is all we have to help us here.'

'Not necessarily,' Gerhard said from behind me, in the suave tone that I have learnt to dread as the hum of his homing mechanism.

'What do you mean not necessarily?' I asked, irritated at

Gerhard's intervention. 'We're lawyers, aren't we, and isn't that what Mr Tomlinson came to us for, in spite of his grave misgivings about the potency of the law?'

'I agree, my dear Nicholas, that we are lawyers, and as such our first recourse is naturally to the law. But where, as Mr Tomlinson has pointed out, the law so manifestly lacks balls, we may have to rely on our own ... devices for a remedy.' I did not dare look round at him, knowing only too well the evil expression I would find on his face.

Luc Tomlinson was looking at Gerhard for the first time. His evident interest in Gerhard's argument, and his innocence of Gerhard's probable motive, did indeed make him seem like an earnest angel attentively giving a very polished devil a fair hearing. 'Call me Luc,' he said.

'With pleasure,' Gerhard said. 'Luc.'

'And how exactly do you propose to retrieve *Luc*'s baboons by extra-legal means?' I asked.

'That I cannot say *exactly* as yet,' he replied grandly, 'but I'm sure three resourceful young people like us can come up with something.'

'Four,' I said cattily. 'Don't forget Clive.'

'Of course. Thank you for reminding me.'

'Then you don't know how?' Luc asked sensibly.

'Not *exactly* was what I said. We'll have to work on the details.'

'Well, then,' Luc said. Gerhard's up-beat optimism was affecting him; his chin was regaining something of its pugnacious tilt.

'Well, then,' I said, anxious to regain at least the semblance of control over my own client, 'why don't you leave things in our hands for the time being? I'll phone your mother, and when Gerhard here has worked out the details of his scheme we'll contact you.'

'How?' he asked.

'How what?'

'How will you contact me?'

I swallowed my irritation. 'I keep forgetting that you are romantically inaccessible. Perhaps you'll have to make a point of phoning me every day ...'

'I have an idea,' Gerhard chipped in.

'Yes, Gerhard?' I asked in an elaborately patient tone.

'That cell phone that you ... that someone left in your car. Do you still have it?'

'Yes, it's right here.' I took my would-be apprehender's abandoned cell phone out of my drawer. I'd bought a charger for it and a SIM card, but I'd not wanted to use it. Apart from having an old-fashioned aversion to the idea of being followed for every waking moment wherever I went by anybody who cared to phone me, this particular phone had unpleasant associations for me. I felt it could somehow phone home and tell its original owners where it was.

'Perhaps Luc can borrow that, then we will know where to get hold of him when we need him,' Gerhard said in his most brightly helpful tone, the one, no doubt, that he had used to seduce the scoutmaster.

'Sure,' said Luc. 'I don't mind.'

'That's excellent, then,' I said. 'Don't call us, we'll call you. We have your number.'

'Do you know how to work a cell phone?' the ever-helpful Gerhard asked.

'Sure thing. Fiona has one.'

'Then ... ' I said.

'Then?'

'Then why can you not use hers?'

'I'm not seeing her any more. Not much anyway, only when she comes out to do the chakra. She's met another guy, an Australian. She says he has a more musical aura than me. He plays didgeridoos. So she dropped me.'

'I do sympathise with your ... disappointment,' Gerhard said, with all the sincerity of Norman Bates showing Janet Leigh to her motel room.

'Yes, well. It's no big deal. I was getting a bit pissed off with having to mind her chakras all the time, and having mine analysed. She said she was attracted to me in the first place because I had such beautiful chakras, but then later they seemed to fade or whatever happens to chakras when they stop, you know, radiating energy. It's a bit like a battery discharging.' He attached the cell phone to his belt so that it

261

dangled perkily above his loins. I noticed because I knew Gerhard was noticing.

'And how does she reconcile her chakra with her cell phone?' I asked.

'She was worried about that, because she knew somebody who started receiving calls from her own chakra. So she tested the cell phone first to make sure it was transmitting on a different frequency to her chakra.'

'Sensible girl. Well, we'll be in touch – and if there's anything you need, remember, we're only as far away as your cell phone,' said Gerhard.

'Yes, well,' said Luc, failing to rise to Gerhard's innuendo.

'How did you get here, by the way?'

'I cycled.'

'All the way from Cape Point.'

'Sure. It's a brilliant day. After the rain.'

'And you're cycling all the way back?' Gerhard asked, with offensive innocence.

'Maybe. Maybe I'll crash in town somewhere.'

'You have a place to stay?' Gerhard asked.

'Sure. Lots.' For once I enjoyed Luc Tomlinson's monosyllabic impenetrability.

'Well, then,' I said.

'Well, then,' Luc said and got up to leave.

'Don't forget to charge your battery – I mean on your cell phone,' Gerhard said.

'No,' Luc said, and left.

'That was disgraceful,' I said to Gerhard.

'Why? I was just being helpful.'

'If Luc Tomlinson thought you were just being helpful, he's even thicker than I thought. Your motives stuck out like … like …'

'Like a hard-on in running shorts?'

'I'll find my own metaphors, thank you. Like a rottweiler at a cat show. But that's your business – yours and Clive's …'

'Clive doesn't object to my making myself useful when the opportunity arises.'

'I don't want to hear about it. I was going to say if you really have a constructive suggestion I'd be pleased to hear it. Left to

262

my own better judgement I'd have told Luc Tomlinson that lawyers are not in the baboon-tracking business and that would have been that. Now you've gone and involved us in this *impossible* business.'

'My dear Nicholas, think positively.'

'I don't even know where to start.'

'Start with what we know or assume. Brick Tomlinson prevailed upon his old pal Johanna van der Merwe to abduct his son's baboons. They are now being kept in the research laboratory at Silvermine. We must get them out.'

'You make it sound so easy.'

'Hold your sarcasm and listen. We have two possible approaches. One is Joyce Tomlinson …'

'You heard what Luc said.'

'He said his father had forbidden his mother to talk to him. That does not necessarily mean she won't talk to you.'

'It should, but I agree that it doesn't *necessarily*. And what's the other approach?'

'Johanna van der Merwe. Colonel Johanna van der Merwe. The Black Widow.'

I could see from the flourish with which he produced the name that he was going to make the most of this one, so I sat back and said, 'Go ahead. Bring on The Black Widow.'

But it wasn't going to be that straightforward. 'I think I'll get her to speak in her own words. Why don't you try to get hold of Joyce Tomlinson, while I nip down to my office to find a certain document?'

'By all means. Let's not spoil the case for a lack of suspense, intrigue and special effects.'

'You're learning.'

Joyce Tomlinson's vaguely scented card was still in my drawer. I dialled her number; she picked up on the second ring.

'Hello, Mrs Tomlinson – Joyce – this is Nicholas Morris.'

'Nick, ah, yes, hello, how nice to hear from you.' The manner was not exactly cold, but it had barely had the chill taken off it.

'I'm phoning, as you may have guessed, about your son's … trouble.'

263

'Yes, and I'm sure he's told you that I am not in a position to discuss his trouble with him or with you. I told you when I first came to see you that my first loyalty was to my husband. I helped you with Luc's case against my own better judgement, and I am not going to jeopardise my husband's ... esteem once again, just for a few baboons.' She was playing the repentant-wife-determined-to-transgress-no-more.

'Then your husband was responsible for removing them?'

'I did not say he was.'

'You implied it.'

'Listen, Nick, I don't have to submit to cross-questioning from you. You know that if I have information that I think you need I'll give it to you because I want to, not because you drag it out of me.'

'I'm sorry.'

'That's all right, I suppose you can't help your profession. But please just let me be for the time being. I've been through a very hard time after the trial.'

'I am sorry.'

'So you've said, and I believe you. I'm going to ring off now.'

'I hope that if you feel we need to know something that you can tell us without infringing your commitment to your husband ...'

'Just talking to you infringes my commitment to my husband.'

'Would it be impossible for you to tell me what you know about the Silvermine laboratory?'

There was a short silence. 'Yes, totally impossible.' Another short silence. 'I mean, given that my husband built it.'

'Your husband ...?'

'Built it. That's why it's impossible for me to discuss it with you. But you have a job to do. I won't say anything more, except just to ask you to give Luc my love.' She was now the loving mother sacrificing her son.

'I'll do that. And thank you.'

'I can't imagine why you're thanking me. I've not given you anything.'

'No, of course not. I mean thank you for talking to me.'

'I do not recall talking to you,' she said, and put down the phone.

Gerhard came into my office carrying a tabloid-sized newspaper.

'Any luck with La Tomlinson?'

'Not much. She refuses to talk to me, but did let slip that Brick Tomlinson built the Silvermine laboratory.'

'Well, we knew there was a connection there, but this makes it more definite. The usual combination of services rendered and contract-farming.'

'And the Black Widow?'

'Yes, the Black Widow. In her own words.' He flourished the newspaper at me, a limpish publication entitled *The Gayest Cape*.

'Johanna van der Merwe writes for the poofter press?'

'Please watch your language. Under the new Constitution it's illegal to discriminate on grounds of sexual orientation. But no, not exactly.' He paged through the paper and placed it in front of me, pointing at a classified advertisement. 'There.'

'*Hello Mr Chips,*' I read, '*Firm disciplinarian seeking fractious pupil for correction.*' Is that the Black Widow?'

'No, you dummy, the display advert below it.'

I read: '*Sick of being gay? Reorientation of your sexual drive IS possible through the most advanced technology, administered by a medical specialist. Free to selected subjects. No aversion therapy. Phone during office hours* ... There's no name here – how do you know that's Johanna van der Merwe?'

Gerhard had the grace to look embarrassed. 'A friend of mine tried it.'

'Do I know this friend?'

'You know *of* him.' Gerhard came as close to blushing as he ever did, which is to say his ear lobes swelled slightly.

'You mean *Clive* volunteered for reorientation of his sex drive?'

'Yes, if you must know. He is a young man of essentially conservative instincts: he had moral and religious qualms about sodomy, which he suspected of lacking a spiritual dimension.'

'How eccentric of him. And what happened?'

'He responded to the advertisement, and made the initial contact. But he pulled out, in a manner of speaking, before the actual treatment.'

'Why?'

265

Gerhard smiled modestly. 'Well, he met me.'

'And you cured him of his qualms before Dr van der Merwe could cure him of ... his sodomitic tendencies?'

'I would hesitate to claim a cure. At most I would say that I have helped him accept with equanimity the sheer carnality that almost always lurks beneath the surface of a qualm. It's well known that nobody fucks like a Puritan let loose.'

'I don't want to hear about it. Tell me rather how this is going to help us rescue Luc Tomlinson's baboons.'

'I – we – still have to figure out the details, but the basic principle is that we gain access to the baboons through the Black Widow, to whom in turn we gain access through this advertisement.'

'You mean you go for treatment?'

Gerhard smiled unpleasantly. 'No. I mean *you* go for treatment.'

'Are you're out of your *mind*? Why should I go for treatment? I'm not even gay.'

'That is exactly *why* you should go: you're immune to her therapy. I mean, what if I went and the treatment *worked*?'

'I'm sure you'd make a very good heterosexual.'

'Thank you, and I'm sure you'd make a very good astronaut; but you happen not to want to be an astronaut, right, and spend the rest of your life in outer space? Well, I don't *want* to be a heterosexual and join the PTA and the Rotarians and go to dinner dances at the golf club. Whereas you, apart from being a ready-made, off-the-peg heterosexual, are also Luc Tomlinson's lawyer.'

'It is not part of the client-lawyer understanding that I should have my orientation technologically tampered with for the sake of Luc Tomlinson's baboons.' I stopped. 'Come to think of it, why can't Luc present himself for treatment? I can't see why we should do it for him.'

'That's because in fact you're not thinking. You'll remember that the Black Widow is a friend of Brick Tomlinson's. That means that she is more than likely to have seen young Luc around and will most certainly smell a large rat if he presents himself as a suitable case for treatment just after she's obligingly abducted his baboons.'

266

'Look, there's no way I can pretend to be gay. I don't even know what gays *do*.'

'Yes, you do. I've told you often enough.' He leered at me offensively. 'But if you like, I'll show you.'

'Oh, for heaven's sake, Gerhard, be serious.' I decided to change my tack. 'Look. You muscled in on this case for reasons that insofar as they are apparent are entirely unprofessional. From this I deduce that you have some interest in this matter. That being the case, you can handle this aspect of it, or else I phone Luc Tomlinson now and tell him to take his case to Animal Welfare or Greenpeace. And I am serious.'

He considered. 'Yes, I can see you are; you have that peculiar sharpness to your nose that you get when your moral faculties are agitated.' I said nothing, and he continued, 'Right. I'll volunteer for treatment on condition that you go with me.'

'Don't be ridiculous. You mean I go along to hold your hand?'

'No, it says no aversion therapy. Look, the way I see it, this is our way of getting access to the laboratory, right? And presumably if I'm going in for treatment I'll be strapped to a slab or confined to a cage or something; so we need a free agent to snoop around and open the cages, that sort of thing.'

'*Assuming* that I go along with this entirely ridiculous scheme, how do we sell my presence to the Black Widow?'

He thought for a while. 'Ah. I know. You are my lover.'

I sighed. 'Gerhard, I've just explained to you that ...'

'Wait, wait, *wait*. I'm not suggesting that you should go and present yourself for treatment; what I am suggesting is that you go and volunteer *me* for treatment. You make an appointment with the Black Widow and tell her that you want your lover treated ...'

'And why on earth would any gay man want his lover to be turned into a heterosexual?'

'Because ... your lover is dabbling in heterosexuality, is wondering if he is not perhaps straight; you can't stand the uncertainty, not to mention the various experiments your lover is conducting with his own sexuality, so rather than live with his indecisiveness, you want him to be classified one way or the other by scientific means.'

'And you really think she'll believe that?'

'She'll believe that because she will have no reason not to believe it. As far as she's concerned, there is absolutely no reason why the two of us should want to approach her, except for the reasons we give. And you must remember that people like Johanna assume that everybody wants to be heterosexual, and that even homosexuals would rather be involved with heterosexuals than with other homosexuals.'

'Who exactly is this Dr Johanna van der Merwe, and why do you call her the Black Widow?'

'Dr Johanna in fact prefers to be called Colonel Johanna van der Merwe. She was a Medical Officer in the South African Defence Force, in fact, I think somebody told me she was the personal physician of the minister of defence. In her Defence Force capacity she was in charge of some highly controversial experiments, the full details of which are only now coming to light. I'm vague on the exact nature of her research, but Mhlobo should be able to tell us, because there has in fact been some coverage of her in the press.'

'But why is she called the Black Widow?'

'Well, she is a widow, of some army type I believe, and she does favour black. And you know of course that the Black Widow is a reputedly fatal spider.'

'How reassuring. Have you seen her?'

'Yes, several times. She frequents the more exotic gay clubs. She's about as tall as I am and dresses in what looks like black razor wire. Anywhere but in a gay club she would be as conspicuous as the Statue of Liberty – as it is, she's often mistaken for a drag number; I've heard it maintained by some ever-optimistic gays that by day she is a crane driver on the docks. She smells of Dune and formaline.'

'How come she's accepted in gay clubs if she's openly recruiting candidates for reorientation?'

Gerhard shrugged. 'We're a queer bunch. We would seem to be titillated by the truly atrocious. You know, apparently in Germany there are now gay clubs in the Gestapo's torture chambers ...'

'That's appalling.'

'True, but my point is that the Black Widow has something

of the same allure, the fascination of the abomination, flirting with evil, dallying with death.'

'Is this why you want to risk this crazy venture?'

'Not entirely. My first consideration, you will remember, was Luc Tomlinson's baboons –'

'Which is to say Luc Tomlinson's butt.'

'I'm shocked by your vocabulary and your imagination alike. I was moved withal by Luc Tomlinson's plight, poignant though that plight might be rendered by what you inelegantly call his butt. I will admit, though, to a certain entirely decadent *frisson* of excitement at the thought of matching my wits against this Boer Boadicea, this bastion of militant Christian National heterosexuality.'

'You forget that I altogether fail to feel this *frisson*.'

Gerhard got up from my desk and came and stood behind me. He leaned forward, pressed his cheek against mine from behind, and whispered, 'Sweetheart, your alliteration redeems your lack of imagination.'

I phoned Mhlobo at the *Mail & Guardian*. 'For the price of a beer at the Pig and Wen, will you tell me what you know of Colonel Doctor Johanna van der Merwe?'

He whistled. 'Hey, man, Colonel Doctor Johanna van der Merwe will set you back at least two beers.'

'So be it. After work?'

'Your work or mine?'

'Mine.'

'You're on. Wig and Pen at five thirty punc-tu-ally.'

'Just when I thought I'd managed to have a whole conversation with you in monosyllables.'

As I was on the point of leaving my office for my appointment with Mhlobo, my mother phoned.

'How are you, dear? I've been worried about you. You're never at home.'

'I'm almost always at home, mother, except when I'm at the office.'

'I phoned yesterday afternoon, but there was no reply.'

'Yesterday afternoon? Yes, I went out to lunch.'

'There you are, then. I was worried.'

'Mother, you worry when I don't go out, and you worry when I do go out.'

'Yes, dear. These are troubled times.'

'Come on, mother, you've been through more troubled times than this.'

'Yes, dear, but then I had your father to support me.'

'Mother, you know that father was responsible for most of your troubled times.'

'You mustn't talk like that about your own father. He was a good man in his way.'

I glanced at my watch; I was going to be late to meet Mhlobo if my mother went into her mode of nostalgic recollection, which was to say a mode of sentimental distortion.

'Was there anything in particular bothering you, mother? Something that I can help you with?'

'It's not something you can help me with, but I've been so upset on poor Iris's account.'

'Why? What's gone wrong now?' My sister, apart from having had every disease known to science and a few that were still fluttering the medical journals, was notoriously accident-prone. In her horse-riding days she fell off her horse so often that the riding stables refused to stable her horse unless she wore a crash helmet when she went riding.

'Well, you know how fond Iris is of animals.'

'Yes, I do. It makes up for how nasty she is to people.'

'Now, dear, that's not nice. Anyway, on Saturday morning Iris was going into Durban to the races, a friend of hers, Bridget Murphy, I think you know her, had a horse running, and on the N3, just after our turn-off, she saw this dog – a big Rott ... Rottmiler ...'

'Rottweiler.'

'Yes, Rottweiler, next to the road, looking, Iris says, very lost.'

'Bad place to get lost.'

'Well, exactly. Iris was worried that the dog was going to try to cross the road and get killed, you know what the traffic is like on that stretch. So she stopped on the verge of the road ...'

'Dangerous.'

'Yes, but she says she couldn't just drive past knowing the dog was probably going to get run over. So she stopped and reversed and got out. The dog seemed friendly enough, nice dog, she says, well bred, though bewildered, of course, so she called it and opened the back door of her car for it. She says he was obviously used to cars because to her relief he immediately jumped in and sat bolt upright on the back seat, looking quite at home. Then ... are you listening, dear?'

'Yes, of course, mother,' I said, though I was in fact rather anxiously keeping track of the time.

'Good. Well, Iris felt quite pleased with this, and went round to her side of the car. But the moment she touched the front door the dog leaped over onto the driver's seat and started snarling at her, she says, most viciously.'

'How ungrateful.'

'Yes. And also inconvenient, because now she couldn't get into her own car. Every time she touched the door the dog tried to attack her through the window, you know, leaped up against the glass, and left her, she said, in absolutely no doubt as to what he would do to her if she opened the door.' She paused for effect. My mother liked to be prompted, otherwise she suspected I wasn't listening.

'But how ... presumptuous of the beast.'

'Yes, my words exactly. But point is, there was Iris on the N3, next to her car, and no way of getting into it without, as she says, being torn limb from limb by a mad Rottwiener.'

'Rottweiler. Didn't she have her cell phone with her?' My sister Iris goes nowhere without her cell phone.

'Yes, dear, only it was inside the car with the Rottwiner. Along with her handbag and everything else.'

'That was short-sighted of her.'

'Yes, dear. Only she couldn't have foreseen that the dog would turn out so vicious.'

'I suppose so. So what did she do?'

'Well, she tried to stop a passing car, only of course she didn't want to stop just *any* car, you know ...'

'You mean she tried to stop a white car.'

'Yes, dear, or Indian, they're sometimes quite nice, but nobody would stop for her, she says they all just looked at her as if she was mad, and the children laughed at her. You know, my dear mother used to say all the gentlemen were killed in the War. Anyway, eventually a man did stop, an Aff-ricander, you know, but still, and he said he'd shoot the dog for her, but obviously she couldn't have that, I mean she was trying to save the dog's life, and now to have it shot on her front seat, so the man said' – my mother assumed a bad imitation of an Afrikaans accent – '"Well, madam, looks like you'll have to wait for it to die of hunger." He offered her a lift into town but she says she didn't like the look of him, he was wearing shorts, you know the way they do ...'

'They?'

'Aff-ricanders. So he drove off, leaving her to her mercy right there in the middle of nowhere.'

'How did she get out of the mess?' I asked, hoping to bring my mother to the end of my sister's tribulations on the N3.

'Yes. Well, to cut a long story short, she stayed there for quite a while, with the dog sleeping quite peacefully inside the car, except it went mad every time she tried to open the door. Then it started raining and she got hysterical, and a taxi stopped, you know one of those ... Bantu taxis ...' She pronounced it *Barn*-too.

'A minibus taxi?'

'Is that what they're called? Well, you know how full they always are, but they offered her a lift into town and at this stage she was desperate, but she didn't have any money on her, and the taxi driver said that was all right as long as she promised to pick up the next black man she saw standing next to the road. So she promised and he took her to her friend Bridget's, and they got hold of the SPCA, but the SPCA said they didn't do road calls, and in the end Bridget phoned a friend who's a dog psychologist and they drove out to the car, and the dog psychologist opened the back door and got in and the dog jumped into the back and licked her face, which of course made Iris feel very foolish.'

'And what did they do with the dog?'

'They took it to the Animal Welfare.'

'So it will be put down after all?'

'No, dear, that's where you're wrong, because the story got

into the Sunday papers and now there are any number of people who want the dog, as a sort of car alarm and anti-hijacking device, you know.'

'Well, then, all's well that ends well, isn't it?' I tried to inject a note of cheerful closure into my voice.

'Yes, dear. Except, as Iris says, what kind of country are we living in where you can't even trust the dogs?'

CHAPTER TWELVE

Mhlobo was halfway into his beer when I arrived at the Wig and Pen. The place was packed, as always after work, but he had managed to annex two stools at the bar.

'I'm terribly sorry ...' I started, but he waved it away.

'Don't be agitated,' he said. 'I always tell my colleagues I'm willing to make concessions for white people who have not had our opportunities to acquire a sense of time. Let me order you a drink. The barman owes me a favour, I did a story on his employer.' He raised his finger and the barman, a short, harassed-looking man, trotted over and took my order.

Mhlobo had brought a folder of newspaper cuttings along. 'It hurts me to conclude that you do not read our invaluable publication,' he said, opening the file.

'I do – sometimes,' I said. 'But some Fridays I exempt myself from the duty of being well-informed.'

'And now you need me to relieve you of the burden of ignorance. Was there anything in particular you wanted to know about Dr van der Merwe?'

'No, just some background. I may have to make her acquaintance soon.'

'As long as you're neither black nor ho-mosexu-al you should be safe enough.'

'I have been told she rehabilitates homosexuals, but what does she do to blacks?'

Mhlobo went into his factual, reporting mode. 'Strong rumour has it that she was involved under the previous government in developing a range of products intended to keep down, shall we say, the black population. The most ridiculed project was a sterility drug apparently intended to be added to foodstuffs favoured by black consumers. Realising they'd decisively lost the battle for the hearts and minds of the people, the government went for their balls instead.'

'Why was it ridiculed?'

'Not for its aim, which was hardly a laughing matter, but for the nature of the research.'

He took out a cutting headed *Bizarre experiments in State lab*. 'Apparently the drug was tested on baboons; but, of course, there is some difficulty in telling a sterile baboon from a fertile baboon, except by taking semen samples. Now as you can im-ag-ine, taking semen from a baboon can be a slow and not a very dignified process – apparently if you don't do it just right they bite you, and in any case the laboratory workers objected that jerking off baboons wasn't in their job description. So Dr van der Merwe developed a technique of stimulating the prostate with electrodes to effect e-jac-ulation.'

'And did it work?'

'Well, in the sense that the baboons ej-ac-ulated cop-i-ously, yes, but as far as is known no sterility drug had been developed when the tests were stopped.'

'So she is in fact a bit of a joke?'

'Not ac-tu-ally.' He selected another cutting from the file. The headline proclaimed: *Black Widow 'implicated' in chemical warfare*. 'She was more successful in developing contact poisons, which could be administered through any skin lotion and would remain undetected. To my knowledge the poison was used, with some success, on political activists who fell foul of the Civil Cooperation Bureau's murder squads. I take it you do know about those?' he asked pointedly.

'Yes. I'm not entirely out of it.'

'You'd be surprised how many white South Africans would claim not to know of the death squads. Anyway, as State physician, Johanna cooperated closely with the security establishment, more specifically the CCB; invaluable in signing death certificates citing death by natural causes or misadventure or anything but the real cause. She was quite a powerful person. She also brought in quite a bit of money ...' He selected another cutting. The headline read: *Trade in chemical weapons and drugs: the Cape connection*.' Apparently our rulers financed some of their projects by selling off the Black Widow's inventions to foreign buyers …'

'Drugs too?'

'Yes, one of the quainter notions of the security establishment was that the black populations should be demoralised by being fed huge quantities of Ecstasy. Unfortunately the Ecstasy made available cheaply in the townships immediately found its way, at hugely inflated prices, to the white clubs, where it proceeded to demoralise the white teenagers. So our very moral government became drug pushers to the world. You must remember that by this time, the late eighties, the South African government had established intimate relations with almost every black market on earth, having had to rely on the scum of the earth to bust the sanctions that were by now pretty firmly in place. So they had ready-made contacts. I think it could be said that the South African government did its bit to teach the world to sing. Ironic, when you think about it.'

'But why is the laboratory still operating?'

'Oh, *officially* it isn't. *Officially* it's been closed down. In fact, it's been privatised, and is now running a very lucrative export trade in *medical supplies* – for which read drugs, laboratory animals, probably still chemical weapons. It also undertakes privately funded research of a dubious nature.'

'And Johanna is behind it all?'

'Not quite all, and not quite behind, but she was an important link in a tremendously lucrative chain. Her personal fortune must be considerable, presumably safely stashed away in Switzerland.'

'But … how come she's still allowed to practise?'

'There is a massive inquiry under way, but it's a tricky business; even under the new dispensation witnesses are reluctant to testify, and the old dispensation is still dug in so inex-tri-cably in every state and parastatal structure that you can't remove it without dismantling the whole thing.' He sighed. 'A peaceful transition is a wondrous thing, but it does leave a lot in place that we might have been better off without. And, between us, some of the new bunch are not exactly eager to have the whole truth revealed.' Mhlobo was paging through his cuttings as he talked. He took out one and passed it to me. 'This one might interest you. Or if it doesn't it should.'

It was quite a small item. The heading was *Black Widow inherits Hit Man*.

I scanned the report. It said that Johanna had 'acquired the services' of an ex-member of the Civil Cooperation Bureau, Bernardus ('Boetie') Bester, notorious for his involvement in the activities at Vlakplaas, the rural headquarters of the CCB. He was now her 'personal laboratory assistant'; the report notes sardonically that he is not known to have any scientific training or experience.

'Boetie Bester is likely to be in close attendance if you make contact with the good Doctor. Her many activities ne-ces-sitate the services of a bodyguard. He is not a pleasant character.'

'Do you know him?'

Mhlobo's deadpan expression fleetingly registered a grimace. 'I know of him. He was personally responsible for the death of one of my best friends. A stupid, ruthless, overweight, under-educated man. He's by no means unique in the annals of Vlakplaas – one of the operatives given a gun, a bottle of brandy and a free hand to deal with subversives, real or imagined – the goons to which the security of the state was entrusted by a paranoid government. They tortured and killed at will, and were protected by the generals and the politicians as long as they were useful, but they're now being jettisoned by their political masters, and will probably have to take the rap for the fat cats and the big fish who are out to save their own asses. Boetie Bester is one of the lucky ones who still have a job.'

'Sounds great.'

'May I ask ex-act-ly why you want all this information?'

'Yes, very confidentially. Johanna's laboratory has abducted Luc Tomlinson's baboons. We want to steal them back.'

He whistled. 'Now that is what I call very au-da-cious. Let me get you another drink.' He raised a long finger and the barman came scuttling over.

On Tuesday morning I filled Gerhard in on what Mhlobo had told me.

'Mmm,' he said, 'charming woman. Science in service of the community.'

'What I still don't know,' I said, 'is what we do once we're inside the lab.'

'Quite simple, really. The Silvermine laboratory is in the middle of nowhere, which is to say on the mountains above Scarborough, that area. All we do is release the baboons into nature, and let them find their own way home.'

'That's miles from Cape Point. They'll get lost.'

'Listen, would you rather get lost, or be used to test the efficacy of fire-resistant clothing?'

'Is that what they do?'

'That's one of the more rational. There are others. For instance: they take a baboon mother and baby and put them in a cage, then start heating the cage floor. The aim of the experiment is to see at what point the mother drops the baby and gets on top of it to get out of the cage.'

'But what's the point?'

'The human need to know, the scientific pursuit of knowledge for its own sake.' He adopted his quoting stance and declaimed: 'And God said unto man, have dominion over the fish of the sea, and over the fowl of the air, and over every living thing that moveth upon the earth, and kill them and maim them and torture them as compensation for all the disease and war and famine I intend to visit upon you.'

'That's not what the Bible says, is it?'

'Not quite, but that's what it implies. Now I suggest you get on that phone and make an appointment with the Black Widow.'

'Can't you do that?'

'And how are we going to explain to her that the appointment was made by somebody with a heavy Makwassie accent and kept by somebody with a poncy Natal accent?'

'You're also going to attend the appointment, remember.'

'Yes, but only under duress from you, remember.'

The phone rang for a long time. Eventually it was answered by a male voice; 'Huhlo,' it said in a peculiarly uninflected, uninviting tone.

'Good morning. I'm responding to the advert in the newspaper.'

'What?' The monosyllable had never sounded as monosyllabic, the interrogative never as incurious, as in the mouth of my charmless interlocutor.

'I said I'm responding to the advertisement in the newspaper.'

'What newspaper?'

'Well, *The Gayest Cape*, actually.'

'Yes?'

'Yes, and it says to phone this number for more details.'

'For more details of what?'

'Well, you know, of changing your sexual orientation.'

'Changing my *what*?' The flatness yielded marginally to a readiness to take offence.

'Not yours, one's … anybody's … sexual orientation?'

'You're not phoning about the Skyline?'

'What Skyline?'

'The Skyline I advertised in the *Burger*.'

'Listen, I think I must have the wrong number, I'm sorry I bothered you, I … '

'Are you looking for the Colonel?'

'Yes,' I said, and then bethought myself that I was not supposed to know the identity behind the advertisement. 'Yes, I think so, it's about the advertisement for volunteers for a scientific experiment.'

'The *moffie* treatment?'

'Yes, yes I imagine so.' My knowledge of the Afrikaans vernacular, though not extensive, did encompass this particular term, thanks to Gerhard.

'Hold on.'

'Thank you,' I said, but my courtesy was acknowledged only by the empty clunk of the abandoned receiver hitting the wall at the other end.

I waited for several minutes, listening to what sounded ominously like the humming and whining of the technological advances mentioned in the advertisement. At length I heard the click of high-heeled shoes on a hard floor; then a deep female voice said, with somewhat more telephone manner than her predecessor, 'Hello.'

'Oh, hello, good morning, I'm phoning about the advertisement in *The Gayest Cape* …'

'Yes. So my assistant told me. You are interested in my re-orientation programme?'

'Yes, well, that is, it's not for myself actually, it's for a friend …'

She sighed. 'It always is. But you need not be ashamed. You are doing a very brave thing, and there is no *need* to hide your identity. In any case, in order to treat you I shall need to see you, not your friend.'

'Of course, but it's just that this really is for a friend.'

'Then why does your friend not call himself?'

'It's quite a complicated story, and one that I would rather discuss with you face to face if that is possible –'

'I shall expect you to bring your friend to the discussion.'

'Yes, of course, it's just that I promised him I would set up the meeting. He is … quite shy.'

'My subjects often are. I interpret it *as* the socialised self trying to avoid the confrontation with the true nature of the individual.'

'I'm sure … you must be right. I'll be sure, then, to bring my friend. Where should we come to?'

'The therapy is done in my laboratory, but I always have a preliminary meeting with the subject in an unthreatening environment *in* order to establish whether he is suitable for my method. Not everybody is.'

'Then where shall we meet?'

'At the Brass Tack. Tonight at eight.'

'The Brass Tack?'

'Yes. It's in Loop Street.'

'I'm sure I can find it.'

'Your friend will probably know it. What is his name, by the way?'

I hesitated. We had neglected to invent incognitos for ourselves. I went completely blank for a moment, then came up with, 'It's Wouter … Wouter Theron.' Wouter Theron had been the name of my Afrikaans master at school, a complete sadist.

'I knew a Wouter Theron once,' Johanna said in a softened

tone. 'But he was killed on the Border.' Then she snapped back into her professional manner. 'And what is your name?'

'It's … Morris Nicholson.'

'And I take it you will be accompanying your friend?'

'Yes, I will have to. To make sure that he attends.'

'You realise that I don't treat subjects against their will?'

'Yes, of course. No, he's quite willing really, but just … as I say, very shy.'

'I hope he gets over his shyness. My methods are quite invasive. Not painful, but … intimate.'

'I'll warn him.'

'Don't call it a warning. Think of it as a spiritual preparation. Eight o'clock in the Brass Tack. Loop Street 27.'

'Yes. And how shall we know you?'

She laughed again, a low vibration more suggestive of hunger than amusement. 'You can't miss me, as they say. My name is Dr Johanna van der Merwe. My friends call me The Colonel.'

Gerhard and I conferred; if we met the Black Widow that evening, we could meet Luc the next day to discuss whatever plan seemed plausible in the light of the Black Widow's schedule. We agreed that we would try to gain access to the laboratory on a Saturday, when there would not be ordinary staff around.

'I can say I'm self-conscious about being exposed to the stares of outsiders,' Gerhard suggested.

'Yes, but will she be prepared to work on a Saturday?'

'I gather this therapy thing is more a hobby than her regular job. She may prefer to do it after hours.'

'Well, we can but try. I must warn you that she says the treatment, though not painful, is quite invasive.'

'I imagine she means it's psychologically invasive. I can deal with that; my psyche was invaded at an early age by the paranoid doctrines of Christian National education, and it has resisted annexation reasonably well, apart from the odd weird prejudice which I still discover lurking in its darker recesses from time to time.'

'Good, I'm pleased you're feeling robust. And by the way, your name is Wouter Theron.'

'I met a Wouter Theron once. He was *weird*.'

281

I phoned the cell phone number. It rang for a long time. I assumed that Luc had lost or mislaid the phone, and was about to ring off when a rather flustered voice came on. 'Yes?'

'Luc? This is Nicholas Morris.'

'Yes. Hello. Sorry, I couldn't figure out how to switch this thing on. Why does it play *Nkosi Sikelel' iAfrika*?'

'I don't know. I think you can set different tunes somewhere.'

'No, this one is okay, once you're used to it.'

'Good. Listen, can we meet to plan strategy?'

'You have a plan?'

'Gerhard has a plan. It's not exactly foolproof, but it may be worth a try. We'll need your help, though.'

'Well, yes. Of course. When do we meet?'

'Tomorrow afternoon, after work. Do you know the Wig and Pen?'

'That fake place in Burg Street?'

'That's it. You'll just have to bear with the fakes.'

'No problem.'

'Good. Five-thirty, then. Oh, and one more thing. According to your mother, your father built the Silvermine laboratory.'

'I don't know. If she says so.'

'Does your father keep his old building plans?'

'I don't know. Yes. Yes, he does. There's a little room next to his study.'

'Can you retrieve the plans to the laboratory?'

'I told you my mother isn't allowed to talk to me. I'm not allowed to go home.'

'Would it be impossible for you to get in anyway?'

'No. I have a key, if that's what you mean.'

'And isn't there a time when your parents aren't at home?'

'I could hang around. Mom usually goes out in the morning.'

'Well, then, if you could remove the plan for us tomorrow morning, that would be a great help.'

'Are you telling me to burgle my own home?'

'Yes. This is the new South Africa.'

I wanted Gerhard to accompany me to the Brass Tack, but he was playing squash with Clive, and said he would meet me there. 'It's quite safe, really, you won't get accosted unless you invite it.'

'What must I wear?'

'Leather or rubber, preferably.'

'Don't be silly. Can you imagine me in leather?'

'I often do. It's one of my favourite fantasies. But failing leather, go for denim. Preferably faded in the crotch area.'

'I can't arrange to have my crotch area faded by tonight.'

'Just don't blame me if nobody asks you to dance.'

CHAPTER THIRTEEN

The Brass Tack, though situated in central Cape Town, turned out to be hard to find. There was no name, no visible sign of an establishment of any kind, only an unadorned metal board with a small number 27. Apart from this, there was nothing but an inscrutable grey façade, blank except for a grey metal door. It had no knob or any other opening mechanism, but next to the door was a tiny bellpush. I pressed the button and waited. A light went on above the door; a closed-circuit camera swivelled out of an alcove above the door and peered at me for a moment. It must have been satisfied with what it saw, because it withdrew into its alcove and the door clicked once and opened, very slightly. I pushed at it and it swung open to reveal a heavy leather curtain, blood red, held in place with massive brass rivets. I pushed aside the curtain.

In front of me was a counter, halfway between a ticket office and a hardware store. A young man in dungarees and boots perched on a high stool, smoking and chatting to two other young men, these less industrially clad in black leather waistcoats, pants and boots. Their bare arms and chests left one in no doubt as to the bulk of their muscles; indeed the suppleness and tightness of the leather left very few features of their considerable bodies undefined. One was operating what looked like a TV console, presumably the door-screening and opening device. The other was peering into the mirror surrounding the counter area, adjusting one of the studs in his left nostril.

'Hi,' said the dungarees. 'You're early.'

'Am I too early?' I asked.

'Never too early for me,' he said archly. 'It's just that you won't find much action in there yet,' and he gestured to his left, from which direction a loud thumping beat suggested that the inaction was at any rate not silent.

'That's no problem,' I said, 'I have to meet a friend.'

'Don't we all?' he shrugged. 'That'll be 40 rand. Early bird special. Not that there's much in the line of worms as yet. I hope your friend's nice.'

I gave him a 50-rand note. He slid my change along the counter, and took hold of my right hand. I resisted: whereas I was perfectly willing to enter into the spirit of the place, I didn't feel called upon to submit to the caresses of the door staff.

'Relax, sweetie,' he said. 'Just a little stamp. It won't hurt.'

He took a largeish rubber stamp and applied it firmly to the inside of my wrist. It left a purple impression of a pair of handcuffs. 'Your first time?'

I nodded.

'Enjoy.' He reached behind him to a shelf, took off a small packet and passed it to me. 'A little present from the management. Tuesday evenings tend to be quiet, but you never know. All it takes is one.'

'Thanks,' I said, glancing at the packet. It was wrapped in shiny cellophane; gaudy lettering, for some reason in heavy Gothic script, said 'Rough Stuff', and in smaller lettering, 'Will not break or leak even under extreme conditions.' There was also a little sachet, which at first I took for shampoo, but the lettering said 'Greased Lightning'.

'Use that,' the young man said. 'If you need more, they're five rand each. It's that way,' and he gestured towards his left again.

I thought I would wait somewhere inconspicuously till Gerhard arrived, but the bar, raised slightly above a small dance floor, had clearly been designed for the purposes of people who wanted to see and be seen, and I was about as inconspicuous as a giraffe on a skating rink as I crossed the floor and presented myself at the gleaming metal counter. The lighting was soft but firm: detail was bathed in a flattering glow, but outline was sharply delineated. You could get away with a wrinkle or two but not with a sagging waistline. The music, which was deafening on the dance floor, was slightly muted here by a canopy over the whole bar area, festooned with saddles and stirrups.

There was no barman in sight, but exuberant laughter from an alcove behind the bar area suggested that life was not so much absent as otherwise occupied. The place was, as the doorman had intimated, not full; but leaning against the counter was a very tall woman in a very short dress, revealing a pair of sturdy but well-shaped legs. This I took to be Dr van der Merwe. In the first place, she was the only woman in the place; in the second, she corresponded in essentials to Gerhard's description. Her gleaming black hair was sprayed into whipped-cream curls, if it's possible for whipped cream to be black; and her sturdy frame – square rather than curved, but firm and clearly in good shape – was contained in a tight-fitting dress in a blue-black metallic material. She was sipping at a bright purple drink. As I moved closer I got a whiff of perfume – Dune mixed with formaline, Gerhard had said. At close quarters her hair, too, seemed metallic, and her eye shadow matched the dress. She was talking to a young man, very slight, nervously and inexpertly puffing at a cigarette. He was dressed like a construction worker and seemed scared of her.

On the other side of the nervous young man stood another young man of a distinctly different mould. His clothes, a conventional grey two-piece suit, were crumpled, even though they were made of a supposedly wrinkle-free synthetic: he had the kind of body that would wrinkle anything you put onto it. His face was as featureless as his body was shapeless: a little button of a nose, small pale-blue pig-like eyes, a mouth slashed downward like a shark's, only less generously proportioned, three chins stepping down to his chest in an incongruously matronly manner. His hair was swept back in an attempt at leonine dishevelment that was foiled by the sparseness of his mane, to issue in a little fringe at the back of the neck, draped over the collar like a greasy doily over a milk jug. His most salient feature was negative: he had no neck, his head rising out of his massive shoulders like a freakish outcrop out of a plain. I wondered what *recherché* fantasy he represented; I had by now recognised that the clothing in the place was so much fancy dress, wish-fulfilment costumes rather than actual functional dress. A polyester suit did not strike me as anybody's erotic fantasy, but I was also learning that erotic fantasies were by definition esoteric. Who knows, perhaps No-Neck was by day what everybody else here pretended to be by night – a crane driver, a mechanic – and indulged himself by night with dreams of being what everybody else was by day – a clerk in a building society, an assistant at Boardmans Interiors.

Johanna was saying to the young man she was talking to, 'Well, Mr Duncan, that is, as they say, your problem. Come and see me if you change your mind.' The deep timbre was unmistakably that of the voice on the telephone.

'I'll do that,' the young man said, very unconvincingly, given his evident anxiety to extricate himself from the conversation. He moved off, tripping once over his own bootlaces, and I moved closer along the bar. No-Neck looked at me warily; Johanna lifted one heavily pencilled eyebrow and said, 'Have we met?'

'Only by telephone – that is, if you're Dr Johanna van der Merwe.'

The full lips parted in a gracious smile. She extended her hand, and I was conscious of a slight frisson of electricity as my hand touched hers. In a dark room, no doubt, we would have produced a sizeable spark.

'Mr Nicholson,' she said, 'I am pleased to meet you.' Her voice was very deep; her accent was almost imperceptibly tinged with Afrikaans, her tone politely formal. She could have been welcoming me to the weekly meeting of the Women's Christian Association. 'But tell me, where is you friend Wouter?'

'He should be along very soon,' I said, hoping fervently that I was right. I did not want an extended tête-à-tête with this razor-wire confection.

'Good. I must tell you I had my doubts *about* your story. It seems strange that you should want to help your friend to cure himself. I'm assuming that by *friend* you mean *lover*.'

'He ...' I began, but she held up a hand to stop me. 'BRUCE!' she yelled over her shoulder in the direction of the activity in the next room, her tone startlingly at variance with the suave huskiness of her demeanour to me. 'Bring the gentleman a drink!'

An over-muscled and under-dressed young man appeared

behind the bar, tightening or otherwise adjusting a nut-and-bolt assembly adorning his navel. 'Sure, Colonel,' he said. 'What's it going to be, mate?'

I wanted a beer, but I thought I'd better ask for something homosexual. 'White wine, please. Dry.'

'From the bottle or in a glass?' His tanned features, so curiously featureless in their bland perfection, relaxed into a blinding grin. 'Just joking. As a rule the regulars don't go for wine. But we serve anything.' And he winked at me again.

'One of the disadvantages of homosexual establishments is that the service tends to be very forward,' Johanna said, her tone making no concession to the proximity of the functionary in question. 'They're selected according to criteria that bear no relation to their function.'

'Wrong, Colonel,' Bruce said cheerfully, placing a large glass of white wine in front of me. 'My function is to please.' He rippled the muscles of his abdomen, evidently to demonstrate his qualification for this vocation.

'Function,' Johanna said to me, ignoring Bruce, 'is not something determined *by* the subject itself; it is imposed *from* outside the realm of subjectivity. This is why I am dedicated *to* the reorientation of homosexual deviants in terms of their natural function.' Her eccentric prepositional stresses made her sequences seem purposeful and coherent.

'And what is that?' I asked.

'The fact that you have to ask that testifies to the decadence of the human species. Do you find any other species questioning its own function?' She threw out the question challengingly, then took a sip of her purple drink. 'Think about it,' she insisted, 'in all of nature the only species that questions the meaning *of* its own existence is the human.'

'But what *is* the natural function of human beings?' Johanna's erratic stresses were proving to be catching.

'I judge the matter *in* the light of my objectivity as a scientist, my intuition as a woman, and my faith as a Christian. I believe my intuition takes me where no male scientist can go, and my religion guides me not to go where I am not Supposed to go. And *in* terms of all three of these paradigms, the function of the human species is to procreate itself responsibly, and to create

288

the best possible environment – *under*, of course, the circumstances, such as they are.'

'The best environment for human beings, I take it.'

'I believe, of course, that *as* the Bible tells us, we have been instructed and empowered to rule over creation. The human being is the crown of creation, and as such is entitled to use the rest *of* creation *for* his benefit – *within* certain limits, of course.' She surveyed the club in a leisurely way, as if to establish the limits there and then.

'Who determines the limits? I mean, on the one hand you use nature as your criterion, and on the other you claim that humans are superior to natural creatures.'

'Ah, fortunately, to decide such questions we have been given *dis*crimination, rationality, and discretion. Trust to your reason and you will not be able to abuse your God-given attributes.'

She said this in an encouraging sort of way, looking into my eyes and putting her hand on mine where it rested on the bar, as if she was reassuring me personally. She had emerald-green eyes.

I looked around me, mainly to escape the forceful regard locked into mine. The grip of her hand with its well-manicured, razor-sharp nails, was more difficult to evade. Two men, bare-chested except for leather waistcoats, were performing an elaborate ritual on the tiny dance floor; they were attached to each other by two chains, clamped with crocodile clips to the earlobes of the one and the nipples of the other.

'And this?'

'That? That is an abuse of reason, a travesty of human ingenuity. When God gave us reason, he also gave us the ability to misuse our reason. Adam was free to eat the fruit *of* the tree of knowledge, and fell through abusing his freedom. The sons of Adam are still abusing that freedom every day and every night. We were not given intelligence in order to devise new styles of nipple-clamps.' Her suave tones assumed a sibilant outline, her consonants like steel under her velvet vowels, and the indulgent huskiness of her voice opened up into darker tones. 'Human inquisitiveness *into* God's secrets brought about our expulsion from Paradise; now Science, the beautiful if misbegotten child of inquisitiveness, will collaborate with Nature, which is God's gift *to* humanity, to reclaim humanity from its own corruption, and to re-establish that harmony *from* which we were estranged by the Fall.' Her face shone with the eerie glow of conviction that I had seen on the faces of preachers and dieters; I had a rare misgiving about Gerhard's safety as I considered that this was the woman to whom he would be entrusting his sexual orientation, and whatever part of his psyche or body that she assumed it to be anchored to or manifested in.

'Watch out, mate,' said Bruce, sashaying past us and admiring his buttocks in the mirror behind the bar. 'She'll have yer balls in her cocktail.'

'Shut up, Bruce,' Johanna growled, and returned to her exposition. 'Unfortunately, so far the collaboration between Nature and Science has resulted mainly in over-population, indiscriminate breeding unhindered by the positive checks of the past.'

'Isn't breeding natural?' I permitted myself to ask.

'It's natural only in the sense that the procreation of rabbits and chickens is natural. Nature in that sense is an accident, without plan or purpose. That is the creation *over* which the Lord gave us dominion. The higher nature is guided by divine wisdom as manifested *through* science and technology, and informed *by* a sense of individual and national identity.' Then, abruptly, she changed her tone. 'As I was saying, Mr Nicholson,' she said, 'what *puzzles* me about you, Mr Nicholson, is what interest you have in this business of your partner's re-orientation.'

'Well, yes,' I said, conscious of a very searching glance from under the mascara, 'I suppose it seems odd – I mean ... you see ... my friend – Wouter – is not altogether sure of what he is, if you know what I mean.'

'Of course I do. Half the men in South Africa are not quite sure what they are. That is why I am so necessary.'

'To tell them what they are?'

'To tell them what they should be, and to help them assume their rightful identities.'

'And does your method work on everybody?' I asked, relieved to be asking rather than answering the questions.

'No, alas. I like a challenge, but I recognise a waste of time when I see it. As I say, I am an expert in my field, or perhaps I should say in any number of fields. My present most active interest is sexual deviance. I have been awarded a Human Sciences Research Council grant to produce a report on the remediation of deviance amongst sexually hyperactive men.'

'Why only the hyperactive ones?'

'It is my theory, *for* which I have considerable evidence, that sexual hyperactivity is an indicator not, as is often assumed, of an excess of sexual appetite, but *of* profound dissatisfaction: to put it bluntly, homosexuals fornicate ceaselessly because they're never satisfied.'

Bruce, overhearing this on one of his sorties past us, interjected, 'You mean straights fuck just once and die in bliss like bumble bees?'

'Shut up, Bruce. And the reason,' she continued to me, 'why they're never satisfied is that they are looking for something that homosexual relations can't give them.'

'Like a heterosexual relation?'

'Like a heterosexual relation. But of course, they have been programmed to believe that the next man they meet will be the perfect one, no matter how often they're disappointed. You must understand,' she said, looking into my eyes so intensely that I wondered whether she was trying to hypnotise me on the spot, 'that you were not *born* a homosexual; you were conditioned into it. And what can be conditioned in can be conditioned out.'

To my relief her eyes released mine and strayed to a point in the middle distance behind me. I sensed that I had lost her attention. Experience suggested that my friend Gerhard had just entered. Looking round, I found this to be the case. Pausing in the doorway, Gerhard dominated the room, partly with his sheer size, partly with a kind of sexual magnetism even I could recognise. There was something animal about him, but intelligently animal, elegantly simian; with his high cheekbones, the almond-shaped, hazel-coloured eyes, neat ears, the slightly grizzled hair dense and fine like fur on the compact skull. On his nights out he reverted, as he put it, to his roots, and dressed in the boots, khaki and leather of his farm youth, to considerable effect in this pseudo-chunk setting. Amidst the self-consciously revealing skin-tight leathers and too-shiny metal appurtenances, the blow-dried wind-swept haircuts, the anxiously styled crew cuts, the carefully gauged one-day stubble, he looked what in a sense – but only in a quite limited sense – he was, a farmer astray in the city. Nothing in his appearance betrayed the considerable mileage he had derived from that image since discovering its potential.

'Forgive me,' Johanna breathed, returning her attention to me with an effort, 'I thought I recognised that young man. I think I must have met him somewhere.'

'That is Wouter,' I announced. 'My friend.'

Her eyes turned a dark green. 'Ooooh,' she half-growled, half-purred. 'I can see your problem.'

Gerhard spotted us across the room and crossed the dance floor with the elaborate unself-consciousness which always marked his more calculated effects. The two dancers paused in their slow gyrations to stare at him, with the overt hostility with which homosexual men seem to express their interest in each other.

Even the neckless hunk shifted restlessly as Gerhard approached, but his interest was evidently entirely professional; he came over to Johanna and muttered, in the flat interrogative I now recognised from the telephone, 'Shall I check him, Colonel?'

'Relax, Boetie,' she said, in a tone one would use to a loyal but stupid dog, 'I'm expecting him. Why don't you go and ask somebody to dance?'

He looked at her uncertainly, with the dim insecurity of somebody who suspects a joke at his expense but can't see the point. 'Cheez, no, Colonel, I dunno, with so many *moffies* round a man just doesn't feel safe. You feel you have to stand with your back to the bar.' He giggled at his own joke, an unpleasant mirthless cackle.

'That's nonsense, Boetie, you're absolutely safe; one thing about homosexuals, they have aesthetic standards if no others.'

Gerhard had now reached us. I could see from his gait and his bearing that he was adopting his aw-shucks-ma'am manner for the occasion, the one he reserved for non-sexual purposes, which is to say women. He extended a hand the size of which was usually enough to cow any new acquaintance.

'Good evening,' he said, 'Dr van der Merwe?'

'Of course,' she purred. 'You must be … Mr Theron.'

'Call me Wouter,' Gerhard said, with the faintest flicker of an eyebrow at me.

'Hi, I'm Bruce,' the barman said. 'What can I get you?'

Johanna proved to be an efficient negotiator and acute questioner. Though clearly more than taken with Gerhard, she did not abandon the spirit of scientific enquiry.

'I need to be quite sure,' she said, after we had covered the preliminaries, 'that you absolutely want to be part of this treatment.'

'Of course,' Gerhard said, 'why else should I be here?'

'Oh, you'd be surprised at how many people come to me against their will because they're having pressure put on them. Do you have any particular reason for wanting reorientation?'

Gerhard looked convincingly uncomfortable. 'Well, of course, you realise that it is a matter of some delicacy between Nick here and myself …'

'Of course,' she said, 'Mr Nicholson has explained to me …'

'Call me Morris,' I said to her, in a tone sufficiently emphatic, I hoped, to make an impression on Gerhard's obtuseness.

'Morris has explained,' she said, 'that you are not entirely convinced that your present orientation is natural and permanent.'

'That's right,' he said.

'Why is that?'

'Well, I just feel … you know … different to what I used to feel.'

'Do you now feel less attracted to men or more attracted to women?'

'Or just less attracted to me?' I asked, in what I thought was a creditable imitation of waspish reproach.

'Well, a bit of both – that is, in answer to your question, Doctor.'

'If you have any doubts, just come and see me, mate,' Bruce said, passing Gerhard the Black Label he had ordered.

'Shut up, Bruce. Women in general or any particular woman?'

'Oh ... both ... yes, both.'

'Which particular woman?'

'Which ... well, there is this woman that I have ... that I think I might have a relationship with.'

'What is her name?'

Gerhard was clearly not prepared for this question. 'Leonora le Roux,' he said, and I stopped myself just in time from throwing my wine glass at him.

'Mm. Sounds like an *Afrikanermeisie*. Does she know about your deviance?'

'My ...?'

'Your deviance. Your perversion.'

'Oh, that. Yes, I have told her.'

'And what are her feelings?'

'Oh, very understanding, but ... well, not entirely reconciled to it.'

'One would not expect her to be.' The Colonel gave Gerhard what one could only call an assessment, inspecting him with no more reticence than if she were judging stud bulls at an agricultural event. Then she said, 'Of course, she will have to be present during the treatment.'

'*What*?' Gerhard and I asked at the same time.

'Yes,' she said. 'I believe in informed consent.'

'Consent is one thing,' Gerhard objected, 'which I might well be able to arrange, but actual presence is quite another thing. You must realise that Leonora is quite a conservative girl, and Nick – Morris – here tells me that your procedures are quite ... invasive.'

'That is so, and for that reason I would not want her to be present while I administered the actual treatment, which is of a nature perhaps too personal for some young women. But she needs to be there *in* a position of support and *as* positive reinforcement immediately after the treatment. It is all a matter of associations.'

'Does this mean that I am not allowed to be present?' I asked.

'Not after the therapy, no. But before the therapy, yes, so that you can be associated with the pre-treatment set of mind.

294

an aversion-object and an attraction-object. The aversion-object needs to be somebody closely associated with the subject's pre-therapy life.'

'It's nice to think that I will be useful,' I said.

'You must not take this personally,' Johanna said. 'Science is impersonal and impartial.'

'And may I ask exactly what this therapy entails?' Gerhard asked.

'You may ask, but I must warn you that techniques which in the clinical atmosphere of the laboratory are perfectly impersonal may strike you here, in this setting' – she gestured at the dance floor, which by now looked like a blacksmith's convention getting out of control – 'as very ...'

'Invasive?' I suggested.

'Intimate,' she said to Gerhard, ignoring me, and lightly raking the back of his hand with her nails. 'So I propose that we leave the technical details until we are *in* a more scientific ambience.'

'But I need to know what I'm letting myself in for,' Gerhard objected. 'I mean, you said yourself, informed consent ...'

'But of course, of course. You will be able to withdraw *up* to the very last moment. But for the time being I expect you to trust me.'

Apart from this slightly open-ended clause, we managed to negotiate, without seeming to negotiate, almost exactly what we had hoped for: an 'initial' therapy session at the Silvermine laboratory, with nobody present other than the subject, his 'lover', his 'girlfriend', and, as assistant and no doubt security, Boetie, whom Johanna at length condescended to introduce to us as 'my assistant, Boetie Bester'.

Boetie extended a hand like a small plump blind animal. 'Bester,' he said in his flat tone that deprived fact and interrogation alike of their point, 'Breker Bester'. His handshake, though every bit as clammy as the rest of his appearance would have led one to expect, was unexpectedly powerful, a bone-crushing reminder that somewhere under the blubber and bluster there were still the muscles acquired on the rugby field, in training camp, somewhere where boys were taught to be tough and men were taught to kill – where Brothers became Breakers. He seemed eager to make an impression on Gerhard – rather oddly so, given his probable opinion of homosexuals, but explicable perhaps by a veneration for masculine bulk, of which he seemed doomed to increase his own share only by lateral expansion.

'I'll show you round the laboratory,' he said. 'It's the best equipped in the southern hemisphere.'

'Equipped for what?' Gerhard asked.

'For experiments,' Boetie said darkly, and Johanna laughed.

'It used to be involved in many strategic developments which have now been stopped. But it's still very much operative.'

'Anything else for anybody?' Bruce asked, but directing his question at Gerhard.

'No, thank you, Bruce, we have everything we need,' Johanna said firmly.

'Speak for yourself, Colonel,' the barman said.

CHAPTER FOURTEEN

Trying to scrub the print of the handcuffs off my wrist the next morning in the bath, I wondered at the process through which I had allowed myself to become embroiled in a mess that seemed to have the capacity to complicate itself exponentially over time. What had been a relatively simple environmental case now involved bizarre sex experiments and meetings in seamy nightclubs with the sort of people that a month ago I had not known existed. And now Leonora of all people, Leonora the one retreat of sanity from the improbable world of Luc Tomlinson and his baboons, had also become implicated in the web of intrigue and lies. I wondered uncharitably whether Gerhard had deliberately done this: it was the kind of thing that would divert him, for Leonora to find herself part of a lurid sex experiment. But then, recalling the circumstances, I had to concede that he had probably come up with her name on the spur of the moment because he could not think of any other – though it was a bit provoking that he could not have produced Dikeledi or Angie or one of those women friends homosexual men are supposed to have so many of.

I was musing along these lines, not getting much further with cleaning the handcuffs off my wrist, when the phone rang. I sighed. The only person who would phone me so early in the morning was my mother, who, having given birth to me, assumed she had retained exclusive rights to me in perpetuity.

'Hello,' I said in my least encouraging tone, dripping on the bedroom floor.

'Morning,' a male voice said. 'Sorry to bother you at what is clearly not a good moment.'

The apology half-mollified me, half-reinforced my irritation. 'No problem,' I said, 'what can I do for you?'

'This is Andrew Conroy.'

'Oh, I'm sorry, I assumed it was a client. Where are you phoning from?'

'From my house. I wouldn't normally phone so early, but I'll be in court all morning, and I wondered if you'd like to have lunch today?'

'Lunch?' I considered, but I was too surprised by the invitation to think clearly. 'Yes, that sounds good.'

'Good. How about the Gardens? It looks as if it's going to be a lovely day.'

'The Gardens will be fine. What time?'

'One o'clock?'

'One o'clock.'

It was only as I put down the receiver that I realised I'd intended to lunch with Leonora, to fill her in as tactfully as possible on the role she was going to be expected to play in Gerhard's re-orientation. She would have to be part of our planning meeting in the afternoon, and a preliminary conversation would certainly have helped to get her used to the idea of being the girlfriend-in-waiting of a homosexual-in-transit. It was not the kind of thing that was easy to explain over the telephone to anybody; I had no idea how I would do so to Leonora.

In the event, I didn't attempt it. I simply phoned Leonora, before leaving for work, and told her that Gerhard and Luc Tomlinson and I needed to discuss something with her, and would she be at the Wig and Pen at five-thirty.

'Is it anything … important?' she asked.

'Yes. It has to do with Luc's baboons.'

'I'd be very pleased to help,' she said, 'but how?'

'We'll explain it all to you this afternoon. It's rather complicated.'

'That's all right, then. See you then.'

It occurred to me, as I rang off, that I had not considered the possibility that Andrew Conroy might invite Leonora as well. So far all our meetings had been triangular, as it were; and yet there had been something in Conroy's invitation that had confined itself to me alone. I found I was pleased about this and ashamed of being pleased.

As I got out of my car to close my gate, Tornado came over to greet me, as he now did every morning, apparently feeling he had established a stake in my welfare. I patted the huge head, hoping his slobber would not drip on my newly polished shoes. I often wondered if I owed it to a creature that had saved my life to allow it to drool on me.

'There you go, Tornado,' I said. 'I love you too, but come and see me when I'm wearing old clothes.'

'Hi, Nick!' somebody shouted brightly from across the way. It was Sharon, sveltely on her way to work, with little Samantha, somewhat less sveltely on her way to play school.

I waved back. 'Lovely day,' I shouted, in a tone that normally terminated our conversations.

But not this morning. Sharon parked Samantha in the baby seat of the car and sauntered over. I had no choice but to remain standing outside my car, Tornado nuzzling my hand.

'He's so fond of you,' Sharon said.

I couldn't say what I thought, which was that I was probably the only human being he got to talk to all day. 'Well, I am of him too,' was all I could come up with.

'Oh, good,' she said, with more enthusiasm than the sentiment or the occasion really demanded. 'I just wanted to share our good news with you. Our papers have arrived.'

'Your papers?' I asked blankly. I couldn't imagine what papers could inspire such joy: had a lapsed subscription to the *Cape Times* been revived? Then I remembered. 'Oh, your *papers*. Your Australian papers.'

'Yes, isn't that just brilliant? We're leaving for Perth next month.'

'That sounds great,' I said insincerely. 'Do you like Perth?'

'Oh, we've never seen it, but everyone says it's absolutely fabulous. Like Port Elizabeth, only much cleaner, you know. And *no crime*.' She paused and recomposed her face. 'Actually, we hate to leave.' She gestured towards Table Mountain, which was glistening in the early morning light. 'I mean this will always be our country, but we feel we owe it to Samantha to move to a safer environment.' As if to register her opinion of this indebtedness, Samantha started screaming in her baby seat, but Sharon was too absorbed in her own act to notice. 'It will take a lot of courage to start afresh so far away from our family and friends.'

'I thought your family and friends were all over there already?' I asked. She had told me on a previous occasion that they were being forced to emigrate because everybody they knew was leaving.

She looked hurt. 'Oh no, we'll be quite alone, Stu and little Sam and me.'

'And Tornado?' I suggested. The dog wagged his tail at the sound of his name.

Her face dropped even further, from pathos into the realms of tragedy. 'Oh, that's the saddest thing of all. We can't possibly take him. Australia has a quarantine period of nine months, and we couldn't possibly expect him to survive that, could we, Tornado?' she said brightly to the dog, who responded but moderately, as if guessing that he was being asked to agree to his own superfluity. 'Besides,' she added, 'in Australia one doesn't really need a dog, does one?'

'Not?' I asked, nonplussed at this new light on Australian self-sufficiency.

'No, not like here.' She made big eyes at me. 'No ... *crime*, you know.'

'Oh. So what will you do?'

'I suppose we'll have to have him put down,' she said brightly, 'unless ...' and she looked at me coyly.

'Unless?'

'Unless a kind neighbour would like to adopt him?'

I realised too late what the whole conversation had been leading up to.

'You don't mean me, do you?'

'Well, I must confess, I thought that you might like to be given the first opportunity to ... you know, take over Tornado. It would be so much the most suitable solution, don't you think?'

I thought. The inconvenient thing was that she was right: there was a lot to be said for her proposal, indeed nothing to be said against it except that I did not want a dog. I was not the kind of person who had a dog.

'Well,' I said, 'that's a thought.' Tornado looked up at me as if waiting for me to reply. 'The problem is,' I continued, relieved to find that I had a valid problem, 'is that I'm at the moment considering a move to London.'

'Oh?' she said, her brightness acquiring a slightly sceptical edge. 'You haven't mentioned that before?'

'No, well, it's by no means certain, but it's a possibility, and I obviously wouldn't want to commit myself at this stage to something that might complicate my departure.' I found I was explaining myself to Tornado rather than to her. He seemed even more sceptical than she.

'Well,' she said, becoming aware of Samantha's wailings in the car, 'I thought I'd tell you about it first. Think about it, you needn't decide immediately.'

'I will,' I said. 'I mean think about it.'

'Please do.' A last flash of brightness and she was gone, Samantha staring at me accusingly through the back window, no doubt hating me as part of the unsafe environment that had been so unfairly imposed on her at birth.

I found to my irritation that I did think about it on my way to work. There really did seem to be no reason for me not to return Tornado's favour and save his life – and I did not for a moment think that Stuart and Sharon would go to a great deal of trouble to find an alternative home for a dog that they hardly noticed while he lived with them. All my habits, domestic as well as emotional, objected, their lips pursed, their eyes averted in disapproval, to the invasion of my home and my life by a large, demonstrative, dependent, drooling dog. It would not be fair to the dog to be left on its own all day, I assured myself, but without altogether convincing myself that, given a choice, Tornado would prefer to be put down.

So I returned to the real enough question of whether I might go to London. Mr McKendrick had not mentioned the matter since our initial discussion, but I knew well enough that this silence was perfectly compatible with his planning the matter to the last detail before informing me, as he had done with the company car. Having shown me the bloom of his intention, Mr McKendrick might well present me with a fully flowering decision one morning.

The traffic was again slow enough to give me time to turn over this question, and to contemplate once again the city that I would be leaving. Always at its best in winter, at least to my kind of temperament, Cape Town was sparkling in the damp sunshine of the early morning, sea and sky and mountain all looking impossibly fresh. And yet, of course ... I drove past a *Cape Times* poster: *Elderly man battered to death in flat*. Did one want to live to be battered to death in one's own home? My mind was turning over this matter so actively that it seemed appropriate to have Myrah say to me as I arrived in my office, 'Mr McKendrick would like to see you as soon as you come in.' I knew that it would be the London option.

And so it proved. With his usual tension-inducing pauses, cautions, reservations and provisos, Mr McKendrick let it be known that the firm was going to open an office in London and that (almost) all the partners agreed that with my knowledge of English law, and my good track record locally, I would be the most appropriate person to head such an initiative – 'as full partner in the firm, of course,' he added, as if this had not been the most anxiously discussed aspect of the whole matter: spending a fortune on opening a London office was a relatively minor matter compared with admitting a fresh piglet to the feeding trough.

'You do have a British passport, I take it?' he asked.

I nodded. 'Through my parents.' My parents had come from England after the War, when South Africa was a land of opportunity, and had forgotten to go back when it ceased being that.

'Good. That will make it simpler. Can I take it then, that you are accepting the position?'

Absurdly, I thought of Tornado. 'I wonder if I can ask for a day or two to think this over,' I said. 'I'm aware of course that this is a unique opportunity, but there are personal considerations which I have to think through.'

'Of course, of course. I'm not pressing you for a reply,' he said, though it was clear that he was hoping I'd give him one anyway. 'We were hoping to get going by October or so, but plenty of time, plenty of time.'

'I'll give it my most serious consideration, of course,' I said, 'and let you know as soon as I have reached a decision.'

'Dikeledi,' I said, popping into her office on my way back to mine, 'give me one good reason to stay in this country.'

She gave me her what's-with-this-white-shit look. 'I could say because we're trying to make a go of it, but that's not going to do it for you, so I'll just say because you've still got it better here than you'll have it anywhere else.'

'For how long?'

'I don't know, Nicholas. We're not handing out guarantees.'

'We?'

'The New South Africans. The Dark Peoples. Whoever it is that you see yourself as distinguished from.'

On my way from Dikeledi's office to mine, I met Angie, who uncharacteristically hardly returned my greeting.

'Anything wrong?' I asked.

'No. Yes.'

'Tell me about it.'

'It's just ... hell Nick, are all South African men like that?'

'Like what? Like Trevor?'

'Not Trevor. Kevin.'

'What's wrong with Kevin?'

'Just what's wrong with every South African man I've met since I've come to this place. They're all just after one bloody thing.'

'That's supposed to be true of all men, isn't it, not just South Africans?'

'You don't understand. What they're after is a bloody British passport. They all want to marry me!'

She burst out crying.

I was early for my lunch appointment with Andrew Conroy, so I strolled more slowly than usual through central Cape Town, reflecting on the demise of the English-style department stores, and the rise of the informal traders. On Greenmarket Square, originally the site for sober Dutch burghers to sell their produce to their fellow-burghers, were spread out the craft and cunning of a continent, all flooding to the new trading opportunities in the South, intent on reversing the processes of history: where three hundred years before European settlers

303

had brought trashy trinkets to trade for produce, cattle and land, now the natives were bringing the trash to trade for the hard currency of the European tourist. All the glass beads and copper wire were being returned to source, having had curiosity value added to them by being turned into ethnic jewellery; all the animals wiped out by the colonists were being commemorated with serried rows of funeral statuary: tall giraffes (the despair of airlines), massive elephants, kindly hippos, snarling lions, carved in wood and stone, etched on copper, worked in beads, painted on t-shirts, reproduced on greeting cards, all posing as authentic African produce to satisfy the needs of visitors who were used to satisfying their needs by shopping.

In one corner, possibly the Antipodean fringe, was a stall selling didgeridoos. A young man was performing on one of his products, lost to all but the sound of his instrument. On the ground next to him sat a young woman in beads, lots of beads, whom I recognised as Fiona. She was holding a small drum as if it was trying to run away, and beating it as if it was misbehaving. I tried to catch her eye, but she seemed lost in the waves of sound and rhythm she and the young man were generating. I wondered what she would do if her cell phone rang.

While I was watching her, she seemed to become aware of my presence, and focused on my face. Assuming she was trying to place me, I said, 'Hi. I'm a friend of Luc's.'

Not greatly to my surprise, she did not acknowledge this social nicety; merely intensified her stare. For one terrible moment I thought she was going to go into a trance as she had done over the avocado, but she merely started blinking rapidly, and said, drumming rapidly, and chanting in time to her drumming, 'I know you, I know your aura.'

I have heard dog owners complain that at doggy occasions they are recognised only as the owners of their dogs; I had a pang of sympathy with this displacement as I realised that to Fiona I was merely the bearer of my aura.

'I hope my aura is in good order,' I said, possibly a trifle facetiously to her taste, because she frowned, while drumming more slowly. Then she started drumming more urgently, and said, 'Your aura is blocked.' Then she repeated, 'Your aura is blocked,' and I hoped she was not building up to a chant on the subject of my aura.

Three German tourists were listening with earnest attention to this diagnosis, and regarding me with evident misgivings as the owner of a blocked aura; no doubt, like faulty plumbing, a blocked aura could pollute the surroundings and cause the mystical equivalent of typhoid. They said something to each other and moved away from me.

I was going to ask whether it would be expensive to fix, but opted for, 'Is there anything I can take for it?'

Fiona stopped drumming, and reached into the bodice of the loose robe she was wearing. She brought out a piece of coloured crystal and gave it to me. Her companion sustained his tuneless wailing.

'Your second and fourth chakras are out of balance,' she said. 'Wear this next to your heart, and say to yourself "I accept all that I am" ten times a day.'

'What is it?'

'Rose quartz. It will help you to love yourself.'

'I thought we weren't supposed to love ourselves,' I objected, still half-facetiously.

'That's bullshit,' she said in surprisingly down-to-earth tones, a businesslike daughter of the suburbs rather than an Earth Mother. 'The Christian cringe fallacy. Wear the quartz next to your heart. Get yourself a ruby to wear for passion. The rose quartz will be ten rand.'

I handed over a note, which she pocketed adroitly. Then she started drumming again and lapsed into mystical communion with her chakras, oblivious to my presence. As I left Green-market Square I heard her drumming start up again under the thin sound of the didgeridoo. I put the rose quartz in my shirt pocket.

'It's a way of makings sense of the universe, like any other,' said Andrew Conroy. I had told him about my encounter with Fiona. We were sitting out of doors under the huge trees in the public gardens; relic of the colonial ambitions of the Dutch, who established here a sensible vegetable garden to victual their ships, and of the English, who turned the vegetable garden into a botanical garden.

'Do you believe in it?'

'Not for a moment. But nor do I believe in the Biblical account of creation, and yet I can appreciate a certain consistency of metaphor in it. All our systems – Platonic, Ptolemaic, Newtonian, Copernican, Einsteinian – what are they but attempts to make sense of that' – he waved expansively at the mountain, the trees, the garden – 'and this' – and he pointed at his own heart – 'and of course that?' – and he pointed at my heart, where the piece of rose quartz immediately throbbed painfully, as if in response to the attention.

'But surely Fiona's ravings don't rate with Plato and Newton?'

'Well, for her they do, and given the efficiency of modern communication systems, they probably do so for more people than ever believed in Plato or Ptolemy. Not, of course, that mere numbers mean anything.'

'Numbers make up majorities, and majorities win elections.'

'The majority doesn't judge, it reacts.'

'Can't the majority judge the best interests of the majority?'

'Absolutely not. One intelligent, well-informed, well-disposed individual could judge much more wisely of the interests of the majority than the confused members of that majority.'

'A philosopher ruler?' I asked with light irony, but he ignored my tone and replied factually, 'Yes.' He pointed at the lawns surrounding us, on which various people had spread themselves out, having pulled out the 'Please Keep Off the Grass' notices. 'The majority of those people believe that it is in their interests to lie on the lawn. In the long run, this will destroy the lawn and there will be no more lawn to lie on. Who knows best? The scoff-law or the killjoy?'

'Anyway,' I said, 'Fiona seems to think I need to crank up my passion. She recommended a ruby worn on the body.'

He smiled. 'Passion again. The great goat-bleat of the modern age. Most people, when they talk of passion, mean the craving they have for ice cream or, if they're more sophisticated, cashmere sweaters. But they also want to believe that they are capable of the ultimate transport, of multiple simultaneous orgasms, of shuddering screaming eruptions of bliss, the

306

meaning of life contained in a spasm of the loins, everything that they've read about in the magazines and seen in the soap operas. So they talk of passion as if it was a holy duty, an ennobling state, a higher mode of being.'

'But ... it exists, surely,' I said. I had never experienced such a state of consciousness, but had assumed this to be a failing on my part rather than a misrepresentation on the part of the media.

'Yes, it exists, but it's far rarer than they want to believe, those seekers after g-spots and orgasms. Does our Fiona strike you as a truly passionate being?'

'Well, I suppose not; she seems too unfocused somehow ...'

'Exactly: she's so unfocused that she would forget whether she was making love or beansprouts salad. But she thinks she has passion.' He paused, apparently looking critically at a young couple on the lawn who were getting progressively more interested in each other. 'Perhaps people haven't learnt to distinguish between passion and prurience,' he said, lapsing into the slight didacticism to which he was prone. 'Prurience, from the Latin *prurire*, to itch. Now you,' he said, 'strike me as less avidly in pursuit of physical sensation than most young people your age.'

He was on the point of carrying on, but our food arrived, and in the fuss of arranging everything on the smallish table, he seemed to reconsider his own intention.

'You'll wonder why I'm lecturing at you,' he said. 'You must forgive me. We all think we have wisdom to impart, but forget that young people have their own ideas.'

'I don't know,' I said, 'I'm not sure that I have very many ideas of my own.'

He put down his fork. 'You have some very good ideas,' he said. 'I read your thesis.'

I could feel myself blushing with surprise and pleasure. 'Where on earth did you get to read it?'

'I was the external examiner. I was lecturing at UCT at the time.'

'I'm flattered that you remember.'

'It was a very good thesis.'

'Still, what a coincidence that we should meet like this.'

307

Conroy seemed to be considering his words more carefully than usual. 'Not really,' he said after a pause, 'I mean, given the smallness of the legal circles here. But I must confess, too, that it wasn't entirely a coincidence. Over the years I had noticed your name coming up in cases, and I'd kept track of your movements. And then, when Luc was looking for an environmental lawyer, I suggested to his mother that she should tell him about you. And afterwards I asked her to arrange a meeting between us.'

'I remember she said she had a friend who wanted to meet me, but of course, I didn't take that too literally.' I thought for a while; then asked what I most wanted to know: 'But why? I mean, as they say, why me?'

'I was intrigued by your thesis. It suggested the kind of conservatism that I admire. It also showed, if you'll forgive my saying so, a kind of immaturity that called out for guidance, a kind of ignorance about life that needed to be informed. If I'd had a son, that was how I would have wanted him at that age: fundamentally sound, but open to influence, a challenge and a responsibility for an older man.'

I reflected on this. 'So you chose me?'

'Yes. Do you mind?'

I considered. 'No, I'm flattered. But I don't know if I can live up to your expectations.'

'Oh well, if you don't …!' he laughed.

It was true that I thought Conroy's choice of me was a compliment; but it was also true that there was something disconcerting about being selected so entirely involuntarily, indeed unwittingly. I reached across the table for the salt.

'What's that?' Conroy asked, his tone sharply inquisitive.

'What?' I looked down at where he was pointing and felt myself blushing again. On my extended wrist the purple handcuff stamp I had been given the night before was still clearly visible.

'That looks like a night club stamp,' he said. 'I didn't know you were a raver.'

'It's a complicated story,' I said, 'but I had to go to a night club, a place called the Brass Tack, last night on business, believe it or not.' I wondered whether I could tell him the story, then decided against it: though apparently on Luc's or at any rate Joyce's side of the dispute with Brick Tomlinson, he was still a friend and associate of Brick's. So I left it at that. He seemed pensive.

'Did you go with your friend Gerhard?' he asked.

'Yes, as it happened. It's much more his kind of territory than mine.'

'So I would have assumed, yes,' he said rather dryly. He seemed put out, though I couldn't quite understand why. Admittedly the Brass Tack was not a place I would normally frequent, but I did not feel compromised by a single visit. Of course, he did not know it had been a single visit.

Conroy changed the topic to some point of law he had come across that morning, and the rest of the lunch went smoothly, his conversation engrossing as always. Still, it was as if the incident, so petty in itself, had placed a slight strain on the conversation. As we prepared to leave – Conroy insisted on paying – he said, 'Listen, I'm sorry if I've been slightly preoccupied. Why don't you come round over the weekend and I'll play you that Bach Suite I promised you?'

'That would be wonderful,' I said, sincerely enough, but strangely apprehensive. 'When would be a good time?'

'Whenever suits you,' he said. 'Saturday evening?'

'Saturday evening will be fine,' I replied.

It was a good thing that I had the planning meeting after work to think of, otherwise I might have spent time wondering about Andrew Conroy. It was clear that he wanted to establish a special relationship of some sort between us. Whereas I gave no credence to my friend Gerhard's theories – he was incapable of imagining a relationship that was not sexually motivated – it was true that Conroy now no longer seemed to want to include Leonora in the friendship. Whereas this of course did not necessarily mean that he had sexual designs on me, it did seem to imply a friendship that was in some sense exclusive of other people. Time would tell; Saturday evening would almost certainly bring a clarification of motives. But for the time being his motives were obscure – almost as obscure to me as my own feelings.

The Wig and Pen was packed, as it usually was at that time of the afternoon. Gerhard and I arrived together, to find Luc Tomlinson and Leonora confronted at a little table. They were an incongruous couple: she neat as always in a two-piece suit, he flamboyantly out of place in this stronghold of young professionals in his faded jeans and shapeless but colourful cotton jacket. She was drinking a sparkling mineral water, and he seemed to be drinking straight water. I was surprised to note that they were having a lively conversation, though I couldn't have imagined about what; perhaps Leonora was telling Luc that he reminded her of Brad Pitt.

The meeting was not made easier for me by the fact that Gerhard had decided to leave explanations to me. 'I'm going to be dealing with the Black Widow,' he said, 'you deal with Rageltjie de Beer.' I explained as best I could, making much play of the need to rescue the baboons at all costs. As I had anticipated, Leonora was well disposed to the scheme, but puzzled at her own role in it, and as I had also anticipated, explaining in finer detail the nature of the occasion to a person who was even more inhibited than I about references to matters sexual, as well as constitutionally resistant to any form of subterfuge, was well-nigh impossible.

'But why must I pretend to be Gerhard's girlfriend?' she asked, quite clearly appalled at the very idea.

'Well, you see, in order to make the whole thing plausible he has to pretend to have a girlfriend, and we needed somebody, you know, whom we could trust. And you needn't actually *say* you're his girlfriend, you can just, you know, allow the impression to be formed.'

'A lie is no less of a lie for not being spelt out,' she persisted. 'Am I going to have to *do* anything?' she asked.

'No, of course not,' I assured her, though not entirely convinced of this. I had no idea what Johanna's procedures entailed. Luc did not improve things much by choosing this moment to suggest with uncharacteristic helpfulness, 'I suppose he'll have to fuck you to prove that he's cured.'

There was an awful silence during which it was clear that both Gerhard and Leonora were refraining with difficulty from betraying their nausea. 'Oh, nonsense,' I tried to laugh, 'the therapy is purely orientational, it has no practical component.'

'What does that mean?' Luc asked, which I couldn't tell him, having absolutely no idea.

'Listen, let's forget the therapy; it's just a way of getting us into the lab,' I said. 'What we have to plan is how to go about getting the baboons out of the lab. You've brought the plans? Good man.'

'Yes, well,' he said. 'I had to sneak in and steal it while my mother was at gym.'

'I must say,' said Leonora with uncharacteristic firmness, 'I don't like all the dishonesty that we have to commit. I mean, if our scheme is a good one, it shouldn't be necessary to lie and steal.'

I could see Gerhard getting restless with irritation, and in truth I also thought that Leonora was being very inconveniently moral about the whole thing. While I was drafting a diplomatic but firm reply, Luc Tomlinson to my surprise made another contribution: 'If other people lie and steal you're not going to get anywhere if you don't also lie and steal.'

'And what happens to society if everybody lies and steals?' she asked.

'Listen,' Gerhard said, 'I take your point absolutely in a general philosophical sense, what about the fabric of society and all that, but in the mean time there's a troop of baboons sitting out at Silvermine being subjected to heat tolerance tests and organ rejection tests and infant deprivation tests …'

'Infant deprivation tests?' Leonora asked.

'Yes, they test the effect on mothers and infants of being forcibly separated just after birth,' Gerhard said brutally. Leonora paled visibly.

'But why do they need to test that?' she asked. 'Surely they know that it will cause trauma?'

'Somebody probably needed a subject for a PhD,' Gerhard said. 'But the point is while we sit and agonise about telling a few lies in order to release the baboons, the baboons are suffering.'

'Release the baboons?' asked Luc Tomlinson. 'Where are we going to release them?'

'I thought,' I said, 'that if we can just get them out of the cages and the laboratory, we can release them right there in the mountains at Silvermine. Look, here, on the plan, there's this back entrance ...'

'No,' said Luc, in a tone that might have struck a more sensitive person as rude. 'No way.'

'What do you mean, no way?' I demanded. 'What else can we do?'

'We have to take them back to Cape Point. They won't find their way back from Silvermine. They'd have to go through Dido Valley or Kommetjie or any number of other places where baboons aren't exactly welcome.'

'And how do you propose we transport a troop of baboons – how many are there anyway?'

'Only about twelve, eight adults and four young.' Luc's angelic composure was turning into a major irritant.

'And how do you propose we transport only about twelve baboons to Cape Point? I've got a BMW, and Gerhard has a Golf, and Leonora has a Mazda, and you have a bicycle, and it's not as if the baboons are going to sit still like a bunch of senior citizens on an outing to the seaside ...'

'Relax,' Luc said.

'Relax? What do you mean relax?'

'Relax,' he said again in his provocatively imperturbable way.

'And while we relax who rescues the fucking baboons?' I shouted at him, to Leonora's profound horror. I never swear, believing as I do that swearing is an admission of weakness in the face of adversity, and also an unnecessarily overt expression of one's own loss of control. It seemed to me, though, that an overt expression of some sort was called for by the circumstances. 'Relax?' I shouted at him. 'You mean we all go into meditation and levitate the fucking baboons out of their cages with ... with drums and fucking didgeridoos?'

'Please, Nicholas,' said Leonora. 'Your language.'

'Yes, really, Nicholas,' Gerhard chipped in. 'I'm quite shocked.' I kicked him under the table and he yelped more loudly than necessary.

'Listen,' I said, 'we're supposed to be planning a constructive plan of action, not thinking up objections to everything that gets suggested. So if we can attend to one thing at a time, Gerhard, I promise not to offend your maiden sensibilities again. Now, Luc, what exactly do you mean by your injunction that we should *relax* in the face of your insistence that we steal twelve baboons from the laboratory and transport them in luxury to their natural habitat?'

'I mean relax,' he said. 'I'll arrange for that if you can get me into the lab.'

'You mean all we need do is open this back door and give you access to the cages?'

'Well, yes,' he said, 'and of course if you can arrange for the personnel to be otherwise engaged ...'

'That's my job,' Gerhard said with a grimace. 'We must hope that that Neanderthal type, whatsisname ...'

'Boetie Bester.'

'Boetie Bester?' said Leonora. 'I was at school with a Boetie Bester. He was not very clever.'

'Sounds like our man. I mean we must hope that Boetie Bester will be in attendance at the therapy session, otherwise he's hardly going to allow us free run of the lab. Insofar as any of the bulges on his person was more eloquent than any other, I could have sworn the one under his jacket was a largeish firearm.'

'Do you have a gun for me?' Luc Tomlinson asked.

'We're not going to use guns,' I said. 'Somebody will get hurt. None of us even knows how to use a gun.'

'I know how to use a gun,' Leonora said. 'I did a course in small-arms handling as part of Youth Preparedness at school.'

'For heaven's sake, you object to telling a lie or two, but you're prepared to shoot your way into the place ...'

'I didn't say we should use guns,' Leonora said, 'all I said was that I ... '

'Exactly,' Luc said, cutting across her protest to address my argument, 'if we have to use their methods, we have to go all the way.'

'You can go all the way,' I said, 'I'm not going into a shoot-out with Boetie Bester. The man was a Civil Cooperation Bureau operative, it was his business to kill people.'

'Well, yes, sure, if you don't want to you needn't,' he said. 'But you know where I can get hold of a gun?'

313

'No,' I said firmly, then relented. 'There's a gun in my safe at home,' I said, 'the one the hijacker left behind.'

'Can I borrow it?' Luc asked.

'I suppose so,' I said. 'But I still think we should keep firearms out of it.'

'Relax,' Luc said again, and I suppressed my desire to kick him, too. 'I won't do anything foolish.'

I refrained from pointing out that just carrying a firearm was, under the circumstances, foolish. 'I'll bring the thing to my office tomorrow,' I said, 'if you'd like to collect it.'

'Sure,' he said, 'if you don't want me to come to your place.'

'Look, it's not ...' I started, then just shrugged. 'You're on a *bicycle*, for heaven's sake.' This was not the time for Luc Tomlinson to develop sensitivities nor for me to minister to them. 'Can we just coordinate our actual movements on Saturday?'

This proved to be about as easy as organising a Sunday school picnic or a D-Day landing: everybody insisted on a different configuration of personnel. I suggested that Gerhard and Leonora should arrive in one car, as the couple to be united by the proceedings, with me arriving in a separate car, to leave me free to help Luc Tomlinson, though how was he going to arrive ...?

'Relax,' he said, 'I'll have transport. You can come with me.'

'No, I can't,' I said, 'I have to be present before the therapy as aversion-object. And Leonora has to be present afterwards as attraction-object. So ...'

'But can't I travel with you to the laboratory?' Leonora asked, transparently reluctant to travel with Gerhard.

'No,' I said, 'can't you see that from Johanna's point of view we are the two with least reason to like each other? I mean, we're supposed to be in love with the same man ...'

'Which would be very flattering to me, as the man in question,' Gerhard said, 'except I get to be the wimp who doesn't know his own mind or whatever faculty is deemed to be responsible for one's decisions in these matters.'

'Well,' I said to Gerhard, probably with an unnecessary edge to my voice, 'if you want to make clear to the world in general and Doctor Johanna in particular that in fact you know your own mind, you could always get Clive to drive you to your appointment.'

'Now, Nicholas,' said Gerhard, 'that is unworthy of you. You know that that would blow our cover. Not to mention what it would do to Clive ...'

'You haven't told him?'

'You don't expect me to tell him that I'm subjecting myself to therapy that, if successful, would terminate or at any rate radically change the nature of our relationship?'

'I don't know what I expect from your relationships,' I said. 'But for the time being I expect you to help us plan how we're going to get twelve baboons out of an extremely well-fortified laboratory. Looking at this plan ...' I unrolled the plan again on the tiny pub table.

I managed by what I secretly thought was some skilful diplomacy to get the company to agree to my original suggestion: Gerhard and Leonora would arrive together. I would arrive in my own car, which would give me the option of leaving at the same time as Luc, who would arrive after the rest of us in the mystery transport that he kept on enjoining us to relax about. Leonora came up with the unexpected suggestion that she might be useful as a way of occupying Boetie Bester.

'If it's the Boetie Bester I'm thinking of,' she said, 'he used to quite like me at school.'

'And did you like him?' I asked.

'Not really, but I was sorry for him. We were in the same Sunday school class. He had a thing about being too short, and the other boys called him ...' she blushed, 'ugly names.'

'What ugly names?' Gerhard asked. 'It might help to get us out of a tight spot if he pulls his pistol on us – you know, call him names.'

'I can't ...' she began, then made a visible effort to force herself to something supremely distasteful. 'They called him *Mossiepiel*.'

I looked at Gerhard in mystification. 'Sparrowprick,' he translated for me. 'Apparently Boetie is less heroically endowed than he would want to be. Makes sense of his career choices, in an obvious sort of way.'

'Not that it makes me any more eager to face him,' I said. 'I can't see that shouting *Sparrowprick* at an armed man is going to make him drop his pistol. Will you be all right with him, Leonora?'

'Oh yes, thank you,' she said. 'I've done a course in Self-defence for Women.'

I've never thought of myself as a brave person. By definition bravery means taking a risk against the odds, and that has always struck me as intelligible only in the light of a clearly defined and self-evidently worthwhile objective. Since most human enterprise is actually surprisingly deficient in this respect – I have never been able to admire the man who climbed Everest 'Because it was there' – I have seldom felt called upon to risk my own safety and security beyond the limits and stresses of everyday living. In the two days preceding our intended infiltration of the Silvermine laboratory, though, it occurred to me that without intending to I had committed myself to an act of bravery, indeed folly. Doctor Johanna, for all that it was tempting to dismiss her as a comic monster, had been an efficient functionary of a ruthless and sanguinary regime; and Boetie Bester, for whatever pathetic reason, was armed and dangerous. There were times when I asked myself why I had allowed myself to be drawn into a project of which the objective – rescuing a troop of baboons from almost certain torture and death in the interests of science – seemed Quixotic, to say the least.

'Why are we doing this?' I said to Gerhard on the Thursday morning, after our less than reassuring planning meeting.

'I'm doing it because I can't resist a strong man in distress,' he said. 'And you are doing it because your concern for the environment extends also to the dumb creatures not protected by our new constitution, admirable as that document is in all other respects.'

'Thanks for telling me. And does my concern not extend itself to the human beings who may benefit from the experiments to which the dumb creatures are sacrificed?'

'Not until there's a clear code of conduct regulating the treatment of laboratory animals. The point is that whereas there may well be necessary and useful experiments, nothing obliges the likes of the Black Widow to measure her objectives against the rights of the animals, because animals have no rights. There is no control over the use to which they are put in these secret laboratories. And you may have picked up in your researches into the Silvermine laboratory that it was mainly used to test out different kinds of poison on animals – for use on human enemies of the state.'

'All this sounds rather glib to me.'

'The alternative is to believe that you're doing it because you too can't resist Luc Tomlinson. Nothing wrong with that, of course. You can call it sublimation if you like.'

Luc Tomlinson came to collect the gun from my office. I gave it to him wrapped in a dishcloth in a Woolworths packet.

'I hope you know what you're doing,' I said.

'Sure thing,' he said. 'Relax.'

'I wish you'd stop telling me to relax. I think I'm about as relaxed as is compatible with a proper sense of the seriousness of our enterprise.'

'Well, yes,' he said. 'You don't want to make too much of it, though.'

'In other words, relax.'

'You said it, not me.'

'And you've still got the cell phone?'

'Sure thing. I'll stay in touch. Just …'

'Relax?'

CHAPTER FIFTEEN

Saturday dawned as wet and cold as only a July morning can dawn in the Cape. I thought that this might render our exploit less risky, in that most people tend to be less conscientious about security when it entails getting wet. By the same token, though, it was likely to render our job more damp, muddy and generally unpleasant. I selected my warmest clothes: corduroy pants, woollen shirt and walking shoes, bearing in mind that as far as Johanna was concerned I had no reason to be dressed as if I was going on an outdoor endurance trial. Yielding to atavistic impulse, I slipped the rose quartz crystal into my shirt pocket.

We had arranged with Johanna to be at the laboratory at two o'clock, and I had impressed upon Gerhard the importance of being punctual for once. 'Never fear, I'll have Little Dorrit to get me there on time,' he said.

'Even Leonora can't physically extricate you from the kind of complications you tend to get yourself into at crucial moments.'

'That is all behind us. Clive has reformed me.'

Between them, then, Leonora and Clive would have to manage to get Gerhard to the laboratory at the appointed time. As I negotiated my way through the heavy rain along a winding, unknown road to an uncertain destination I found myself envying Gerhard and Leonora the company of each other, how little each other might have been what either of them would have selected if given a choice. On my own, with no company other than Leonora's Schubert tape, I could not escape gloomy forebodings: the fatalistic folk imagination infusing most of the songs imparted an air of mythic invincibility to the Black Widow and her goblinesque henchman. My normal guarantees and safeguards had been left behind; I was about to venture beyond the culture of burglar alarms and deep freezes into a realm of secret potions and processes.

318

The approach was not reassuring. The road narrowed to a track, and then stopped short at a high razor-wire fence. A large red sign said: '*Restricted Area; No entry to unauthorised Personnel.*' Slightly inconsistently, another, newer sign below this one, pointing to the right of the complex, said: '*Deliveries and Service*'. The gate was controlled from a guard hut, unmanned at present. Indeed, there was no sign of any human presence: either I had been right in my surmise that even security personnel were discouraged by such weather, or the laboratory was no longer deemed to merit the protection of guards. I got out of my car, reflecting that at least security guards had their uses in opening the gates that they guarded. The gate was not locked; I pushed at it, and it opened readily, with the ominous smoothness of those gateways to peril in literature and cinema. As I got back into my car, Gerhard's car, to my considerable relief, appeared behind me. I gestured to him to follow me and drove down a paved track leading to a small parking area, in which was parked a large Mercedes Benz and a dented blue Nissan Skyline. The laboratory, as I knew from Brick Tomlinson's plan, was largely underground, but at one end of the parking lot was a kind of glassed-in vestibule, again provided with a guard hut, again unmanned.

I waited for Gerhard and Leonora to get out of their car, and the three of us splashed towards the entrance. I smiled at Leonora; she was looking pale, and even Gerhard seemed unusually subdued. 'How are you feeling?' I asked.

He grimaced gamely. 'A bit exhausted. I made the most of my sexual orientation last night, just in case.' I realised that he was more anxious than he had allowed himself to show, and squeezed his arm.

The vestibule was as deserted as the rest of the approach, but there was a door at the far end with a bell push. Gerhard gave me a *Morituri te salutant* raised-hand greeting and pressed the button. After a longish silence the door was opened by Boetie Bester, still clad in his rumpled suit, and no friendlier than he had been at the club, though again apparently anxious to ingratiate himself with Gerhard. He also seemed to feel that the presence of a woman obliged him to make a show of strength or at any rate authority, and said, 'I'll have to search you for weapons and drugs.' I wondered why anybody would try to bring drugs into the laboratory, but submitted to Boetie's clumsy search.

'Sorry, lady,' Boetie said to Leonora, and then stopped himself and blushed bright red. For a moment he looked like the awkward schoolboy he must once have been.

'Hello, Boetie,' Leonora said.

'Leonora!' he breathed, with an expression closer to beatitude than I had expected ever to witness on Boetie Bester's face. Clearly Leonora, characteristically, had understated the extent of her hold on the man. He seemed quite at a loss. Then he recovered himself and said, 'I'm called Breker now. Not Boetie.'

We were ushered into the maw of the building by a now very attentive Boetie. He showed us into a reception area sparsely furnished with government-issue chairs, back copies of *You* magazine, the *Reader's Digest*, and *Paratus*, the official publication of the Defence Force. At the far end of the room was a door marked *Dr Johanna van der Merwe: Director of Research*.

'The Colonel will see you at two-thirty,' he said, but without explaining why the appointment had been deferred by half an hour. 'You can wait here,' pointing at the uninviting interior of the waiting room, 'or perhaps, if you like' – and this was directed at Leonora – 'I can show you around the laboratory.'

Since this was what we had been counting on, it was fortunate that the suggestion did not have to come from us. Leonora accepted the offer with proper enthusiasm, and Boetie led the way down a long, brightly lit corridor, a sterile succession of closed doors labelled with the names of researchers of one kind or another. At the end of the corridor was a barred door.

'This is normally locked,' said Boetie, 'but over the weekend there's nobody around. Except the animals.' He opened the barred door and led us into another corridor, indistinguishable from the first, except that the doors, instead of bearing the names of occupants, were labelled and numbered as Store Rooms.

'What's in here?' Gerhard asked.

Boetie grinned and winked. 'Stores,' he said. 'Emergency stores.'

'Medicines?' Gerhard asked, playing dumb.

Boetie giggled. 'You could say so.' He hesitated in front of one door. 'I'll show you something you've never seen before,' he said. He selected a key from his bunch, opened the door, and switched on the light. We peered in apprehensively. All we could see were shelves from the floor to the ceiling, housing hundreds of tins such as chemists use to store pills in large quantities.

'Medicines?' Gerhard asked again.

Boetie nodded. 'Medicine for bad moods. Ecstasy.'

'That's all Ecstasy?' Gerhard asked.

Boetie nodded. 'Lots, hey? We were going to feed them to the … you know, the Bantu, so that they couldn't make any more trouble, but that didn't work, so now we're selling them to other countries. The Colonel says it's a good source of foreign exchange. She doesn't mind if I help myself now and again – not to use myself,' he explained anxiously to Leonora, 'but to sell for a bit of pocket money when we go to those clubs.' He opened a tin and took out a foil leaflet with ten tablets. 'I can make more than a thousand rand out of that,' he boasted, pocketing the shiny leaflet. 'Plenty more where that came from.'

We continued our guided tour. Some of the doors had large warning notices on them; they said, simply, *Highly dangerous*, without specifying the nature of the danger. 'Poison,' Boetie said, and winked again. 'For people you can't get with bullets.'

One door had an extra sign that said *Do not enter without protective clothing.* 'Anthrax,' Boetie giggled. 'The colonel says there'll be a lot of money in that soon.'

He paused in front of one unmarked door. 'Emergency supplies,' he said. 'The Colonel thought if the elections … you know, went wrong, we might spend some time down here. She thought of everything.'

He unlocked the door: again shelves from floor to ceiling, but these stacked with a wide variety of groceries, though tinned bully beef and toilet paper seemed to predominate.

'And who's going to eat all that bully beef now?' Gerhard asked.

Boetie shrugged. 'I suppose we'll give it to the kaffirs when it reaches its Best Before date.' He locked the door. 'Come and have a look at the animal section. It's quite something. You want to see that?'

'Yes, why not?' said Gerhard, at his most casual.

'Do you want to see the dogs and cats or the baboons?' Boetie asked, as if he was offering us a choice of treats.

'Oh, the baboons, I think,' Leonora said, with admirable restraint. I knew how distressed she must be at the prospect of a tour of a collection of captive animals.

'Yes, they're more interesting,' Boetie said. 'The dogs just lie there, now we're no longer testing the poisons. It was different then, I can tell you. Some of them took a week to die.'

We became aware of the smell before we reached the cages; not just the usual smell of animals in captivity, urine and faeces and stale food, but the smell of chemicals and fear, a blend of the technologically advanced and the primitive. Then there was the sound: the whimpering, gibbering, chattering of unhappy animals.

The cages were arranged down two sides of a long shed-like room, brilliantly lit by fluorescent tubes. At the far end was a door that, if my reading of the plan was accurate, gave direct access to the outside of the building. I was relieved to see a key in the door. The baboons were for the most part alone, one to a cage, and the cages were arranged so that no contact was possible between cages. The cages all seemed very new.

'Clever buggers, baboons,' Boetie said, 'we have to place the cages so that they can't get to each other, otherwise they will, you know,' he made an apologetic gesture at Leonora, 'right through the bars.'

'But don't they get very bored?' Leonora asked.

Boetie giggled again. 'I don't know. What do baboons know about boredom?'

To judge by their behaviour, they knew all about it. The arrogant, assertive air that had so annoyed me on my visit to their home ground was gone. The baboons, adults and young alike, sat staring gloomily at us, as if we were manifestations of some unavoidable but uninteresting fate. One female was chewing at her own paw; a male was masturbating, but half-heartedly, as if he did not expect much joy from it.

'What are they being experimented on for?' I asked.

'This lot is lucky,' Boetie said. 'The Colonel has a contract to try out different ways of restraining laboratory baboons. You see, they found out that if the animal is too unhappy, it interferes with the results of the tests, so now they're comparing the different ways of holding them still while they're being experimented on. Some of these cages are bloody clever. This one,' he said, walking to the first cage, 'has what they call a squeezeback. You see, the back is loose – so you can move it forward, so – you see – and force the baboons to come to the front of the cage' – he demonstrated the action; the occupant of the cage, a large male baboon clearly used to the procedure, cowered to the front of the cage – so you can inject them or whatever.' He prodded a finger though the cage; the baboon snarled at him ineffectually.

'No way, José,' Boetie said. 'You don't get to me that way.' He turned to the next cage. 'Then we have these boards,' he said, pointing at a board equipped with straps at the four ends and in the middle. 'You just strap the baboon down with its legs and arms and waist, so it can't move. They don't like it, mind you; you should see them struggle.' He moved to a chair-like contraption, again fitted with straps. 'This one is also quite clever – we call it the ... *Gemakstoel* –' he looked enquiringly at Leonora.

'Easy chair,' she said.

'Yes, easy chair. You see the baboon actually sits in the chair and gets strapped to it by the neck and waist. They don't carry on like on the board, but the Colonel says they pass out. I think they're just pretending to pass out, you know how clever baboons are.'

'Anyway,' he said, 'we must go, the Colonel will be waiting for us. There are all those other things too –' he pointed at nets and tethers hanging from the walls, 'that we're also testing, but they're more old-fashioned, not like these things.'

'So you're basically testing out cage designs at the moment?' Gerhard asked.

'Yes, all these cages were specially designed for these tests. They even have a special lock' – he showed it to us – 'which doesn't need a key, but which the baboons can't open themselves, so we don't have to walk around with huge bunches of keys.'

'And what will happen to these baboons when you've done the tests?'

'I don't know, now they've stopped testing the poisons, they didn't last long then, you can imagine. We're exporting quite a few to France, their army does tests with baboons. I reckon we should help the French, they were good to us when the rest of the world was against us. And the English also take quite a few for their transplant experiments.'

On our way out I noticed a cage slightly separate from the others. It was also distinguished from the others in that it housed two baboons, the only cage in the room containing more than one baboon. The two baboons were grooming each other, but I noticed something odd about their actions. They were using only their right hands; both baboons lacked a left hand.

'And this?' I asked.

'A little mistake.' Boetie giggled. 'Somebody was trying to get these baboons to swap hands – you know, transplant from one baboon to the other – those baboons are sisters, so he thought if you cut off one's hand and sewed it to the other's arm it should take. But it didn't. You can't win them all.'

As we left the animal room, Boetie leading the way with Leonora, Gerhard said to me in a low voice, 'Do you still wonder why we're doing this?'

'No,' I said, 'but I'm still wondering how we're going to do it.'

We were taken back to the waiting room. Boetie knocked respectfully at the door harbouring Dr Johanna van der Merwe, then opened it and stood aside to allow us access. I could not entirely divest myself of a feeling of having a pistol trained on my back as we entered. The office was large and plushly furnished. Dr Johanna van der Merwe got up from her desk. She was dressed in a white laboratory coat, somewhat shorter and tighter than was entirely consistent with its protective function.

'Ah, Mr Theron, Mr Nicholson,' she said graciously, reverting to her more formal mode, 'and this must be Miss le Roux. Please have a seat; I'd like us to have a little chat before the actual therapy.'

Behind us the door was closed from the outside. Boetie would presumably stand guard. We sat down like obedient schoolchildren in front of her desk. On the desk, next to an angular arrangement of Strelitzia reginas, was a large framed photograph of a man in uniform, nondescript except for a large dark moustache. Johanna caught me looking at it and nodded.

'My dear late husband,' she sighed, 'Cornelius, Major Cornelius van der Merwe. A brave soldier and a devoted husband – alas, not two duties one can fulfil at the same time. *In* the end his duty to his country came first, I am proud to say. I would not have wanted a husband who stayed at home just to please me.'

This was a tricky opening line: insofar as it invited a response, it was difficult to tell whether it was most congratulation or condolence that was required. Gerhard adroitly combined the celebratory and the elegiac by murmuring, 'A fine-looking man.'

Gratified, Johanna visibly divested herself of her tender memories and said, 'Well, we must not dwell on the past. I have had my consolations, after all,' gesturing towards the wall behind her desk, where there were various photographs of her receiving awards and degrees, including one of her in full uniform, having a medal pinned to her ample bosom by a slightly perplexed-looking PW Botha.

'The Star of South Africa,' she said, as factually as was compatible with her evident pride. 'They can't take that away from me.' I couldn't imagine that anyone would want to, but contented myself with nodding in what I hoped was an impressed-looking way.

'My normal procedure is to encourage the subject' – she smiled tersely at Gerhard – 'to interact freely *with* me and *with* the two objects, the aversion-object and the attraction-object, *in* order to establish an atmosphere of absolute trust and acceptance.'

'And how,' Gerhard asked, 'how do we interact?'

'In any way that you find meaningful,' she said, 'but I normally encourage people to talk *through* any aspect of the situation that has been or may be traumatic. I am a fully qualified stress counsellor, so I can deal with any tensions that may come *to* the surface. *In* particular,' she said to Leonora, 'I want you to talk *through* your anger.'

She sat back as if, having given us this reassurance, she now expected us to start interacting, producing on command stresses and tensions for her to deal with. I glanced at Leonora, who sat pale with shock and embarrassment. Constitutionally averse as she was to lying, this injunction to act out the details of her lie must have struck her as an atrocity.

'Well, actually,' Gerhard said, 'it's remarkable, but there has been no stress or anger; we have all three from the start agreed to this therapy.'

'A most convenient belief for you, Wouter,' Johanna said, 'since you are the object of the anger *in* the other two. All the more reason for you to listen while they express that anger. Let us start with you, Leonora.'

'To tell the truth,' Leonora said, clearly relieved at being able to do so, 'I think Gerhard is right. Speaking for myself, I feel no anger.'

'Gerhard?'

'I mean Wouter. I call him Gerhard.'

'Ah!' Johanna said triumphantly, 'can't you see that your denial of his true identity reveals your suppressed anger, at having to accommodate the doubts of the man you're *in* love with as to whether you really are basically, and I do mean basically, what he wants?'

'Well, that is a problem, of course,' Leonora valiantly battled on, 'but I don't think I need take it personally.'

'But that is your mistake, surely?' persisted Johanna, whose idea of defusing tension seemed to be to foment it first. 'After all, can we separate the personal *from* the ideological in this instance? Should you not learn to access your own anger, to stop blocking it, and to express it to its object, to make it the basis for a new relationship in which you are not merely the object of his choices, but the subject of your own?'

Leonora looked at me for guidance, which I was hardly in a position to give her. I decided nevertheless to intervene. 'I think,' I said, 'if anybody has reason for a grievance it must be me.'

'There you are,' Johanna said to Gerhard, gratified but not

surprised at being vindicated. 'You must understand the anger of others before you can get *in* touch with your own feelings. The danger, Morris, is that your weak self-regard will internalise your rejection so completely as to accept it *as* your punishment for placing your affections unwisely. It is not a condition I am qualified to deal with, but I will recommend you to a psychiatrist I know, who has been very effective *in* restoring the confidence of members of the former government who were ousted from their positions by the new political dispensation.'

'Thank you,' I said weakly, aghast at the thought of being classified with the goons and murderers from whom we had so recently been delivered, and in whom low self-esteem might have been commended as a salutary approach to self-knowledge.

'The next step,' Johanna announced briskly, 'is for me to deal on my own with the subject – well, not entirely on my own, since I prefer to have my assistant on hand to avoid misunderstandings. I will no longer need the aversion-object, but the attraction-object, as I have said, will have to be present for positive reinforcement after the therapy session. Are you all here in the same car?'

'No,' I said, 'I am in my own car.'

'Excellent. Then this is the appropriate time for you to depart, leaving Leonora behind to ease Wouter into his new identity. All that will really be necessary is for the attraction-object to accompany the subject *on* the journey home. The symbolic significance of such a journey, I have found, plays a profound subliminal part *in* the reorientation process.'

I gave a pale-looking Gerhard a thumbs-up sign as Leonora and I left. Boetie took up a position just behind Gerhard, presumably to ensure his cooperation at all times. To him it was probably not much different from the interrogation sessions he must have attended in the same capacity in his years as an operative.

In the bleak waiting room outside I asked Leonora, 'Will you be all right?'

She smiled wanly. 'Of course. I'm a *boeremeisie*. I'm just sorry I can't help you rescue those poor baboons.'

'That's fine, you're doing your part here. And if Boetie should come out, just do your best to keep him here.'

'I'll do that. It shouldn't be too difficult.'

'What do you mean?'

She smiled again. 'He's already told me that he's still in love with me. While you were looking at the baboon cages.'

'Bloody cheek! Who does he think ...?'

She shrugged. 'Remember, he thinks I'm in love with Gerhard, who can't make up his mind between you and me. But you must go now, Luc will be waiting.'

I made my way back along the deserted corridors of the Silvermine laboratory. Things were going almost too smoothly – Boetie's absence, my dismissal, the free access to the animal room ... but then, the rest of the operation was dependent upon Luc Tomlinson's mysterious plans, which for all I knew would bring disaster upon us and our scheme.

The baboons did not even look up at me as I re-entered their quarters. They seemed gloomily resigned to the living death which had come to them from nowhere. 'Hang on,' I said to a large male, which I fancied was my old tormentor Petrus, 'we'll get you out of here in no time. Just don't ask me how.'

I unlocked one of the large double doors at the end of the room. It opened, as I had surmised, into the delivery area at the back of the laboratory. A wave of cold air and rain hit me as I pushed open the door, and the baboons chattered excitedly as they smelt the fresh air. I stepped outside, and collided with a tall figure in a waterproof cape. It took me a few seconds to recognise Luc Tomlinson.

'Am I glad to see you!' he said in a low voice. 'What kept you?'

'Johanna's procedures,' I grimaced.

'Are the chacs okay?' he asked; he was evidently very tense.

'Yes – well, they're right here in their cages. Shouldn't we just ...' and I pointed at the surrounding mountainside – 'you know, let them find their own way?'

He shook his head. 'They'll scatter and get lost. It's okay, I've got transport.' He pointed at a vehicle parked behind him. It was a white minibus. Under the back window was painted the legend *Halfway to Hell and Back*.

'You got a taxi? How on earth?'

'Well, yes. I borrowed it,' he said. 'With the help of your friend's firearm.'

'You hijacked a taxi?' I demanded. 'Are you out of your mind?'

'Cut the moral outrage,' he said, 'and help me with the chacs.'

'And I suppose you're going to point a gun at the baboons and tell them to get into the taxi?'

'Nothing as antisocial as that,' he said. 'I've got the juice.' He took out from under his cape a large cardboard container. 'Sleep juice.'

'Are you going to drug the baboons?'

He nodded. 'Ketamine.'

'Ketamine?'

'Don't worry about it now. It works. Take me to the chacs.'

We went back into the animal room, where the baboons were now more restive. They started jabbering excitedly when we came in.

'They can smell me,' Luc said. 'We'll have to be quick.' He took off his cape and put it on the floor. 'I'll need both my hands.' He put his right hand under his shirt and under his left arm for a moment. 'Just getting my smell on my hand,' he said, 'so the chacs recognise me.'

He opened the box; inside were several little bottles and syringes. 'Enough here for all the baboons in Africa,' he said.

'Do you know how to give an injection?' I asked.

'Sure, I know many things. I was a teenage junkie. I could find a vein at midnight in a coal shed. Except I'm not going for the veins now. Beauty of Ketamine is you can go intramuscular; takes a bit longer to work but lasts longer too. But we've got to be quick even so – quarter of an hour to half an hour is all we've got to get them back to Cape Point.' He walked to a cage in which a young baboon was whimpering, excited by the general commotion amongst the animals.

'I'm going to start with the young ones; after four minutes, you carry them out to the taxi. Don't wait for them to go to sleep. They won't close their eyes. Ketamine is a dissociative agent.'

'Won't they bite you?' I asked as Luc opened the first cage.

'They shouldn't. They know me pretty well.' He extended

his hand for the baboon to sniff, then took hold of the young baboon and gave it a quick jab. 'There,' he said, 'Three to four minutes.'

I watched the young baboon. As Luc had said, it didn't close its eyes, didn't seem to go to sleep; but it didn't react to my presence, and when I put a cautious hand on its paw, didn't respond at all. I lifted the small body; there was something strangely vulnerable about the unconscious baboon, seeming to look at me with open eyes.

Suddenly Luc, so calm up to now, exploded. 'Fuck, will you look at this!' He was pointing at the two female baboons with missing hands.

'Boetie told us that somebody was trying to transplant their hands. It obviously didn't work.'

'Can you *believe* the arrogance of these so-called scientists?' I was surprised to see tears in his eyes; then he visibly collected himself. 'Well, no use getting upset about that now. Let's just get them out of here before some Dr Moreau type finds us here.'

The adult baboons were strangely tractable under Luc's confident grasp: either they recognised and trusted him, as he claimed, or their spirit had been broken in the laboratory. We carried the baboons out to the minibus taxi one by one and arranged them in the back, on the floor rather than on the seats. 'You don't want people to see us transporting a troop of baboons in a taxi,' Luc said. 'There's probably some bye-law against it.' As we left the empty animal room, he looked at the leashes and nets hanging against the wall. 'Might as well take these along, in case.'

'I'll follow you in my car, shall I?' Although there seemed to be no reason for my presence, I thought it would be rather flat to return to Pinelands and not see the release of the baboons.

'Of course. We must celebrate.' He gave me a hug, his tension clearly feeding into his exhilaration, and jumped into the taxi and slammed it into gear. I walked round the building to my car – it was still raining – and followed the *Halfway To Hell and Back* blazon out of the grounds, with a twinge at seeing Gerhard's car parked forlornly in the rain. Who knew what horrors were being visited upon him by the Black Widow?

A few kilometres from the laboratory there was a stop street, where the minor road joined the Ou Kaapse Weg. The taxi was far enough ahead of me to give me time to see a figure walking towards the vehicle from a bus shelter nearby. He went up to the driver's door, and I assumed he was, not unnaturally, enquiring about the taxi's destination. But before I had come to a halt behind the taxi, the man had slammed open the driver's door, and Luc jumped out with his hands behind his head. The man leaped into the driver's seat and the taxi disappeared into the rainy afternoon.

Luc came running to my car and jumped into the passenger seat.

'Follow that taxi,' he said, 'I've been hijacked.'

'You have a gun on you and you get hijacked?'

'What's the use of a gun if somebody else pulls one on you first?' he asked. 'You'll just get shot at close range. Besides, the gun is in the cubbyhole of the taxi. Don't lose sight of him, whatever you do.'

The taxi had taken a right turn at the junction and was heading towards the Blue Route and the southern suburbs. 'Does he know he's got twelve baboons in his vehicle?'

'Of course not. But they'll be waking up soon. One of the side effects of Ketamine is that it makes the subject totally irrational. And with twelve irrational chacs in a minibus taxi he's going to know all about it.'

'Can you tell me now how you came to possess such large quantities of the stuff?'

'Well, yes, if you must know. Friend of mine works at the Red Cross Children's Hospital. She kindly brought home some of it for me.'

'Here we are in a country that I'm on the point of leaving because it's being eroded by crime, and now you tell me that in one day I've been an accomplice to the hijacking of a taxi and the theft of medical supplies from a children's hospital. What's the *point*?'

'The point was to steal the chacs back from the people who stole them in the first place. You can't fight clean when you're fighting filth.'

'So what happens to standards and moral values?'

'Don't ask me,' he said, 'I just live here.'

'It's all right for you; you're a dropout, you're supposed to be antisocial, but I'm a lawyer, I'm supposed to uphold the laws of the land.'

'You told me to steal the plans from my father's office,' he pointed out. 'Besides, who steals more money in this country, the dropouts or the lawyers?'

'I really couldn't say,' I said.

'You couldn't say, but you have a pretty good idea, don't you? I can tell you, some of the things I saw when I was looking for those plans in my father's office ...'

'I'm not sure you should tell me things you found out in an illegitimate way.'

'Suit yourself. But some of it would knock your booties off.'

We were now entering the southern suburbs, and I had to stay closer to the taxi.

'What happens if he stops to pick up passengers?' I asked.

'He won't, not if he has any sense. I don't even know if he wants the taxi; he may just have been fed up with waiting for a bus in the rain.'

'He could have asked you for a lift.'

'Perhaps he was scared of rejection.'

The taxi turned off the Blue Route to Claremont. We were driving quite slowly now, contending with Saturday-afternoon shoppers on their way home in the rain. 'Where is he going now?' Luc asked. 'Don't lose him, he's turning off to the left.'

'He's going to Cavendish Square. Perhaps he just needed to do some shopping.'

We were now right behind the taxi. As it approached the shopping centre, the vehicle veered to the right and unceremoniously stopped, half in the road, half on the sidewalk. Hooters sounded indignantly, pedestrians swore, as the driver jumped out and disappeared into Cavendish Square, closely followed by twelve baboons.

'Oh, shit,' said Luc, 'just as I thought. The chacs have woken up.'

'What now?' I asked.

'Dunno. First thing is to get the taxi out of the way. Let's hope he left the keys in the ignition.' He thought for a moment.

332

'Okay. Tell you what, let me get the taxi and go and park it in the parking garage upstairs. You follow me, and we can try and trap the chacs. The Ketamine should still be in the taxi.'

Luc jumped out and into the taxi. It is an article of belief in Cape Town that nothing a minibus taxi does is out of character, and pedestrians and motorists made way for Luc with grudging promptitude. I followed in his wake, benefiting by the latitude left him by anxious Mercedes owners.

We parked on one of the upper levels. Luc took his Ketamine kit under his arm and passed me the nets and leashes. 'You do the gladiator bit, I'll do Dr Moreau.'

We emerged from the parking area into the shopping mall. I had imagined that finding a troop of baboons in such a large complex would be difficult, but in the event it was all too easy to pick up their trail. Outside the cinema complex a group of six schoolchildren was being hysterical in concert, their teacher trying in vain to calm herself to the point where she could calm them. We gathered that the little group had been robbed of its collective popcorn stocks by a band of baboons. Apparently, though, the popcorn had turned out not to be to their taste, for a trail of discarded popcorn led down to the floor below, where an Italian restaurant and some of its clients were strewn with the remains of the dessert trolley, which had been parked temptingly close to the entrance. Further along, one of Cape Town's better-known fashion designers was nursing a flesh wound incurred when an over-zealous security guard had taken a pot shot at a baboon. The guard was being berated by his superior: 'Are you fucking mad, man? You don't shoot in here, you could damage something and then the firm has to pay.' A woman was trying to reassemble her groceries, which had been ripped out of their bags in her shopping trolley.

Not that all was chaos. There will always be those who shop while the bombs drop around them, who waltz as the *Titanic* goes down, who make love as Vesuvius blows its top; and Cavendish Square had its share of these heroic hedonists. The diners at Gino's continued dining with as much composure as if they had not just witnessed twelve marauding baboons spatter their fellow-diners with tiramisu; the coffee drinkers at Scoozi's sipped their café latte as if a baboon ravaging the delicatessen counter was a vaguely embarrassing misdemeanour which it was one's civilised duty to ignore; the beautiful people in the Young Designers' Emporium lost neither their cool nor their poses; the thin young men in Hilton Weiner tried on floppy jackets over their slight frames, unflappable, unthreatened, restrained.

But elsewhere normality was disrupted and demoralised by the invasion of this excess of the natural: a child screaming in a pram, having been pawed by a creature from its nightmares; an elderly woman clinging to a handrail, having been shoved aside by a discourtesy next to which the younger generation seemed positively well-behaved; a cleaner resentfully taking a mop to baboon droppings mixed with human hair on the floor of the Upper Cut Hair Boutique. And everywhere a steady trail of consumer objects collected and discarded marked the progress of the plundering troop – a pair of bent sunglasses, a cordless telephone, a half-eaten bagel, a single running shoe, a copy of *Men's Health* magazine, a wig, a teddy bear with its entrails torn out – followed by the distracted migration of a desultorily rubbernecking crowd, generating, accumulating and disseminating rumour as it went.

'They say it's a publicity stunt by an advertising company.'

'I've been told that they escaped from the kitchen of Pies for Africa downstairs.'

'They say that the baboons on Table Mountain are so hungry that they're coming down into the city for food.'

'Someone saw them getting out of a taxi; the *sangomas* are using them for medicine.'

'*Ag* shame and sis, they have no hearts, these kaffirs.'

Two security guards, having read into our nets and leashes some professional connection with the baboons, were following us around, clearly torn between arresting us and offering to help us. Deciding that if we didn't catch the baboons they might have to, they approached us warily.

'Are you catching the baboons?'

'Trying to,' Luc replied. 'Do you want to help us?'

They looked at each other. 'Sure,' said the braver of the two; the other said, 'Depends.'

'Well, come along,' said Luc to the first; to the second he

said, 'Depends, my arse,' which the man seemed to accept as a persuasive argument. With the addition of two uniforms to our paraphernalia, we were immediately accorded the recognition of the public at large as 'the baboon-trappers', and generously plied with advice.

'My grandfather used to cut a hole in a pumpkin and then the baboons grabbed the pips and couldn't get their hands out again.'

'My grandmother caught a baboon in her house once by putting a mirror in front of it and it fell in love with its own reflection.'

'They say baboons will never harm a baby, you can catch them easily by putting a baby down in front of them.'

'They say baboons have to screw every half-hour and you can catch them then.'

Few of these suggestions could readily be implemented, but at least the public interest kept us informed on the where-abouts of the troop, which fortunately seemed to be keeping quite close together. Their presence in the normally sedate shopping centre generated a spirit of anarchy, and some shop-keepers, wary of looting, were starting to shut their shops. One man, arrested for lifting a cell phone, claimed that he'd taken it off a baboon and was returning it; a child accused of stealing a Sweetie Pie said a baboon had given it to her; two boys were quarrelling violently for possession of a skateboard abandoned by a baboon.

Led by rumour, surmise and the walkie-talkies of the security guards, we made our way back to the top floor of the complex. There a large gathering of rowdy shoppers was trying to crowd into Sweet Treats, one of those overpriced little sweet shops which display their wares in bright plastic bins to trigger the impulses of passers-by. The sweet-shop owner was desperately trying to keep the crowd out of his store, and just as desper-ately trying to get the baboons out of it; but the animals had discovered the joys of the help-yourself bins and were impos-sible to dislodge; indeed, it seemed that some of them were emulating their pumpkin-trapped ancestors and had got their hands stuck in the bins. The place was strewn with cashew nuts and jelly babies and peanut clusters and every variety of

Sweet Treat on offer. Children were helping themselves from the floor, from which it was but a short step to helping themselves from the shelves and the bins, to the fury of the owner, who was swiping at baboons and humans indiscriminately with his *Weekend Argus*. 'Get the fuck out of my shop!' he was screaming. 'My insurance doesn't say anything about baboon raids!'

The security guards proved useful in clearing the crowd out of the little shop. Their threats of violence – 'Get out if you don't want to get hurt'; 'Clear the shop, please, we're going to release tear gas' – had no effect; then one of the guards took an empty toffee carton and went around saying, 'We're collecting money for Animal Welfare', and 'Please give generously', which dispersed the crowd like a bomb scare. Once the humans were outside, the guards slid shut the glass door of the shop. The owner was but moderately relieved.

'That's great,' he screamed, close to hysterics, 'now get the fucking monkeys out of here!'

Luc, assuming an unusually courteous tone, tried to calm the man by saying, 'We'll have them out of here in a minute, sir. We're from the Parks Board.'

'Are these your fucking monkeys? I'll sue the Parks Board all the way to hell!'

'You can try, sir,' I said, 'but then we'll have to stop our operations immediately.'

'Oh, *fuck*!' the man screamed, 'just get them of here, will you?' He took a swipe at a baboon dismantling a chocolate model of Table Mountain, and the baboon bared its teeth at him.

'Careful, sir,' Luc said, 'they bite.'

'Can't you shoot the fuckers?' the man demanded from the security guards.

'We could try,' said the more sardonic of the two, 'but in here the bullet would bounce around like a flea in a matchbox, you know? Could hit your sweetie bins or yourself.'

Luc put his box of anaesthetics on the counter and said, almost languidly, 'If you all will please start behaving like rational creatures we'll get the chacs out of here in no time.' He opened his box, which seemed to have a calming effect on the sweet-shop owner. 'Are you a *doctor*?' he asked.

'No, don't worry,' said Luc cheerfully. To the security guards he said, 'Why don't you two gentleman collect us about four shopping trolleys so long?' The two men went off, not quite sure whether this was the most heroic of missions. 'You come and pass me the juice, Nick,' Luc said. 'They're a bit excitable, but the sweets are distracting them.'

The baboons were more tractable than I had feared they would be, partly because they knew Luc and partly because they were literally stuck in the bins. By the time they had all subsided into unconsciousness the guards were back with four large Woolworths trolleys, and we could arrange the baboons as decorously as possible inside.

'That's great,' said Luc, 'now, very quickly, follow me to the car.'

Our little procession created considerable interest, not to say outrage. Now that the baboons were unconscious, but with their eyes wide open, draped demurely in the trolleys, they looked vulnerable, even cuddly, like woolly toys, and awoke every compassionate impulse that their undisciplined behaviour had effectively suppressed.

'They say they can them for export to the Rest of Africa,' one woman said. 'The natives eat their brains.'

'Shame, look, that one doesn't have a hand.'

'Yes, they cut off their hands for fly swats.'

'A cheek, I call it, using Woolworths trolleys, you'd think they could use Pick 'n Pay or Shoprite. Tomorrow, who's to tell, you or I could get one of those trolleys.'

'I've read that they export them to Lagos as prostitutes.'

'They say those buggers get R80 for every baboon they catch.'

'It's a crying shame, isn't it, that people should enrich themselves at the expense of dumb animals?'

This seemed so outrageously unfair that I could not restrain myself from a rejoinder. 'We're rescuing the baboons, you fool.' This, though, hardly placated her or any of the other members of the growing crowd, and we might have been at best disastrously delayed, at worst lynched, had Luc not stopped dead, and, taking advantage of his considerable height, announced: 'Ladies and gentleman, we appreciate your concern, but we must warn you that these baboons have escaped from a laboratory where they were infected with the Aids virus. We would welcome your help in restoring them to the laboratory, but of course entirely at your own risk.'

Most bystanders only heard the word Aids, but that was enough to disperse the crowd of concerned citizens, and give us a free run to the car park. Here we thanked the security guards profusely, and congratulated them on clearing the centre of a potentially hazardous situation so promptly. 'All in a day's work,' said one modestly; 'More exciting than patrolling the toilets,' the other said.

'Shall I follow you again?' I asked Luc, after we had once again transferred the unconscious baboons to the taxi.

He considered. I had to admit that Luc under pressure was more impressive than Luc laid-back. 'Nope,' he said, 'why don't you leave your car here, and drive the taxi? That way I can sit with the chacs and inject them again if necessary.'

'I've never actually driven a taxi.'

'It's easy. You just pretend you're the only vehicle on the road.'

'Not quite my style, but I'll try.'

I got the taxi going after a few false starts; after the BMW the controls of the minibus were harsh and rudimentary, the steering strenuous, the suspension like wood. The off-ramp of the parking garage was as narrow and as low as economy dictated and the building regulations allowed, which did not make for easy driving; once or twice I nearly scraped the sides as I took a sharp curve.

At the bottom of the off-ramp we came to the boom barring the way, with next to it the control box into which one is supposed to feed one's ticket, duly paid for inside the complex.

'Oh, shit,' I said, 'we haven't paid for our parking.'

'We haven't got time to go back,' Luc said. 'Keep going.'

'But ...'

'Just keep going.'

I shut my eyes and kept going. There was the shock of impact as the boom resisted; then it splintered, and we were through. 'How many laws have we broken today?' I yelled at Luc.

'Don't tell me you're not enjoying it,' he rejoined. 'Perhaps you're an outlaw at heart.'

'Which way to Cape Point now?'

'Left in front … oh, *shit!*'

'What's the matter?'

'It's after five. Cape Point will be closed by the time we get there.'

'Can't we just crash through the boom there as well?'

'You're learning fast, but let's not get too enthusiastic. The boom is a bit more solid than here. We might get stuck in the rain. Besides, I don't want to have to give the chacs another shot of dope right away – they've already had about as much as they can take.'

'Then what?'

'Where do you live?'

'Pinelands. *Why?*'

'Have you got a room – a garage, anything, where we can lock up the chacs for the night?'

'I don't have a garage. Just an attic room. But it's my guest room.'

'Well? The chacs can be your guests.'

'Do you know what you're asking?'

'Yes, I know what I'm asking. But I'm asking very nicely. Please.'

'Oh, hell, Luc.' I was approaching the traffic light on Rhodes Drive: the road to Cape Point was to the left, to Pinelands to the right. At the last moment I veered to the right, prompting the car behind me to an hysterical outburst of hooting, such as I had often been provoked to by a minibus taxi. I looked in my rear-view mirror; the gesticulating driver, all moral outrage and righteous indignation, looked comically unattractive in his futile remonstrations. For the first time it occurred to me that taxi drivers and their passengers probably had a good deal of fun at the expense of the irate middle classes.

'Good man!' Luc shouted. 'Give it stick!'

'Pinelands, here we come!' I shouted back, curiously exhilarated at the thought of invading my own domestic retreat with a taxi-load of baboons.

Pinelands is so close to Cavendish Square that by the time we arrived there the baboons were all still unconscious. I stopped outside my gate. Tornado, waiting in the rain for

Stuart and Sharon, came trotting over to investigate the strange vehicle. He relaxed when he saw me, and came up for the pat which I nowadays condescended to bestow on him; but when he came close to the vehicle he must have smelt the baboons, for he went into a paroxysm of barking and seemed about to tear the taxi to pieces to get to the contents.

I did not even try to soothe an antipathy as ancient and elemental as that between dog and baboon, merely rushed to open the gate, drive the minibus into the yard, and close the gate with Tornado on the other side. 'Good boy,' I said, 'but they're wild and you're domesticated. Sort of.' I unlocked the side door to my house, and Luc and I did a quick inspection of the guest quarters upstairs.

'Remove everything that can break or tear,' he said, 'and even then, I'm afraid, you're going to have to do some redecoration. Let's get them in before they wake up. And have you got some fruit or something we can leave them?'

'I bought some apples and bananas for the weekend.'

'That'll be great. Let's get going.'

Carrying a fully grown baboon up a flight of stairs is not an easy feat; fortunately Luc's well-defined muscles proved to be functional as well as ornamental, and he managed the larger animals. By the time we had cleared the room and lifted out the baboons, they were all still unconscious. With one last look at my meticulously neat guest room, now stripped of bedding and even curtains, I closed and locked the door.

'Great,' he said. 'Now it's just a matter of getting them back first thing tomorrow morning, collecting your car at Cavendish, and returning the taxi.'

'Returning the taxi?'

'Yes, well. I told the owner he could collect it from the Mowbray police station on Sunday evening.'

'I don't know why you didn't just hire a truck in the first place.'

'You don't know how full of shit those hiring places are about transporting animals. And I've always wanted to hijack a vehicle.'

'It's people like you who are making our roads the hell-runs they are.'

'And you. You drove that taxi like a pro.'

'Thanks.'

Suddenly, after the tension and the hectic activity of the day, I felt drained. We were standing in the kitchen, from which the staircase ascended to the attic. Outside it had grown dark, and it was still raining quite hard. It was cold in the kitchen. We were both wet and dirty.

'And now?' I asked. 'Would you like …?' I was wondering whether I should offer him a cup of coffee before he returned to whatever mysterious commune or house of ill repute he frequented when he drifted around the city.

'What I'd like is a hot shower, and if you have a fireplace I'd like a fire, and a plate of pasta and a bottle of wine and a bed.'

'Oh,' I said. 'At least that's clear.'

'You have a problem with that?'

'No. No, I suppose not. Except with the bed.'

'You don't have a bed?'

'Yes, but it's upstairs with the baboons. That's my only guest room.'

'We can deal with that later. Mind if I have a shower now?'

'Let me find you a towel,' I said, adding slightly sarcastically. 'I'm afraid my clothes won't fit you …'

'That's okay. I've got some dry clothes in my rucksack in the taxi.'

He went out into the rain and came back with a small rucksack, one of those that I have always regarded as the mark of the truly rootless, too big to be merely a convenience bag, too small to contain a complete change of clothing.

I showed him to the shower, and started making a fire, half irritated, half amused at myself for following Luc Tomlinson's instructions to the letter. I was not used to having guests in my house. Gerhard sometimes visited but complained that the place felt uninhabited, and objected to the ornaments I had inherited from my grandmother; Leonora felt that it was not proper for a young woman to visit a young man's place on her own. As a consequence I did not often make a fire; it hardly seemed worth the trouble of cleaning up afterwards to make a fire for myself alone.

341

I was cleaning up the chips of bark around the hearth when Luc Tomlinson came in from his shower. He had apparently found a clean t-shirt in his rucksack, but was still wearing his damp jeans, and was barefooted. He was drying his hair with a towel. He squatted next to the fire, rubbing his hair, coppery in the glow of the fire. He smelled of my Body Shop shampoo. It was a good thing that Gerhard ...

'Oh, heavens,' I said. 'Gerhard and Leonora.'

'What about them?'

'I must find out if they're all right. Have you forgotten that they were last seen entering the den of the Black Widow?'

'Well, no,' he said, though he did not seem much concerned. 'How will you find out?'

'I thought they would phone here. I'll try them at home.'

Neither Leonora nor Gerhard was at home. Leonora's flatmates told me what I knew, which was that she had left early that afternoon, but they had no idea where she was; at Gerhard's number I got only his slightly flirtatious answering machine, urging me to leave my name and *especially* my number. I left my name without my number and asked him to phone me immediately when he returned.

'I don't know,' I said, 'I feel like a beast sitting here in front of a fire when they're out there somewhere.'

'Not too much you can do about it, is there?'

'I suppose not, but ...'

'Relax. This fire is very good.'

'I think the next item on your wish list was a bottle of wine,' I said. 'I didn't know you drank wine.'

'I don't normally. But it seems right tonight. A bottle of red wine.'

'Any particular year or cultivar?' I asked, but my sarcasm was lost on him.

'No, I don't care much about that shit. Long as it's good.'

'Would you know?'

'Yes, well. I'll know if I don't like it.'

I had two gift-packed bottles of wine that I had given my father for Christmas one year and that he had never drunk; after his death my mother had given them back to me apologetically: 'Your father appreciated the present, but he never

342

drank anything but whisky.' It seemed like an appropriate revenge on my father for his non-appreciation of my gift, serving it to this equally unappreciative young man. Come to think of it, the only person I'd ever met who took more for granted than my father was Luc Tomlinson.

I brought out the wine and poured him a glass. 'You don't mind if I have a shower now?' I asked him.

'No, suit yourself, I'm happy right here on my own.'

My bathroom looked as if the baboons had invaded it. Luc had managed to flood the floor, and had unpacked my bath-room cabinet, presumably in search of my shampoo, which was standing open on the rim of the washbasin. The rest of the contents of the cabinet was stacked on the cistern of the toilet. My Body Shop Face Scrub had been opened, used, and left open. My first impulse was to storm back into the sitting room and tell him to come and tidy up, but I decided that he wouldn't understand why I was so excited and would in any case just irritate me further by making a rotten job of cleaning up. So I tidied the bathroom, dried the floor, had a shower, removed what seemed to be three pubic hairs from the soap, and found dry clothes. Smiling at my own irrationality, I transferred the rose quartz to the clean shirt.

Returning to the sitting room, I found Luc sprawled in front of the fire, nursing his wine and cleaning his toenails with a splinter he'd broken from a log. 'What took you so long?' he asked. 'I could have had five showers in the time it took you to have one.'

'I had some tidying up to do. Anything I can get you while I'm up?'

'Some pasta would be great, but come and sit down first and relax. There's plenty of time.' He patted the carpet, spilled a splash of wine, and blotted it up with my towel.

I did as I was told and debated with myself whether to throw Luc Tomlinson out or to relax, as he kept on urging me to do, and try to enjoy his company. The thing was that he was so outrageous that one more or less *had* to relax or explode. I decided to keep the explosion option open, but to relax in the mean time. I took a large sip of my father's wine. It tasted very good; just about the only worthwhile thing I had inherited from my father, I reflected. And it might help me to relax. I had half a glass and then said, 'You ordered pasta.'

'I can see you're not going to relax till you've had your pasta.'

'You're the one who wanted pasta.'

'Yes, but it's not as if I ordered takeaways at Gino's pronto pronto.' He got up all the same. 'Let's see what you've got in your kitchen.'

'Not much, I'm afraid. But there is pasta.'

I'm not what you could call a great cook or even a cook at all, as that term is defined nowadays. It seems to me that the relentless pursuit of what are called natural ingredients is in fact a highly unnatural activity in a civilisation such as ours, based as it on a culture of processing. So my own cooking is an unassuming affair based on what is available at the Pinelands Superette on a Saturday afternoon.

In the kitchen Luc Tomlinson inspected my groceries with the same lack of inhibition as he'd displayed in unpacking my toiletries. 'Tinned tomatoes, good, we can use that; Aromat, yuck, pure MSG; onions, fine. You have any garlic?'

'No, I don't like garlic.'

'I didn't think you would. Chillies?'

'There's some chilli paste in the fridge, and some leftover chicken.'

'No chicken. I'm a vegetarian.'

'Oh, I beg your pardon.'

'No sweat, I just don't eat chicken. But we can make a good pasta with what's here – there's some elderly mushrooms and green peppers here we can have.'

'Help yourself, don't be shy.'

'What's this margarine shit? Don't you have any butter?'

'No, I don't. I prefer margarine.'

'You can't possibly. You're just too stingy to buy butter. Olive oil?'

'No, just sunflower.'

'That will have to do. Why don't you boil the water for the pasta, and I'll get the sauce going?'

'You sure you can trust me with boiling the water?'

He laughed. 'Sure thing, I bet you boil a mean pot of water. Don't get uptight. I'm a natural organiser.'

I filled the kettle. 'For a natural organiser you were pretty helpless when you first came to see me.'

'Yes, well, I was much younger then.' He started chopping the onions. 'This is a shitty knife, you should get yourself a decent set. And then, I can organise well, you know, things I know, but things like the law, that sort of shit, I'm no good at.'

'We all have our talents, I suppose. I do law and that sort of shit, you chop onions.'

'Sure thing. And I chop them fucking well, you'll admit.'

He chopped for a while, then stopped and said, 'Hey, listen.'

I switched off the kettle and listened. Through the drumming of the rain outside there was a constant scurrying noise, like some very large mice scampering in the ceiling.

'The chacs have woken up.'

'Should we go and have a look?'

'Let's not. We don't want to excite them any more than is necessary.'

'I suppose they're trashing my spare room.'

'Probably. Give you a good opportunity to get rid of all that Laura Ashley stuff.'

I switched on the kettle again. 'Didn't know you knew about Laura Ashley.'

'Yes, well. I pick up the odd bit of culture here and there.'

If Luc Tomlinson was an infuriating person to have around, he himself was almost frustratingly even-tempered. His equanimity may well have been the corollary of his unshakeable self-confidence: he did not feel challenged enough by anybody else to lose his temper. This in itself might be irritating to less glacially self-assured people, but it did at least mean that one was unlikely to have a flaming row with him, even if one wanted one.

The meal was, given the sparseness of the ingredients, good; Luc Tomlinson pronounced his own sauce 'brilliant' and the wine 'good stuff'. We sat in front of the fire with our food and wine, and I tried not to notice the spills on the carpet. He kept up an amiable enough stream of conversation, and by the time we opened the second bottle of wine I thought I was at last starting to relax.

For such a self-centred person Luc was surprisingly interested in my origins and history, my family, my time in England, my relationship with Leonora, my friendship with Gerhard; though here, too, his technique was that of a baboon in a pantry, displaying a complete disregard of traditional restraints and no-go areas.

'Do you fuck each other?'

'I *beg* your pardon?'

'You heard me. You and Gerhard – do you …?'

'Sure I heard you, but I didn't think it was a question you had a right to ask me.'

'Why not? It's not a sin, it's not even a crime any more.'

'Don't you have any sense of privacy?'

'Privacy? You mean like not peering through people's bedroom curtains?'

'Yes, like that exactly.'

'I don't do that. But I don't mind if people know personal things about me. So I can't see why they mind if I know about them.'

'Well, I mind.'

'Suit yourself.' After a short pause he asked, 'What's he like?'

'What's …?'

'What's he like? Gerhard.'

I thought this was the moment to explode. 'Listen, it's none of your bloody business, but for your information Gerhard and I do not in fact sleep together, have never slept together and never will sleep together.'

'Well, then, why get so excited when I ask you if you do?'

'Because whether we do or not is none of your business.'

'Business, business, your business, my business, I don't buy all this business talk.'

'That's because you can afford, through your grandfather's business acumen, to affect this completely unsocialised ethos.'

'You reckon it's affected?'

'You didn't grow up in Constantia cleaning your toenails in front of the fire.'

'No, I grew up with my father badgering me all the time to become a good little Bishops boy and then despising me for it. He wanted me to be what he'd never been, but he hated thinking I thought I was better than him.' His tone became more

346

conversational, and I followed his lead, abandoning my probably futile attempt to educate him in the proprieties.

'And did you? I mean think that you were better than he?'

'No, why should I? But I fucking well thought I was better behaved than him. He treated me like shit. And he wasn't that great to my mother either.'

'Is he still not talking to you?'

'Naw. D'you know that he's in financial shit?'

'He did say that the Cape Point thing was going to ruin him, but I thought he was exaggerating.'

'Yes, well. I don't know about ruining him, but it cost him a shit-load of money, and he's got all sorts of contracts with people who now want to sue him for breach of contract.'

'Are you sorry now that you took him on?'

'No ways. He was trying to get at me, and got burnt. That's how it goes.'

'Why doesn't he like you?'

He laughed. 'You should know, you don't like me either. But my father's different. Mainly he doesn't like me because my grandfather liked me.' He had finished eating. He pushed aside his plate and stretched himself out on his back.

'Did you like your grandfather?' I asked, making myself as comfortable as I could in the remaining floor area.

'He was an old bastard but I loved him. He was very good to me. I think that's because I inherited his red hair.'

'And your mother?'

'What about my mother?'

'Do you … you know, get on with her?'

'Yes, well. I did before she stopped talking to me. She's all right, a bit full of shit at times, you know, playing the great lady, but yes, basically we get on very well. She says I have no culture.'

'And do you … have culture, I mean?'

'Well, what's culture? If it means music and painting and all that shit, then it doesn't do too much for me, no, but if it's just, you know, the way you get on with what's around you, then I'm all for it. I'd say the chacs have culture, the way they play and interact with one another.'

'Most people would define culture in human terms, I suppose.'

347

'Yes, well, and I suppose if chacs could talk they'd define culture in baboon terms.'

'Fact remains that we can talk and they can't.'

'Sure, as long as we don't think talking is everything. Most people think they're the fucking ornaments of the universe, when as far as I can see they're what's wrong with it.'

Our conversation meandered along in this style, skirting major disagreements, cautiously exploring new territory before returning to the exploits of the day. The combination of the wine, the heat of the fire and the relaxation of the tension of the last few days was very soothing; and when Luc Tomlinson was not being abrasive he could be almost pleasant, his normally over-assertive self-possession mellowing into a companionable ease. His disregard of other people's body space seemed to matter less in a context that normalised and domesticated it; he could have been a large dog stretched out on the carpet. At about ten o'clock he yawned and stretched himself. 'Well, it's been quite a day. Time to hit the sack, I'd say.'

'Good idea,' I said. 'Will you be all right here in the sitting room? I'll bring you a pillow and some blankets.'

'Like hell I'll be all right here,' he said. 'D'you expect me to sleep on the floor?'

'The sofa …?' I offered, not very hopefully.

'I couldn't get onto that sofa if I folded myself double. Look, what's your problem? You've got a perfectly good double bed, haven't you? I saw it when I went for my shower.'

'Yes, but I'm not in the habit of sharing it with … just anybody.'

'Well, then, start a habit. Besides, I'm not just anybody.' He got to his feet and walked towards the bedroom.

I stayed behind, thinking that I might opt to sleep on the sofa. Then I rebelled against the idea of being driven from my own bed – my parents' double bed, in fact, passed on to me when my mother moved into her town house after my father's death – by the presumption of Luc Tomlinson, and I followed him to my bedroom.

He was in the bathroom, brushing his teeth.

'I hope you're not using my toothbrush.'

348

'Relax, I brought my own.' He gestured at his rucksack lying on the floor, half its contents spilled out. He finished brushing his teeth, then walked to the toilet, unzipped, and started urinating loudly.

'Listen. Do you mind?'

'Mind what?'

'Mind closing the door when you use the toilet.'

'No, I don't mind,' he said, 'if you have a problem with people pissing.' Staunching the flow with two fingers, he walked to the bathroom door, closed it and went back to his now slightly less audible business.

I thought this a good opportunity to change into my pyjamas, but I had only succeeded in wriggling into the jacket when he walked in.

'Pyjamas?' he said. 'Jeez, do they still make them?'

'No, I have them made specially by a little old granny I know about,' I snapped back, my mellow mood of earlier now thoroughly dispelled.

'Whatever for?' he asked, missing my sarcasm again, and stripping off his jeans and t-shirt.

'For warmth, decency and hygiene,' I retorted. 'And what's more, if you're going to sleep in my bed you're going to wear some form of clothing.'

'Sure thing. I'll wear a t-shirt.'

'I mean some sort of ... other clothing.'

'You mean I must cover my willy.' He fondled himself unnecessarily and grinned, and for a moment he reminded me of Gerhard. 'Sure thing, I've got a pair of rugger shorts.'

'Good,' I said. I was now fully clad in my pyjamas and felt to some degree protected from his unsparing regard.

'Gawd,' he said, 'you look like something from Noddy.'

'We can't all look like something from ... from the Planet of the Apes.' I looked at the piece of rose quartz I'd put on the bedside table, and said, 'I accept all I am.'

'You sound like Fiona.'

'I wondered if you'd notice.' He had still made no effort to put on the promised t-shirt and shorts. I went into the bathroom to prepare for bed. My toothpaste was lying open on the washbasin: it had been squeezed in the middle with such force that it looked like a strangled mouse. I opened the door. 'I thought you had your own toothpaste.'

He was examining his physique in my full-length mirror. 'Nope,' he said. 'I said toothbrush.'

'Oh, my mistake.' I closed the door, counted to ten, did my best to revive my toothpaste, brushed my teeth. I noticed the toilet had not been flushed after Luc had used it. I counted to ten, flushed, used it, waited for the cistern to fill and then flushed again and went back to my bedroom.

Luc was still at the mirror, apparently examining a minor blemish on the perfection of his right shoulder. He was naked except for a thin gold chain round his neck from which dangled what looked like a ruby pendant.

I got into bed. 'Try not to pop your pimples on my mirror,' I said.

He laughed. 'Only nerds have pimples,' he said.

'Well, then, get into your t-shirt and shorts and get into bed.'

'Relax, what's your hurry?'

I ignored this innuendo, and turned my back to him. I could hear him scratching around in his rucksack, for longer than I would have thought necessary, given the size of the sack. At length I heard the reassuring sound of clothing being put on, and deemed it safe, indeed advisable, to turn round and check.

'Where on earth …?' I said. 'I mean, what on earth have you been doing in those shorts?'

'I was wearing them to fix the septic tank at Rocklands,' he said. 'But they're quite clean.'

'No, they're not quite clean. They're filthy. You're not getting into my bed in those shorts.'

'Please yourself,' he said. 'You're going to have to choose between dirty shorts and a clean arse.' He took off his shorts and got into bed.

I counted to ten, then sat up straight, and shouted at him: 'Luc Tomlinson, fuck out of my bed and my house this minute!'

He also sat up, looking hurt and surprised. 'Relax,' he said.

'And don't ever fucking well tell me to relax! I'm not going to relax until you've got your clean arse out of my bed and my house, and as far as I'm concerned you can take your fucking baboons with you and go and camp on fucking Rondebosch common.'

'Hey, what's got into you? You don't normally use such language.'

'No I don't, but this isn't normal, this is fucking lunatic abnormal and I'm not going to put up with it! You walk into my house and make yourself at home and use my shampoo and my toothpaste and ...'

'Relax,' he said again and put his hand on my leg.

'Don't ... !' I almost shrieked, and jumped out of bed. Unfortunately my anger had perversely manifested itself as an insurrection the nature of which even my pyjamas were not designed to conceal. The last thing I wanted was for Luc Tomlinson to notice, or heaven forbid, comment on a reflex that he was bound to misinterpret. So, somewhat inconsistently and to his evident surprise, I got back into bed.

'Don't tell me to relax,' I said, trying to camouflage my capitulation as a mature concession. 'And don't touch me.'

'Why not?' he asked, in a tone I'd heard Gerhard use when the devil was prompting him. 'Scared I'll notice your hard-on?' And he put his hand on the area in question.

I now had a choice between jumping out of bed again with an erection like a barber's pole protruding from my Noddy pyjamas, phoning the police, or physically expelling Luc Tomlinson from my bed. The first was undignified, the second impractical and the third impossible. Fortunately Luc removed his hand before my indecision had matured into the appearance of consent. 'Hey, listen,' he said, pointing up at the ceiling. We were right below the attic where the baboons were, and it was obvious from the crashes, squeals, growls, barks and shrieks that they were now either having a party or waging a battle to the death.

'What are they doing?' I asked, my anger stopped in its tracks.

'Making whoopee. Playing. Fucking. Having a ball.'

'Well, there goes Laura Ashley,' I sighed. I'd lost the impetus of my own fury, and the invasion of my bedroom and my bed seemed almost tame by comparison with the havoc being wrought upstairs.

'You're not really angry with me, are you?' he asked.

'I don't see why you should find it so impossible to believe that anybody could be angry with you,' I said, and then realised that that was exactly what he did believe, with all the bland naivety of a child who has been brought up to imagine his very failings loveable. In that case, there was little point in remonstrating with him. 'But it's all right,' I said, 'let the baboons rage it out on my behalf.'

'You mean you're not angry any more?' He snuggled into bed, for the moment actually looking like an angel, his red hair glowing like a halo around his contrite face, his blue eyes wide with concern.

'I suppose not,' I said, and lay back against my pillow. And indeed, my irritation lifted, diffusing itself in the uproar upstairs, leaving me pleasantly conscious of having drunk the better part of a bottle of wine, and of being in bed on a rainy evening.

'Good,' he said. He turned on his stomach, half on top of me, and put his face up against mine. In the dim light his pupils were very large, the blue of the iris forming only a narrow rim to the darkness. 'Let's fuck.'

I like to think of myself as a consistent person. I had not reached the age of 28 without learning most of what there was to know about myself, and I was content that there were no major surprises waiting in my life. I knew, amongst other things, that I was a normal heterosexual male with no more than a statistically insignificant attraction to other males; an attraction certainly not strong enough ever to lead me into a compromising situation with a member of my own sex. Furthermore, as members of my own sex went, Luc Tomlinson had from the first day of our acquaintance made himself particularly objectionable.

I counted to ten, trying not to identify the shape pressing against my thigh. Luc lifted one arm and put it across my chest. It was the closest I had ever been to another human being. The smell of toothpaste – my toothpaste – was not strong enough to counter the pungent herb-and-musk of his sweat. The baboons were cavorting above our heads. The rain lashed

352

against the windows. Luc Tomlinson's firm body was smooth and warm. 'Please remove your body from its inconvenient proximity to mine,' was what I intended to say. What I in fact said was, 'Oh, what the hell, what am I saving myself *for*?'

Over our heads the baboons were caterwauling and somersaulting. The stone round his neck glowed a wicked red. He put his nose in my armpit and said, 'I've been wanting to do this ever since I got a whiff of your pheromones that day when I dragged you up the mountain starkers.'

Luc Tomlinson, though hardly circumspect, turned out to be more considerate and well-mannered in this relation than in any other I had yet seen him in; or perhaps it was just the light touch of experience. There was no way he could make the breaching of my inexperience painless: my body reacted as if by reflex to this intimate invasion, but after the initial spasm Luc settled into a rhythm that transmuted the pain into something else, too intense to be pleasurable exactly, and yet by no means unpleasant. He leaned forward and kissed me. I flinched. 'Don't you like that?' he asked.

'It ... takes getting used to,' I said.

'I'll get you used to it.' He increased the rhythm of his movement, gauging his own arousal against mine, controlling my responses with his hands. We were gathering momentum when the telephone next to the bed started ringing.

'Oh, shit,' I said.

'Let it ring.'

'I can't. It will be Gerhard. I told him to phone.'

'Well then, answer it,' he said, grinning. 'I can amuse myself.'

'Yes, but can you, you know ...?'

'Pull out? No ways. I was here first.'

'This is very embarrassing,' I said, lifting up the receiver. 'Hello.'

'Nick, what the hell took you so long?'

'I was asleep, I'm sorry.'

'You sound out of breath. Are you all right?'

'Yes, I'm fine. But are you okay, you and Leonora?'

'I suppose so. Time will tell. I am certainly a wiser man than I got up this morning. Do you want to hear the story?'

353

'No, not now, I'm rather sleepy, as long as you're okay –' Luc Tomlinson grinned and tensed his haunches, and I yelped.

'What's that?'

'Nothing, just a cramp – *ow*!'

'Had I not known you so well I'd have suspected you were being fucked.'

'Don't be silly, Gerhard.'

'Sorry. I'm still not quite myself. Shall we get together tomorrow?'

'Yes,' I said. 'Why don't we meet for *lunch*?' My voice went out of control into another yelp as Luc put on the pressure.

Gerhard laughed. 'I've got a lot to tell you, but I suspect you've got something to tell me too. See you at Blues at one?'

'Make that two o'clock.'

'By all means. And if you're late I won't mind.'

I put down the phone.

'You think I could have your undivided attention now?' Luc asked.

'Sure thing,' I said, 'relax.'

'No ways,' he said, and increased both the frequency and reach of his thrusting. To the sound of the baboons orgying and the rain pelting down, Luc and I were climaxing noisily, energetically and simultaneously in my parents' marital bed, when I remembered, in the throes of my first-ever shared orgasm, that I had missed my appointment with Andrew Conroy.

CHAPTER SIXTEEN

It is not to be presumed that the habits, emotional and physical, of 28 years can in one night be abandoned for a radically new set of attitudes; but it must be said that Luc Tomlinson did his best in this regard. We woke, after not very many hours of sleep, to one of those sparkling days that in the Cape often follow a rainy spell. I got up, opened the curtains, looked at the disarray of the room, at the strange person in my bed, and asked myself what he was doing there. The morning sun flooded the bed, lighting up the coppery-red hair on the pillow. Luc opened his eyes, smiled, and stretched himself indulgently.

'Well, then,' he said. The blanket slipped off his chest; the smooth skin with the dusting of red-gold down gleamed in the morning sun.

'The Angel of Dawning,' I said.

He smiled again, and pushed the blankets all the way down. 'You mean this one?' he asked. 'We used to call it a Morning Glory.'

'So did we,' I said, 'but Angel of Dawning is better.'

I could not hide from myself the disruptive effect of such unrestrained intimacy upon my hitherto carefully shuttered, gated and signposted existence. Having initially profoundly resented Luc Tomlinson's invasion of my home, I had willingly given him access to the most secret places of my hitherto unexplored body, and he had availed himself of that permission with exuberant disregard for the merely decorous, urging me, too, to explorations of his body that a day before I would have found abominable, had I found them thinkable at all. Such physical licence was impossible without the connivance of the emotions; indeed, after an initial token resistance, they seemed to collaborate all too vigorously with the intruder within the gates.

355

It was fortunate, then, for my equanimity, that my own inex-perience had been supplemented by years of vicarious partici-pation in Gerhard's exploits. However life-changing I might be inclined to find my maiden foray into the forests of the night, I knew that in the received wisdom of experience it was simply what is known as a *one-night stand*, or a *bed-and-breakfast*; I knew that I had been Luc Tomlinson's *trick for the night*, and that he was probably a *double adapter*, or *a closet case*, or perhaps just availing himself of that undistinguished *port that will do in a storm*; as for myself, I had been *testing the waters* or *taking my temperature*. I knew that any expectations I might have con-ceived were *first-timer's fantasies* or *Stardust*, and I knew that I'd *got the fuck and shouldn't expect the phone call*. Above all I knew not to ask *When shall I see you again?*, the question above all others which not to ask was to hear no lies. It was useful and at the same time dispiriting to find such a ready vocabulary for an experience that one might have wanted to regard as unique. Everything was packaged and labelled in advance, all the clichés were lined up, ready to protect me against my own naivety. For this reason I knew that I didn't want to tell Gerhard about this development.

In any case, any inclination I might have had to take too romantic a view of what Gerhard had once called physical jerks with closure, would have been effectively discouraged by Luc Tomlinsons's own laconic demeanour. I looked at him lying back, totally relaxed in post-coital complacency, and asked him: 'How do you feel?'

'Fucked out,' he said, in a tone that did not invite a compar-ative discussion of our degrees of fulfilment.

It is possible that my hesitations on the brink of euphoria were reinforced by the knowledge that I had to explain myself to Andrew Conroy – and that without having anything to offer that could in any way mitigate the rudeness or assuage the hurt of my not turning up. It was not auspicious that my first venture into the realms of passion resulted in the breach of a commitment to someone whom I liked and respected.

I decided to get the explanation, such as it was, out of the way as soon as possible. It was very early in the morning to phone anybody, but I persuaded myself that an early call would testify more eloquently to my remorse than a leisurely before-lunch call later. I took the opportunity of Luc's absence in the shower to make my call; I had no desire to have him listen in on a conversation that he would have regarded as at best unnecessary, at worst abject. I had told him the night before about my missed appointment. He had, of course, told me to relax.

I dialled the number, looking at the piece of quartz still lying on the bedside table. *I accept all I am*, indeed. How bloody magnanimous.

'Hello, Conroy.'

'Andrew? This is Nick.'

'Hello, Nick.' The tone was neutral, controlled, unreproachful.

'I'm sorry to phone so early on a Sunday morning.'

'That's all right. I was awake anyway.'

'You know why I'm phoning – about last night.'

'Yes, I thought that might be it.'

'Listen, I really am most awfully sorry, it was just such an impossible day, I can't explain to you in detail now …' I hesitated. I couldn't really tell him that I had forgotten about our appointment till … well, till it had come to me; nor could I tell him that I had spent the evening with Luc Tomlinson. 'I don't really know what to say except I'm terribly sorry.'

'Well, don't hate yourself too much for it. I won't deny that I was disappointed, but by nine o'clock, when you hadn't turned up, I played the Fifth Cello Suite anyway, and I must say I don't think I've ever played better.'

'I'm very sorry to have missed it then.'

His voice regained some of its ironic warmth. 'Ah, by my logic it wouldn't have been as good if you'd been here. Unless of course it had been even better.'

'Of course,' I said hardly knowing what I was saying. Mainly I was aware of the impossibility of dealing with a disappointment that I myself had caused, for no reason that could alleviate the hurt. As I was trying to think of something appropriate or even just adequate to say, Luc shouted from the bathroom: 'Hey, can I have another towel? We used mine last night.'

The telephone was ominously silent.

357

'Andrew,' I said, 'you still there?'

'Yes, Nicholas, I'm still here. Where else would I be? But you have company. Phone me any time when you'd like to come over.'

'I'll do that.'

I put down the phone, feeling wretched. I had never in my life stood anyone up. The idea of Andrew Conroy playing the cello to himself was almost unbearably sad. I got up and took Luc a towel.

'I was talking to Andrew Conroy.'

'You explained to him?'

'I tried to. But what does one say?'

'One says sorry, but I was fucking my heart out.'

'You would say that. It's not my kind of line.'

'Hang around, you'll get there.'

I hoped not. But perhaps my inhibitions were just sops to my own conscience: was Andrew Conroy any better off for my not telling him the truth, for in fact finding out that I'd not been telling him the truth? Luc Tomlinson came and stood in front of me, lifted my face, kissed me lightly and said, 'You're worried.'

'Yes, I am. But don't tell me to relax.'

'Don't relax, then. Get yourself through the shower so we can get the chacs back home. They sound relatively quiet at the moment.'

'Fucked out, I suppose,' I said, rather bleakly.

He smiled. 'You are learning fast. But don't get bitter.'

The return of the baboons, after the previous day's mishaps and complications, was comparatively straightforward. The animals were calm when we opened the attic door, though the state of the room testified to a night of activity at least as energetic as ours downstairs. My neatly kept, hardly-ever-used guest room was in the kind of disarray that cannot be remedied by a superficial rearrangement of furniture; it would have to be refurbished from the carpet to the ceiling.

'Laura Ashley meets Africa,' Luc said. He took out his syringes. 'And now Africa meets modern science.'

I drove the minibus, and Luc tended to the baboons, who needed what he called a top-up on the long drive to Cape Point. The gatekeeper at Cape Point knew Luc, of course, and waved us through. Luc directed me by a route, no more than a track, that took us to a spot very close to the baboons' habitat, above Rocklands. We unloaded the unconscious baboons.

'Let's sit and wait for them to wake up,' said Luc.

We sat on a rock in the silence and the early morning light, the sun gleaming on the wet vegetation, the water of the magnificent bay extending blue and placid under the huge bowl of the sky to the crisply peaked mountains on the far side of the bay.

'I'm thinking of taking a job in London,' I said.

Luc Tomlinson looked at me. 'Why would you do that?'

I shrugged. 'To get away from the chaos.'

He pointed ironically at the sea, the sky, the distant mountains. 'What chaos?'

'I know, it doesn't seem like that here. But this is a nature reserve on a Sunday morning. This is not where I live and work.'

'What's to stop you from living and working here?'

'You're not serious.'

He didn't deny this, and we sat in silence, enjoying the mild heat of the sun. The baboons were regaining consciousness groggily; they explored their surroundings, found their mates and their parents and their children, and started chattering and scrounging and grooming. They seemed little the worse for their travails, although the two females who had lost their hands were clearly having difficulty adapting to the handicap.

'Suit yourself,' said Luc Tomlinson. 'If you think London will help you to escape from the chaos.' He subsided into silence, engrossed in the increasingly confident antics of the baboons. Then he leaned across to me, put his arm around my shoulders, and kissed me on the cheek.

'The chacs say thank you.'

'The chacs are welcome. We'll have to make sure that they don't get carted off again, though.'

'I'll shoot anybody who comes for them.'

'There are more legal methods than that. I'll get onto Felix Hartshorn first thing in the morning. As you know, he's pretty well disposed to us now. I'll persuade him to apply for an urgent interdict against the Silvermine laboratory, prohibiting them from entering any of their areas.'

'Good man.'

'The law has its uses.'

'Well, yes. I never said it didn't.'

'You came pretty close to it on occasion.'

'That was before I'd fully explored the uses of the law.'

'And you now have?'

'I don't know about fully.' He smiled and put his hand down the back of my pants. 'Shall we go down to the house?'

My old instinct of caution reasserted itself. 'I don't know,' I said. 'I have to collect my car from Cavendish, I suppose, and then ... you said you had to return the taxi ...?'

'Yes, well.'

'So perhaps we should get back.'

'Suit yourself.'

We both stood up from our rock. 'I mean,' I said, 'I have to be in Camps Bay for lunch with Gerhard and probably Leonora. Are you joining us? You're very welcome.'

'Yes, well. I don't think so. I'll spend the day checking out the chacs, I guess. You go and talk to your friends, I'll talk to mine.'

'If you prefer. Shall we get going, then? I'll bring you back here after we've dropped the taxi.'

'Not necessary. I'll chuck a bicycle in the back; we can fetch it from the house now.'

There is something forlorn about a conversation in which there seems to be nothing to talk about because all you really want to say is out of bounds. I had learnt from Gerhard that *a post-mortem presumes a corpse* and not to *regurgitate the meal*; I knew to *make love, not conversation* and not to *take a fuck for an introduction*: again I benefited by the hard lessons gleaned from countless encounters that had foundered on the simple human need to talk. Luc had made clear enough, I thought, that he had no wish to analyse or evaluate or otherwise reflect upon our night together, and I had no wish to intrude upon his reticences. As a result we had a relatively taciturn trip back to Cavendish. He was driving, humming softly to himself.

'Is your cell phone still operative?' I asked, as he stopped outside Cavendish Square.

'Guess so. Check if it's still in the cubbyhole, will you? The bugger who hijacked me didn't have time to find it, I should think.'

The phone was still where Luc had left it. 'Well, give me a ring sometime,' I said, as casually as I could.

'Sure thing. You'll be okay, or should I take you up by car?'

'Not to worry. I'll be fine.'

'Thanks again, man.'

'Thanks to you.'

'Anytime.'

He drove off, ignoring the appeals of a couple of aspirant passengers hailing him.

My car was where I had left it, what felt like years ago. Somebody had put a flier under the windscreen wiper, advertising Natural Weight Loss. Somebody else had stolen my aerial. I retrieved my parking chit from inside the car, went into the centre, paid the exorbitant fee, and exited by the already repaired boom. I felt I was driving back into normality after an extended expedition into uncharted territory.

At home I phoned Leonora and invited her to join Gerhard and me for lunch.

'I hope it wasn't too traumatic for you,' I said.

'No, it wasn't traumatic at all. It was … interesting. But I'll tell you at lunch.'

I wondered how I could ever tell someone my relationship with whom had been posited on the implicit understanding that my chastity was the glorious and necessary complement to her own, that I had surrendered this anxiously guarded jewel to the depredations of a young man who smelt of baboons. I was not even sure how this relinquishment would affect my relationship with Leonora. To know that I would have to know how it would affect my relationship with myself.

I spent an hour cleaning the worst filth in the baboon-ravaged guest room, and another hour changing the linen and otherwise tidying up my bedroom and bathroom, trying to squeeze the toothpaste tube back into shape, cleaning the soap. I washed the dishes, tidied the sitting room, tried to remove the wine stains from the carpet, and left for lunch. I had already locked the front door when the phone rang. I rushed back and picked up the receiver. It was my mother.

'Hello, dear, I'm just phoning to find out how you are.'

'I'm very well, mother, only I'm on my way to lunch with friends.'

'That's nice, dear. Which friends?'

'Leonora, mother, and Gerhard.'

'Oh. Yes. You have a lot of Afrikaans friends, don't you? I've often thought it's funny that your girlfriend and your best friend are both Afrikaans. Iris says perhaps you're rejecting your background.'

'That's just coincidence, mother. I'm not rejecting my background.'

'Yes. Still, I sometimes think you'd be better off with a nice English girl.'

'Yes, mother.' If it's any consolation to you, mother, I've just been fucked silly, in a very precise sense of the word, by a nice English boy.

'Yes, dear. Not that I have anything against Leonora. I just sometimes wonder whether she isn't a bit of a bluestocking?'

I recognised here the fears of my sister Iris, who thought that any sedentary occupation that couldn't be practised on horseback was 'intellectual' and thus suspect. 'Well, she reads books, if that is what you mean.'

'No, dear, I also read books. But does she read anything else?'

'Do you mean *Horse and Hound*, mother? Or *The Lady*?'

'I think you're slightly peppery this morning, dear.'

'No, I'm not, mother, it's only that I have to get going, otherwise I'll be late for lunch.'

'Run along then, dear. You don't want to be late for your lunch with your friends.'

I drove off, reflecting on the processes whereby those dearest and nearest to one become members of an alien culture observing bizarre and antiquated rituals, and wondering what exactly I had replaced them with. The two people supposedly closest to me on earth were meeting me for lunch, and I couldn't tell them what had happened to me the night before, at any rate not with the forthrightness that one would normally expect in such a relationship. I slipped Leonora's tape into its slot. The perky, celebratory rhythms of *Ganymed* mocked my self-conscious melancholy: *Wie im Morgenglanze Du rings mich anglühst* .... I fast-

362

forwarded to the more congenially gloomy tolling of *Death and the Maiden*, and then wondered why, having arguably made an important and liberating discovery about myself, I should shy away from the ecstatic towards the obsessive.

The California-come-to-Cape Town ambience of Blues, on the Camps Bay seafront, was well served by the cool, brilliant day, all ozone and seagulls, almost imperceptibly spiked with petrol fumes. Gerhard and Leonora were seated at a window table; seeing them before they saw me, I was struck by the ease and even warmth of their rapport – another consequence, then, of the previous day's events.

'You're looking a wee bit fragile,' Gerhard said, 'in spite of your early night.'

'Was it early?' I asked.

'It was only half-past-ten when I phoned.'

'Perhaps I slept too much, then,' I said, a bit wanly. 'Have you ordered?'

I assumed that Gerhard and Leonora would by now know each other's story; but it transpired that, considerately, they had saved the details to share with me. 'We thought it would be more pleasant to share the stories,' Leonora said, and I guessed that she had been self-conscious either about telling her story to Gerhard or about hearing his without my mediating presence. We agreed, after ordering our lunch, that we would take turns to recount our version of the day's events, starting with mine and ending with Gerhard's.

I kept my account as neutral as I could. Fortunately there were enough complications in the simple narrative of events to fill out my story decently without too much dwelling on the aftermath. By the time our food arrived, I had brought the narrative to its conclusion, with Luc's returning the minibus to the police station.

'So the baboons spent the night in Pinelands?' Gerhard asked, his eyebrows raised in the sceptical way I dreaded.

'Yes – we had no choice.'

'And Luc?'

'He too, obviously.'

'Mm.' I could see that it was only Leonora's presence that kept him from pressing for precise details.

'And the baboons are quite all right?' Leonora asked.

'Yes, they seem fine. Luc's watching over them today. He sends his regards and his regrets, by the way.' This was a lie, one I couldn't have accounted for except as a way of smoothing over Luc's absence, which in any case nobody but myself was much concerned about. 'And now your story, Leonora.'

'Yes,' she said, overcoming her natural shyness. 'It's not as exciting as yours, but it did have its interest. You see, I thought I would just have to sit and wait for Gerhard.'

'Reading *Paratus*,' he said.

'Yes. But after … I suppose about half an hour …'

'Forty minutes,' Gerhard said, 'of which you will have a full and hair-raising account.'

'Forty minutes, the door opened and Boetie came out. He was, how shall I say, agitated, excited, worked up. At first he didn't say anything, just paced up and down, and said that the Colonel had sent him out. I asked him why and he said, "She says it's because I'm distracting the subject, but if you ask me it's because she wants him to herself." He seemed quite upset about this, and I said but surely it doesn't matter if the doctor does the therapy on her own, and he looked a bit embarrassed and said, "Yes, but this is otherwise therapy." I didn't want to ask him about the therapy, but he still seemed very agitated, and then he said …' – Leonora blushed – 'you must forgive me, but I'm just repeating what he said, he said, "Jesus, I've never seen a … a *disselboom* … a shaft like that."'

Gerhard shrugged modestly. 'Perhaps he just hasn't had many opportunities of comparison.'

'He seemed very upset about this, and I asked him why that should bother him, and he said, "You don't know what it's like to be always teased about being short and small and I won't tell you what my nickname was at school," and of course I didn't have the heart to tell him that I knew.'

'So Gerhard's imposing proportions sent Boetie Bester into a convulsion of jealousy?' I asked.

'That was part of it, I think, but gradually, you know, as he talked, I gathered that it was more basic than that. There was the thing, of course, of being smaller than other boys, but then there was also a kind of admiration of Gerhard mixed with his jealousy and resentment. He kept on saying, "If I looked like that I wouldn't be a bloody *moffie*." I'm sorry, but you know, that's how he talks.'

'I don't mind,' Gerhard said. 'If I'd looked like him I'd also have gone for straight. I don't see him making it in the Meat Rack stakes.'

'Are you saying that Boetie Bester was admitting to homosexual tendencies?' I asked, amazed as much at the fact that I was discussing such things with Leonora as about anything else.

'No, I don't think so, not at all, he just meant that Gerhard's talents were wasted and that he, Boetie, would have made better use of them.'

'Well,' said Gerhard, 'if he means he might not have been a death squad operative if he'd had a bigger dick, that's something he can save for the Truth and Reconciliation Commission.'

'I'm coming to that – I mean the Commission – but there was also this other thing.' She looked uncomfortable. 'I don't know exactly what that woman was doing with you …'

'I could tell you,' Gerhard suggested. 'Should I fill you in on meantime in the laboratory?'

'Excuse me,' our waiter, an earnest young man of about twenty, asked, 'is everything in order?'

Gerhard glanced at him for slightly longer than necessary, smiled in a way I had known to make waiters drop plates of soup in customers' laps, and said, 'Everything is just fine.' The waiter nodded, slightly flustered, and disappeared. Gerhard repeated, 'Shall I come in with my part of the story now?'

Leonora nodded. 'I think my story would make more sense with your background.'

'Are you absolutely convinced that you want to hear the whole unexpurgated account?'

'No,' I said. 'Perhaps you can judiciously cut where necessary.'

'And how am I to judge the need?'

'If you're worried about me,' said Leonora, 'you needn't be. I think I've seen and heard … more things than I thought I would ever see and hear, and I can't say that I feel, you know, overwhelmed.'

'Good woman. Then hear ye ... right, where did we part company?'

'With me and Leonora being sent out of the Doctor's office.'

'Yes, right. Well, I assumed this therapy session, as she kept on calling it, would take place right there in her office, with me sitting in a chair at her desk, that kind of thing. I was, I will admit, apprehensive. Whereas I am not, I think, timid in dealing with men, I don't mind telling you I feel at a disadvantage with women, especially sexually aggressive women. And Colonel Johanna is not called the Black Widow for nothing. Anyway, my initial misgivings were in no way assuaged by her announcement that we would repair to the "reorientation laboratory" for the treatment. I don't know if you noticed another door in the far wall ...'

'Just next to the photo of the Star of South Africa,' I said.

'Exactly. Well, she ushered me in there, with Boetie not coincidentally in close attendance, and there, all gleaming tiles and mirrors and chrome and pipes and dials, was what seemed like a fully equipped interrogation chamber. Or perhaps that was just a superficial impression, derived from the fact that all the laboratory equipment and furniture seemed dedicated to *restraint*: everything seemed to have a strap or a buckle or a clamp attached to it – including and especially the centrepiece, which was what I can only describe as a kind of *throne*, come to think of it an upmarket version of that chair they have to restrain the baboons ...'

'The *gemakstoel*,' Leonora said.

'That's it. Anyway, there in the centre of the room like a dentist's chair for recalcitrant patients was this contraption, humming quietly to itself ...'

'Humming?'

'Perhaps it was just the fluorescent light, but it sounded like the chair, one of those smug triumphs of technology and design. Anyway, as you can imagine, I was starting to get very cold feet indeed at this point, especially as Boetie was becoming a very visible, not to say obtrusive, presence. To be honest, I suspected him of an unhealthy interest in the proceedings, which Leonora's account has now gone some distance to explaining. Theoretically, you remember, I could terminate my

366

participation at any stage, but practically, of course, the problem was that I had to stay in there for as long as I thought you'd need to get the baboons out of there. So I was meeker, I tell you, than was entirely natural under the circumstances, indeed, all my instincts were telling me to up and run.'

'So were you in The Chair at this stage?'

'No, Johanna made me sit down on an ordinary chair first to explain to me, as she said, the scientific basis of the therapy. It turns out to be what she calls positive conditioning, the opposite of aversion therapy: heterosexual relations are, as she put it, conceptually redefined by being associated with pleasurable sensations. To this end, she explained, I would first have to render myself pharmaceutically receptive ...'

'What on earth is that?'

'In a word, Ecstasy, which she said I would be taking in a strictly controlled environment.'

'The Chair.'

'The Chair. She asked me whether I was prepared to submit to that aspect of the therapy, and I thought what the hell, it's not as if I've never taken E before. Furthermore, I would be *electronically stimulated*.'

'Sounds ominous.'

'Indeed. It transpired that in the course of the celebrated sterility experiments conducted by the laboratory while it was still labouring for the preservation of our traditional way of life, I don't know if you know about them ...'

'Mhlobo told me about it,' I said, and explained to Leonora, 'apparently they tried to develop a sterility drug to feed to the ... superfluous population groups.'

'Right,' said Gerhard, 'and they tested these drugs on our friends the baboons. One of the technical problems, though, was collecting baboon semen without getting, as it were, too personally involved with the baboon.'

'I know,' I said, 'Mhlobo told me about that.'

'Yes. It caused a certain amount of sensation in the press. So Johanna and her technical advisers developed a system whereby the prostate is stimulated by a mild electric shock administered via electrodes connected to ... well, to the prostate. Not to put too fine a point on it, the baboons were electronically jerked off.'

367

'Excuse me,' said our waiter, 'can I take your plate?'

'Absolutely,' said Gerhard. 'Help yourself. We'll let you know if we want anything else.'

He waited for the waiter to clear the table before continuing. I could see he was watching the young man's forearms. 'Now, when the baboon experiments were stopped, Johanna, ever resourceful, and loath to waste a good idea, redirected this technology to her new field of interest, and incorporated it into the process of positive conditioning.'

'So you ...'

'Yes, so I. This is where the Chair comes into it. I was invited – *invited*, mind – to divest myself of my clothes behind a screen, though heaven knows why the screen, since I then had to appear from behind the screen in a state of nature and submit to being strapped into the chair by Boetie, but with Johanna assisting as necessary. I was at this stage, as you can imagine, in no state to appear in public. "You must not think of me as a woman," Johanna said to me, donning an ominous-looking pair of rubber gloves, "not just yet, anyway. For the time being, think of me as a doctor and trust me." Upon which she stepped on a switch which flipped the chair backwards, rendering my nether parts totally accessible, and stuck a fingerful of KY jelly up my bum.'

'Do we need quite so much detail?' I asked.

'Yes, I think so. You need to know what I went through for our friend Luc and his baboons. Anyway, while I was still recovering from the psychological shock of this invasion, Johanna produced an ugly-looking probe which she proceeded to install, as it were, inside the newly prepared area, after which she plugged me into the wall like a Snackwich maker.'

'But ...' said Leonora hesitantly.

'But what?'

'But I thought the theory of positive conditioning was that you were subjected to pleasurable experiences.'

'My thought exactly, as I lay there trussed like a chicken with a meat thermometer up its cavity: isn't this supposed to be pleasurable? I said as much to Johanna, and she explained to me that the conditioning takes place in two stages, the dissociative phase and the associative phase. In the dissociative phase one is encouraged to distance oneself from one's former pleasure objects, by which I assume she meant the KY and the probes, which no doubt figured to her somewhat rudimentary imagination as an approximation to homosexual intercourse.'

'And then the associative phase,' I prompted.

'And then the associative phase. The associative phase is not much more sophisticated, and I'm not sure that it is much more pleasant. But it is the phase with the sweeties and the balloons. First, still in the guise and garb of a medical worthy, Johanna administered a little tablet of Ecstasy. Only, as she explained with some pride, her laboratory is something of a pioneer in skin absorption, and they had perfected a technique of making Ecstasy directly absorbable through the lining of – you've guessed it – so the pill followed the electrodes up the Khyber.'

'At this stage the electrodes were ... dormant, as it were?'

'Oh, yes, I hadn't been switched on yet. The next dimension, as Johanna called it, was the *ambience*.'

'You mean flowers and candles?'

'No, although here too there was a *Strelitzia regina* and a photograph of PW Botha – I mean, who needs Ecstasy? But *ambience*, it turned out, was music, which in this relation is deemed not so much to have charms to soothe the savage breast as to arouse the timid breast to savagery.'

'Which music?' asked Leonora, with a music lover's interest.

'Well may you ask. I was given a choice; Johanna said that considering her clientele, she had to have a good selection of music, mainly disco and opera. I said I wanted the *Liebestod* from *Tristan and Isolde*, which always gives me a hard-on, but she didn't have that; she says most of her subjects want Maria Callas, but as you know I've never been *that* stereotyped, so we settled for the *Ride of the Valkyries*.'

'All this while you're strapped to the chair?'

'Absolutely, though this is the point to tell you that the chair is in fact voluptuously comfortable if not exactly dignified. Possibly as a result of the absorption of the Ecstasy, I was in fact starting to ... relax at this point, which is the point at which Johanna metaphorically as well as literally took off the white coat. As she did so, she explained – Johanna is a great explainer, she could make a fortune as a sex consultant on TV – she explained that normally she used a sex worker, a very reliable and skilled professional whom she knew from her army days, but this being a special case, she would in the interests of science and the nation make herself available as associative object. In short, the various stimuli would all contribute to my greater pleasure in, if you'll pardon the phrase, bonking Johanna.'

'Bonking Johanna?'

'Bonking Johanna. Indulging in sexual intercourse with the Black Widow. Now I know what doubts are crossing your mind: how do I, a man of pronounced homosexual tendencies, manifest enough of an interest in Johanna to become susceptible to said pleasurable associations? In other words, how do I get it up?'

'The thought did cross my mind,' I contributed.

'Well, that's where the Ecstasy helps, and of course the electrodes and the chair, and then the music. And this is where I intersect with Leonora's story. You see, duly drugged and stripped and trussed and plugged, and with the Valkyries pouring out of a very powerful sound system I was getting very … you know, responsive, when Boetie intervened.'

'You don't mean he … ?'

'Interposed his own body? No, heaven forbid. But he put it to Johanna that she was being untrue to the memory of Major Cornelius, you remember, her ex-husband, the wimp in the moustache. He seemed really upset, which of course did rather detract from the magic of the moment, so Johanna sent him out of the room, quite like a mother sending a naughty boy to his room.' He paused dramatically. 'Which is where we rejoin Leonora in the waiting room.'

'Should I carry on?' Leonora asked.

'I think so,' Gerhard said. 'Then I'll give you the rest of mine later.'

'Well, as Gerhard was saying, Boetie was very upset about what he called the Colonel's conduct, which according to him was disrespectful to the memory of the late Major van der Merwe.'

'Why does he have this thing about the Major?'

'That's just it, you see. I asked him that, and he told me that when he first joined the Civil Cooperation Bureau he was very young and inexperienced, just out of police college, and very scared, because they had to go on these night-time raids to "take out undesirables", and Boetie of course didn't want to say that he was scared, but the Major must have known, and he took a personal interest in Boetie, he says like a father in a son, and stayed by him on the first night out and showed him what to do and after that always showed an interest, with the result that Boetie became, as he said, one of the crack members of the squad. The Major personally recommended him for a medal, which the minister conferred on him. But then the Major was killed when his vehicle caught fire, Boetie says sabotaged, and Boetie says it was the greatest loss of his life, because his own father had beaten him to make him tough and never showed an interest, but Major Cornelius had looked after him and *educated him*, he says.'

'I suppose if education means preparation for one's chosen walk of life, Boetie did in fact receive an education from his Major,' Gerhard mused.

'Yes, except that after the Major's death, it seems, he was at a loss and became a kind of personal killer for an unknown person, somebody he calls Pluto, who used to send him on missions, where he missed, he says, the personal element. Which is why he was pleased to become personal assistant to Colonel Johanna, though I gather he still works for Pluto too. So when Johanna, you know, took part in your therapy, he did see it as a betrayal of this heroic father figure, whom obviously he sentimentalises. I suppose it's a bit like seeing your mother in, you know, a compromising position.'

'It makes one feel quite sorry for Boetie,' I commented.

'It does,' said Gerhard, 'and then it also does not. I mean, I know that background, I come from it myself. It's bloody awful and it fucked up a whole generation of young men. But we didn't all become killers; I mean, how many people did Boetie personally kill in pursuit of the approval of Major Cornelius?'

'Yes,' said Leonora, 'and now he feels something of that, though to be honest I'm not sure how much of it is, you know, remorse and how much of it is fear that he will be summonsed in front of the Truth and Reconciliation Commission, and now, he says, all the generals and cabinet ministers, the people who used to hand out the medals, are quietly withdrawing and leaving people like Boetie to take the responsibility. That's another reason why he stays with the Colonel; he says at least she'll never betray him.'

'So while I was baring my all to Johanna, Boetie was opening his heart to you?' Gerhard asked.

'Yes. He ... he's not very rational at the moment, of course, and he claims that seeing me again has made him want to get out of it all, as he puts it. I seem to be, you know, a reminder of what he thinks of as a better time. He's actually quite sentimental. And that's really all I have to tell. He asked me for my telephone number, and I couldn't very well refuse.'

'If he's sentimental it's a good thing that he didn't stay to watch Johanna's whole performance with me,' Gerhard said. 'I think I can say she entered into the spirit of the therapy with commendable thoroughness. There I was, lashed to my chair, humming with Ecstasy, with Johanna towering over me, by now divested of her laboratory coat and all other manner of covering, keeping firm control not only of me but also of the electric current being fed to my G spot, and adjusting, as she put it, supply and demand through manipulation of the rheostat. I literally had my volume adjusted, which through a strange effect of the drug seemed to be intimately connected with the keening of the Valkyries. Johanna, as you may have noticed, is a vigorous and energetic woman, but also a surprisingly agile one; add to this the fact that I have always had a penchant for a little light bondage, and ... well, to cut a long story short, it was, as far as it went, a successful session.'

'Are you sure it didn't work?' I asked.

Gerhard enacted an exaggerated shrug of universal doubt. 'Who can be sure of anything where the human psyche is concerned?' Then he relaxed into his usual mode of acute engagement with his environment. 'But I must admit, for instance, to an undiminished interest, albeit an entirely hypothetical one, in the remarkably mobile muscles playing under our waiter's Chinos. But let me not be distracted from my story – of which, however, little remains to be told. Johanna expressed great satisfaction with the session, but felt that a positive reinforcement session would have to be arranged quite soon.'

'So you also exchanged telephone numbers like Leonora and Boetie?' I asked, possibly a bit waspishly.

'Well, I have hers. She doesn't have mine. If Johanna wants to hang around with gay men she'll have to learn not to hold her breath while waiting for a phone call.'

I winced. 'So you weren't reoriented?'

'No, I said it was successful as far as it went, which was right there and then and no further.'

'How do you know?' I asked. 'After all, it was only a few hours ago.'

'And what do you think I've been doing in those few hours?'

'Sleeping, I'd have imagined.'

'No such thing. Giving Clive the benefit of the remains of the Ecstasy. And if I've been reoriented neither of us noticed a thing. Coffee, anybody?'

Leonora looked at her watch. 'I'm afraid I must go. I told my flatmates I'd go for a walk with them.'

'I'll phone you tomorrow,' I said.

She leaned over and kissed me lightly. 'Good,' she said. 'How much do I owe?'

'Not to worry,' I said, slightly taken aback; she didn't normally initiate the farewells. 'My treat.'

We ordered coffee from the waiter, whose attention was sharpened by Leonora's departure, and whom Gerhard did nothing to discourage.

'I don't understand you,' I said.

'I know,' he said, 'but what aspect of my conduct is it that mystifies you at present?'

'How you can pretend total commitment to Clive and then sit here and flirt with that waiter.'

'My dear Nicholas, total commitment has never precluded flirtation. It's what makes total commitment bearable, indeed possible. It also makes that young man's job considerably more interesting.'

'That's just a rationalisation.'

'That's also true; but a rationalisation is not necessarily untrue. But do I detect a slightly morose tone in our Nicholas today?'

'That's possible.'

'Nothing to do with the baboons' night in Pinelands, by any chance?'

I sighed. 'I wasn't going to tell you, but if I can't tell you, who can I tell?'

'Precisely.'

Gerhard listened to my story with more seriousness than I had expected; I had imagined that my plight might strike him as ridiculous, but he listened with a minimum of interjections, nodding sagely at times and saying 'How very interesting' from time to time.

When I'd reached the end of my story, for the second time that afternoon, with Luc's return of the taxi, he said, 'A wonderful story. But why the depression? You spend a night with a spectacular young man, spend it by your own account in a state of blissful discovery, and now you look as if in fact you'd spent the night watching home movies with Stuart and Sharon.'

'I don't know,' I said, 'it's left me feeling very uncertain.'

'Uncertain about yourself or about him?'

'Both.'

'If he were to phone you now, would you leave and rush to wherever he was?'

I considered. 'Yes.'

'Then you need no longer be uncertain about yourself. Next question: is he likely to?'

'Phone me? No, I don't think so.'

'Then you're uncertain about him.'

'Well, yes. You know him – he's so ... so uncommitted. I mean, here's this ... thing that's happened to me, and it's obviously a big thing for me, but for him it was just another Saturday evening.'

'I'd be less than a friend if I tried very hard to persuade you otherwise. Look, I've been through it myself, and I'm afraid I may even have taken several young men through it by showing them a course on which I had no intention of accompanying them beyond the first decisive steps. This may have made them unhappy for a while, but I believe that in the long run they were the better off for having been introduced so gently and efficiently to something they were destined to discover some time in any case.'

374

'I'm not sure that I'll be the better off in the long run.'

'What was the alternative? Dragging on your painful relationship with Leonora, who by the way is much nicer than you ever allowed her to be in your company?'

'Thanks. So I was sodomised by Luc Tomlinson to bring home to me what a rotten lover I was to Leonora.'

'There are worse ways of making such discoveries. Some people get married.'

I laughed. 'I'm not sure that you're helping.'

'Look, all that will *really* help is for somebody to tell you that Luc Tomlinson is waiting for you at home and is going to devote the rest of his life to the single-minded pursuit of your pleasure and comfort. Now that unfortunately I can't do for you; all I have for you is advice, for what it's worth.'

'What *is* it worth?'

'Not much, in the lonely hours, but in the long run useful as a sign that somebody has travelled that road before and did not fall by the wayside.'

The waiter was hovering with the bill; we were the last lunchers. Outside the short winter's day was drawing to a beautiful close, the sun plunging into the sea without much fuss. 'Excuse me, sir,' the young man said, 'but I'm about to go off duty.'

Gerhard took the bill. 'I'll pay,' he said to me, 'so you can't tell me to shut up when I give you my last piece of advice.' He glanced at the bill and put his credit card on top of it, the waiter whisked it away, and Gerhard continued. 'You must not confuse a bad need for a good fuck with the pangs of unrequited love, but you must also not underestimate the disruptive potential of a bad need for a good fuck. In either case, a little art is a great aid to nature, in the sense of a well-dissembled equanimity. In other words, you can suffer, but don't mope.'

The waiter brought the credit card slip for signing, with the original bill. Gerhard looked at it again, added a tip, handed it back to the young man, and said, 'Thank you very much. You are a joy to behold and a credit to the establishment.' The young man blushed and said, 'Thank you very much, sir.'

As we left, I asked Gerhard, 'What was that all about? Wasn't that a bit florid?'

'Perhaps. Art coming to the aid of nature.' We were outside the restaurant now. He showed me the bill. It was signed 'Warren', with an underlined telephone number next to it.

'He'll be disappointed when I don't phone. But at least he won't think I didn't like him.'

On my way home I rewound the tape to *Ganymed*, and hummed along as best I could to the half-understood words:

Dass ich dich fassen möcht'
In diesen Arm! ...
Ick komm', ich komme!
Ach, wohin? Wohin?

It occurred to me that I'd been introduced to the music by Andrew Conroy and given the tape by Leonora, the two people most betrayed by my present application of their gift.

CHAPTER SEVENTEEN

I'm one of the few people I know – my secretary Myrah is another – who don't really mind Monday morning. In some ways I even prefer it to the coerced good cheer of Friday afternoon, and the implicit imperative of the weekend: thou shalt have a good time lest thy neighbour mock thee on Monday morning. Above all, Monday morning, once I have negotiated the irrationality of the traffic jams, means a return to an existence ordered by my diary, policed by Myrah, circumscribed by the walls and door of my office. Of course, interruptions do happen, unscheduled visitors turn up, unexpected phone calls break into the routine; but those can be dealt with from a position of strength, my own chair behind my own desk.

This Monday morning was no exception. The shocks and surprises of the weekend seemed more manageable, more finite, when contained in the two relatively small blocks of my week-at-a-glance diary. Admittedly I felt a twinge at seeing '*Andrew Conroy: supper*' entered for Saturday evening; also '*LT: baboons*' for the afternoon. I had kept one appointment and not the other, and as a consequence my existence had temporarily fallen apart; I now had to reassemble it.

My first act was to phone Felix Hartshorn. I was interested and intrigued to find that the telephone was still under the firm control of Brenda. If she recognised my name, she did not say so; ever the impeccable secretary, she simply said, 'Mr Hartshorn will speak to you now,' as if I was being granted an audience

Felix Hartshorn was, for Felix Hartshorn, cordial. I explained to him what we wanted. 'That's splendid,' he said. 'We have to regain control of our natural resources, and demarcate the legitimate boundaries of scientific research. We have, in fact, managed to effect, as it happens, a moratorium on the export of baboons to foreign laboratories.'

'So you will consent to an application for an interdict in the name of the Department?'

'Definitely. I have, as you may have noticed, the greatest respect for scientific method, but at times I do sense in the scientific mindset a certain arrogance in the face of God's simple creatures. And I have of course heard of Dr Johanna van der Merwe.' I thought I could detect a shudder in his voice, which surprised me. Given his affinity for Brenda, he should have found Johanna irresistible.

The second item on my list of things to do to get my life in order was to phone Leonora and arrange to meet her for lunch. I had decided that whatever my encounter with Luc Tomlinson had meant, and I had no idea what that was, it had brought home to me with unignorable cogency that there was no future in my relationship with Leonora: indeed, that there had been and was neither past nor present in it. This was not something that I looked forward to telling somebody of whose life I had arguably occupied something like four years; but I could not see that an occupation of that kind would be much redeemed by being made permanent. It seemed only appropriate that we should meet at Michelangelo's: having tolerated its bad food and disgraceful service for so long, this was not the time to break new ground. There was even a sense in which its uncomfortable wooden seats could serve my penitential frame of mind, in reminding me painfully of Luc Tomlinson's energetic incursions.

I was, for once, earlier than Leonora. 'Table for one?' the depressed-looking owner asked.

'No, table for two as usual, please.'

'You can sit anywhere.' He did not bother to try to make this sound like an exciting liberty.

Leonora was slightly late, but not late enough for me to develop a grievance that would have made my announcement easier to deliver. We ordered our usual chicken mayonnaise sandwiches from our usual unenthusiastic waiter. I was trying to think of a way of launching my topic, when Leonora said, 'I suppose you can see I'm a bit tense.'

As a matter of fact, I had seen nothing of the sort, being too

378

much preoccupied with my own burden, but I said, 'Well, yes, but I didn't want to say anything.'

'It's a pity you didn't, it might have made it easier for me.'

'Made what easier for you?'

'What I have to say to you.'

'You have something to say to me?' This was almost unprecedented in my relation with Leonora, but I did not think it diplomatic to say so.

'Yes. It's ... well, to get to the point, it's just that I don't think we should continue to see each other, not like this anyway, as if ... as if it meant something. I think it's time we recognised that, that, you know, we're not meant for each other.'

It took me a while to register that Leonora had just seized the initiative. My first instinct was to link this startling development with recent events. 'Were you offended by yesterday's conversation? I mean all those details ...?'

'No, not at all. I'm not very experienced in such things, but I've read enough to know that the things I don't know are not, you know, inhuman. I always thought your friend Gerhard was a bad influence on you, but now ... I don't know, I was trying to blame him for the fact that our relationship was not developing, but now I think I just didn't want to face the fact that there was nothing in our relationship to develop.'

Slightly petulantly, I said, 'Is it Boetie that made you aware of my shortcomings?'

But Leonora was not to be drawn into the parting-with-mutual-recriminations mode. 'I'm not talking about shortcomings,' she said, 'either yours or mine. And I could never love Boetie. He is a murderer and quite a limited person. But it is true that seeing him made me realise that ... it is possible to be loved, rather than tolerated. I'm not blaming you for it, but I think you have tolerated me, and perhaps I have tolerated you.'

Given how reluctant I had been to initiate the break, I should have been grateful to Leonora for taking it upon herself to do so; but whereas I could rejoice in not having to sever relations with a weeping Leonora, I could not help feeling slightly cheated by this change of role, which left me little scope for anything other than dignified acceptance. I could not even tell her that I myself had been on the point of terminating the relationship, without seeming to want to grab the advantage. I certainly did not have the starring role in this break-up.

Still, it may be preferable to play the amiable minor character than the villain, and I did, on reflection, feel the good fortune of having been released at so little cost to myself. Predictably, with the release of tension came also a much less constrained communion, and the rest of our lunch was unusually relaxed. We even felt free to admit to the deficiencies of Michelangelo's. 'This place does make rotten sandwiches, doesn't it?'

Leonora laughed. 'I always thought so, but didn't want to hurt your feelings by saying so.' I reflected that trying not to hurt each other's feelings was probably admirable as a component of a relationship, but not as its sole constituent.

The waiter did not ask us whether our food was in order – Michelangelo's is not a restaurant that can afford to invite complaints – so I had to create my own opportunity. As we left, I said to him, 'This place makes the worst sandwiches in Cape Town.'

The man looked at me without surprise or resentment. 'I know,' he said. 'I could never figure out why you kept coming back.'

I went back to my office and attended to routine business, my life once again in order and under control. I phoned Mhlobo and gave him an edited version of our exploits.

'Good,' he said. 'But there's talk of the good doctor not being with us inde-fin-ite-ly.'

'Johanna?'

'The same. Evidence is mounting from the TRC that the experiments conducted at the Silvermine laboratory were ... irregular, even given the nature of the institution. The prosecutors and courts have rather more to cope with at present than they are equipped for, but in due course the law may well turn its dignified regard upon Johanna van der Merwe.'

'She certainly seems to have had a free hand up to now.'

'She is by no means the only one. And of course, we must not expect the law to be infallible; there are quite enough corrupt judges left over from the previous lot who could be persuaded to think it their patriotic duty to acquit Johanna. But I'm glad you got your monkeys back.'

'Baboons.'

Angie came into my office, looking slightly sheepish. 'You remember Kevin,' she said.

'The one who wants to marry you for a British passport?'

'Yes. Only it turns out that that's not why he wants to marry me.'

'Why *does* he want to marry you, then?'

'Oh, come on, Nick, is it so impossible to believe somebody could want to marry me for myself?'

'I thought it was your complaint that nobody did.'

'Well, Kevin does. And what's more, he not only does not want a British passport, he wants me to apply for a South African passport.'

'Why on earth?'

'As proof of my commitment.'

'To him or to the country?'

'Both.'

'Couldn't you apply for a South African passport and keep your British?'

'Yeah, sure. But that's hardly total commitment.'

'Who says total commitment precludes all other options?'

'I'd have said so, Nick, wouldn't you?'

'I have no idea,' I said. 'I don't know the first thing about total commitment.'

One more thing remained to be done: I had to phone Andrew Conroy and present myself for re-invitation. I thought I would leave that till about Wednesday. I had promptly enough expressed my apologies: I needn't seem too abject – or, for that matter, too eager. Now that I'd been initiated so thoroughly into the possibilities of male relationships, I wondered whether, if that was indeed what Andrew wanted, I wouldn't be better off with him than with Luc, with whom I had almost nothing in common, and who seemed purely heartless by comparison with the older man. I seemed to be learning fast, I said to myself, to adjust my desires to my possibilities.

It occurred to me that I'd better find out whether the baboons were all right after their peregrinations. I hesitated for a moment, then phoned Luc Tomlinson's cell phone number. The phone rang and rang, naggingly but ineffectually, without even the barren consolation of an invitation to leave a voice mail message. Luc Tomlinson was not the kind of person who walked around with a cell phone strapped to his belt. In fact, he was not the kind of person who lived in terms of phone calls; baboons did not need telephones.

On Wednesday morning Leonora phoned me at work, something which she had always avoided as 'unprofessional'.

'Nick, I'm sorry to bother you at work, but I'm terribly concerned, and I think you should probably know about it.'

'Tell me, then.'

'It's Boetie, only it's not only Boetie. You know, he said he was thinking of getting out of his involvement with this mysterious person ...'

'Pluto?'

'Yes, Pluto, and then on Monday he phoned, and he was quite excited and he said he knew who this Pluto was, and he might get amnesty if he told the TRC everything he knew, and he was going to get out of his job at the laboratory too, because the Colonel had disappointed him, and he wanted me to know, you know, that meeting me again had made him see the evil of his ways. But that's not really the main thing I wanted to tell you; he then said that he'd been given a job by Pluto, which he was going to refuse to do, because it wasn't a political job and he could never claim amnesty for it, and when I asked him what this job was, he said it was to kill Luc Tomlinson.'

'Kill ... ?'

'Kill Luc Tomlinson. He called him the Baboon Boy. So I said to him but who *is* this Pluto, and he said he couldn't tell me that yet, because it was now his only asset, this knowledge that he had.'

'And he definitely said he wasn't going to kill Luc?'

'Yes, he said he'd already refused, he sounded quite proud

of it. But whoever Pluto is won't stop there. We should warn Luc.'

'We should indeed. I'll try his cell phone first and then get back to you.'

Without very much hope, I tried the number that I by now knew at heart. As usual, it rang to no effect; I thought of *Nkosi Sikelel' iAfrika* tinkling into silence somewhere.

I called Leonora. 'How can I get hold of Boetie?'

'He said he was going to be at home today, now that he's decided to resign his job.'

'And where is home?'

'In Plumstead somewhere, a flat. He gave me the address ... wait, here it is.'

I made a note of the address. 'Listen, I'm going to see if I can get hold of him to find out more, and then I'm going to try to find Luc at his home in Cape Point. But will you keep phoning his cell phone number every twenty minutes or so, just in case he's somewhere nearby, and warn him?'

'Of course.'

'And if anything goes wrong, phone Gerhard.'

I put down the phone. It seemed fairly obvious to me that Pluto was Brick Tomlinson, outraged at the disappearance of the baboons, still smarting because of the financial beating he'd had to take. Admittedly, I'd not have imagined his vindictiveness to stretch to killing his own son; but then, his resentment of his son had seemed badly out of control at times. And if he'd found out that Luc had burgled his study, his natural irrationality might have been provoked beyond all restraint. Besides, the assassination of Sam Stanford, so soon after his testimony in the Rocklands case, now made sense as the work of Boetie Bester acting on the commands of an irate Brick Tomlinson.

I explained to a surprised Myrah, who believed that her proximity was an absolute condition of any productive labour on my part, that I had to go and interview a client who could not come to my office, and drove to Plumstead.

I found the address Leonora had given me. Boetie's flat was in a more luxurious block than I'd expected, but then I remembered that he'd boasted of the money he made selling Ecstasy;

besides, I had no idea what hit men were paid. His flat was on the ground floor. I rang the doorbell twice, but there was no reply, although I could hear music inside. I tried the door. To my surprise it was not locked. I opened it and found myself in the small entrance hall of what seemed to be a large one-bed-roomed flat. The sitting room, which led directly off the entrance hall, was sparsely furnished: a large television set, a coffee table, two imitation leather easy chairs, and an elaborate music centre, pumping out Julio Iglesias singing *To all the girls I've loved before* at very high volume. There was a display cabi-net in the corner containing, as far as I could tell, little trophies of the kind one was given at school, and some ornaments: a Dutch shoe in gaudy porcelain, a Voortrekker monument in flimsy-seeming metal. There was no sign of Boetie.

The bedroom door was ajar. I knocked gently; there was no reply, and I pushed it open. Boetie Bester was lying on his bed, a narrow army-style cot. He was sprawled on his stomach and he was completely naked. His posture made it all too evident that he had inserted into himself what I took to be one of the electrodes Gerhard had described. The other end was plugged into the electrical outlet on the wall, and the control box lay on the floor next to Boetie's limp hand. An open bottle of Vaseline stood on the bedside table; next to it lay a little foil envelope such as he had shown us in the laboratory, containing Ecstasy. Boetie did not move nor breathe. On the bedside table was a framed photograph of himself with Major Cornelius van der Merwe, clearly taken at some team-building outing: they were drinking beer, and the Major had his arm around Boetie. Boetie's open eyes seemed to be staring at this reminder of happier days.

I approached, absurdly quietly, and was about to touch Boetie when I realised that if he was dead he had probably been electrocuted. I switched off the outlet and pulled out the plug. I took Boetie's arm; it was still warm, but there was no pulse. The control unit on the floor said *Approved by the South African Bureau of Standards*; I wondered how exactly they had tested it. I looked at the over-muscular corpse, the unprepos-sessing remains of a man who had died in pursuit of the ulti-mate sensation: who knows what transcendent fantasies had embellished his final convulsions? One could only wish for him that the Ecstasy had had time to kick in before the electricity did.

I decided to leave Boetie for the time being to his dreams; I needed to get to Cape Point without the kind of delay visited upon the first person on the scene of a death. As I closed the front door behind me, the CD player eerily shuttled to the next selection, obedient unto death to the wishes of Boetie Bester. Frank Sinatra breezily implored an anonymous lover: *Fly me to the moon* ...

At the gate to Cape Point I asked, 'Has Luc Tomlinson gone in or out today?'

The man shook his head. 'No. Last time I saw Luc was yesterday. He came in with his bike.'

'Thanks.' That at least was good news. I had no idea what I was going to say to him when I saw him: *Your father wants to kill you*? I could hear him say, 'Yes, well. Relax.'

Rocklands was basking serenely in the winter sun; there was no sign of life, no motorcars, but that was normal: Luc left very few marks of his passage. I parked at the foot of the steps leading up to the house, and paused for a moment, recalling Luc's effulgent appearance that Sunday morning long ago. Now there was nothing, only the steps; but the front door was open, which was a good sign: Luc would have closed the door if he'd gone walking or hakea-hacking, to keep the baboons out of the house.

I pushed at the front door; it seemed wrong, somehow, to knock at the door, as if Rocklands was some suburban bungalow. Besides, it was not as if Luc Tomlinson knocked at doors before entering. The house was quiet. I heard no sound of activity, and walked down the passage, glancing into Joyce's room. The portrait of Brick had disappeared, as had other signs of her habitation, but the painting was still on the wall.

The kitchen door was closed, which was odd: Luc was not a closer of doors. I hesitated, momentarily taken aback at my own temerity. I turned the knob, opened the door and went in. The kitchen seemed empty in the morning light; but as I ven-

385

tured into the room, a voice by my side said, 'Good morning, Nicholas.' It was Andrew Conroy.

I started. 'Andrew! How …?'

'How what?'

Not quite knowing what aspect of Andrew's presence most required explanation, I asked, absurdly, 'How did you get here? You car isn't outside.'

'By sea. From Kalk Bay.' He was wearing a dark-blue waterproof jacket and jeans; also thin leather gloves. His face was flushed with exercise and the open air, and in the dim light of the kitchen his eyes seemed shiny and black. 'You remember my little boat. It was such a splendid day, and I had no court session today, so I thought I would get a bit of exercise and come and visit my godson. I did not expect the pleasure of your company.'

'And where is …?'

'Luc? I have no idea. I've only just arrived; I suppose he's talking to his baboons.'

'Oh. I'm rather desperately trying to get hold of him. It's … it's not what you think.'

'How do you know what I think?' Andrew Conroy's dark eyes were mocking me.

I stood in confusion, quite unable to figure out what Andrew Conroy did or did not know. 'Oh, what a tangled web,' he said, smiling his ironical smile. 'Never mind what it is that I think; why is it that you're looking for him?'

I calculated the chances: Andrew was a friend of Brick Tomlinson's and yet it was inconceivable that he could be party to the man's insane plot to have his own son killed.

'I know it sounds crazy,' I said, 'but someone is planning to have Luc killed.'

'Who on earth would do that?' he asked in a tone of polite enquiry. I could see that he was incredulous.

'I don't know. A man called Pluto.'

'Pluto?'

'Yes – like Mickey Mouse's dog.'

'Or the god of the underworld.'

'I suppose so. Anyway, Pluto ordered a man called Boetie Bester to kill Luc, only now Boetie is also dead …'

'How do you know that?'

'I went to his flat on my way here, and he … he electrocuted himself by accident, but …'

'Boetie Bester has electrocuted himself?'

'Yes, in rather a … novel way. But he'd already decided not to kill Luc anyway, so now I'm here to warn Luc.'

'But if this man Boetie is dead, there is presumably no immediate danger – not unless Pluto knows that Boetie is dead.'

'Well, I gather that Boetie told Pluto that he was not going to kill Luc, so Pluto must already know that much at least, and may …' I petered out.

'And may?' Andrew Conroy asked, his dark eyes glowing with amusement.

'May already be on …'

'On …?'

Somewhere in another room, muffled by distance, *Nkosi Sikelel' iAfrika* started tinkling in the uninflected tones of a cell phone.

'On his way here,' I said.

'That is a possibility you surely thought of before you came here.'

'In the abstract, yes, but I was in such a hurry to warn Luc that I …' I shrugged, helplessly.

'That you didn't take precautions? That was unwise.'

The cell phone was still ringing. 'Excuse me,' I said, 'I must find that phone. Perhaps Luc is unconscious or something somewhere.'

'I wouldn't worry about that if I were you.'

'But why not?'

'There's nothing you can do for your friend.' Conroy's ironical tone had sharpened into something much less accommodating.

'Is he …?'

'Dead? No, if you must know. But he will be, fairly soon.'

'How …?'

'You are very inarticulate today, Nicholas. How what?'

'How do you know?'

'I know because, as seems to have been dawning on you in the last few minutes, I'm Pluto – after, I must insist, the god of

387

the underworld. But I suppose we live in a post-modern world where even the gods have become the dogs of mice.'

The phone stopped ringing. We were still standing in the kitchen. I looked around, more to cover my confusion than for information. On the table were what seemed to be the remains of Luc's breakfast things: a cereal bowl, two coffee cups. The rest of the room was, for Luc, relatively tidy.

'You'll oblige me by giving me your car keys,' Andrew Conroy said. 'Just to make sure you don't decide to make a run for it.'

'Would that not be unwise of me?' I asked, trying to borrow something of his almost bantering tone.

'Under the circumstances, no. Under the circumstances it would in fact be more unwise not to give me the keys.'

'The circumstances?'

'The circumstance, if you insist. This one.' He produced a gun from the pocket of his jacket, showed it to me, and then replaced it. 'Your keys, please.'

I gave him the keys; he took them with his left hand and put them in his jacket pocket.

'That gun …'

'You recognise it? Yes, I took it from Luc. I'd rather not use it, but if need be I will.' He looked around the kitchen. 'You must be thirsty after your exciting morning. Why don't you make us a cup of tea while we chat? I would do it myself, only I'm slightly – only slightly, mind – hampered by these gloves which I have no intention of taking off.'

I obeyed mechanically, wondering if I could throw a kettle at Conroy, find a knife in a drawer, in some way take command of the situation. 'I must warn you not to try any tricks. I've got the gun trained on you in my pocket.'

'But …?' I asked as I filled the kettle.

'But what, Nicholas?'

'But why? Why are you Pluto, why are you involved in this, why do you want to kill Luc? It just doesn't make sense.'

'It doesn't make sense to you because you see only a very small part of the pattern. But there is a pattern. Shall I explain it to you?' I hesitated. He smiled. 'Don't bother to reply; I'm not actually giving you the choice. I've been wanting to tell you my

388

story – I hoped at some stage as a willing confidant, but that was not to be.'

I switched on the kettle, and looked around for the teapot. He moved around with me, so that he was facing me all the time. 'And I've always appreciated an intelligent audience. One of the frustrations of being a judge is that one so often delivers judgement on people who are incapable of appreciating the elegance of the judgement.'

I opened a cupboard.

'The teapot is on that shelf over there, if that is what you are looking for.'

'Thank you.'

'The pattern, I'm afraid, derives its coherence entirely from its relevance to my personal history; only artists make patterns that transcend the personality of the subject. And yet I did try to achieve something of the impersonality of art.'

Andrew Conroy sat down at the kitchen table, his right hand still in his pocket. 'Like all personal histories, mine should probably begin with my childhood, but I'll spare you the David Copperfield bit, pausing only to note that my childhood was in fact nearly as destitute as that of David Copperfield, even to the detail of my stepfather, who was a man of quite Dickensian inhumanity. Fortunately I was clever, and found in books a refuge from a world obviously not arranged for my convenience. Accepting naively the dictum that knowledge is power, I indiscriminately collected knowledge, without this noticeably conferring power upon me. It did, however, enable me to win bursaries, which took me away from home and to university. I don't know if your intimacy with the Tomlinson family has put you in possession of the history of my relationship with that family …?'

'Joyce did tell me the essentials, I believe.'

'Good, then that saves me the recounting of a tedious tale. Did Joyce say I was still in love with her?'

'I do believe she implied something of the kind. It was in any case the impression I got.'

'You needn't equivocate. I know Joyce well enough to understand exactly how she would romanticise my history so as to cast a golden glow over her own. Besides, in a certain sense it is true that I have remained in love with her, but only in the sense that love is an obsession to have power over the loved object. In my case the obsession was probably intensified by the fact that she chose Brick Tomlinson over me – Tomlinson, who represented all the privileges I had never had, and all the unthinking arrogance and complacent ignorance of the very rich. Of course, one could say that she never chose Brick, in that she had to marry him ...'

'She *had* to marry him?'

'Yes, as it was quaintly put in those days. She didn't tell you that she fell pregnant in her last year at university?'

'No, she did not mention that.'

'Well, that's a woman's privilege of omission, and perhaps I should not have told you something that apparently she did not want you to know. But it matters very little now, and in any case, as I said, I am explicating the pattern as it falls into place from my perspective. From that perspective, Joyce's pregnancy was one of the epic desecrations, Leda and the swan, Europa and the bull ...' he paused, thinking, then corrected himself '... except, of course, that those were very precisely not desecrations but annunciations, visitations from the gods. And there was nothing godlike about Brick Tomlinson.'

'She may have thought there was.'

'I'm sure she did; and, Joyce being Joyce, she would have seen herself as the fount and foundress of a line of pagan demigods. She certainly worships Luc as if he was one.' He paused as I passed him a cup of tea. He took it with his left hand, keeping his right hand in his jacket pocket. 'Thank you. Sit down at the other end of the table and keep your hands on the table.' He took a sip of tea and continued. 'And you, I suppose, share her perspective – *mutatis mutandis*, of course.'

'Her perspective on ...?'

'Her infatuated regard for that inarticulate young animal. No, wait,' he said, as I tried to protest against this characterisation of my assessment of Luc, 'I know that you have had carnal relations with the man. He boasted to me about it.'

'What ...?'

'Not to worry about that now. We may get to it. I was telling you about Luc's origins, in which I am more interested than in his present conduct. You see, he was in a sense the cause of my loss of Joyce.'

'It was hardly his fault, surely.'

'Not by the bland dicta of the law which hold that intention is decisive in determining culpability. But I adhere to the more ancient view whereby we are responsible for the events caused by our actions or even just by our existence, whatever our intentions or motives or even ignorance. There is such a thing as an abomination to the gods. Luc, in coming into the world, frustrated my romantic idealism and destroyed it; but of course Brick was the cause of Luc's coming into the world. And Joyce was not the progenitrix of a line of gods; she was a talented, graceful creature taken captive by the Philistines to preside over their sacrifices to Mammon.'

'But weren't you at Oxford by the time Luc ... arrived?'

He smiled. 'Yes, fortunately my absence coincided with the first few years of what the world politely regards as married bliss. At that distance, it was easy to consent to being Luc's godfather, and to the gesture of appeasement it was intended to be; and by the time I came home, I could pretend to be what Joyce wanted me for, a trusted and loyal friend of the family, and somebody for Joyce to talk to when ... well, when she needed somebody to talk to. It was generally assumed that I'd got over my disappointment at Oxford, but I had in fact just got better at living with it and converting it into energy to drive my revenge. I suppose all that places like Oxford can really do, for all the importance that is attached to them, is to activate some potential you have already acquired from deeper, darker, earlier sources. What Oxford activated in me, apart from a determination to succeed that I had in common with most people there, was a pronounced cultural conservatism; I felt nothing but impatience with the privileged young Oxford students in their scraggly beards earnestly protesting against their own privileges – this was in 1973, remember, with the events of 1968 filtering through their influence from France, as usual five years late. My sympathies, or antipathies, allied me with some people whom I would not necessarily now countenance as friends – political conservatives make such awful dinner guests – but who have since been very useful.'

'What surprises me,' I said, 'was that in this country you were known as a liberal, even quite a radical lawyer and judge.'

'That's partly perspective – to be liberal in South Africa at the time was not in fact incompatible with being a conservative in England – and partly my opportunism. I came back from Oxford to a teaching post at the University of Cape Town, an institution where anything other than a liberal opinion was most illiberally discriminated against. And then, as you know, the National Party regime was such as only a fool or a knave could support. Not, as you also know, that I am a democrat. My resistance to the Nationalist regime was as much aesthetic as it was moral: I was appalled by their blunt heavy-handedness, their lack of style, their paunches, their wives' hats, their bestial stupidity, their pig-eyed venality. But it was contempt I felt, rather than disapproval. So it was not difficult to deliver pronouncements heavily critical of the regime. At the same time, though, through my contact with Brick Tomlinson, I was meeting some of the more powerful members of the government socially.'

'I should imagine that was quite embarrassing – I mean, meeting people about whom you were so outspokenly critical.'

'No, not at all. It so obviously meant nothing to them. The Nationalists were strong because they did not mind being disliked. So these pocket potentates, heavily genial behind their brandies and their red wine, shrewdly tolerant of what they patronised as liberal pretence, some of them intoxicated with the conceit of being more sophisticated than their benighted colleagues, tolerated me partly through vanity, partly through political instinct. They knew that an enemy who can't be eliminated must be cultivated.'

'But why did you consent to being cultivated?'

Conroy sighed, shrugging ironically. '*Que voulez vous*? On the one hand I was ambitious, and was cynical enough to know that for the time being the Nationalist controlled the passages to power; on the other I believed that a democratic government would mean an end in this country to that Western civilisation which I am still convinced is the highest expression thus far of the human spirit – at least the highest expression that is intelligible to me.'

'But what ambitions did you have that weren't satisfied by your being a successful and respected academic?'

He smiled. 'My dear Nicholas, that is your most naive question yet. Academics in this country – in most countries probably – have no power, very little standing, and almost no influence. This is because they have no money. So, to answer your question, what ambitions did I have that were not satisfied by my being a successful academic? *Limitless!* I wanted power, and in order to have power I wanted money; above all, I wanted to wipe out the insult of having to concede to Brick Tomlinson dominion over Joyce and all she represented, and the ignominy of having to endure his condescending hospitality.'

He got up from the table, still facing me, not forgetting, as I had hoped he might, that I was being held by his coercion rather than by his narrative. 'So,' he continued, 'I left the university, started practising as an advocate, took some controversial cases, and even won some – partly, no doubt, because here and there a judge resisted his brief, which was to apply the apartheid laws as they stood. When I was made a judge, it was hailed as a victory for the independence of the judiciary in a country where, more and more, independence of any kind was oppressed viciously. In fact the Nationalists, blunt as they were in many relations, were subtle enough to realise that a known liberal in a prominent position could be more useful to them than yet another Broederbond appointment churning out time-serving judgements.'

'You mean they were actually responsible for your appointment?'

'Let's say they turned a blind eye to it; and once I was on the bench, they approached me from time to time with propositions of various kinds.'

'What kind of proposition?'

'Usually an arrangement, shall we say, that certain of my dissident judgements would be tolerated in order to give me credibility as an independent legal mind. Then it came home to me that I was in fact being *encouraged* to release some of these accused, I assumed at first because it suited their purposes to maintain the illusion of an independent judiciary; but of course in the long run that is a dangerous kind of illusion for

393

a totalitarian regime to cultivate. And it soon became clear to me that my judgements were serving the purposes of the regime in other ways – that I was being fed selected political accused who were in fact police informers and needed the credibility of being charged in open court, and who were then released as heroes, their usefulness much enhanced by their trial. And of course I became, as you know, something of a hero of the liberal press – and of the forces of liberation that I was starting to realise would soon be in control.'

'So you were preparing for the transition to the new by collaborating with the old.'

'Yes, it was an arrangement that suited all parties at the time – of course, I didn't tell my employers that I was preparing for their downfall, but I suspect they realised that; many of them were doing the same thing in their own way. At the same time my special relationship was becoming extremely lucrative for me and useful to them, in that I was in a position to broker certain deals with some of my erstwhile Oxford acquaintances and their network. Conservative people are useful in that they are so predictably selfish; they're much easier to manipulate than people who are more indifferent to their own wealth and welfare. So they were only too ready for the various propositions that I was now in a position to put to them.'

'Trade agreements?'

'Yes, generally speaking. More specifically, arms trading.'

'What happens to your ideals of Western civilisation when they have to depend on arms trading?'

'They always have, in one form or another. Western civilisation has had to defend itself by force, which means by force of arms, often enough. Oh, and medical research, for which purpose I participated, I'm afraid, in the large-scale export of baboons to that centre of Western civilisation, greenest Cambridgeshire. Ever heard of the Huntingdon Life Sciences laboratory?'

'No – should I have?'

'Not really – very few people have. The Brits don't advertise its existence. Suffice it to say that it radically redefines the concept of Western civilisation. I had some qualms, I suppose, but it's easy enough to adopt a view of civilisation as larger than individual taste or morality. If culture is a trophy that the victor presents to himself, a monument built by power to itself, then the man of culture will see to it that he is on the side of power. Power is to be used.'

'But surely power was using you?'

'Yes, it was, but I believed that I was cleverer than the people using me.' He smiled wryly. 'I'm not so sure now; most of them seem to have survived the transition at least as successfully as I. One thing I did discover was that the price of power is eternal vigilance. To have a secret is to become its slave, and potentially the slave of anybody who finds it out; and of course, here and there were informers who knew of my part in their release; and who, as is the nature of informers, threatened to sell their knowledge to the highest bidder. I mentioned this problem to one of my powerful friends, who gave me a phone number and a name, and told me that the person behind the name would have instructions to execute my instructions as to the removal from society of anybody whom I felt to represent a threat to my security or my usefulness to the state.'

'And that name was Boetie Bester?'

'Yes, although he insisted on being called Breker Bester. It was a small concession to make to the vanity of a stupid but useful man.'

I thought of the muscular bulk of Boetie Bester, the hulkish, brutal protector of this elegant and sophisticated man. 'You didn't feel ... compromised by having to use the services of such a man?'

'No, why should I? People have dogs to protect them; I had a human being.'

'People have relationships with their dogs; the dogs are motivated by loyalty, not money.'

'Sentimental anti-anthropomorphism. Dogs are motivated by whatever it is that dogs feel for the person who feeds them; so was Boetie Bester, until he inconveniently met your charming friend Leonora.'

I started. 'How do you know?'

He sat back and laughed, the first quite uninhibited expression of amusement I had witnessed from him. 'My dear Nicholas, you and your friends have provided me with more

395

entertainment than I thought I was capable of in my fallen state. I have mentioned that one of the advantages of the otherwise quite intolerable social occasions *chez* Tomlinson was the useful people whom one met. Amongst them was Johanna van der Merwe, who took an unaccountable liking to me. She seemed to feel that I embodied a certain sensitivity that in the nature of her job she often had to forego in her colleagues. Be that as it may, we have become quite – shall I say *confidential* with each other, and on this occasion, not for the first time, we found our information to complement each other's usefully. I suspect she would have seen through your absurd little scheme on her own, in any case – Johanna may be mad, but she's not stupid – but in fact you yourself were responsible for the discovery. You remember the day we had lunch together, you and I in the Gardens?'

'Yes, of course.'

'Yes, of course. And you had a stamp on your wrist, a night club's admission ticket, a pair of handcuffs?'

'Yes, I remember.'

'Recognising the stamp from having seen it on the wrist of my friend Johanna, aware of the nature of the club, and conscious of the fact that you are not the kind of person who frequents clubs of that kind, I simply asked her whether she'd met a young man called Nicholas Morris on one of her outings. Your *nom de guerre* was hardly such as to conceal your identity, and your friend Gerhard was all too recognisable from her description of him. Apart from that, I knew, of course, of your acting for Luc Tomlinson, and that Brick Tomlinson had used Johanna to abduct the baboons. It did not take a genius to figure out what you were after.'

'And Johanna knew?'

'Of course Johanna knew. You don't think you would otherwise have had the run of a top-secret laboratory and more or less been invited to remove the baboons?'

'I did in fact think that it was too easy to be true. But there seemed to be no reason why Johanna should make it easy for us. What was in it for her?'

'Gerhard. Johanna is a woman of strong appetites, and her crusade to, shall we say, *recycle* homosexuals is, as far as it goes, sincere, however dubious scientifically. So it was not particularly important to her what Gerhard's motives were; what she wanted was Gerhard in her chair, and that was what she got. Indeed, your friend performed so impressively that I must admit I wondered whether Johanna's therapy wasn't more effective than I had given her credit for.'

'Did she tell you this?'

'She did express her satisfaction, yes, but in fact it was quite obvious to me that he was, shall I say, participating quite vigorously.' Conroy paused in his pacing, then sat down at the table. 'I was, in case you were wondering, watching from behind a one-way mirror – the partner to the one from which I watched your valiant effort in Johanna's office.'

'But this is ... despicable.'

He held up one finger, and for the first time seemed to lose his ironic control. 'Do you dare despise me? You who entered into the silliest of schemes in order to please a worthless young man for whom you had conceived an irrational passion ...'

'I had not conceived a passion for him; he was my client.'

'And for how many of your clients would you spend a Saturday rounding up baboons? How many of your clients do you spend the night with? For how many of your clients would you miss an appointment with me?'

'That was ... oh, I can't explain how it happened, and I don't suppose it matters.'

He visibly made an effort to regain his composure. 'You're right, it doesn't matter, not any more.'

I thought it safer to get the conversation back to the details of my own humiliation. 'But what about the baboons? Did Johanna not mind the loss of the baboons?'

'There are plenty of baboons to be had. These particular baboons she took as a favour to Brick Tomlinson, but she did not feel obliged to sacrifice her own pleasure and her own pursuit of scientific data to Brick's continued satisfaction.' He had regained his air of superior detachment from the farce he had witnessed. 'I must admit there was something satisfying, something almost tragic, with the humour of great tragedy, in the spectacle of your illusion of independent action.'

'It must have been like playing God,' I said bitterly. The

thought of Andrew Conroy witnessing my pathetic performance in front of Johanna van der Merwe was profoundly
humiliating.

'The situation had satisfying elements of omniscience to it.
But I'll be honest with you. Even I miscalculated. I mention
tragedy, but in fact there is something almost comic in the ruth-
lessness with which fate interposed passion and sentiment of
the most vulgar kind between my design and its execution: on
the one hand your coupling with that young animal; on the
other hand Boetie conceiving an adolescent infatuation with
your friend Leonora– he told me he could not execute my commission because he had *seen the light*! And all this made possible by Johanna's lusting after your friend Gerhard. Truly, your
baboons are a model of rationality compared with their human
masters. And to crown it all, by coming to the laboratory, I
enabled Boetie Bester to recognise me. He had seen me at a distance, but on this occasion he was close enough to me to recognise my voice as that of Pluto.'

'So that it is in fact very convenient for you that Boetie electrocuted himself.'

He laughed as heartily as his civilised, restrained manner
permitted him. 'Boetie did not electrocute himself.'

'You electrocuted him?'

'No. Reconsider your assumptions. Why do you take for
granted that Boetie was electrocuted?'

'Well, he was ... plugged in when I found him.'

'And no sign of any other possible cause of death?'

'You mean the tablet of Ecstasy was poisoned?'

'No, the Ecstasy was Boetie's own addition to my plan.
Think again.'

'He was naked. There was nothing else around except a
photograph of Major van der Merwe ...'

'Ah yes, poor Boetie's father fixation. Harmful but not lethal.
And nothing else?'

'No, just a jar of Vaseline.'

He smiled. 'I'll stop playing games with you. You were right
up to a point in assuming that Boetie killed himself. In a world
of specialists, the judge judges, the lawyer makes law, and the
murderer murders. Appropriately, the murderer gets to

murder himself. You see, it was clear to me from my vantage point that Boetie, for all his moral disapproval, indeed perhaps *because* of his moral disapproval, was, to say the least, impressed with the effect of Johanna's stimulator on your friend Gerhard. I judged that if he were to be given one of these as a present he would be curious enough to try one; it is a cherished piece of received wisdom amongst farmers that a baboon will play with any object you present it with, a triumph of curiosity over experience that has cost many a baboon its life. So I suggested to Johanna that she might present Boetie with one; whereas he would of course profess horror, he would probably take it home with him. I included in the gift pack a bottle of Silvermine Vaseline – an unfortunate concoction of Johanna's, which she developed in her ever-zealous search for new ways of disposing of enemies of the state. The main ingredient is an organophosphate – something called paraoxon – that is soluble in petroleum jelly, only, of course to be released virulently upon contact with the skin. It was tested with some success on animals and activists in the eighties, but was never developed in commercial quantities, owing to the misgivings of the legal department about possible lawsuits from the makers of Vaseline. So there are several thousand jars of lethal Vaseline stockpiled at Silvermine. One of Johanna's less elegant experiments, I thought. Still, Boetie took the hint and covered the electrode probe with Vaseline before inserting it – a kind of toxic suppository administered by himself. There is, you'll agree, a certain poetic justice to it. I am grateful to you, incidentally, for informing me of the success of my plan, and thus saving me a visit to Boetie's residence.'

'Poor Boetie.'

'Alas, poor Boetie. Console yourself that if I had told him a week ago to eliminate you, he would have done so without demurral or compunction.' He shook his head, an ironical half-smile on his mobile face. 'Boetie and his henchmen – the clowns of death – cabinet ministers, state presidents with their little hats and their big stomachs – the clowns and dupes of death, thinking themselves powerful, not knowing which master they serve until he comes to call. It's like a morality play. But Boetie was a minor player in it, achieving such prominence as he had in the pattern only through his unexpected and inconvenient refusal to remove Luc Tomlinson.'

'But I still don't understand why you should want to remove somebody by and large as harmless as Luc Tomlinson.'

'I have already told you that he has always been an abomination to me, that graceless young animal – no, why should I pretend to you? – that extremely graceful young animal. Indeed, if any aspect of him infuriated me more than any other, it was his reminding me so much of his mother at his age – combined with his indifference, nay, antipathy to me. I've never had what used to be known as a crush on the young man – I'm just not that way inclined, and even if I had been, I would have been bored with the type, I think – but I have wanted some recognition from him of my superiority. But he seems just bored with me and with what I represent, and would rather sit and jabber to that brainless flower child. But what made him finally intolerable was his seduction of you – a pointless, heartless exercise in power, defiling what he was too self-centred and limited to appreciate in any other way.'

'How do you know that?'

'I'm sorry if I am destroying any illusions you may have about my godson's interest in you; I have known him for long enough to have taken the measure of his involvements. Insofar as they are not purely carnal indulgences of the most superficial sort, they are manipulations, a child's delight in its own power to get other people to do its bidding.'

'You resented the fact that you had no power over him.'

'That, too; but his fatal error was in exercising his power over you, whom I had marked as my own. Having once had to yield a prized possession to Brick Tomlinson, I was not prepared to give you up to Brick's son.'

'And what did you do with Luc?'

'Ah, not so fast. I'll tell you that only when I'm convinced that there is no possibility of your interfering with my plans. No possibility whatsoever.'

'And that will be …?'

'Not so fast. You seem to have lost interest in my narrative.'

'Not at all. It's just that I thought we had now reached – you know, the present.'

'You don't have a literary imagination, otherwise you would have sensed a digression from – call it the narrative principle, that without which there would be no narrative, the reason for it all, the golden thread of my design, the reason for your being here today.'

'You mean your revenge on Brick Tomlinson?'

'Yes, to put it somewhat bluntly. I would describe it rather as my rectification of the scheme of things that gave me so much and yet deprived me of Joyce Tomlinson. Which is not to say that I was trying to regain Joyce Tomlinson. What I resolved to do was to achieve mastery over myself and others, partly through self-control, partly through control of them. And whereas control of the self is a matter of discipline, control of others is a matter of money. Of this, as I have remarked, I soon had large sums, thanks to my contacts in countries officially hostile to South Africa. I allowed Brick Tomlinson to have just enough of an inkling of this to temper his contempt with the respect that the Philistine will always have for money, however obtained. This respect was intensified, in due course, by Brick's need of the financial assistance I could give him in the tight spots in which, as an impulsive entrepreneur, he was prone to find himself. Being myself somewhat more prudent in my dealings, I made sure that this assistance was in the form of well-documented and well-secured loans, or otherwise joint ventures in which my contribution was secured by watertight guarantees. It used to be true that whom the gods wished to destroy they first made ridiculous. In a commercial world, they first make him financially dependent.

'With the advent of a new dispensation in 1990, a bit earlier than generally anticipated, Brick's stake in the so-called independent homelands, dependent as those were entirely on the central government, came under pressure; the building contracts for lavish government offices and grandiose casinos in puppet states dried up, the influential dinner guest suddenly seemed less secure, more likely to call in old debts than to provide new ones. Brick badly needed money; I, on the other hand, was better placed than ever before. As a well-known dissident judge, I had credibility with the new government, and my old allies were only too willing to use me as a go-between.

So I was in a position to render assistance to my old partner in business, and even to advise him; to encourage, for instance, the bold idea of developing his family property at Rocklands, preferably while there were still enough of the old guard in place to smooth the passage of the project. In addition, I had the loyal support of the ministers of Defence and Nature Conservation and Development, secured, apart from anything else, through my possession of some photographs I had had the foresight to take of some of the more uninhibited festivities at Rocklands in the good old days before Luc took occupation.'

'You took those photographs?'

'Yes, I'm afraid to say. Appalling excesses on the part on the guardians of our country's well-being.'

'And you gave them to Joyce Tomlinson?'

'Yes, with the specific request that she should pass them on to you.'

'But ...'

He held up his left hand. 'Patience, dear Nicholas, all shall become clear. I must tell my tale as it unwinds, otherwise we shall lose hold of the golden thread. In addition, then, to facilitating the process through my special relationship with certain role-players, I encouraged Brick Tomlinson in the most tangible way possible, by making large loans available on easy but always well-secured terms. I also encouraged him to commit himself and his firm to an entirely ruthless American firm of developers, providing huge guarantees to secure their interest and cooperation. On the home front, I helped him to buy the planning permission he needed – for instance, through bribing that discredited stooge Visser. All this you know as much about as I, through your skilful exposure of poor Visser in open court.'

'But ... you said, that day in the Gardens, that you suggested me to Joyce Tomlinson.'

'True. All unbeknownst to himself and of course to you, Luc Tomlinson walked into your office as my emissary.'

'You mean,' I asked, and I could feel myself reddening with embarrassment and anger, 'that you selected me because you were counting on me to lose the case?'

He shook his head. 'No, my dear Nicholas, nothing as

insulting as that. Admittedly, had you lost the case, I would have had my compensation in the form of a major share in a lucrative development – one for which, incidentally, I had already arranged the exclusive casino rights at a considerable price. But I was not interested in more money; what I wanted was for Brick Tomlinson to lose every penny he had, every stick and stone, and as a consequence, Joyce Tomlinson. In short, I wanted to ruin him, as they used to say. And for this I needed your help. Luc Tomlinson was a most convenient agent of his father's ruin, but if he hadn't been there, I could quite easily have arranged it in some other way.'

'So even in the capacity of puppet I was not indispensable?'

'Don't be bitter, Nicholas. We are none of us indispensable; we may be useful in the designs of others, but the design, if it has any aesthetic merit, is always larger than the detail.'

'What I don't understand is why, if you wanted Brick Tomlinson to lose the case, you had Sam Stanford assassinated for testifying, in effect, against him – unless I'm wrong, of course, and it wasn't your doing.'

'You're right as far as it goes – Boetie killed Sam Stanford – little knowing that it was to be his last job for me. But your mistake is in interpreting every detail of the design in the light of your place in it. I did not have Sam killed because he testified in the Rocklands case – as you suggest, that was in fact most useful for me. But you see, it seems the bright young man you briefed in the case ...'

'John Scheepers.'

'... yes, John Scheepers, revealed to Sam the public circulation of certain photographs I had taken. Incensed at what he regarded as my betrayal, he was threatening to expose me, denounce me – a threat that I had to take seriously, now that he had so little to lose by such an exposure. So his death had very little to do with what he said in court, and everything with what John Scheepers said to him before the court case.'

'And as far as it went, you were successful in your design. Brick Tomlinson is ruined.'

'Yes, as far as it went. But again I failed to take into account the inconsistency of human beings. Joyce Tomlinson, having for years found it quite compatible with her love of her husband to scheme against him, was moved by his destitution to side with him against all outsiders, including myself.'

'And including her son.'

'Yes, so that Luc and I ironically end up together in the outer darkness.'

I felt that my life quite literally depended on my keeping the narrative going, a role-reversed Scheherazade: while Andrew Conroy kept talking, something could happen, somebody might turn up. 'And my contribution to this large design was to help to drive Brick Tomlinson to bankruptcy and despair,' I said, hoping to engage him in the topic that seemed most to obsess him.

'Yes. At least, that was the original intention. But then, after our first meeting, I amended the design in order to accommodate you as a more central strand. As you know, I had been taken with your dissertation some years ago; I had retained an interest in you and your career; and now, I thought, with the proper encouragement and training, you could take the place of the son I never had. You could be a disciple, a follower, an equal, a companion, an heir. You reminded me of myself at your age: ascetic, high-principled, civilised, and without the weakness of my poverty and hunger. At last, I thought, a young man in whom passion and restraint are gracefully balanced. For the first time my sterile obsession with avenging myself on the world for what I had missed yielded to a vision of what I might yet have.' He sighed. 'All that you destroyed on Saturday night.'

'I really don't know what to say. I am sorry, of course, that I let you down by not keeping our appointment. But insofar as your disappointment presupposes my participation in what you call your grand design, you would have been disappointed sooner or later in any case.'

'You no doubt imagine yourself too morally fastidious to benefit by money derived from an evil regime. I need hardly point out that for decades every white South African to a greater or lesser degree benefited by the policies and practices of that regime. But more to the point, like many a founder of a benevolent dynasty before me – consider, for instance, the philanthropy of the American robber barons – I would have passed on to the second generation nothing of the taint attached to the money, only the power to do good. You would not have *participated*, as you so delicately put it, in my nefarious dealings with the now defunct regime; you would have been my helper in working towards a new society built on reason and judgement and reflection, relationships built on trust and restraint, authority based on wisdom.'

'Reason, trust, wisdom – out of the death squads?'

'Yes, if need be, out of the death squads. Reason, trust and wisdom have come forth from worse atrocities in the past. But all this is so much hypothesis; we are left with the question of where to go from here. I shall not hide from you the fact that after Saturday I had decided not to see you again, or that if I ever did see you again, only with the purpose to terminate our relationship, such as it has been. You have complicated matters by turning up here and obliging me to share with you knowledge so very dangerous to its possessor, as Boetie Bester and your friend Luc have discovered.'

'What have you done with Luc?'

'You must really not try my patience by harping on the subject of Luc Tomlinson. I am about to put a proposition to you which would be jeopardised by your showing or feeling any concern for his fate.' Conroy got up from his chair, and moved around the table till he was facing me. 'It is this: I am prepared to continue my patronage and support of you in return for your undertaking to honour my principles and practices. I shall not involve you again in any illegal action, but in order to secure your loyalty in future, I shall share with you, and more to the point you will share with me, full knowledge of and consent to my godson's death. In short you will be a party to his death.'

'You mean I will be expected to kill Luc?'

'Nothing as crude as that. But by knowing about it and condoning it, you will become an accomplice.'

'And if I don't consent to this proposal?'

'Then of course I shall have to kill you. It is not something I willingly do, but it is not something I shall shrink from.'

I hesitated. It seemed unthinkable that I could consent to Luc's death in order to save my life; and yet by consenting to my own death I would not be saving his life. I am not, as my father pointed out so long ago, of heroic mould; self-sacrifice has always seemed to me a misguided sort of virtue. And certainly dying for a cause or a person has always struck me as a singularly pointless thing to do. Though Andrew Conroy was a deeply duplicitous person, he was in a position to do good to more people than he had ever harmed by his actions; and he was a considerably more interesting person than most of the law-abiding people I knew. Besides which, I did not want to die, I did not want to witness the process of my own violent extinction, to look into the barrel of the gun that is about to discharge a bullet into my flesh and tissues and organs, to feel, perhaps, the pain of existence being abruptly terminated. It was my life and it was the only one I had.

'What do you say, Nicholas?' Conroy asked, taking the gun out of his pocket almost absent-mindedly. He was still wearing gloves. I took a deep breath, as a way of not saying anything just yet, and while I was exhaling, the cell phone somewhere recommended its absurdly jaunty tune. Leonora was, true to my instruction, still trying to reach Luc; Luc may well be hearing the telephone, may even think that it was me trying to get in touch with him; and I was considering severing my connection with what that telephone represented, the fragile effort to reach out and help someone in distress.

'No,' I said. 'I can't do it. I can't be part of your murder of Luc Tomlinson.'

He flexed his right wrist. 'You realise in that case you will have a somewhat unenviable part in your own murder? The starring role, as it were?'

His facetiousness helped me, in forcing me into a correspondingly flippant mode. 'Oh, you will have that. You are dressed for the part.'

'Let's not bandy words.' I thought he was going to shoot me point blank. But he threw my car keys on the table in front of me and said, 'There. We're going for a scenic drive.'

CHAPTER EIGHTEEN

Andrew Conroy, being a man who savoured a certain appropriateness in things, would have been pleased to learn, had I told him, how fitting it was that I should be invited to drive to my own death. Driving was the one activity above all that I had most resented in my life, the most abject subordination of natural rhythms to mechanical principles, the most foolish sacrifice of the end to the means yet devised by technology. Of course, if there is one thing worse than driving, it is being driven: at least having a steering wheel to hold on to gives you an illusion of choice, however much you are constrained by roads and human expectation from exercising that freedom. As passenger you are at the mercy of the death wish of the driver, or at best the victim of his incompetence. So driving with a pistol held, almost literally, to one's head, was to combine the strain of being a driver with the helplessness of being a passenger. I had, for one, no idea of our destination.

'Where am I driving to?' I asked Andrew Conroy, as we got into my car.

'Not to worry about that. I'll direct you.'

I reached to fasten my seat belt, then reconsidered. There seemed little point in safeguarding myself against injuries in order to keep myself intact to be shot. If I had to die, I would die liberated from the anxious restraint of the seat belt. I resolved also to disobey as many traffic rules as I could; it was unlikely, given the present state of law enforcement, that we would be stopped by a traffic policeman, but at least I would savour for once the licentious pleasures of the scoff-law.

As we drove away from Rocklands, Andrew Conroy said, as pleasantly as if we were discussing a fishing trip, 'Incidentally, I did once before make an attempt on my godson's life, an attempt that I believe you were witness to, indeed I must assume almost a victim of. I was not to know that Luc would have guests to breakfast.'

'The avocado?'

'The avocado. You may recall that Joyce left behind a gathering of her husband's business associates, people her scorn for whom she made no effort to hide – to go and visit her son at Rocklands. I was one of these associates, as was, as it happens, your friend Johanna van der Merwe, who used the opportunity to pass on to me a sample of a new poison formulated by her laboratory. The idea was that I should, in my turn, pass this on to an interested foreign buyer. I pleaded abjectly with Joyce to stay, for my sake if not for that of the rest of the company, which was abysmal enough in all conscience. But she refused, thereby making it clear that she valued her son's taciturn ill manners more highly than my company – a display of bad taste which you are not in a position to deplore as you should.' He paused for only long enough to let this reproach settle and bite, then carried on: 'As you will have discovered today, the one thing that infuriates me, literally to the point of murder, is being undervalued. One can, of course, make allowances for the feelings of a mother, but I was not inclined to make any allowances whatsoever for the young Luc, who took her preference for granted as if it was his by right. I was talking to Joyce in the kitchen, where she was assembling provisions for her spoilt son's breakfast. I knew that she herself did not eat avocados, so on the spur of the moment, indeed I'm afraid rather impulsively, I injected the avocado with the poison. In the event, all it did was kill a baboon. Ironically, the baboon ended up in Johanna's laboratory for an autopsy, and, even more ironically, they could not identify their own poison.' He laughed, genuinely diverted by this absurdity.

'How amusing,' I said. I wondered whether I was also going to be poisoned, that apparently being Conroy's preferred method of disposal; and if so, whether I would end up on Johanna's slab for my autopsy, a further twist of irony which no doubt Conroy would relish. We were waved through the exit gate at Cape Point without as much as a token peek or prod; I reflected bitterly that for all the control actually exercised by the boom, they might as well just leave it up permanently.

Outside the gate of Cape Point, the road joins the circular route that runs along the perimeter of the southern peninsula; thus, coming from Cape Point, one either turns right to Kalk Bay and Muizenberg, or left to Hout Bay. I paused at the junction. 'Right or left?' I asked.

'Ah, by rights I should give you the choice. But let's go left, it's so much prettier.'

'And you're still not going to tell me where you're taking me?'

'No. Relax and enjoy the scenery.'

This was a tall order, even given my by now extensive experience of driving around Cape Town with a gun pointed at me. But the scenery was undeniably if not all-engrossingly beautiful. The road from Cape Point to Hout Bay is a much-photographed scenic drive, comprising as it does the Big Three of Mountain, Sea and Sheer Drops. The first stretch is a relatively mild run along the beaches of Scarborough and Kommetjie, attractive but not breathtaking. In the winter sun on the water, some surfers, black specks in their wet suits, were waiting for a wave; a pair of baboons appeared next to the road; a roadside stall was selling African curios of dubious origins; a girl on a horse was galloping along the beach. Normality had never seemed so normal and yet so extraordinary, so vivid with light and life. I took my sunglasses from the dashboard and put them on.

'Those baboons,' Conroy said. 'Isn't it amazing that after all they have suffered at the hands of humans, they still saunter out and stare at us as if we were so many animated teddy bears?'

'I suppose that statistically very few human beings will harm a baboon.'

'Yes, but do the baboons know the statistics? Besides, statistically very few people get mugged or raped or murdered, and yet we are always aware of the danger. Nor can we say that baboons are trusting animals, as dogs are. They clearly take a dim view of human beings; it's just that they've decided not to live in fear. That I find quite admirable, unattractive as baboons are in almost all other respects. They are human in all the worst ways.'

'Did it not perturb you, as a civilised person, that you were involved with a system that was deliberately inflicting the most appalling suffering on baboons and countless other animals?'

'No, it did not. As a civilised person I value life forms that are capable of improving themselves through creative self-expression. No baboon has ever written a sonata or a novel or painted a picture or devised a mathematical formula. The most meaningful thing they can do is to die in a laboratory, under controlled conditions for a well-defined reason.'

'Like testing poison to kill human beings?'

'Yes, for instance. Whether one agrees with the aim of the experiment or not, the death is still in the pursuit of some clearly-defined aim, which is more than can be said for most human beings. A human being dying of cancer or in an earthquake or in a car accident dies meaninglessly, which is why humans have had to invent a vindictive God who *wants* them to die.'

We drove in silence for a while. Conroy seemed to be thinking; I dared to hope that he was reconsidering his intentions in the light of my valiant refusal to live in fear. But he said, 'That is the favour I'm doing you, Nicholas; I want you to die, and in executing my purpose I give meaning to your death.'

If this had been a good time to be sarcastic, I could have produced any number of trenchant retorts. As it was, I said, 'Then any murder is meaningful, because the murderer wants the other person to die.'

'The murder is at any rate not accidental or arbitrary. But most murderers are thugs, whose reasons do not confer dignity upon their victims.'

'And you ...?'

'I am most certainly not a thug.'

'I will be every bit as dead as if I had been killed by a thug, by ... by a hijacker, for instance.'

'All deaths are equal, biologically speaking. The difference is a matter of aetiology. But thank you, you have given me a brilliant idea. I will make your death seem like a hijacking. That will account for both the body and the motive very convincingly.'

410

'I'm surprised and a bit disappointed that my death should be such a spur of the moment matter.'

'Oh, I had some alternatives in mind, but none perhaps as elegant as this.'

'As a matter of interest, what will you do with my motor-car?'

'I shall abandon it in some back street and make my own way home.'

We were beginning the winding ascent to Chapman's Peak, the most spectacular part of the route. If one were to nominate a route by which to reach the Final Destination, one could hardly do better than this for sheer effect. If one preferred not to be reminded of what one would be missing once there, one could hardly do worse.

'What music are you listening to nowadays?' Conroy asked, pushing in the cassette protruding from the tape deck. Abruptly, like a scream in a supermarket, the Maiden's indignant protestations cut across the engine noise:

Vorüber! ach, Vorüber
Geh, wilder Knochenmann!
Ich bin noch jung, geh Lieber!
Und rühre mich nicht an …

'How appropriate,' Conroy smiled, 'and how pleasing that you followed up our discussion.'

'Yes, Leonora made me a recording of some of those songs. What is a Knochenmann?'

'A skeleton – that, I hope, is not appropriate. *Und rühre mich nicht an* … how universal, the plea for immunity – *noli me tangere*, pass me by – *Ich bin noch jung*, as if youth is a safeguard,' Conroy mused; he seemed quite moved by the pathos of this. The song resolved itself into the enthralling blandishments of Death – '*Sollst sanft in meinem Armen schlafe*' – and for a moment there was only the soft hissing of the tape, longer than normal. I thought of Leonora considerately leaving a pause between songs so that I should not be rushed headlong into the next, and felt a tenderness for her I had not felt before.

We had rounded the highest point of the Chapman's Peak

pass, and were now winding down the narrow road gouged out of the mountainside high above the blue water of Hout Bay. It was a view both serene and disquieting: the quiet water, the placid reflection of the Sentinel across the bay, and yet the dizzying height between the road and the sea, the terrible depth of the sea soughing at the rocks far below. Leonora's pause was broken by the drumming rhythm, the opening of *Erlkönig*, with its anxious questioning: '*Wer reitet so spät durch Nacht und Wind?*'

'Hardly night and wind for us,' said Conroy, 'but the rest will do.'

'*Mein Sohn, was birgst du so bang dein gesicht?*'

'I'm not aware of hiding my face in fear,' I said.

'Very good,' he said, 'you've learnt the words.'

'I listened to them with translations.'

'You know, it really is a pity that you're being so obstinate. I could have taught you so much, you could have given me so much pleasure.'

'*Du liebes kind, komm, geh mit mir!*'

'What have you done with Luc?'

He laughed. 'He will die as he lived, a slave to his passions.'

He will die ... so Luc was not dead yet.

'It's not too late for you to change your mind, you know.'

'*Mein Vater, mein Vater, und hörest du nicht,*
Was Erlkönig mir leise verspricht?'

'Don't tempt me. I'm not a hero.'

'Well, then, be tempted.'

'*Willst, feiner Knabe, du mit mir gehn?*'

I shook my head. 'It's absurd, but of all the pious claptrap I was brought up with, what has remained is a ... suspicion that we can't live at the cost of somebody else's death.'

'Pious claptrap indeed. All life is posited upon the death of others. Every breath you draw is paid for somewhere by somebody else's suffering.'

'Perhaps. But you're asking me to say yes to the death of somebody I know. And I can't.'

'If that's your final answer,' he shrugged, 'you leave me no choice.'

'*Ich liebe dich, mich reizt deine schöne Gestalt;*

412

Und bist du nicht willig, so brauch ich Gewalt.'

I took a sharp corner at speed; the rear wheel slid out onto the dirt, then corrected itself.

'Aren't you driving rather too fast for this road?'

'Does it matter how fast I drive?' The music's relentless progress, the boy's terror ever more urgent, the father's fear ever more evident, the Erlking's appeal ever more insistent, was releasing a reckless sense of power in me. 'You don't sentence somebody to death and then tell him to drive carefully.'

'Even a man sentenced to death will cling to life to the last.'

I was approaching a sharp curve, the road separated from the drop into the ocean only by a low stone wall. If I struck it at an angle, we would be deflected back onto the road. But there were observation areas at intervals, jutting out over the precipice. If I turned in, then struck the parapet wall at speed …

'Mein Vater, mein Vater, jetzt fasst er mich an!
Erlkönig hat mir ein Leid's getan!'

An observation area was coming up. I accelerated and turned the wheel sharply. The car leaped forward, hit the wall and somersaulted. The music seemed to be suspended in time and space as I felt myself going over …

'Dem Vater grauset's, er reitet geschwind …'

'You have surprised me,' said Andrew Conroy.

… I opened my door and jumped, blindly …

I opened my eyes. I seemed to have landed on a ledge below the parapet. It was very quiet. Far, very far below me, my car was lying on its roof in the sea, slowly sinking. I thought, but could not be sure, that I heard the joyful opening of the *Ganymed*, and then I heard nothing except the slow fretting of the waves at the rocks. I became aware of a presence near me, a human shape. It was a baboon, squatting peaceably next to me, trying on my Ray-Bans. It looked up at me as I shook myself, dusted the dirt off my clothes. 'Relax,' it said.

On the road above me the powerful growl of a tourist bus subsided to a purr as the vehicle drew up and stopped, idling, at the lookout point, next to what must now be a gaping hole in the wall. The bus door opened. Over the wall peered what seemed to be hundreds of faces; each face produced a camera;

413

each camera swivelled, paused, and sprouted an erection; shutters clicked, films advanced, click, advance … I took my cue from the baboon next to me, who was now chewing the earpiece of my Ray-Bans pensively, and pretended not to notice.

The tour bus was conveying a group of Japanese tourists from a luxury cruise ship in the harbour. They were spending 24 hours in Cape Town, and had a lot of ground to cover. The driver explained to me that in terms of their contract they were not allowed to transport pick-up passengers. He appealed, though, to the tour leader for permission to waive this rule, and after lengthy negotiations with the legitimate passengers, the tour leader announced that his charges would be honoured to extend the hospitality of their bus to me. This they did most graciously all the way into Cape Town, at the small enough price to me of being asked to pose next to whatever landmark they stopped to photograph. It is a comfort to think that in a hundred Japanese homes I am now a permanent part of the scenic beauty of the Cape Peninsula, although I suspect that they would have preferred the baboon. And I never did get my Ray-Bans back.

'What on earth happened to you?' asked Gerhard as I rushed into his office, having been dropped downstairs to the fond and courteous farewells of my fellow-passengers. 'You look as if you've been fucked by a warthog. Or have you been messing around with baboons again?'

'I can't tell you now. Have you got your car here?'

'Yes, as it happens. Why?'

'Take me to Cape Point. It's urgent.'

'If you say so. I won't even ask you where your car is, or what makes Cape Point so attractive, or where you have been all day, or why your left elbow is bleeding …'

'Don't. Let's go. Or wait, can I use your telephone?'

'Help yourself. It's a minor inconvenience compared with the trauma of being dragged from my day's work to Cape Point.'

I phoned Leonora. She said that she'd been phoning Luc's number ever since I spoke to her. 'That's wonderful,' I said. 'Please keep it up for a while longer. I'll explain later.'

414

On the way to Cape Point I told Gerhard as much of the story as I could coherently recollect.

'Well!' he said. 'Pray God that that will be a lesson to us all.'

'And what does it teach us?'

'To stay at home in Pinelands and cultivate our gardens. And not to hop into bed with Angels of Dawning.'

'Don't joke. Where can he *be*?'

'Didn't Andrew Conroy give you any indication?'

'Only what I told you, that he will die as he lived, a slave to his passions.'

'Well, what were his passions? You should know.'

'Nothing out of the ordinary, as far as I could tell.'

'You seem to have expanded your notion of the ordinary since we last discussed the matter.'

We reached Rocklands in the late afternoon. The house was as we had left it. In the kitchen were our tea cups and the two coffee mugs, one only half drunk. We searched every room in the house, under every bed, in every cupboard, and made our way back to the kitchen. As we stood staring at each other helplessly, the faint tinkle of *Nkosi Sikelel' iAfrika* reached us.

'The cell phone,' I said. 'But from where is it coming?'

We moved closer to the sound. It seemed to be coming from the outside wall of the kitchen; when we got there, it seemed to be coming from under our feet.

'It's under the floor,' I said.

'Of course,' said Gerhard. 'How stupid of us. The cellar in the photographs. It must be down there.'

We searched for a trap door, but could find none. I opened the kitchen cupboard again and pulled at a shelf. All the shelves swung out, leaving the back of the cupboard accessible. Near the top was a latch; as I pulled at it, the back of the cupboard swung backward, revealing a stone staircase leading down into the foundations of the house.

The phone was still ringing as we entered the cellar. It was indeed the room we had seen on the photographs, equipped as if for a dungeon or torture chamber: iron staples in the wall, slings with handcuffs and foot-irons, leather hammocks that seemed to be able to double as straitjackets, complete suits of leather armour. Against one wall, suspended by his wrists from two iron rings in the wall, tied by his feet to the floor, gagged and masked, recognisable only by his red hair, was Luc Tomlinson.

'Lord,' Gerhard said. 'I thought I had seen kinky.' He went to Luc and started untying him.

'Is he alive?' I asked, as Gerhard took off the mask and gag.

'Relax,' said Luc Tomlinson, but very weakly.

Gerhard ruled that both Luc and I were too exhausted and too weak to face the kind of questioning that the police would subject us to; after all, I had the potentially tricky situation to deal with of having driven a car in which another person was killed.

'Relax,' said Luc, 'we can't get out anyway. The gate closed half an hour ago.'

'You mean we have to spend the night here?' Gerhard asked.

'Yes, well. My mother's room is there. It's quite clean.'

'Good,' said Gerhard. 'I don't usually spend the night without my toothbrush, but I'll have to make an exception for a special occasion.'

'But there's just the one bed in there,' I said.

Luc looked uncomfortable. 'I thought you might want to share ...'

'It's all right,' I said, 'I can sleep on a sofa somewhere.'

'Suit yourself,' said Luc.

'Let me interpret you to yourselves,' said Gerhard. 'Luc here thinks you and I sleep together, Nicholas, or otherwise he does not want to seem to assume that we don't.' He turned to Luc. 'Nicholas, on the other hand, thinks that you don't want to sleep with him. I suggest that you both consider the strong possibility that what you both want is to sleep together, and since this is in fact perfectly possible, do so as soon as we have managed to find something to eat in this rather bare-looking kitchen. In the meantime, before it is quite dark, I want to go and look at that attractive little beach I noticed when we arrived, so please excuse me.'

At this point Luc and I, by all accounts, should have entered into a mutually enlightening explanation of our feelings, during which it would have become apparent that only pride and vulnerability had prevented us from recognising that the other's need for reassurance had been as great as our own. Luc not being Elizabeth Bennet, however, and I not Mr Darcy, and it even being possible that our feelings on the subject were not in all respects exactly similar, such conversation as we had centred on the rather more pertinent fact that one of us had spent the day in a semi-comatose state suspended from a wall, and that the other had discovered a murder, survived a murder attempt, and committed a murder.

Luc filled us in, over a creditable supper of pasta and vegetables, on the details of his visit from Andrew Conroy, or such of them as he could remember.

'Sure, I was surprised when he turned up. We're not exactly mates, as you know. But he spun me the line that he was out rowing and wanted a break and how about a cup of coffee, so I reckoned okay and made us both a cup. And all I remember was that he started asking me about you' – he nodded in my direction, looking a bit embarrassed – 'wanting to know all sorts of things ...'

'What sort of things?' Gerhard asked, as I had known he would.

'Yes, well, whether we fucked or not, and I said it was none of his business, and then he reckoned well he knew that we'd slept together on Saturday, and so I said well if you know, why bug me about it, and what's it to you? And the next thing I knew, I started feeling limp and the next thing after that I remember is my cell phone going crazy and me dangling from the wall for ever.'

'The hand of Johanna again,' Gerhard said. 'The Silvermine laboratory produced what they call a muscle relaxant, which was used to some effect in getting rid of enemies of the state. Some were dumped into the sea from a helicopter, I believe.'

'Well, then, that's what he slipped me. If you hadn't turned up, I'd have died hanging from that wall. My old folks never visit me any more and nobody else knows about that cellar. It's not as if I ever use it.'

My second night with Luc Tomlinson was useful in establishing that the first night had not been a one-night stand.

Whether it was going to be more than a two-night stand would have to remain an open question until we spent a third night together. And so on. It was a curious thing that for the time being that seemed about as rational a basis for our relationship as any other.

When I said so to Gerhard, he said, 'That seems very cold-blooded to me.'

'Just because after a youth of extreme promiscuity you've settled down to a bourgeois existence, don't begrudge me my timid venture into unconventionality.'

'I do not begrudge you your timid venture into anything for one second. Indeed, if the truth be known, I was responsible for your giant leap into passion.'

'I'm sorry, but you were not. I remember distinctly that it was Luc who said ... well, whatever he did say on the occasion.'

'Yes, but how did you get into a position for Luc to say whatever it was that he said and that is making you blush in that unbecoming fashion? You remember when he came to your office to weep and wail about his baboons, you were prepared just to let him leave? Remember?'

'More or less.'

'Yes, and I insisted that we help him? And why?'

'Because you were sorry for him and found him attractive.'

'No. Because I was sorry for him and found him attractive *and* could see that he had the hots for you and that if you had brought yourself to have anything as undignified and un-Nicholas as the hots you'd also have the hots for him, and therefore I reasoned that if the two of you could be brought into near proximity and kept there for a substantial period of time, the probability was very high that you would end up where you did.'

'Oh, for heaven's sake, Gerhard, sleeping with Luc was the one aspect of my life that Andrew Conroy did *not* plan, and now you tell me *you* planned it?'

'You should be grateful. Greater love hath no man ...'

'You mean sacrificing Luc Tomlinson to me?'

'No. I mean sacrificing you to Luc Tomlinson.'

The complications arising out of the deaths of Andrew Conroy and Boetie Bester were less strenuous than I had feared. Gerhard had on occasion remarked that it was more difficult to get away with a parking offence than with a murder, and this proved to be the case. There seemed little point in trying to get Andrew Conroy convicted of the murder of Boetie Bester, so I suppressed what he had told me about that, and the inquest found that Boetie had died of heart failure induced by a combination of electricity and Ecstasy. ('*Vlakplaas hit man eliminates himself*' was how Mhlobo headed his report in the *Mail & Guardian*, having with great reluctance agreed not to print the full story.) As for Conroy's death, Luc and I decided simply to tell the truth, or a simplified version of it, namely that Conroy had been jealous of our relationship. Somewhat unusually as far as the law is concerned, the truth turned out to be quite effective, possibly because there were no lawyers involved other than myself, and the inquest went off with a minimum of fuss. ('*Human rights judge dies tragically in love triangle*' was Mhlobo's angle on that one; this was picked up by the *Sunday Times* as '*Sexual intrigue ends in death crash*'.)

My mother phoned to express her shock, concern and incredulity.

'Nicholas, what is this absolute *nonsense* in the papers? Iris brought me the paper this morning and we can't make head or tail of it.'

'Yes, mother, I don't expect you to understand; it's a rather complicated story.'

'There's nothing wrong with my understanding dear, it's just that the paper seems to be saying that this judge got killed because he was jealous of your relationship with another man. Iris says she's never heard of anything like it.'

'No, mother, I'm sure she hasn't. Nor had I, until recently.'

'Then you mean it's *true*?'

'It's about as true as anything else you read in the newspapers, which is to say it's got the facts more or less right and everything else more or less wrong.'

'But what about Theodora?'

'Leonora, mother. She's very well.'

'Yes. And you're no longer seeing her?'

419

'Not really, no.'

'Well, perhaps that's just as well. Tomlinson is quite a good surname. And as long as nothing happened to you, dear.'

'No, mother, nothing happened to me.'

'That's good, dear. Iris sends her love.'

I invited Leonora to an after-work drink at the Wig and Pen and told her as much of the story as she seemed interested in hearing, which was just about all of it: our range of reference had certainly expanded dramatically since we had stopped pretending to be interested in each other.

'So poor Boetie was murdered?' she asked; that seemed to be the part of the story that occupied her most.

'Yes, in effect.' I had not thought it necessary to give her every last detail of Boetie's death, had merely said that he had been killed by a skin-contact poison.

'Shame,' she said, 'and he was hoping to be given amnesty if he confessed. Was he any worse than the people who used him?'

'Surely not. But he wasn't as clever.'

She considered this. Then she smiled one of her rare smiles and said, 'I am pleased about you and Luc. He's nice.'

'Thanks for mentioning that. I'm not sure that I would have had the courage.'

'It shouldn't take courage. We've come a long way.'

'You've come a long way. I'm not sure about myself.'

She laughed. 'If you're not sure, you should read last week's *Sunday Times*. You've come a very long way indeed.' She looked at her watch and swallowed the last of her passion fruit and lemonade. 'I must go,' she said, 'I'm doing an Assertiveness Training course.'

Joyce Tomlinson phoned me the day after Andrew Conroy's funeral, a well-attended and well-publicised event.

'Nicholas,' she said, 'I hoped to see you at the funeral.'

'That would have been hardly tactful,' I said, 'considering my relation to the deceased and the manner of his decease.'

'I suppose so. I don't quite know why I'm phoning you like this, only all of a sudden it seems so lonely. I've lost my only son and now I've lost my only friend ...'

'Fortunately you still have your husband.'

'Yes, thank God, and don't think I don't. Incidentally, I don't know if you've been watching the press, but you may be interested to hear that Brick has been given the contract to build I forget how many, oh *thousands* of new houses on the Cape Flats. All part of the Reconstruction and Development Programme, you know.'

'I'm very pleased for you.'

'Oh, I don't matter, but it's wonderful for Brick. It more than makes up for his losses on the Rocklands project. And, of course, it situates him very well in terms of the new dispensation.'

'It's business as usual, then.'

'You could put it like that, though Brick thinks of it more as a mission than as a business. But what I really wanted to say to you is that, in spite of our differences in the past, I wish you very well, and I hope that you and Luc can between the two of you get some sort of relationship together, because it's not something that either of you were particularly good at on your own. And please tell Luc that I love him, even though I cannot see him.'

'Isn't that rather hard? Not seeing him?'

Her voice descended an octave, to the timbre of tragedy. 'Yes, it is rather hard. But that is what marriage means, when you take it seriously.'

The insurance payout on my BMW was such as would have bought me a handsome mountain bike. The firm would normally have replaced the car with no more than a grumble from the accountant, but in my case there was the possibility that I would leave for London in the not-too-distant future, and they obviously did not want to have to present my successor with a previously-owned vehicle. This was inconvenient, because for all my hatred of motorcars, commuting by train was slow, dirty and dangerous, public transport in Cape Town being second only to private croquet as lowest funding priority. Also, not having Luc's training, I found the prospect of cycling out to Cape Point to see him quite daunting; besides which, undertaking a two-hour cycling trip for a night of passion has about it an avid purposefulness to which I was not yet ready to commit myself. Luc did not seem to mind cycling out to Pinelands, but there comes a time when practicality takes over from passion, and against that time I judged it prudent to acquire motorised transport.

'Borrow my car,' said Gerhard. 'I usually walk to work anyway, and over weekends we can use Clive's car.'

This was what I did, but it did remind me that the London issue needed to be resolved one way or the other. Not being a naturally decisive person, and this being after all a more momentous decision than whether to have a chicken mayonnaise or a cheese and tomato sandwich, I was preoccupied with the question to the point of absent-mindedness.

'Excuse me, Mr Morris, but have you had time to look at that contract I put on your desk yesterday?' Myrah would ask me, with as much reproach in her voice as Myrah could ever muster in her dealings with me.

I could not discuss the matter with Gerhard, because he was intolerant of what he called Emigration Vacillation. 'If you don't know whether you should go or not, you shouldn't,' he declared. 'The only good reason to emigrate is one that presents itself either irresistibly or inexorably, a grand passion or a pogrom.' Nor could I discuss it with Luc, who would simply have said 'Suit yourself,' which, as far as it went, was perfectly sincere advice: that was what he himself did in all his relations in life. I was not doing too well at seizing control of my own destiny. What I did know was that I was more likely to retain control over my destiny, for what that was worth, by going to England than by staying in a country with as uncertain a future as South Africa. It was all very well for Gerhard to enthuse about our new democratic government; I knew that democracy counted heads, not costs.

At times I wondered if I was suffering from delayed shock: my existence, though pleasant enough, and livened up considerably by Luc's presence in it, seemed oddly aimless, as if, now that I was no longer subject to Andrew Conroy's design, I had become a character without an author. At such times I would tell myself that I was experiencing the burden of free action, and should make use of this in an enlightened way. The problem was to know what, in a given situation, the enlightened course of action was.

I like to think of myself as a rational person. In most situations, I believe, it is possible to withdraw oneself from one's own involvement and weigh up the considerations objectively; in really tricky cases I tend to make two columns on a clean sheet of paper, and list the considerations for and against in terms of a scale from one to five. This was what I did in this instance: I sat down at my desk, got a sheet of paper, and drew two columns. One I headed *Cape Town*, the other I headed *London*.

	Cape Town	London
Scenery and Nature	4	0
Friends (Gerhard)	3	0
House	3	?
Family (Proximity of)	-2	0
Crime and Security	-5	4
Traffic	-3	Not applicable
Public Transport	-5	4
Luc	4	0

This produced a score of 8 for London and –1 for Cape Town, which should have been decisive but wasn't. It told me what I already knew, which was that all of Cape Town's pleasures were as nothing against the fact that one's tenure on them was so insecure; as for the pleasures of London, they were too abstract to become part of the equation for me.

Perhaps there is a rule or a law or a principle somewhere, the Wishy-Washy Principle, that holds that one's susceptibility to the designs of others increases proportionately to their determination multiplied by one's own indecisiveness. One afternoon as I arrived home, Tornado, by now used to the initially unfamiliar car, came trotting over for his pat and chat, as he did every afternoon. What was unusual was that Stuart and Sharon were home, and seemed to be taking Tornado for a drive; he had come over to me while they were covering their back seat with an old cloth to protect it against the terrors of dog hairs and spit.

Sharon waved at me, then came over. 'Hi,' she said, as blindingly bright as always. 'It's so nice that you're here to say goodbye to Tornado.'

'Oh? Where is he going?' I was surprised to discover how disappointed I was. 'Have you found him a home?'

'No, alas,' she said. 'You know, there's just nobody who wants a fully grown bull mastiff?'

'Then where is he going?'

'To the vet. To be put down. We thought that would be the kindest in the long run, even though it *is* quite expensive. It's quite painless, you know.'

'I believe so,' I said, not quite knowing what I was saying. 'Listen, can't you hang on just a day or two until I've got clarity about my own plans? If I don't go to London, I'd gladly take Tornado, but I don't know yet ...'

'Alas, no, we really can't wait. We've started packing for Perth already, and we won't have time later, apart from the fact of course that it's just too sad living with a dog with a death sentence hanging over his head. We'd rather just get it over with and cope with our grief now. And then, you know, to be honest, he's a bit of a nuisance when estate agents come to show people around the house. We're getting just a tiny bit worried that we won't sell the house before we leave. Come Tornado, come boy, walkies!'

I realised that I was probably being blackmailed, but Sharon's strong suit was the fact that she was so obviously, perfectly, brightly sincere in her intention to take Tornado off to his death.

'Listen,' I said, 'why don't I just take him?'

That evening, sitting at my dining room table with Tornado lying at my feet as if that had been his place since birth, I took out my score sheet again, and under *Cape Town* I wrote, 'Tornado: 5'. At the bottom of the page I wrote: 'Score now: Cape Town 4, London 8.'

'I'm not quite sure what we're going to do with you if the score remains in London's favour,' I said to Tornado, but he just wagged his tail slightly, as if I'd promised him a treat. Then he sat up, alert, his ears and his nose twitching, and his huge bark filled my house.

The front door opened and Luc appeared. 'Relax,' he said to Tornado. Tornado growled; I said, 'That will do, Tornado,' and he subsided.

'What's this, then?' Luc asked.

I told him the history of my acquisition of Tornado.

'That's cool,' he said, 'he's a great dog. Aren't you then?'

Tornado nodded and flopped down at our feet again.

'Have you seen the *Argus*?' asked Luc.

'No, I've been avoiding the press. Why?'

'Just this,' and he took a cutting out of the pocket of his windbreaker. The heading said: *Baboon moratorium revoked: Animal groups up in arms*. The report explained that the new Minister of Nature Conservation and Development had announced that the moratorium on the exportation of baboons for laboratory purposes had been suspended until further notice, following talks with the French military on matters of mutual strategic interest. The paper mentioned that there were rumours that French scientists were using baboons in research into the nature of injuries sustained in car accidents. As a postscript it mentioned that a farmer had applied for a licence to can baboon meat for export to poor countries as a cheap form of protein.

'What do you think that means for the chacs?' he asked me.

'Well, there's no doubt that it's bad news for baboons everywhere,' I said. 'Of course I don't know how this will affect your – our – baboons, but what's bloody depressing is what it says about the new government, and its susceptibility to just the kind of deals that the old lot used to strike. Mutual strategic interest, indeed. We give you baboons, you give us arms, and fuck any principle or consistency.'

'What makes them think they can trade baboons as if they were bales of wool?'

'The fact that a baboon has no more protection under law than a bale of wool; indeed a bale of wool, as belonging to somebody, is better protected than the baboon.'

'Why don't you bloody lawyers do something?' he asked, his belligerent tone mitigated by his putting his arm round my shoulders.

'As I said to you so long ago, when you were making a

nuisance of yourself in my office, because baboons don't have money to instruct lawyers.'

'Well, then. I'm instructing you on behalf of the baboons.'

'Money up front?'

'In a manner of speaking.'

I disengaged myself and went to the table. On my list, under *Cape Town*, below *Tornado*, I wrote 'Baboons: 5'. At the bottom of the page I wrote 'Final score: Cape Town 9, London 8'.

Early the following morning I went to see Mr McKendrick to inform him that I was no longer available to open the London office. He listened gravely.

'Well, Nicholas,' he said, 'it is of course your decision entirely.' He paused, then repeated, with more conviction, 'Entirely. I am sure you have carefully weighed up the welfare of the firm against your own considerations. May I ask you what those considerations are?'

'To be honest, Mr McKendrick, they are of a rather personal nature.' I couldn't bring myself to tell him that I was staying in order to save a dog from extinction and to fight for the right of baboons not to be canned.

He nodded. 'Of course. I understand.' I realised that what he understood was that I was staying in order to be with Luc Tomlinson, my relationship with whom had so recently been aired in the national press. My first impulse was to explain that this was not in fact the case; then I shrugged and said, 'I'm pleased and grateful that you do, sir.'

'Of course. We have always prided ourselves on being a tolerant firm. Incidentally, do you think your friend Gerhard Naudé might be interested in the London option? He also has an English training, I seem to remember.'

'Yes, he does. If you wish, I could mention it to him in passing, but I must tell you, sir, I know his views on leaving the country, and I suspect he would not want to go to London at this stage.'

'No, don't mention it to him just yet, if you don't mind. I shall discuss it with the other senior partners first. I have to inform them of your decision in any case. They will be disappointed; they all, almost without exception, think very highly of you.'

426

I noticed again the conscientious qualification. As I got to my feet, I said, 'If I may make so bold as to ask, sir, what is it that Mr Watts has against me?'

Mr McKendrick was too honest a man to pretend that he didn't know what I was talking about. 'Well, Nicholas, it's not something you should take personally; indeed, I'm telling you this exactly to persuade you that it is not personal. You see, when you first came to us, you remember, we approached you with an offer …'

'Indeed, sir, and very flattering it was, too.'

'Yes. The reason why we made the offer was that we had received a warm recommendation from a highly respected legal academic and lawyer. It was, however, a man of whom Cedric, whose political views, as you know, are on the conservative side, disapproved, and I'm afraid he has allowed that consideration to colour his opinion of you.'

'And this academic and lawyer was, of course …?'

He nodded. 'Yes, Justice Andrew Conroy. The late Justice Andrew Conroy, I should say.'

I went to Gerhard's office to tell him that I was no longer going to London. I walked in, looking forward to his pleasure, which would no doubt take some acerbic or scabrous form; but at the door I paused. Gerhard was sitting at this desk, neither working nor reading the newspaper – he was simply sitting, looking more wan than I had ever seen him.

'Gerhard! what on earth …?' I went up to him and put my hand on his shoulder.

He looked up with a wry smile. 'What was it I said about total commitment?'

'That flirtation made it bearable and possible.'

'Good. I wonder if one could extend the definition of flirtation to encompass the act of giving a stranger a blowjob in a bus shelter.'

'You haven't …'

'No, I haven't. Clive has. Did. Late last night while out jogging on the Sea Point promenade.'

'But I thought Clive …'

'Was the steady one, and I was the slut. Yes, I thought so too.'

He smiled, not very convincingly. 'To think that I had to climb Table Mountain before I got what this other bloke got for making his way into a bus shelter. But that's not really the worst, though I must admit it's what most occupies my thoughts. The worst is that Clive was quite badly beaten up by a couple of sensitive types who took exception to having to witness such flagrant immorality. They also removed Clive's watch and his ... acquaintance's wallet as a token of their disapproval.'

'And is Clive badly injured?'

'He lost a couple of teeth, and his lip and nose are quite badly cut. He was also kicked in the ... groin.'

'How appalling.' I took his hand. 'And how awful for you.'

'You might take the view that the one atrocity cancels out the other. If the thugs hadn't beaten Clive up, I might have been tempted to do so myself. Now my function resolves itself into tender loving care.'

'Much more appropriate than the other one.'

'Thank you. But enough of domestics. What brings you to my office with such bright eyes?'

'I wanted to tell you that I'm not going to London.'

He got up and hugged me. 'That is the best news I've had all week, which doesn't say much given that the other news I had was that my boy friend was beaten up for public cocksucking, so let me rephrase that – that's the best news I've had all year. You couldn't have found a more effective antidote to my unaccustomed gloom if you'd tried.' He hugged me again, then said, 'All that pisses me off is that that bean-pole of a Luc Tomlinson managed to do what I couldn't.'

'You mean get me to stay?'

'Yes. What else could I conceivably mean?'

Feeling very foolish about it, I had Fiona's piece of rose quartz set in a pendant that I wore round my neck. I forbore to spell out the symbolic implications to myself; partly because it was so difficult to take seriously anything emanating from Fiona, partly because there was a part of me highly sceptical of my surrender to sentimentality. But in an obscure way I associated the crystal with the day we rescued the baboons and Luc made his way into my bed. And there was certainly no possibility of Luc's presenting me with a token of that event.

'And they say,' said Kitty Jooste at the coffee machine, about a week later, 'that millions of rand in taxpayers' money is being spent on praise singers. Every cabinet minister wants a praise singer, and now the cabinet ministers' wives and husbands want them too, and the main praise singers, I kid you not, now have their own praise singers.' She paused for effect.

'It's a cultural thing,' said Willy Wilson.

'Yeah, like the poet laureate,' said Dikeledi. Kitty Jooste looked at her uncertainly, not knowing what a poet laureate was.

'Have you noticed,' asked Dikeledi as we walked to our offices, 'how *it's a cultural thing* has taken over from *you can't teach them anything*, I mean as an expression of the general hopelessness of the dark people?'

I laughed. 'Well, I suppose you could say there's a different spin on the hopelessness.'

'I'm not sure. You've heard all this talk about a culture of entitlement and a culture of appropriation, which basically means that blacks don't pay for what they get and steal what they want. As part of their culture.' She paused outside her office. 'In-cid-*dent*-ally, as Mhlobo would say, we are getting married.'

'Congratulations,' I said, 'When? Or should I say why?'

'The when hasn't been decided, the why hasn't been discussed. Just say it's a cultural thing. Also known as It Takes Two to Toyi-toyi. And we're moving out of the flat. We're tired of having our door knobs and our hub caps stolen.'

'Where are you moving to?'

'Don't know yet. Any suggestions?'

'Well, the house across the road from mine is for sale.'

'Pinelands? Do you think they know the Group Areas Act has been scrapped?'

'This might be a good way of informing them.'

'I don't know. You can't teach them anything. But I like the idea.'

I phoned Mhlobo to congratulate him.

'Well, yeah,' he said, sounding slightly embarrassed, 'there comes a time when a man has to *commit*, you know.' He paused. 'And when a woman has to have children.' He laughed loudly to dissociate himself from his statement. 'By the *way*,' he said, 'speaking of childbearing, have you heard that your old friend Johanna The Black Widow van der Merwe is pregnant?'

'*No.*'

'*Yes.* By person or persons unknown.'

'You mean ... could it be ...?'

'...that our other friend Gerhard is about to become a father? Sounds plausible to me. And in-ci-*dent*-ally, my sources say that the case against Doctor van der Merwe is so complex and so contradictory that the most likely outcome is that they'll drop all charges.'

'There's no justice, is there?'

'I'm the journalist, you're the lawyer, and *you*'re telling *me* there's no justice?'

Gerhard was less amused than I'd expected him to be.

'God forgive me,' he said, 'if I've really contributed to the creation of some poor little creature to be brought up by that woman. With my fucked-up genes and her screwed-up notions the kid's got nature and nurture lined up against it from the first breath it draws.'

'What's wrong with your genes?'

'Nothing a bit of genetic engineering can't fix. But in the meantime they're all blood, soil and drought. Come to meet my parents sometime.'

We were sitting in the Wig and Pen, Gerhard having suggested a drink – 'for a change, now that you're so domesticated.' He had seemed preoccupied, even before receiving the news of his impending paternity.

'How is Clive?' I asked, guessing that that was what he'd wanted to talk to me about.

'He is fine. His teeth have been replaced and the rest of him has been patched up.'

'And how are you?'

'Fine. Patched up.'

'Then what's bothering you?'

'Something I must tell you.'

'Do I want to hear it?'

'I suspect not. But here goes anyway. I'm going to take the London job.'

'You're ...'

'Your jaw has just dropped, my dear Nicholas, retrieve it immediately. Yes. Mr McKendrick spoke to me a couple of days ago, and I told him this afternoon that I would take it.'

'But *why*? Why the *fuck*, if you'll excuse the expression?'

'In a word or more precisely, in a sentence: because Clive wants to go. He can, quite easily, because he has a British passport.'

'But why *now*, all of a sudden?'

'Well, the attack shook him, as you can imagine. He says if you can't even go jogging without getting beaten up, that's a wake-up call.'

'He was hardly jogging when he was beaten up, if you'll forgive my saying so.' I was not in a mood to be compassionate to Clive.

'I said so myself. In fact I pointed out to him that even in London they take a dim view of people giving each other blowjobs in bus shelters. It's not as if England is exactly Poofter Heaven, from what I hear.'

'And what did he say?'

'He said it's not that, it's that South Africa had a culture of violence which made such things possible. He seems to think that in London they might have pushed him around a bit but they wouldn't have broken his teeth. You haven't met Clive. He's quite ... dogmatic. You must remember he's from missionary stock, from which he's inherited the assumption that the mother country is by definition more enlightened than the colony.'

I knew the assumption from my own parents, but thought that it had died out in the younger generation. 'Need you be ... you know, led by Clive's assumptions?'

'You mean given that I feel betrayed by him?'

'I suppose that's what I do mean. If you feel you can't trust him ... '

431

'I don't know if that is what I do feel. Clive is no less worthy of trust now than when I trusted him; he hasn't changed; I have, if you know what I mean.'

'No, I don't. What has changed is that he told you he was going for a jog and then went for a blowjob.'

'Strictly speaking, of course, and this is what he maintains, he did go for a jog, and the blowjob just sort of took him unawares. And don't look sceptical, it happens, I have often enough been, as it were, for unwary passers-by, the Unforeseen Blowjob in the Bus Shelter, the Faceless Fuck in the Forest, the Whimsical Wank in the Woods …'

'Please,' I said, 'spare me the alliteration. I get the point.'

'… so knowing that Clive is capable of being waylaid as I have waylaid, no doubt, the lovers and husbands of many a trusting man and woman, must not change my belief in his essential loyalty and commitment.'

'Total commitment?'

He smiled. 'Perhaps we shouldn't expect total commitment from any creature other than our dogs.'

I sat staring into my beer. I wasn't particularly interested in Clive's capacities and potentialities, except as they affected Gerhard, and, through Gerhard, me.

'So you're going to London to please Clive.'

'Yes. Do you feel betrayed?'

'I feel … deserted. And undervalued. And fucking angry.'

'I'm more sorry than I know how to say. But you would have done the same to me.'

I sighed. 'I know. Andrew Conroy said our destinies are the accidental consequences of the designs of others.'

'By that logic *somebody* knows what he's doing and is originating everybody else's destinies.'

'Clive?'

'The person who beat up Clive?'

'God?'

We both tried to laugh and Gerhard bought us each a beer. A young man at the counter gave him a look that in earlier days would have left me alone with my drink for at least twenty minutes, but Gerhard seemed not to notice.

As he sat down with our drinks, he said, 'Quickly – what's

the main difference between human beings and other animals?'

'The consciousness of inflicting pain.'

He thought for a moment and nodded. 'Not bad.'

'What's yours?'

'The ability to give and receive a blowjob at the same time.'

I went home and fed Tornado. On the dining room table was my balance sheet. I deleted *'Gerhard'* from the Cape Town column and put him in the London column. I changed the Final Score to Cape Town 6: London 8. I thought for a while, then added a column which I called *Commitment*; I gave Cape Town 3 and London –1, and amended the Final Score to Cape Town 9: London 7.

The following Friday evening I undertook to cook a meal for Luc and myself, to disprove his contention that I couldn't cook anything that didn't come out of a can or a packet. 'See you about six,' he said, 'just to make sure you do it right.'

'Trust me, I'm a lawyer.'

'That's what scares me. See you then.'

I asked Gerhard's advice and he gave me a recipe for a vegetarian curry which took forever to make but was supposed to be delicious. I bought the ingredients – most of which I had never heard of – at lunch time, and left work early to avoid the worst of the Friday rush hour. It was a beautifully warm early summer's day, and I opened the French doors onto my little lawn, now Tornado's main stomping ground. I put a CD in the player – Bach's Complete Cello Suites, which I had bought as a kind of gesture of posthumous propitiation to Andrew Conroy. I would take it off when Luc arrived; he didn't like the Cello Suites. By six o'clock I had prepared the ingredients, and was ready to submit to Luc's strictures on my cooking.

By seven o'clock Luc had not arrived. He had probably been delayed on the road, but if so, it was odd that he hadn't phoned; he still had the cell phone, and usually even remembered to take it with him. I phoned the number that I knew so well.

A woman's voice answered. 'Yeah?'

433

'Oh. I was looking for Luc Tomlinson ...'

'Is that Nicholas?'

'Yes.'

'Oh, hi, this is Fiona. Listen, Ell's not here right now, he's strolled down to the beach for a swim. Shall I get him to call you when he comes in?'

'Yes, if you wouldn't mind.'

'No prob. Bye.'

I put down the phone. The Bach was still playing, serene in its measured grief, its grave joyfulness, each impulse to excess checked and resolved by the constraints of harmony, to be released again by the energy of rhythm. I thought of the darkening beach at Rocklands, and Luc rushing into the waves.

Luc phoned about three hours later, after I had gone to bed without cooking the curry.

'Were you expecting me?'

'Well, yes, since we did have an arrangement.'

'Yes, well, that. Thing is, Fiona's been ditched by her boyfriend' – he broke off, interrupted by a voice in the background – 'okay, yes, well, *sorry*, she wasn't exactly ditched, she says, he's gone back to Australia because his didgeridoo was stolen on Greenmarket Square while he was meditating, so she turned up here in a state' – he dropped his voice – 'and I didn't want to just tell her to bugger off and all. I've had to cheer her up a bit, you know how it is.'

'And she's obviously still there?'

'Yes, well, you know how it is, they lock the gate at night.'

I stood quite still, not knowing what to say or even think. This was what I had wanted to avoid, all those years, this sense of something *happening* to me without my volition, this nameless thing I was feeling. Or perhaps it wasn't nameless at all, was merely a trite old emotion like jealousy or possessiveness. Or betrayal or rejection. Or disillusionment or disappointment. Or helplessness. Or anger. Or relief.

'Nicholas? You still there?'

'Yes. In a manner of speaking.'

'Look, I'll see you tomorrow, how's that?'

'That's just great. Usual time?'

'Usual time.' He sounded quite pleased with this arrangement, as if it disposed of such slight reservations as one might have had about his conduct.

My balance sheet was lying next to the bed. I reached for it to delete Luc's name and recalculate the scores; then I said, 'Oh, what the hell,' and crumpled up the sheet. Tornado looked up from his basket, hoping for a bedtime game. I tossed the ball of paper at him and he shredded it joyfully.

I was on the point of removing the rose quartz from my neck, as part of my process of symbolic divestment, but caught sight of myself in the full-length mirror, and realised how ridiculously solemn I looked. So I left the pendant, with its rather lustreless pink crystal, to exert whatever powers of self-affirmation it might still have. After all, it seemed to have served Fiona quite well.

'Well, then, Tornado,' I said, 'I suppose there's an appropriateness here that Andrew Conroy would have appreciated. You're about the only part of my life that he did not design for me, and you're all that I have left.'

His tail thumped against the side of his basket.

'It's just as well,' I continued. 'They wouldn't have let you into Cape Point anyway. By law dogs aren't allowed into nature reserves. Crazy, when you think about it. Does it tell us most about the law, about dogs, about nature, or about reserves?'

Tornado looked at me with more devotion than comprehension.

'Think about it,' I said, and switched off the light.